P9-CDL-211

THE LAST HOUSE
on the STREET

ALSO BY DIANE CHAMBERLAIN

THE LAST HOUSE

on the STREET

Diane Chamberlain

ST. MARTIN'S PRESS
New York

This is a work of fiction. All of the characters, organizations, and events portrayed in this novel are either products of the author's imagination or are used fictitiously.

First published in the United States by St. Martin's Press, an imprint of St. Martin's Publishing Group

THE LAST HOUSE ON THE STREET. Copyright © 2021 by Diane Chamberlain. All rights reserved. Printed in the United States of America. For information, address St. Martin's Publishing Group, 120 Broadway, New York, NY 10271.

www.stmartins.com

Library of Congress Cataloging-in-Publication Data

Names: Chamberlain, Diane, 1950– author.
Title: The last house on the street / Diane Chamberlain.
Description: First edition. | New York: St. Martin's Press, 2022.
Identifiers: LCCN 2021035221 | ISBN 9781250267962 (hardcover) | ISBN 9781250283177 (Canadian) | ISBN 9781250267979 (ebook)
Subjects: LCGFT: Novels.
Classification: LCC PS3553.H2485 L37 2022 | DDC 813/.54—dc23
LC record available at https://lccn.loc.gov/2021035221

Our books may be purchased in bulk for promotional, educational, or business use. Please contact your local bookseller or the Macmillan Corporate and Premium Sales Department at 1-800-221-7945, extension 5442, or by email at MacmillanSpecialMarkets@macmillan.com.

First U.S. Edition: 2022
First Canadian Edition: 2022

10 9 8 7 6 5 4 3 2 1

Violence is the weapon of the weak.

—RALPH ABERNATHY

THE LAST HOUSE
on the STREET

Chapter 1

———— ≈ ————

KAYLA

2010

I'm in the middle of a call with a contractor when Natalie, our new administrative assistant, pokes her head into my office. I put the call on hold.

"This woman is in the foyer and she says she has an eleven o'clock appointment with you, but I don't have her on your calendar." She looks worried, as though afraid she's already screwed up. "Ann Smith?"

The name is unfamiliar. "I don't have any appointments today," I say, glancing at the time on my phone. Eleven-oh-five. I should see the woman in case the screwup is on my end. I've only been back to work a couple of weeks and don't completely trust myself to think straight yet. "You can send her in."

A woman appears at my open office door as I wrap up my call and get to my feet. She's not at all my usual client—those thirty- or forty-somethings who've amassed enough money to build the home of their dreams. No, Ann Smith looks closer to sixty-five or seventy, though she appears to be fighting her age with vivid red shoulder-length hair. She wears mirrored sunglasses that mask her eyes, but nothing can camouflage the way her red lipstick bleeds into the lines around her mouth.

"Ann Smith?" I ask, smiling and curious as I reach out to shake her hand. "I'm Kayla Carter. Please come in and have a seat. I didn't have you on my schedule today—something must have fallen through the cracks—but I have about half an hour. What can I do for you?"

She doesn't return my smile as she sits down in the red Barcelona chair I offer her. I wish she'd remove her sunglasses. I see only my warped reflection instead of her eyes. It's disconcerting.

"I want to put an addition on my house," she says, folding her hands in the lap of her khaki slacks. Her nails are long acrylics, the red polish sloppily applied, and her voice is deep. *Very* deep, with a bit of a rasp to it. She looks around my office as if searching for something. She seems uneasy.

"Well, tell me about your house," I say. "Where is it?" It's weird, speaking to my own misshapen reflection in her glasses.

"Not far from here," she says. "It's a boxy nineteen-sixties house. Too dark. I want to add a sunroom."

I picture the house, old and airless. I can imagine the way it smells and the tight feeling of the walls as you pass from room to room. It probably cries out for a sunroom and I've designed plenty of them, but I'm not sure I'm the right architect for this project. Bader and Duke Design hired Jackson and me specifically to bring a more contemporary element to the decades-old North Carolina firm. Ann Smith's house sounds like it needs a cozier aesthetic.

"Do you have any pictures of your home?" I ask.

She doesn't answer. Instead, she stares at me. Or at least, I guess, she's staring. Who knows what her eyes are doing behind those glasses? I feel suddenly uncomfortable, as though the power in the room has shifted from me to her.

"No pictures with me," she says finally. "I lost my husband and now the house seems . . . oppressive." She leans forward a few inches. "You know how that feels, don't you? Losing your husband?"

A shiver runs up my spine. How does she know about Jackson? How does she know anything about me? Natalie must have mentioned something to her while she was waiting. "Yes, I do understand what that's like," I say slowly. "I'm so sorry about your loss. But back to your house. How would you like to use the sunroom? For entertaining or—"

"Mine had a heart attack," she says. "He was seventy, which probably seems old to you, but it isn't really. You're what? Thirty, maybe? You'll be seventy in the blink of an eye. Your husband, though. He was way too young, wasn't he?" Her dark eyebrows suddenly pop above the sunglasses in a question. "And to die like he did, falling off the staircase while he was building your new house. Just a shame."

How does she know all this? Any mention of Jackson can throw me off these days, and coming from this odd woman . . . I don't want her to know anything about me. I'll have to have a serious talk with Natalie. "Well." I try to get my footing again. "You're right. It's been difficult. But I'd really like us to focus on your project. Tell me what you—"

"How can you move into the house that took him from you?" She asks the question I've been wondering myself. "No one should've put a house there to begin with. All those new houses. They don't belong. But especially that one. Yours. So modern. And stuck back in the trees like it is."

My palms are sticky on the arms of my chair. At this very moment, we are in an office in Greenville, nearly thirty miles from the Shadow Ridge neighborhood in the outskirts of Round Hill, where my beautiful, newly completed house is waiting for Rainie and me to move into it. How can she know about the house? About my life? What does any of it have to do with her? "How do you know so much about me and what does it have to do with your project?" I ask.

"Shadow Ridge Estates," the woman continues, that deep voice of hers mocking. "Who came up with that pretentious name? All those trees suck the breath out of you. You don't really want to move in there, do you? It's no place for a child. No place for a little girl. Especially one who just lost her daddy."

Oh my God. She knows about Rainie. I don't know how to handle this. She's touching me in my softest, most wounded places and I can't think straight.

I have to get myself under control. I sit up straight, ready to turn the tables on her.

"Would you mind taking your glasses off?" I ask.

"Yes, I'd mind," she says. "Light bothers me." She raises a hand to touch the edge of her glasses, and the loose sleeve of her white blouse slips a few inches up her arm, exposing a pink line across her forearm. Had she tried to kill herself at one time? But I don't think that's it. The line is short and rounded. It looks more like a birthmark than a scar.

"I think you'd better go to another firm," I say, getting to my feet. "I only do contemporary design."

She looks toward the ceiling as if considering the suggestion, then back at me. "If you say so, yes. I guess I'd better." She picks up her purse and stands suddenly, and I step back, afraid of her. Afraid of an old woman. I want her out of my office. I move toward the door, but she swiftly steps forward to block my path. "Do you want to know what keeps me awake at night?" she asks.

"I'd like you to leave," I say. She's too close to me now, so close that I can see the fear in my eyes in the distorted reflection in her sunglasses.

"*Thinking,*" she says. "That's what keeps me awake. Thinking about killing someone."

I push my way past her. Open the door and stand aside. "Leave." My voice sounds firm. At least I hope it does. But Ann Smith doesn't budge.

"I've been thinking about it for a long, long time," she continues. "Years and years and years. And now I have the chance."

My heart thuds against my rib cage. Is she talking about me? Am I the someone? *Years and years and years.* It can't be me. Still, I glance around the room for a weapon, spotting nothing. I think of my three-year-old daughter. Leaving her an orphan.

"Who are you talking about?" I ask, distressed by the quaking of my voice.

"I don't think I want to tell you." She smiles the smile of someone who has all the power. Then she pivots and walks to the doorway. I say nothing as she leaves the room and I watch her move down the hallway with the ease of a younger woman. Shutting the door, I stand frozen for a full minute before my brain kicks in and I rush to the window. I look out at the tiny parking lot we reserve for clients and contractors, watching for Ann Smith, hoping to see what car she gets into. But she never appears and I stand there numbly, the specter of her presence still looming behind me.

Chapter 2

―――――≈―――――

ELLIE

There are moments in life when you suddenly see your future and it's not at all what you expected. I was home from the University of North Carolina for spring break and we were all sitting in the living room. Daddy was reading the paper in his favorite chair, the leather so old it made cracking sounds each time he moved. Buddy was at the fold-down desk by the fireplace, tinkering with some small mechanical part from a car. And Mama sat between Brenda and me on the sofa, the *Brides* magazine open on her lap. Brenda had brought the magazine over and the three of us were admiring the dresses. I had to bite my tongue as Brenda paged through the magazine, though, and I wondered if Mama was biting hers, too. After all, Brenda would not be wearing one of those frothy white dresses, and I, as her maid of honor, would not be wearing one of the beautiful taffeta bridesmaid creations. Brenda's wedding to Garner Cleveland, due to take place next Saturday, would be small and quiet and necessary, with no attendants other than Garner's best friend, Reed—who happened to be my boyfriend—and me.

Brenda turned the page, and the photographs of dresses gave way to the headline of an article: "Sexual Harmony and How to Attain It."

"Don't need that one." Brenda laughed, patting her still-flat belly. She turned the page and if my mother hadn't been sitting next to me, I would have turned it back, curious. I knew next to nothing about sexual harmony. It wasn't that I was a prude. It was just that Reed and I hadn't gone that far, by mutual agreement. I wanted to wait until I was married and although Reed did give me a bit of an intellectual argument about it, he said he admired me for my decision. I hadn't criticized Brenda for *her* decision, though. Every girl had to figure out what was right for herself when it came to that sort of thing. What had shocked me the most about Brenda's pregnancy was that I'd had no idea she and Garner were intimate. I felt hurt that my longtime best friend and dorm mate had kept something so monumental from me.

When I told Mama about Brenda's condition and that she had to marry Garner right away, she expressed sympathy. "That poor girl," she said. "She just cut her freedom short," followed by a stern, "Learn from this, Eleanor. This is what happens when you let things go too far. You and Reed better behave yourselves."

"Mama," I'd said, "I'm not stupid. And we're not as serious as Garner and Brenda are."

"I'd say Reed's plenty serious about you," she said. "That boy adores you."

Reed was a real sweetheart and I'd known him most of my life. He finished college in three years and now worked at Round Hill's biggest bank. He wore a suit and tie every day—a blue tie, to set off his sky-blue eyes and dark hair. He was handsome in a suit, no doubt about it, but now that I was surrounded by college guys in their chinos and madras shirts, Reed sometimes seemed a bit stuffy to me.

I was touched that Mama was sitting with Brenda and me now, kindly oohing and aahing over the bridal gowns as if Brenda might actually be able to select one and wear it to her wedding. Mama loved Brenda, sometimes referring to her as her "second daughter," and Brenda had called her "Mama" for years. Brenda's own chilly mother would never look through *Brides* magazine with her. She agreed to come to the "ceremony," as she called it, even though Brenda's father refused, but she wasn't about to indulge Brenda's fantasies of a fancy wedding when it would be anything but.

"I love this one." Brenda pointed to the sparkly bodice of a beautiful, silver-hued white gown. "I keep coming back to it over and over again."

Mama touched the back of Brenda's hand. "It must be very hard to know you won't be able to have the wedding of your dreams," she said.

I glanced at Brenda. I could tell she was holding back tears. I knew she was happy, though. She and Garner were madly in love.

"Listen to this," Daddy said suddenly, and I shifted my gaze from the magazine to my father. He stubbed out his cigarette in the ashtray on the table by his side and began to read. " 'Reverend Greg Filburn, pastor of the AME church in Turner's Bend, announced today that several hundred white students from Northern and Western colleges will spend the summer in the Southern states registering Negroes to vote. Derby County is expected to host a number of those students. Only—' "

"Oh great," Buddy interrupted him without taking his eyes off the metal part in his hands. "Just what we need. A bunch of Northern agitators."

" 'Only thirty-four percent of Negroes in Derby County are now registered,' " Daddy continued reading, " 'compared to ninety-four percent of the white population, Reverend Filburn said. The voting rights bill, soon to be signed into law by President Lyndon Baines Johnson, will hopefully change that disparity, and we need to do all we can to make sure our folks can register. The program is called SCOPE, which stands for the Summer Community Organization and Political Education project—' " Daddy interrupted his own reading with a laugh.

"That's a mouthful," he said, then continued, " '—and it will send more than five hundred volunteers into seventy-five rural counties with the aim of removing racism from American politics.' "

"What do you think of this bridesmaid dress?" Brenda pointed to a page in the magazine, but neither my mother nor I even glanced at it. Both of us had our attention on my father. Especially me, even though I wasn't yet certain why.

"Are you sure they don't just mean deeper south?" Mama asked. "You know, Alabama and Mississippi where they have all the trouble? Not North Carolina."

"Sounds like they mean here too," Daddy said, "since this Filburn fella's church is in Turner's Bend." Turner's Bend was the town right next to Round Hill, where we lived.

"This sounds exactly like the sort of thing Carol would've done, doesn't it?" Mama asked.

We all automatically turned our heads to look at the empty rocking chair by the fireplace, where Aunt Carol always sat. Cancer took her from us the year before and I don't think anyone had sat in that chair since. I felt her loss every minute of every day. Aunt Carol was the only person in the family who seemed to understand me. Or, as she told me one time, I was the only person who seemed to understand *her*.

"Carol would've hopped right on that bandwagon," Mama continued, and Daddy rolled his eyes.

"That woman never met an underdog she didn't like," he said.

Buddy set down the part he'd been fiddling with. "I don't like the sound of that SCOPE thing one bit," he said. "What gives anybody from the North the goddamned right to come down here and—"

"Buddy!" Mama said. "Your mouth!"

"Sorry, Mama, but this gets my goat," he said. "Let them register if they want to, it's no skin off my teeth, but we don't need hundreds of crazy white kids from New York or wherever descending on Derby County."

He and my parents kept up the conversation, but something happened to me in the few minutes it took Daddy to read the article. For the past two years, I'd been a reporter and photographer for the campus newspaper at UNC. I'd covered the protests as students tried to get the downtown restaurants and shops to desegregate. At first, I wrote my articles objectively, just reporting the facts, but when I proudly showed Aunt Carol one of them, she frowned. "I want you to think about what you're writing, Ellie," she said, in that New York accent she'd never lost despite her twenty years in the South. "Think about what you write not as a Southerner. Not as a Northerner, either. Think about it as a *human being*."

I knew my beautiful blond aunt had long been a champion of civil rights. A year earlier, she'd taken part in the March on Washington, where she heard Martin Luther King, Jr., speak. It was all she could talk about for weeks afterward, making my mother roll her eyes and my father lay down the law, telling her that she could not go on and on about it at the dinner table. Only in the last couple of years had I begun to understand her passion, and talking to her about what was happening on campus changed my work on the newspaper. She made me dig deeper and I began to view events with my heart as well as my head. As I continued to interview the students, their passion and commitment—their belief in the *rightness* of what they were doing—made sense to me. Those students, white and Negro, put themselves on the line, body and soul. They were steadfastly nonviolent, not even fighting back when abused by passersby or dragged away by the police, and my articles about the protests grew more sympathetic toward them even without me realizing it.

Aunt Carol met Uncle Pete, my father's brother, when she was an army nurse and he was a soldier. After the war they moved in with us. I was only a year old at the time, so she was always a part of my life. Sometimes, the best part. She left discipline to my parents, so I knew I could tell her anything—almost—without getting in trouble. Uncle Pete died when I was ten, but Aunt Carol remained with us. She was blunt; I never needed to guess what she was thinking. As I grew older and became aware of the prickly relationship she had with my parents—especially with my mother—I wondered why she didn't move back to New York. Toward the end of her life, when cancer was stealing her away from us, I talked to her about it. "Why did you stay with us?" I asked as I wrapped her shawl tighter around her bony shoulders. She was always cold then, even in the summer. "You never loved North Carolina."

"No, but I loved *you*," she said. "And I think you needed me. I didn't want you to turn into your mother."

"What do you mean?" My mother was all right. She wasn't particularly warm but she was smart. She was a librarian in the Round Hill library.

"She may spend her life around books, but her mind is shuttered closed," Aunt Carol said. "Think about it. There's a reason you share what you're writing for the school paper with me and not with her, isn't there?"

She was right. My mother would have been disgusted by the way I wrote about the protests. The way I now sided with the protesters.

"I'm dying, Ellie," Aunt Carol said, matter-of-factly. "But keep talking to me after I'm gone, all right?" She smiled. "Pretend I'm here. You're a wonderful young woman. Keep writing about injustice. Act on your convictions. Don't let those shutters close your mind. Not ever."

Around that time, I'd been assigned to work on a project with Gloria, the lone Negro student in my pharmacology class. I suggested we talk about our project at the local sandwich shop, but she shook her head. *Let's meet in the library, instead,* she said. *I'm not hungry.* Only in bed that night did I realize that Gloria wouldn't have been allowed to eat in the sandwich shop with me and I felt embarrassed that I'd suggested it and angry on her behalf.

Then last spring, only a few miserable days after Aunt Carol's funeral, Brenda was with me when I was assigned to cover an extraordinary protest for the paper. Students and professors and even some townspeople knelt side by side across Franklin Street, blocking traffic. They held protest signs against their chests, their expressions solemn and sincere. I snapped pictures and felt moved by their quiet courage. Some of the girls wore skirts and I knew the asphalt had to be killing their knees and wrecking their nylons. I could tell from their stoic expressions that they didn't care. Their stockings were the last thing on their minds. They weren't thinking about themselves at all. They were thinking about the segregated shops and restaurants. They were thinking about the segregated grocery store where the owner poured ammonia over the heads of peaceful demonstrators, sending some of them to the hospital with second-degree burns. Aunt Carol had cried when I told her about that.

Gloria was one of the protesters in the street that day. She knelt at the end of the line closest to us next to a young white man, and I made sure to get her in some of my photographs.

Brenda shook her head as I snapped pictures. "This is stupid," she said. "They're all going to end up getting arrested, and what for? It's not going to change anything."

Her words were nothing more than a whine in my ear. Impulsively, before I had a chance to change my mind, I handed her my camera, slung my purse over my shoulder, and stepped into the street myself.

"What are you doing?" Brenda shouted from behind me.

I took my place at the end of the line—which was in the gutter—and got down on my knees next to Gloria. She didn't look at me but kept her eyes straight ahead and I did the same. Pain settled into my knees almost instantly and I felt the stocking on my right leg run clear up my thigh. A young man moved toward me and handed me a sign. I didn't know what it said, but I held it in front of me, as my fellow protesters were doing. My heart pounded but my breathing felt steady. My breathing felt *right*.

There was commotion all around us. Cars and angry drivers. A group of protesters marching on the other side of the street. Townspeople taking our picture. Through the cacophony, I heard Brenda yell, "What the *hell*, Ellie! Get out of the damn gutter!" I tuned her out. I tuned all of it out. I heard Aunt Carol's voice in my head: *Act on your convictions.* Although the physical pain had slipped to the background, I felt tears sting my eyes. Roll down my cheeks.

The police came in a white truck everyone called the paddy wagon.

"Go limp!" someone in the line yelled. I knew that's what you were supposed to do. Don't fight the police, but don't make it easy on them either. I felt the temptation to get up. Walk back to Brenda and disappear into the crowd of onlookers. But the stronger part of me held my ground. The cops began dragging and carrying my fellow protesters toward the paddy wagon. One cop pulled the sign from my hands, lifted me to my feet, and pushed me toward the truck, his hands gripping my shoulders. I couldn't make myself go limp like some of the others. Like Gloria did. She made them carry her, her skirt hiked up to her garters. It frightened me, the thought of being that helpless. Instead, I let myself be prodded along until the gaping rear of the truck was in front of me, and that's when reality began to sink in. I could still hear Brenda shouting to me from the other side of the street as I climbed into the truck, though I didn't know what she was saying. Was I being arrested? How would I explain to my parents that I felt as though I had to do what I did?

We were detained at the police station and later set free without arrest, and although Brenda told Garner and Reed and they both chewed me out for taking such a "stupid risk," my parents still had no idea what I'd done.

Now, Daddy reached the end of the newspaper article. I was only vaguely aware of Buddy saying, *They let that many bleedin'-heart white beatniks into Derby County, they're just askin' for trouble,* and Mama saying, *Only thirty-four percent of Negroes are registered? Sheer laziness. Why don't they just get themselves to the courthouse and take care of it?,* and Brenda saying, *Do you think the neckline on this dress is too revealing?,* because I knew . . . I knew in a way I couldn't explain even to myself . . . that I was going to be one of those white students working to register Negro voters.

I knew it the way I knew my own name.

Chapter 3

KAYLA

"So," the female police officer says once introductions have been made and the four of us—two officers, Natalie, and myself—are all sitting in my office. "Give me a description of her."

I'd hesitated about calling the police, not wanting to overreact, but when Natalie told me she'd given Ann Smith no personal information about me whatsoever, I thought I'd better talk to someone.

"She had red hair," I say. "Very red. Dyed I'm sure. Shoulder length. It sort of fell forward, covering her face." I demonstrate with my dark hair, smoothing it over my cheeks with my hands.

"But her eyebrows were brown." Natalie touches her own eyebrows, as pale as her own long blond hair.

"Could her hair have been a wig?" the male officer—PETRIE, his badge reads—asks.

I hadn't thought of that and I realize now that the woman's hair had looked shiny and thick for someone her age. "Yes, I suppose it could have been."

"Race?"

"White."

"Eye color?"

"That's the thing," I say. "She wore mirrored sunglasses. She refused to take them off when I asked. She said the light bothered her."

Officer Oakley, the female officer, looks at her partner as if that's a telling piece of information.

"She wore very red lipstick and red nail polish. Her nails were long. Acrylics. But . . . sloppy. As though she did them herself. She had on a white blouse and khaki pants."

"You were very observant." Officer Oakley smiles.

"And her voice was deep," I add.

"Croaky," Natalie adds.

"Could she have been a he?" Officer Oakley asks.

Despite the deep voice, there'd been something so female about the woman. "It's possible, but . . . ." I press my lips together. Shake my head. "I don't think so."

"Maybe trans?" Officer Petrie offers.

"I don't know," I say. "I just don't . . . She was so strange. But here's the thing that really got me. Really . . . shook me up." I sit forward. "She knew things about me. She knew about my husband. He was killed four months ago. He was also an architect here and we designed our new house together in a new development in Round Hill. He was working inside the house and one of the construction workers accidentally left a handful of screws on the top step of the staircase before the railing was installed. Jackson didn't see the screws and he stepped on them and fell. The woman knew about it. And she knows I'm about to move into the house. And she knows I have a little girl, nearly four years old. She even seemed to know the lot our house is on. And she said something about . . ." I bite my lip, trying to remember her exact words. "Something like, 'You shouldn't move in there.' "

"When are you moving in?" Officer Petrie asks.

"Saturday." I've had my own misgivings about moving into the house. Will I ever be able to walk up those stairs without thinking of the accident? But Jackson and I had been designing the house for the seven years of our marriage. It was our dream house, a spectacular contemporary on four wooded acres. Jackson would want Rainie and me to create a life in that house, and I truly do want to live there. I just want to feel okay about it.

"Where are you living now?" Officer Oakley asks.

"We're living temporarily with my father in Round Hill. We moved in with him—into the house I grew up in—after Jackson . . . after the accident." It's still too hard for me to put those two words together: *Jackson died.*

"And where is your daughter now?"

"You mean . . . right this minute?"

She nods.

I glance at my phone for the time, suddenly afraid. Is Rainie in danger? "She's at my father's," I say. "She goes to preschool in the morning. Then he picks her up and takes her to his house, where—"

"When we're done here, call him and make sure he keeps a close eye on her for a few days."

"Oh God," I say.

"What's his name? Your father?" asks Officer Petrie. "And his number? Just so we have it on file."

"Reed Miller," I say, and I rattle off his phone number. "What do you think she wants from me?" I ask. "Could I be the person she wants to kill?"

"Fortunately, you're here, alive and well, so hopefully not," Officer Oakley says. "You did a great job. So we have an excellent description of a woman who would stand out anywhere." She hands me her card. "I know you're scared," she says. "You've been through a lot and I don't blame you for feeling a bit paranoid right now."

Officer Petrie looks toward my bookcase. "Was that picture here when Ann Smith was in the office?"

I follow his gaze to the bookcase and see the framed photograph of the three of us—Jackson, Rainie, and myself. I'm grinning in the picture, my arm around Jackson's waist. Rainie, just two at the time, sits on his shoulders, her arms stretched wide, trusting her daddy to hold tight to her legs. Jackson's dark hair falls over his forehead, and his eyes crinkle with joy. The photograph was taken the day we closed on our four wooded acres in Shadow Ridge. We could not have been happier.

"*Yes,*" I say. "Maybe that's how she knew about my daughter? Though it doesn't explain everything else she knew about me."

"Well, if you see her again anywhere," Officer Petrie says to both Natalie and myself, "call us right away. Don't put yourself in any danger. Just call us."

Natalie looks at me. "People say 'I want to kill so-and-so' all the time," she says, reassuringly. "She was probably just—"

"No," I say with certainty. "This was different. She meant it."

"On the one hand," Officer Oakley says, "I wish she'd given you *more* information to help us out, but for your sake, it's good she didn't. I don't like that she knows where you live, or at least, where you're going to be living. It's a new house, so you probably have good locks, a good security system?" It was more of a question than a statement.

"I have a security system," I say. I'd done nothing about setting it up yet, though. You don't think about security systems in a safe little town like Round Hill. "I'll get it taken care of," I say, mentally adding it to my insanely long list of things to do.

Once the police and Natalie leave, I call my father, but he doesn't pick up, which is not unusual. He's terrible with his phone.

"Hey, Dad," I say. "Keep a close eye on Rainie this afternoon, okay? I'll explain later. I'm on my way home."

Then I pack my briefcase and leave my office, carefully locking the door behind me.

≈

I usually enjoy the walk from my office to the underground garage in downtown Greenville, sometimes stopping to pick up a cappuccino for the half-hour drive home to Round Hill, but this afternoon, I look over my shoulder with every step. I reach the garage and shudder as I walk into the shadows. The building absorbs the daylight and I nearly run to my car. Once inside the SUV, doors locked, I feel my heart thudding in my chest. I sit there for a moment, hands in my lap, thinking. Maybe I *should* put the new house on the market. Forget about moving in. Jackson and I had designed the house for ourselves and the family we hoped to create. At four thousand square feet it's far too big for just Rainie and me. But I tear up at the thought of someone else living in the house we designed with so much love and hope.

I close my eyes. Let out a breath. Then I start the car. I'll make the house a happy place. I'll make happy memories there for Rainie.

I drive the car out of the dark parking garage and into the sunlight and it's as if the light washes away my fear. That's the problem with the house. It's full of floor-to-ceiling windows, yet all the trees make it feel closed in. Jackson and I rhapsodized about being surrounded by all that gorgeous thick greenery. From the glassed-in rear of the house, all you can see is green, not another house in sight. Ours is considered the best and largest of the lots in the small development. Yet at that moment, I wish we'd picked a different lot. I wish we'd picked a different neighborhood altogether.

Chapter 4

─────≈─────

ELLIE

1965

That Tuesday, I took Brenda out to lunch at the Round Hill Sandwich Shop. It was a bribe of sorts, although I didn't think Brenda realized it. Her mind was so consumed by the fact that she would be marrying Garner on Saturday that she seemed to have forgotten she'd promised to go with me to Turner's Bend after lunch. I wanted to see Reverend Filburn, the minister who'd been quoted in the newspaper article about the SCOPE program. I tried my best to focus on Brenda's chatter, though. I worried that we were already drifting apart. Brenda would return to UNC with me the Monday after her wedding—no honeymoon for her and Garner—and she'd finish out the year, keeping her marriage and pregnancy a secret so she didn't get kicked out of the dorm. She was moving in a direction I wouldn't be able to relate to.

I watched her now as she added another spoonful of sugar to her sweet tea. She still looked like a teenager: turned-up nose, rosebud lips, and a curly blond halo of hair that set off her big baby-blue eyes. We'd never really shared the same interests: I'd loved school and science and read-ing; Brenda had loved music and movie magazines and boys. Aunt Carol would tease her. *Who's your heartthrob this week, Brenda?* But somehow, Brenda and I connected, even more so once we started dating Reed and Garner. We double-dated all through high school, even after the guys went off to college. These days, we saw them on the weekends when we came home or when they came to Chapel Hill to take us out to dinner. Brenda was really my best and oldest friend. I'd never had many.

Now she looked up from stirring her tea. "Promise me we'll stay friends," she said, as if reading my thoughts.

"Absolutely," I promised.

"I don't know what'll happen to us—to you and me—when I'm married and a mother and you're still a . . . a coed."

"We'll have to make an effort to stay connected," I said. It wouldn't be easy. My pharmacology program was five years, so I still had three more years to go. "And Brenda." I put on my most serious expression. "I know you wish Reed and I were as serious as you and Garner, but we're just not. We've never even talked about marriage, and honestly, until I finish school, I can't imagine marrying anyone."

"You always say that, but that's going to change," Brenda said with un-nerving certainty. "You'll see. Reed is so wonderful. He's only twenty-two and he graduated early and already has that desk job at the bank. He's going to be the manager someday and I just hope you wake up and realize what a catch he is before it's too late."

She didn't have to convince me that Reed was a catch. He was as close to perfect as anyone I knew. Smart. Movie-star handsome. Well respected at the bank, where he seemed to get a raise every month or so. Still, the thought of marrying him—or anyone—held no appeal for me.

When we finished our sandwiches and I'd paid our bill, I looked at my watch. "You ready?" I asked.

Brenda wrinkled her nose at me. "Do we really have to do this?" she asked. "Go to Turner's Bend?"

I nodded, getting to my feet. "Come on," I said. "It won't take long. Then I'll drive you to Garner's."

Brenda stood up and followed me out of the restaurant, walking next to me once we reached the sidewalk. "What's SCOPE stand for again?" she asked.

"Summer Community Organization and Political Education."

"Sounds deadly dull." She slipped her arm through mine. "I just don't understand why you want to do this, honey," she said. "The colored voting thing. I don't get it."

We'd reached my car and I opened the door for her. I'd gotten the red Ford when I started college so I could make that two-hour trip to Carolina on my own. The car was a junker for sure, but Buddy had fixed it up well enough that it did what I needed it to do. My brother was a mechanical genius who'd opened his own car-repair shop when he was barely nineteen years old.

I shrugged as I got in behind the steering wheel. "Because it's the right thing to do."

"I hoped you got it out of your system that time on Franklin Street. What did that get you? Holes in your stockings and a record for being arrested."

"I was *detained*, not arrested. And anyhow, it wasn't about what it got *me*. It made a difference. That café finally opened its doors to *everybody*, so it worked, right?"

"I suppose," she admitted, but I could tell she wasn't convinced.

I pulled out of the parking space. With the car closed up, I could smell the Aqua Net in Brenda's curly hair. I'd been letting my strawberry-blond hair dry straight. It was nearly to my shoulders now and I liked how it swung around my face when I danced.

I glanced at Brenda's beige slacks. I'd asked her to wear a skirt, since we were going into a church, but either she forgot or she hoped she could talk me out of going. I was wearing a cranberry-colored skirt, a white blouse, and my black flats. I looked like I was ready for a job interview.

I'd cut the article about the SCOPE program from the newspaper and taken it to bed with me the night after my father read it to us. I'd read it at least a dozen times since then. The students were all from the North or out west. Mama had been right. It was exactly the sort of thing Aunt Carol would have done as a student when she lived in New York. Would SCOPE take a Southerner? I couldn't see why not, as long as I was committed to the cause. Plus, I knew Derby County better than any of those outsiders ever would.

"This is just so unlike you," Brenda said as we drove down Main Street.

"What do you mean?"

"You . . . caring so much about Negroes all of a sudden."

I shrugged. "I've always cared," I said. "I just never really did anything about it until Franklin Street. Now I can see a real way to help."

"Have you talked to Reed about it?" she asked.

I shook my head. "It doesn't have anything to do with Reed," I said. "And besides, I don't even know if that minister'll say I can do it, yet." We drove past the Hockley Pharmacy, owned by my father and my grandfather before him. The prominent sign in the front window cried out PRE-SCRIPTIONS ARE OUR BUSINESS! We passed the butcher shop and the bakery and the movie theater, where *Beach Blanket Bingo* was showing. Then the shops gave way to the big white houses that belonged to Round Hill's finest.

"Don't you think everyone should have the right to vote?" I glanced at her. She'd opened the car window a few inches and her hair blew wildly around her face.

She shrugged. "They already do, really," she said. "It's not your fault or mine if they haven't bothered to register."

"I don't think it's that easy," I said.

Brenda went quiet. "You'd have weekends off, right?" she asked after a moment. "You'd still get to go to the beach with me and Reed and Garner?"

"Maybe," I said. "I don't know how the program is set up, exactly."

I drove for about a mile and a half to where the road made a right-hand turn, then dropped down a short slope landing us in Turner's Bend, and Main Street became Zion Road, the street no white person ever had a reason to travel. We might as well have landed on another planet. Nobody who looked like us—two blue-eyed blonds—ever went to Turner's Bend. I knew our long-ago maid, Louise Jenkins, lived down here somewhere. My parents would have known where, because they sometimes visited Louise, bringing her our old teapot or toaster, blankets and towels, things we didn't need anymore that Louise could put to good use. Daddy brought her medicine when she had the flu last year, but I'd never had a reason to visit Louise myself.

We drove past houses on the tree-lined street and Brenda rolled her window up and pressed down the lock of her door, surreptitiously, as if she didn't want me to notice. The houses were much smaller than those we'd passed in Round Hill, but they looked well cared for, and I wondered if the people living in them were registered to vote. They had to have jobs to keep their houses up so well. I saw women and children on the porches. Men mowing their lawns. We came to a string of shops—the little downtown area. Then, suddenly, the pavement ended and we were on a dirt road. There were more houses, not as nice as those at the west end of the road. Ahead of us on the right stood a brick church with a tall steeple.

"I bet that's the AME church," I said, but as we neared it, I saw that the sign out front read ZION BAPTIST, and I kept on driving.

"Don't you have an address?" Brenda looked at her watch.

I shook my head. I knew the church was on Zion Road somewhere and I figured it wouldn't be that hard to find, but we were soon in farmland, the houses far apart now, more ramshackle, and the dirt road was rutted and dusty. Dogs and chickens roamed the yards, and men and women were hunched over in every field.

"I think we should go back," Brenda said. "We're out in the middle of nowhere."

She was right and I was losing heart. I should have checked the address, but even so, none of the houses we passed had street numbers on them. A voice in my head told me to turn around. But the stronger part of me kept my foot on the gas. And then, finally, I saw a small, low-slung, one-story white building, its windows clear rather than stained glass. The slender white steeple was topped by a cross no taller than my car's antenna. On the building itself, next to the door, a hand-painted sign read TURNER'S BEND A.M.E. CHURCH.

There was one car in the parking lot, an older-model black Plymouth. Its tires were coated with a fine tan dust, but the rest of the car sparkled in the April sunlight. I pulled into the lot and turned off my car, wiping my sweaty hands on my skirt.

"I'll stay here," Brenda said.

"No, you won't," I said, opening my door. "Come on."

"You're not roping me in to spending the summer out here in . . ."

I got out and shut my door, not wanting to hear what Brenda was going to say. But I waited for her at the side of my car, and when she realized I wasn't going in without her, she slowly opened her door and circled the car to join me. Together we walked across the packed earth toward the church.

The front door was unlocked and we stepped inside. Although the interior of the church was filled with dark wooden pews, much like the Baptist church I'd grown up in, that was the only similarity. The clear windows spread stark white light over the space, unlike the muted colors of the stained glass in Round Hill Baptist. And there was no choir loft, although there were risers in the front of the church behind the pulpit. The pulpit itself was spectacular, the only ostentatious thing in the building. Carved from a beautiful blond wood, it seemed to dwarf everything else in the building.

A man suddenly appeared from a doorway near the end of the risers. I saw the surprise on his face, most likely from finding two blonds in his church. His eyes widened behind dark-rimmed glasses and he stopped walking.

"You lost?" he asked. He was fairly young, no more than thirty or thirty-five, but his voice had the deeper tone of an older man.

Brenda and I hung back by the door. "I don't think so . . . sir." I licked my lips, which had gone very dry. "Are you the minister they quoted in that article about the students coming to register voters?" I asked. "SCOPE?"

"Yes, I'm Reverend Filburn." He made no move toward us and we made no move toward him. The sea of dark pews stretched out between us. "Can I help you?" he asked.

"I read that article and I'd like to help," I said.

The minister studied me for what seemed like a full minute, unsmiling. "Come forward and have a seat," he said finally, motioning to the pews nearest him. Our footsteps made little sound on the old bare wood as we walked toward the front of the church. After we sat down in the second pew, he took a seat in the first, turning to face us.

"What are your names?" he asked.

"I'm Ellie," I said. "Eleanor Hockley."

Reverend Filburn turned his attention to Brenda. "And you are?"

"Brenda Kane, but I'm just here for . . ." She glanced at me, clearly at a loss for words, but Reverend Filburn helped her out.

"Moral support," he suggested with a hint of a smile. I was relieved to finally see some lightness in his expression.

"Yeah." She smiled back at him. "Moral support."

He returned his attention to me. "Well, Miss Hockley," he said, "I admire you for wanting to help, if that's truly why you're here, but SCOPE isn't looking for Southern students. Just from the North. And some from out west."

I'd expected him to say that, given the information in the newspaper article, but it made no sense to me. "But why not, if I'm willing to help?" I asked.

He knitted his eyebrows together. "Why do you want to do this?"

"Because I think everyone should have the right to vote."

"Do you now?"

He didn't trust me. It was disconcerting. "Yes," I said. "Sincerely."

"Are you working?" he asked.

"No, I'm in school," I said. "Finishing up my sophomore year. I'm study-ing pharmacology at Carolina. At UNC."

His brows finally unknit and he nodded. I thought I'd impressed him.

He turned to Brenda. "You a student too?" he asked.

She nodded. "Yes."

He studied her another moment before returning his attention to me. "Where do you live?" he asked.

"In Round Hill." I motioned north of where we sat. "So, you see, I know the area well, and—"

"You may know *Round Hill* well, but I'd bet my church you don't know the parts of Derby County where SCOPE'll be working."

"Well . . . what I mean is, I know it better than any Northerners would. And you wouldn't have to put me up anywhere. I could just go home at the end of the day and—"

"No," He cut me off again, this time sharply. "You'd be treated the same as all the other students. No runnin' home when things got hard. You'd be put up in local homes like everyone else."

That stopped me. I actually felt the muscles of my chest contract with the shock of his words, and next to me, I thought Brenda caught her breath. I remembered the dilapidated little houses we'd passed by on the drive to the church. "You mean . . . to sleep?"

"To sleep. To eat. To get to know the folks you'd be aimin' to help."

Living with strangers was not what I'd imagined and it was a moment before I nodded. "I understand." I thought of backing out right then. I didn't need to do this. Put myself through this. Yet I stayed seated. "I'd want to be treated like everyone else," I said.

He shook his head as if he knew perfectly well how he'd just stunned me. "Tell me about your people," he said, folding his arms across his chest.

I shifted on the hard pew. "Well, we go back a few generations in Derby

County," I said. "I live on Hockley Street in Round Hill in the same house my father and grandfather were born in. My father's a pharmacist and he owns—"

"Hockley?" He interrupted me. "Your daddy owns Hockley Pharmacy?"

"Yes."

His whole countenance softened. He unfolded his arms, stretching his left arm along the back of the pew and turning more fully toward us. I hadn't realized how tightly wound he'd been until he relaxed, and for the first time I thought his smile was genuine.

"Your daddy's a good man," he said. "Sometimes our own pharmacy can't get what we need and Doc Hockley comes through for us. A real good man."

"He is," I said. My father wasn't a doctor, but I knew a lot of people referred to him as "Doc Hockley." I hadn't known, though, that he helped out the folks in Turner's Bend. Maybe Daddy might understand why I wanted to work for SCOPE.

"He helped my own little daughter one time when she came down with something," Reverend Filburn continued. "Carried a special cough syrup all the way down here for her."

"That sounds like him," I said, touched and proud.

"You have to understand something . . . Eleanor, is it?" Reverend Filburn asked.

"Ellie. Yes."

"I'll tell you plain," he said. "I didn't trust you when you walked in here. Not sure I trust you even now. White girl, walking into a Negro church asking to help folk vote? Not an everyday occurrence."

I nodded.

"We've already had threats and SCOPE hasn't even started," he said. "My *church* has had threats. *I've* had threats. My wife and children have had threats. I saw you walk in and I wondered if you're here to plant a bomb in a pew. Understand?"

"Wow," I said.

"For all I knew when you walked in here, you could have been part of the Klan, or—"

"The Klan!" I laughed.

"Not as improbable as it sounds," he said. "The Civil Rights Act brought them out of the woodwork last year, and a Voting Rights Act is only going to make them double their efforts. Right now, North Carolina has more Klan members than all the other states put together."

"I didn't know that." I'd been startled last summer to see a small procession of Klan members, both men and women, dressed in their white satin robes and tall pointed hats, strolling—unmasked, proudly—on the sidewalk through downtown Round Hill. *An anomaly*, I'd thought then, and when I mentioned them to my mother, she said, "Oh, it's more of a social club these days, honey. People like to belong to something." To me, the group had looked silly. To a Negro person, I imagined there was nothing at all silly in the sight of them.

"They're not as . . . violent here, though, right?" I asked.

"Don't bet your life on that." It sounded like a warning. He glanced at Brenda, then back at me. "If you work for SCOPE, you'll have to be watchful. Every place you go. Everything you do," he said. "The thing the Klan hates more than a Negro is a white person who tries to *help* a Negro. Have you really thought this through?" he asked.

"I . . . I think so," I stammered.

"I don't think you have. You thought you'd be able to sleep at home with Mama and Daddy every night. You need to understand what you'll be doing. You might have to walk five, ten miles a day canvassing, trying to get people to come out to vote when they have twenty good reasons not to."

"I'll do anything you need," I promised. I felt Brenda's eyes on me. She probably thought I'd lost my mind.

"The other thing." He shifted his position on the pew again till he was facing me more directly. "The way I distrusted you when you walked in here? No one'll trust you. Not the people you'll be trying to help and not even the other students. The Northern students. They'll be suspicious of you."

"You could put me in an office if you need to hide me away," I said. "But let me help. Please."

"You need to take some time to think it over."

"Maybe that's a good idea." Brenda spoke up for the first time, nudging my arm. I ignored her, but she continued, speaking to the minister. "I don't understand why you'd bring in white Northern students to do this," she said. "It doesn't make any sense."

Reverend Filburn nodded as though he'd been asked the question a dozen times before. "Do y'all remember the three civil rights workers who were killed in Mississippi last summer?" he asked.

I nodded. Beside me, Brenda gave a noncommittal shrug. The pictures of the three young men had been everywhere after it happened. There was so much on the news about them that I even recalled their names: Goodman, Chaney, and Schwerner. I remembered how Aunt Carol wept about their fate.

"You wouldn't remember them at all if they'd all been Negro," Reverend Filburn said. "Two were white. That's why it made the news. That's . . . unfortunately . . . why so many people cared. White SCOPE workers . . . they'll get the attention from the press. But Negro folk won't trust *Southern* whites, so we'll bring these bright, motivated students down from up north."

"I understand," I said.

He tilted his head, looking at me from behind his thick glasses. "Why do you feel so strongly about this?" he asked.

"I know it's unjust that so many people—have a hard time registering," I said. "I can sit home and gripe about it or I can . . . act on my convictions." I imagined Aunt Carol sitting beside me on the pew. "I . . . I see the dirt road we drove in on." I gestured toward the road. "The awful condition of some of the houses and buildings. The fact that your pharmacy can't get everything it needs. And I know voting makes a difference in getting those things taken care of."

He looked at me wordlessly for a moment. "Yes, it does," he said finally, getting to his feet. "Leave me your address. I'll make a call."

≈

Back in my car, Brenda turned to look at me. "You're not seriously thinking of doing this, are you?" she asked.

"I am," I said, turning the key in the ignition.

"It's crazy, Ellie! You'd have to sleep in colored homes! Do you really want to do that?"

I hesitated. "It's hard to picture sleeping in *any* stranger's home," I admitted. I turned onto the dirt road, my car bouncing in and out of a deep rut. "But sounds like it comes with the job. I'd want to be treated like the other students."

"If God had meant us all to live together, he wouldn't have made us different colors," Brenda said.

I looked at her in exasperation. "That's the most ignorant comment I've ever heard you make," I said. But I suddenly remembered back to the year before, when two Negro girls moved into our dorm. We all had to share one large bathroom, and Brenda suggested we put a COLORED sign on one of the stalls so Dora and Midge would only use that one. I thought she'd been making a bad joke. Right now I wondered. We rarely talked about race. We were white girls who'd grown up in a mostly white town. Race didn't come up much in our conversations.

Even if it came up often in my thoughts.

Chapter 5

―≈―

KAYLA

2010

The drive from Bader and Duke Design to my father's home in Round Hill takes thirty-five minutes and I usually listen to pop music to lift my mood as I drive, but I'm so anxious right now that I forget to turn on the radio. I can't get "Ann Smith" out of my head. I keep glancing in my rearview mirror to see if I'm being followed. Maybe I returned to work too soon. Took on too much. Maybe the woman is no threat at all and it's simply that I've come to see life itself as a threat. I never feel safe anymore. Worse, I never feel as though the people I love are safe. My dreams, when I can sleep, are filled with blood and death. I know tonight's dream will be even worse. How am I going to get that bizarre woman out of my head? I shudder when I think of her mentioning Rainie. I can't bear the thought of anything happening to my daughter.

The police hadn't seemed all that concerned about "Ann Smith," but they hadn't been in the room with the woman. They hadn't felt her ma- lignant presence, how she seemed to study me from behind her mirrored glasses as though she wanted to memorize every detail of my face. How she knew about Jackson's death. It would be one thing if she were just some nut threatening to kill someone. Somehow, though, she knew about my life. Did she mention Rainie by name? I don't think so. I'd remember if she had. But she knows that my daughter and I live in Round Hill and that we'll soon be moving into the new house at the end of Shadow Ridge Lane. And as if she'd crawled inside my head, she even knew how I *feel* about the new neighborhood these days: *All those trees suck the breath out of you*, she said. Yes, that's exactly right.

I make the left turn onto Round Hill Road, then another left on Painter Lane, and the house I grew up in is ahead on my right. Rainie and I moved in with my father the week after Jackson died as we waited for the Shadow Ridge house to be completed. Most of my high school friends have left Round Hill and the few who remain are busy with their own families. I need Daddy now, the comfort of him, in a way I haven't since I was a child. The move's turned out to be a good one for all three of us. Daddy's been lonely since Mom died, shortly before Rainie was born, and Rainie's given him a new reason for getting up in the morning. But change is coming. Daddy's downsizing. He's selling our old family home and will soon move into a two-bedroom condo on the other side of town. My old house has sold, my furniture moved to storage. And now the new house is ready for Rainie and me. There's no going back to the way things used to be.

I pull into the driveway of my childhood home and park next to my father's black pickup. I still miss seeing my mother's silver Toyota next to his truck. My heart still hurts when I think that she never got to meet her granddaughter. I hate that I can't call her for advice when Rainie runs a fever or skins a knee. I'm only now getting used to being in our old house without her.

The house is big, baby blue with white trim and a wraparound porch. The perimeter of the yard is dotted with mature dogwoods and redbuds, and in the spring, the beauty is breathtaking. I put aside memories of my mother for now, and my heart rate slows as I lift my briefcase and purse from the passenger seat. Rainie and I are safe here. The red-haired woman said nothing about *this* house, about knowing that Rainie and I live here right now, so I feel a cocoon of safety surround me as I get out of the car.

I can tell that Daddy mowed the lawn this morning, the wide stripes of green a giveaway. At sixty-seven, he still mows it himself even though he could afford to have someone else do it. He still slithers through the crawl space to check the foundation and gets up on the roof to repair the shingles. I wish he wouldn't do that. I know now how quickly an accident can happen. He still walks five miles every morning before breakfast, as he did during the thirty years he was Round Hill's mayor. Even the day after Mom died, he was out there, nodding hello to everyone, stopping only long enough to accept condolences as he made his usual trek through our small town and into the countryside and back again. People like Reed Miller, and he likes them back. He'll easily make new friends in the condo complex.

I hear yelps of joy coming from the backyard as I quietly close my car door, and I smile to myself as I walk around the side of the house, my mood lifting. Standing silently at the rear corner of the house, I watch Daddy and Rainie in the yard, where he's spotting her as she climbs the jungle gym. He's created a veritable playground for her back here, and fortunately the family buying his house was happy to find the jungle gym and swings and sliding board already in place for their own kids.

"Mama!" Rainie suddenly spots me, and Daddy helps her off the jungle gym so she can run to me. She always hugs me as if she hasn't seen me in days instead of hours and I bend low to wrap my arms around her and breathe in the scent of sun in her hair.

"How was your day, love?" I ask her.

She looks over her shoulder at her grandfather. "Gramps made me Mickey Mouse grilled cheese."

"Oh, I bet that was delicious!" I rest my hand on her head, on her sun-warmed hair, nearly as dark as mine.

"Can he make it for dinner, too?" she asks, looking up at me with Jackson's warm brown eyes.

"If he's willing," I say. "But we need to have some vegetables with it to make us strong and healthy."

"Right." She nods. "Carrots." The only vegetable she likes.

"Carrots," I agree.

≈

"Let's go see the new house when you get home tomorrow afternoon," Daddy says as we clean the kitchen after dinner. "I know you haven't felt like going over there, but we really should make sure it's ready for your furniture to arrive on Saturday. Make sure the workers have taken care of the punch list."

"Sure," I say, but my anxiety level climbs another notch at the thought of moving. I remind myself that we'll be less than two miles away from our safe haven with my father, and once he moves, Rainie will still spend her afternoons with him. The condo complex has a playground and even a pool. We'll still have dinner with him occasionally. The only change will be that Rainie and I will sleep in the new house. I shudder at the thought of the dark woods. Ours will be the only completed house on the street so far. The construction crew, many of whom knew and respected Jackson, thought they were doing me a favor by working overtime after his death. "A gift for you," one of them said. The house took my husband from me. It doesn't feel like a gift.

Daddy knows how I feel. He rests a hand on my shoulder. "It's going to be fine, Kayla," he says, and I nod. He thinks I just need time. Maybe I do, but I don't think I will ever be able to live in the house without thinking *These are the windows Jackson special-ordered,* or *This is the quartzite we argued over and Jackson let me win,* or *This is the color Jackson chose for the foyer.*

"A weird thing happened today," I say, as I dry the last plate. I speak quietly, although Rainie is in the living room and I can hear her giggling over a video she's watching. I tell him about the red-haired woman and he frowns when I get to the part about her knowing that Jackson died and that we're about to move into the house in Shadow Ridge.

"Well," he says, "a lot of that information was in the paper after the accident."

"I know, but what does it matter to her? Why did she seek me out? Who does she want to kill?"

"Can it just be that she's crazy and talking through her hat?" he suggests. "Nothing more than that?"

"It's even scarier to me if she's crazy," I say. "If she's crazy, there's no way of predicting what she'll do."

He smiles at me with the calmness I usually love about him, but which is bugging me at the moment. I want him to take this seriously. "Well," he says, "I'll keep my eyes open and my wits about me. And you do the same."

Chapter 6

—————≈—————

ELLIE

1965

We lived in the only house on Hockley Street, on the corner where Hockley intersected with Round Hill Road. Daddy's father named the street after himself—Amos Hockley—and he and his brother built the house. Hockley Street was the only actual "street" in all of Round Hill. There were plenty of roads and lanes and trails, but my grandfather'd thought "Hockley Street" sounded grand. It was decidedly not grand. It had been a dirt road back when the house was built and it was a dirt road now and probably always would be. But our house was big, whitewashed, with black shutters, a red tin roof, and a wide porch with white rockers, one for each of us, and I always felt rich and proud. Our view from the porch was of the kudzu-choked trees and shrubs across the street. "Beautiful monsters," Mama called them when I was small and afraid. They rose up from the earth to the sky in the shapes of dragons and dinosaurs. The kudzu didn't come near our house, so it didn't bother us and it kept anyone else from building on Hockley Street, which was just the way my family liked it. "We have paradise all to ourselves," Mama always said.

Our narrow road ended in the deepest, darkest woods anyone could imagine—straight out of a Grimms' fairy tale—but they didn't bother us. When Buddy and I were younger, we just about lived in those woods, climbing the trees, playing hide-and-seek, and fishing in the lake. I was shy and had few friends other than Buddy and Mattie, who was our maid Louise's daughter, a year younger than me. I loved Mattie. She died when I was eleven and Buddy started hanging out with older kids, and I suddenly had no one to play with. For a year, I was on my own, mourning the loss of both Mattie and my brother, but then Brenda Kane and her parents moved to Round Hill and I suddenly had a friend.

Buddy was smart enough to become a pharmacist like our father, who'd hoped his son would be the third generation of pharmacists in the family, but Buddy discovered cars and that was that. Everyone in town depended on him, not just for their cars, but their washing machines and radios and any other gadget they couldn't get to work right. Once Daddy accepted Buddy for who he was, they grew close. Now they were up in arms together over the idea of a bunch of Yankee kids telling us how to run things down here.

The Sunday after the wedding, Buddy and I strolled up Hockley Street to the woods.

"So how was the wedding?" Buddy asked, putting his arm around me as we walked.

I thought back to the day before and the quiet, sort of sad little wedding at the justice of the peace's office. Garner had looked nervous, perspiring in a dark suit, and I thought Brenda was going to burst into tears at any moment. She wore a pale blue dress I'd seen her in several times before. Her best, I knew. It was a dress she wouldn't be able to get into in another week or two. I teared up during the wedding, remembering how she'd paged through the *Brides* magazine with such longing. She would never wear one of those long lacy wedding gowns. She would never have a string of bridesmaids and groomsmen. Just me as her maid of honor and Reed as Garner's best man.

"Simple," I answered Buddy. "I felt more sad than anything else. It wasn't exactly joyous."

"I can't believe she's going back to school with you like she's not a married girl," Buddy said. "Married woman."

"I know," I agreed. "Still, it's good she can finish out the year. Then maybe she'll pick it up again someday."

"She should've dropped Garner for me," Buddy said. "I wouldn't have let her get in this predicament." He'd had a crush on Brenda since we were all in high school together, but Brenda only had eyes for Garner. "You think she's really after him for his money?" he asked.

"Hell, no," I said. "How could you think that? She adores him." Garner's father was probably the wealthiest man in Round Hill, but I'd never even heard Brenda mention the money Garner was sure to inherit.

"Well, maybe she could talk Garner into telling his daddy to stop raising my rent," Buddy said. Randy Cleveland owned nearly half the buildings in town, including the one that housed Buddy's car shop.

"I doubt she has that sort of clout," I said.

"Well anyhow," he said, "don't you ever let what happened to Brenda happen to you." There was a warning in his voice like he'd break my neck if I came home pregnant.

I rolled my eyes. "I'll be a virgin on my wedding night," I assured him. "Assuming I ever *have* a wedding night," I said. "And you should have waited, too."

"Way too late for that." He laughed. He was ridiculously handsome, my brother. Built like a football player, he had sandy hair, our father's dark eyes, and a lopsided smile that girls found irresistible.

The weather was warm and the kudzu vines were just beginning to green up, rising like towers on either side of the road, trapping us or sheltering us, however you wanted to look at it. I could already make out the shape of a *Tyrannosaurus rex* on the north side of the street and an enormous panther on the south.

"So," Buddy said, "are you and Reed going to be next?" His voice was casual, but I could tell that the words were planned. He worried about me. Even though Buddy had only been three when I was born, he'd been my protector since that day.

"Right now I want to focus on school," I said. "I don't have time for men."

We'd reached the end of Hockley Street, and the dirt road narrowed to one skinny rutted lane that cut through the thick forest. Even now, at two in the afternoon, it was dark in the woods. We fell silent as we brushed away leafy branches and stepped over familiar roots until we reached the massive oak above a round clearing, the ground thick with pine needles and decayed leaves from a hundred autumns. I walked across the clearing and around the oak, where I started climbing the wide boards Daddy'd hammered into the trunk when we were small. He was the one who'd spotted the huge triangle of the oak's branches fifteen feet from the ground. He was the one who built the sturdy little house way up there, adding a deck where we could sit and share secrets or quietly watch the forest in the clearing down below. The plentiful deer. The occasional fox. The birds that flitted from branch to branch around our heads.

I reached the little house, walked through it, and scurried on my hands and knees out to the deck, where I dangled my legs over the edge, high above the clearing. Buddy came to sit next to me.

I'd pictured us climbing up here today. It seemed like the right place to tell him my summer plan. I was afraid, though, of how he'd react. I knew he thought the idea of "Yankee kids" coming to Derby County was wrongheaded. Even though he'd hired a young Negro guy, Ronnie, to work in his car shop and seemed to like him a lot, my brother was still undeniably a bigot. When I told him about the protests at UNC last year, he said to stay out of it. "I don't see what the coloreds have to complain all that much about," he'd said. "They have roofs over their heads. They have their own stores, their own schools, their own churches. It ain't like they're slaves. Why would they even want to come into a white restaurant where they know they're not welcome?"

Now I looked at my loafer-clad feet high above the clearing and took in a breath. "I'm not going to work in the pharmacy this summer," I said.

He laughed. "Good luck gettin' out of it," he said. I'd worked in the pharmacy every summer since I was fourteen.

"You know that SCOPE program?"

"Those Yankee kids comin' down here to tell us how we should be runnin' things?"

"That's not what it's about, Buddy," I said. "The Voting Rights Act is coming and some of the people in poor areas will need help registering. I want to work with SCOPE to help them."

He leaned away from me to look at my face. His blond eyebrows were nearly knitted together in the middle. "Are you messin' with me?" he asked.

"No, I'm absolutely serious. I've already spoken with the minister in charge and—"

"Uh-uh, little sister," Buddy said. "Not gonna let you do that. Think about them three boys that got themselves killed a couple of years ago."

"It was *last* year," I corrected him, "but that was in Mississippi. North Carolina isn't like the Deep South, and you know it. I'll be perfectly safe."

"This is stupid, Ellie."

"I know Daddy's going to be disappointed about the pharmacy."

"That's going to be the least of his objections," he said. "And Reed ain't gonna be thrilled about it either."

"He'll survive without me for one summer."

We were quiet for a moment. Then Buddy said, out of the blue, "I treat Ronnie at the car shop the same way I treat the other guys. No better or worse. That's how it should be."

"I should hope so," I said.

"I ain't no racist," Buddy said.

"That's a double negative. What you just said actually means you *are* a racist."

He stared at me. "What's your problem?" he asked, but then he immediately softened. Put his arm around my shoulders again. "What did you do with my sweet sister, huh?" he asked.

I sighed. Leaned against him. He smelled like motor oil. I'd come to equate the smell with him and I liked it. "I'm just tired of seeing a wrong and doing nothing to make it right, that's all," I said. "I wish you'd give me some support."

He tightened his hand on my shoulder. "How can I support you when I'm afraid you're gonna get yourself killed?" he asked. "Or worse?"

"What's worse than getting killed?" I asked, momentarily sidetracked by his question.

"Think about it," he said, and then I knew. Rape. He meant rape.

"I'm not afraid," I said. "I think I'll be fine . . . if they accept me. The minister I spoke with wasn't all that enthused about having me work with them."

"What's his name? I'll call him up and tell him not to take you."

"You wouldn't dare."

"Have you really thought this through, Ellie?" he asked. "Some parts of Derby County have more colored than white. Would you really feel all right with them being the majority when it comes to votin'? They'd make laws that favor themselves. Before you know it, we'd be the minority."

"I thought you said you weren't a racist?"

"I'm just playing devil's advocate."

"I'm not going to tell Mama and Daddy until I know for sure SCOPE will take me," I said, changing the subject. "But let me be the one to tell them. Okay?"

He laughed. "I promise you I'll just sit back and watch," he said. "With Aunt Carol gone, it's been a while since we had a good fireworks show 'round here."

Chapter 7

———— ≋ ————

KAYLA

My father, Rainie, and I head to the new house late in the afternoon after I get home from work. I'm not excited about going.

I fell asleep easily last night, but that red-haired woman came to me in a dream. She carried a gun and it was clearly me she was after. When I woke up, I had to get out of bed and walk around the quiet house until the image of her—the *memory* of her—was gone, or at least had faded. Then at the office this morning, I constantly looked over my shoulder. I keep wondering if I might one day soon read about a murder in the paper, a murder I could have somehow prevented.

We approach the Main Street intersection. I turn left onto Main and drive past the Round Hill Theater, where my middle school boyfriends and I used to make out in the back row, and the Food Lion, where I worked one summer a lifetime ago. Then I make a right onto Round Hill Road. We pass some newer developments, those clots of homes that seem to spring from the ground overnight, erasing trees and cornfields. That's why Jackson and

I'd been excited about Shadow Ridge, where the developers required the builders to retain so many of the trees.

The new granite entrance signs have been installed since my last visit— SHADOW RIDGE ESTATES in gold script on a dark background. Embarrassingly ostentatious, I think, as I turn onto Shadow Ridge Lane. The first house I see—the first house anyone would see as they drive into this developing neighborhood—is the old Hockley place. Buddy Hockley refuses to sell to the developers, who would like to squeeze two more houses into the wide lot where the big white, red-roofed house stands. The house is ancient, and although it couldn't be more different from the style of house I love to design, I think it's beautiful. There's something appealing about the broad porch with the rockers that look like they've been there forever. It's an inviting "come over and have a glass of sweet tea" sort of porch. But the Hockley house is an abomination to everyone else who is having a house built on Shadow Ridge Lane.

I've heard that Buddy Hockley is terminally ill now—I don't know with what—so I'm sure the developers are ready to pounce on their heirs, whoever they might be.

I'm so used to seeing only a dusty old dark blue pickup in the Hockley driveway that I'm actually startled to see a white sedan behind it. An aide? A visitor? A grown child?

"Does Buddy Hockley have children, Daddy?" I ask as we pass the driveway.

My father seems to be studying the white car as well. "Buddy had a daughter but she passed a few years back," he says. "Wife passed too. Only family left besides his mother is a sister, Eleanor—Ellie—but she lives in California. Left when she was young and never came back."

"Will Daddy be at the new house?" Rainie interrupts our conversation from the back seat. My heart cramps at her question and I can't answer right away.

My father reaches over to touch my shoulder. He gives it a squeeze. *Be strong*, he's saying.

"No, honey," I say. "Daddy won't be there. Remember I told you that he's in heaven?" It breaks my heart that she still doesn't get it that Jackson is gone for good. It breaks my heart that she'll never get to know him, and that he'll never have the chance to see his little girl grow up.

"Oh right. I forgetted," Rainie says, without the slightest hint of pain in her voice. "I wish he'd come back though."

"So do we, honey," I say. "And I know he misses you as much as you miss him."

Both sides of Shadow Ridge Lane are lined with white construction vans, and the sound of hammering and drilling and sawing cuts right through the car windows. I am sick to death of the sounds of construction. The houses are in various stages of completion, and—not counting the Hockley house—there will be nineteen altogether, eight on the north side, ten on the south, and one at the very end of the street. That is ours. Or, I guess, mine. It's an undeniably stunning house—a sleek wood-and-glass Frank Lloyd Wright–inspired contemporary, finished and waiting for the furniture to arrive on Saturday. I wish the furniture would arrive next year, instead, when we'd at least have some neighbors to get to know. I have such a love/hate feeling about our "dream house" now.

"I think you should take out some more trees." Daddy eyes the land around the house as I pull into the newly paved driveway.

I have to admit that the trees look oppressive. Before, I thought they would embrace the house. Now it looks as though the house has slipped inside a deep green cave.

No one should have put a house there. Isn't that what the woman said? Weird Ann Smith?

"Maybe," I answer my father.

Outside the car, I reach for Rainie's hand, but she runs ahead, hopping along the new sidewalk that runs from the driveway to the front door. Daddy and I catch up with her there, and I tap in the code to unlock the door.

Although it's only late afternoon and the walls are more glass than wood, the house is indeed a bit dim inside. I flick on the lights and take a look around. The first story is completely open, the ceiling high. I can see all the way to the kitchen from where I stand. Unobtrusive shelves divide the dining area from the living room, the kitchen from the great room. The walls have now been painted a pale taupe. The new hardwood floors, a rich toffee color, are incredibly beautiful and warm the open space exactly as I'd hoped they would. It's been two weeks since I've been in the house and it looks like it's ready and waiting to be filled with furnishings and family. The architect in me is proud and amazed at what Jackson and I created. The widow in me can barely move.

"Let's look around," Daddy says, as if perplexed as to why I'm just standing there lost in thought in the foyer. His voice echoes in the emptiness. We walk through the great room with its spectacular copper-fronted fireplace. The wall of floor-to-ceiling windows that overlook the wide deck is the rich deep green of the trees. I remember Jackson saying he couldn't wait to see that wall of windows in the fall when the leaves would wash our entire downstairs with color. I wish he would have the chance.

The hand-painted art-deco tile backsplash has finally been installed in the kitchen and it looks even better than I imagined. I know the whole downstairs is absolutely stunning, yet I can't *feel* anything. I don't care about pretty tile. I just want my husband back. I draw in a long breath, doing my best to keep the tears at bay.

We head up the open staircase from the great room to the second story. It's slow going with Rainie, but she hangs on to the railing and doggedly works her way up. When we reach the last few steps, I keep my eye on her, wondering if she understands how that staircase took Jackson from us. But she seems to have no idea how the stairs altered her life, and once she reaches the top, she cheers with the achievement of climbing them. Daddy laughs, and I shake off the horror of memory and join him.

We explore the four large bedrooms, the massive closets, the four bathrooms. I remember the hundreds of hours Jackson and I spent picking out floor tiles and fixtures for those bathrooms. Everything smells of new wood and paint. Rainie knows from our last visit which room will be hers, and she chatters about where she'll put her dollhouse, where her bed will go. Downstairs again, we cross through the great room and outside to the huge deck. We are absolutely, utterly cocooned by trees, so much so that the construction noise fades into the background and we hear mostly birdsong.

"You'll have plenty of shade in the summer," Daddy says. "How far back does your property go?"

"Pretty far," I say. "Jackson and his construction buddies put this circular trail in"—I point to the stepping-stones at either end of the deck—"and he said the property goes all the way back to a little lake, but I never walked that far with him."

"You'll want to fence it off," Daddy says, nodding toward Rainie. "That lake might be small, but it's deep."

"Oh, you know it?" I ask.

"Oh, sure," he says. I shouldn't be surprised. After a lifetime of living in Round Hill, he knows every inch of it.

"I'll get some estimates." I study the trees and for the first time, I notice an enormous oak in the distance. "That tree." I point toward it. "That must be the biggest tree in the neighborhood."

Daddy follows the trajectory of my arm. "Yeah, that tree's been here forever," he says. "The Hockley kids used to have a tree house up in its branches. I hung out there as a kid myself sometimes." He looks a little nostalgic and I smile. I like the idea that this land had once been my father's playground. It makes it feel safe and familiar. That fact and the sweet scent of the forest give me courage about living here.

"Hey, Rainie," I call to my daughter, who is trying unsuccessfully to catch a blue-tailed skink that's running around on the deck. "What do you think of our cool new house?"

Rainie stops chasing the skink. She stands still on the deck, looking up at the house. She stretches her arms out wide. "I think it's the beautifulest house in the whole world," she says, her tone so serious that Daddy and I both laugh. I look at my father and he reaches out to run the backs of his fingers down my cheek.

"Everything's going to be all right, Kayla," he says. "You'll see."

≋

I'm relieved when we leave the house. As we drive back to my father's, I feel trapped. Rainie and I have no choice but to move into the house. Our old house is sold and we can't stay with Daddy any longer; he needs to empty his house for the new owners. Maybe I could put my new house on the market and rent something until I find a house small and cozy and safe for Rainie and me, but the thought is painful. The Shadow Ridge house was our baby, Jackson's and mine. As ambivalent as I am about moving into it, I don't want strangers to live in it either.

When we get to my father's house, I sit on the bed in my childhood bedroom and have a one-sided talk with Jackson. I do this entirely too much. This room awakens all my early memories of him. Even though my personal things have been removed from the room—my yearbooks from high school and NC State, where Jackson and I met and became insepa-rable, the pictures of us at parties and concerts, when our future was wide open—the memories of our early years together still linger. They're in the air of the room. In the walls. In my bed, where we first made love one night when my parents were out. It's both painful and comforting to be in this room.

I remember our first big trip together. We drove ten hours to Pennsyl-vania to visit Frank Lloyd Wright's Fallingwater, that cantilevered con-crete and steel house situated directly above a waterfall. We were two months into our relationship and that's when I realized I had a passionate man on my hands—and not just in our hotel room. While I could appre-ciate the beauty of Fallingwater and the architectural skill that went into its creation, I would have been satisfied with an afternoon's exploration of the building. Jackson, though, insisted on a two-day visit, examining every nook and cranny, peppering the docents with questions as he researched the technical details of the house.

"So is this your dream house?" I asked him that second day, as we stood in one of the building's living areas.

He looked around him, not answering right away. That was Jackson's style, I'd learned. He always thought before he spoke. "Yes and no," he equivocated. "I'm fascinated by the inventiveness. By the skill. But the interior is a bit too cold. I'd like more warmth." Then he pointed to the massive corner window nearest us. "But oh my God, the windows!"

"Totally agree," I said. The enormous window framed the snowcapped branches of oaks and maples and fir trees. "I love how he brought nature inside."

Jackson smiled at me, a smile that made me feel as though I was the only person in the world. "Exactly," he said. "And when you and I design our house together, that's what we'll do. We'll bring nature inside."

I remember him taking my hand then as we continued strolling through the house, while my face heated up from his words. *When you and I design our house together.* I should have felt insulted by his presumption that we'd be together forever, yet I realized, in that moment, that being together with him forever was exactly what I wanted.

Now I sigh, leaning back against the headboard of my bed.

How would you feel if I sold the house? I ask him.

He doesn't bother to respond. He knows I know his answer.

Still, I call one of my good friends, Bets, who also happens to be a Round Hill Realtor, just to test the waters.

"Oh, don't even think of selling it, Kayla!" she says. "It's so beautiful and you and Jackson put your heart and soul into it."

"I know, but—"

"And there's not much suitable on the market right now for you and Rainie to move into."

"We could rent for a while," I say.

"I think," Bets says slowly, "when the worst of your grief is behind you, you'll really regret it if you've let the house go, Kayla."

I sigh. Intellectually, I'm sure she's right.

"Think of Rainie," Bets continues. "What a beautiful gift Jackson's left behind for her. Plus, you'd take a big loss. The house is truly gorgeous, but—and I'm so sorry for saying this—people know what happened there. Everyone knows about Jackson's accident. It was in the news and everybody knows. So for some people, the house is already—" She hesitates, then finally says the word I know is coming. "—already haunted. Forgive me for saying that, Kayla, but I know you want the truth from me."

I wince. "Not really," I say.

"I see this kind of situation all the time," she continues. "People make rash decisions when they're grieving. Please don't do that. My advice would be for you to live in it for at least two or three years. See how you feel about it then. Those Shadow Ridge houses are only going to go up in value. Like crazy. You watch and see."

"My house isn't haunted." I seem to be stuck on that word.

"Oh, I know that. I'm sorry. Poor choice of words," Bets says. "Look, Kayla, I've got an appointment waiting. If you decide you do want to sell, call me. Otherwise, once you move in, invite me over for a glass of wine, okay? I can't wait to see that house with your furniture in it."

I hang up the phone. I'm glad I called her. Glad Bets is a friend who can give it to me straight. Still, I feel shaken. Bets is looking at my situation with her brain. I'm looking at it with my heart. She's right, though. I need to think of Rainie. We created the house for her. For our family. I have no idea what the future holds for my daughter and myself. All I know is that, right now, Rainie and I are going to move into that house.

Chapter 8

―――― ≈ ――――

ELLIE

1965

I had to pull off the road twice on the drive from Round Hill to Chapel Hill to let poor Brenda open the door and heave up her breakfast. She was nearly in her third month and she said her mornings were miserable. Plus she was tearful over being separated from Garner. "I love him so much!" she pined. All I could think to say was that school would soon be over, she'd have her sophomore year behind her, and she'd be living with Garner every minute of every day, for the rest of her life. I was glad Garner was the kind of man who deserved all the love she was showering on him.

"And a few months after that," I added, "you'll be holding your little baby in your arms." That seemed to give her some comfort, I thought, but she was truly a lovesick woman. As she wept, her head leaning against the car window, her eyes closed, I wondered what it would be like to be that much in love. I'd never felt that way. Lovesick.

≈

I focused on my classes for the next couple of weeks. Pharmacology was not an easy major. So much chemistry. So much math. It gave me new admiration for my father. He was much smarter than I'd given him credit for. When the assignments got tough, I pushed myself, fighting to excel. I wanted Daddy to be proud of me. But most of all, I wanted to be proud of myself.

Two weeks before school ended, Reed and Garner drove from Round Hill to Chapel Hill to spend the weekend with Brenda and me. They booked a hotel room and when they showed up in our dorm foyer, Brenda fell into Garner's arms and sobbed and sobbed. I realized then how she'd been holding herself together, not even sharing with me how painful the separation was for her. Garner treated her like she was a delicate flower. I felt moved by the obvious love between them.

Reed hugged me and then nodded in Brenda and Garner's direction. "Listen," he said. "If it's okay with you, we'll let them have the hotel room for the weekend. You and I can get some dinner and then you can sneak me into your dorm room."

Guys weren't allowed in our dorm rooms, plus he was asking to spend the night with me, something we'd never done before.

"Okay," I said, "but . . . you know how I feel about—"

"I know." He cut me off with a smile. "We'll be good."

"Okay," I said again.

Brenda walked over to us. "Are you okay if Garner and I go to the—"

"It's fine," I interrupted her. "Go have a good time with your husband."

She smiled and I realized how long it had been since I'd seen that genuine smile on her face. I grabbed her hand. Squeezed it tight. "Honey," I said, "we only have two more weeks of school. They'll zip by."

She leaned over to hug me, and then she was off with her husband.

≈

Reed took me to the Pines for dinner. It was the most elegant restaurant in town—there was nothing to compare it to in Round Hill. He'd gotten yet another raise and wanted to celebrate. I felt proud of him and found myself looking at him differently. He was so handsome. He kept his thick, dark hair slicked back these days, which seemed to make his eyes even bluer. Those eyes were pretty dreamy, I had to admit. He wore a suit and tie tonight, his banking outfit, and he was carrying a large manila envelope with him.

"What's in the envelope?" I asked.

"Something for you from the AME church in Turner's Bend." He looked curious. "Your mother asked me to bring it to you."

"Oh!" The word fluttered out of my mouth before I could stop it. I'd given Reverend Filburn both my home and school address and I'd been watching my mailbox with mounting disappointment each day. I held my hand out across the table. "Can I have it, please?"

He handed the envelope to me with a chuckle. "You converting to the African Methodist Church?" he joked.

I smiled, shaking my head. "Do you mind if I open it?" I asked.

He shrugged. "Be my guest."

I'd told Reed nothing about my plans, not knowing if Reverend Filburn would let me take part in SCOPE or not. Now I looked across the table at him.

"I didn't tell you about this yet because I didn't know if it would actually happen," I said.

"If *what* would actually happen?"

I opened the envelope and pulled out several sheets of printed information and a typewritten letter from Reverend Filburn. I scanned it. He'd written that if I was still interested in participating with SCOPE, I should read over the attached material, fill out the necessary forms, and show up in Atlanta on June thirteenth for the weeklong orientation, after which I'd be assigned to work in an as yet unspecified county.

"Oh!" I said again, staring at his letter. "Oh, wow!"

"Are you going to tell me?" Reed nudged.

"I'm going to work this summer helping register people to vote!" I said. "There's this program called SCOPE that's—"

"I know what it is." Reed frowned. "There was an article about it in the paper a few weeks ago."

"I've been waiting to hear if I'm in, and"—I held up the papers—"it looks like I am."

"I thought it was just students from Northern schools," he said.

"Mostly, but I went to talk to the minister who was quoted in that article and he says I can do it." I left out all Reverend Filburn had said about the prejudice I'd face as a Southerner and how he'd thought I was going to plant a bomb in his church.

Reed had completely lost his smile. "What will you be doing, exactly?" he asked.

I looked down at the papers. "I'm not certain yet, but I think I'll mostly be canvassing . . . going house to house, hopefully in Derby County, to talk to people about registering." I could hardly sit still. I wanted to read through the material right that second.

"I thought you'd work in the pharmacy with your dad this summer like you usually do."

"This is more important," I said.

"Man," he said, his smile uncertain. "You're somethin' else, Ellie. If that's what you want to do, then I think you should do it. Just save your strength for going out after work."

I looked down at Reverend Gregory A. Filburn's official-looking signature on his letter. I had to be straight with Reed. "I'm not sure I'll have time, Reed," I said. "There's a lot I don't know yet but I think that once you're committed to the program, it's a twenty-four-hour-a-day deal. They'll put me—all the students—they'll put us up in the neighborhoods where we're canvassing."

"Seriously?" he asked. "In hotels or . . . ?"

"People's homes," I said.

His eyes widened. "Your parents will let you do this?"

"I'm twenty. I really think the decision is mine."

"Twenty isn't twenty-one."

The waiter picked that minute to show up at our table and we both ordered lamb. Once he left, Reed spoke again.

"I didn't know you were so passionate about civil rights," he said. "I mean, I know your aunt Carol could get you stirred up, and I know you were really upset over those protests in Chapel Hill last year, but this is really extreme, Ellie. Think about what happened to those people who marched from Selma to Montgomery last month. They were beaten and some were killed, and—"

"That was the Deep South," I said, then added firmly, "I want to do this, Reed."

He studied me with his sky-blue eyes. "Will I ever get to see you?" he asked.

"I don't know," I said honestly.

"Do you care if I ever get to see you?" For a moment, the question hung in the air between us.

"Of course I do," I said. "But this might have to be a summer apart for us."

He leaned back from the table. "Well, I'd be lying if I said I'm happy about it, especially not with those living arrangements. I hope you'll reconsider."

The waiter brought our meals, then, and I slipped the envelope to the floor, resting it against my purse. We ate mostly in silence. My mind was a million miles away.

"I hope your parents won't let you do it," he said, after we'd been eating for a while.

I frowned at him. "Thanks a lot," I said sarcastically. "This is something I really want to do. I wish you'd give me some support on it."

Reed sighed. Looked down at the half-eaten lamb chop on his plate. "I think I'm in this relationship a lot deeper than you are," he said finally.

"If our roles were reversed, I couldn't imagine leaving you for the whole summer. I couldn't handle being apart that long."

I set down my fork again. There was no way I could eat and have this conversation. "I care about you," I said, "but . . . maybe you're right. I want more than just a relationship in my life, Reed. I need something more. Something bigger."

He stared at me. "What can I say to change your mind?"

I shook my head without saying a word.

"So . . . are we breaking up here?" he asked.

My body tensed. I was used to Reed being a part of my life. Selfishly, I still wanted him in it. Before I could think of what to say, he continued.

"How do you expect me to spend my summer?" he asked. "Stay home every night? Every weekend?"

"I think you should do what you want," I said finally. "Go out with other girls." I could barely say those words. I hated the thought of him being with another girl. That told me something. I did love him, but not so much that I'd give up my plan.

"Fine," he said, the word flat as it came out of his mouth.

Neither of us finished our meal, and we passed on dessert. He didn't take my hand as we left the restaurant, and the truth was, I wasn't thinking about him. About us. I was thinking about how I would tell my parents about SCOPE.

⁓

If Reed had had the means to get back to Round Hill on his own that night, I felt certain he would leave, but we were stuck with our original plan. He'd have to stay in the dorm. I managed to slip him into the room I shared with Brenda. It wasn't exactly a romantic setting, and that was just as well. For the first time, I noticed how our room smelled—like hair spray and shampoo and old sheets. I hadn't washed the sheets on my bed in well over a week; I hadn't known I'd be having company. Reed wouldn't be able to use the bathroom at the end of the hall, so I had to empty a bottle of mouthwash so he could pee in it, and we had to speak quietly because the dorm door was paper thin.

"I think, given how we're both feeling right now, I'll sleep in Brenda's bed," he said.

I was relieved. We'd never spent a whole night together. Even during those occasional weekends at the beach, Brenda and I would share a room, and Reed and Garner would share another. Tonight was not the night for us to sleep together.

A few minutes after I'd gotten into my own bed and turned out my lamp, Reed spoke from the other side of the room. "I love you, Ellie," he said.

"I love you, too." It was not the first time I'd said those words to him, and I meant them. Just not the way he did.

≈

It wasn't until the middle of the night when Reed was sound asleep that I turned on my reading lamp and looked through the material Reverend Filburn had sent. There was a mandatory reading list—books about all that Negroes had endured in the United States. Then there was an informative letter from Reverend Filburn, telling me that I'd have to bring a sleeping bag, skirts and dresses—girls were not allowed to wear pants or shorts—and two hundred dollars to cover expenses. Part of that money would go to the local families with whom I'd be staying and who would receive a few dollars a week for my room and board. I'd have to sell my car to get the money. That was going to be a sacrifice, especially since I wouldn't be making any money working at the pharmacy this summer.

I could get a ride to the orientation in Atlanta with some Columbia University students who would pick me up on their way south, the letter said. There was a second letter, this one mimeographed, from Martin Luther King, Jr., himself, which I read three times. How many people had a letter from Martin Luther King? I felt a thrill of excitement course through me. I wished Aunt Carol was alive. She was the only other person who could understand how I felt.

But there were three forms that stopped me cold. One was a medical form that a doctor would need to fill out, stating I was physically fit. I hoped that would be no big deal. I could see a doctor at student health services on campus rather than our family doctor, who might have a word to say with my parents about my plan. The second form was an acknowledgment that I understood I could be injured or even killed. That was sobering, but I figured it was some legal thing that protected the SCOPE organizers. My signature on that form would need to be notarized. But the most troublesome form required my parents' signature, giving me permission to participate because I was not yet twenty-one. I stared at that one, wishing I could change the wording on it. That form could put an end to my entire plan.

≈

I woke up before Reed and sat on the edge of my bed, waiting for him to open his eyes. He saw me watching him and sat up. He was wearing his white undershirt, his hair tousled, his eyes expectant. I guessed it was clear to him that I had something to say that he wasn't going to want to hear.

"I'm going to screw up everyone's weekend, I know," I said, "and I'm sorry, but I need to go back to Round Hill. I have to talk to my parents about SCOPE. It can't wait till next weekend. I need to leave this morning."

He narrowed his eyes at me. "You're kidding," he said. "Garner drove us here and I can tell you, there's no way I'll be able to drag him away from Brenda before Sunday afternoon. What am I supposed to do till then?" I'd never before seen the red blotches that formed on his neck as he spoke. I'd never before seen him really angry.

"You can ride back to Round Hill with me," I said. "We can talk more on the drive."

So, he rode back with me in my little red Ford, but we didn't talk. The tension in the car pressed down on my chest for the entire two hours of our drive. He stared out the side window as if he didn't want to catch a glimpse of me, even in his peripheral vision. I thought of asking *what are you thinking?* but the truth was, I didn't want to know. I didn't want to argue about my decision any longer. My mind was made up.

Chapter 9

My parents were surprised to see me, and I made up some excuse for coming home, too nervous to tell them about SCOPE right away. I was afraid they'd say no and that would be the end of my dream for the summer. At dinner Saturday night, I finally got my courage up. I waited for a lull in the conversation between Daddy and Buddy about the work Buddy was doing on a neighbor's tractor and then, before I lost my nerve, I blurted out, "I've decided to do volunteer work this summer."

For a moment, no one said anything. From across the table I felt Buddy stiffen, his eyes on his fried chicken leg. He knew where I was going with this. Then Daddy turned to me. "That's good, Ellie," he said. "Volunteer work will look good on your application to graduate school."

"You still need to give your father some hours in the pharmacy, though," Mama said. It sounded like a warning.

I licked my dry lips, but before I could figure out how to respond, Daddy spoke again. "What's the volunteer work, sugar?" He sounded calmer than my mother. More willing to listen.

"Remember that article you read about SCOPE?" I asked. "The white students helping to register people to vote?"

The three of them were silent. I felt my parents' eyes on me, and Buddy shot me a look across the table that I couldn't read but imagined said, *There is no way in holy hell they're going to let you do this.*

"You're not thinking of volunteering with *them*, are you?" Mama asked.

I nodded. "Yes. I've already spoken to the minister about it. The one who was quoted in that article. I can probably work right here in Derby County."

"This is ill advised, Eleanor," Daddy said in the calm voice he'd used my entire life when he was laying down the law. "You'll only be asking for trouble if you try to help out with that sort of thing. No one wants that program here. Not the white folks. Not the colored folks. They're fine with things the way they are, so—"

"How could they possibly be 'fine with things the way they are'?" I asked. "I think you just tell yourself that to feel less guilty about their situation." I couldn't remember a time I'd spoken back to my father and for a moment no one said anything. Buddy finally broke the silence.

"It's too dangerous," he said. "The Klan's probably gearin' up to make those students turn tail and go back where they came from."

"And exactly how are they going to do that?" I asked.

"You're being naïve," my father said. "Buddy's right. No one in Derby County is going to take kindly to that sort of interference and you have absolutely no need to be a part of it." He set down his fork and leaned toward me. "Why the hell would you put yourself in that vulnerable position?"

"Daniel!" my mother admonished him for the curse word. I thought it was the first time I'd ever heard my father use it. His voice was still deceptively calm, which made his words that much more intimidating to me.

"Let the Martin Luther Kings of the world sort it out," he continued. "It's not your battle. If you feel so strongly about wanting to do volunteer work this summer, you could work at the Girls' Club in town. Teach little girls how to sew or whatever they do over there."

"I want to do something more important than that, Daddy," I said. "I want to do something that makes a difference on a bigger scale. Not teach a girl how to hem a skirt."

"Well, you're not doing this," my father said. He got to his feet, tossing his napkin on the table. "That's my final word."

It had been years since my father'd raised his voice to me. Buddy was the rebel in the family, not me. I felt close to tears and was angry with myself for my weakness. Right now, it seemed there was nothing else I could say. I could sit there and be cowed or I could leave the table. I folded my own napkin in silence, set it on the table next to my plate, stood up, and walked slowly and deliberately to my room, their silence following me like a ghost.

≈

I was climbing into bed that night when my mother came into my room. She sat on the edge of my bed. Smoothed my covers. I couldn't remember the last time she'd done that. Tucked me in. She smiled down at me.

"We love you more than anything in the world, you know that, don't you?" she asked.

"Of course. And I love you, too."

"And the volunteer work you're talking about is unnecessary, Ellie. There's that new bill coming soon that'll make it easy for Negroes to vote, so what is the point of this SCOPE program?"

"It'll take more than that bill to make it easy for them to register, Mama. A lot of them won't know how to go about registering, or there'll be obstacles in their way. They could lose their jobs or their homes or—"

"Why on earth would that happen?"

"Because their bosses or landlords don't want them to have any power."

She sighed but when she spoke again, her voice was harsh. "You'd be beating your head against a brick wall, trying to change things," she said. "This is the way God made the world. Most Negroes know their place. Like Louise. We all loved Louise, didn't we? But she never tried to overstep. She understood—"

"Mama, it makes me crazy to hear you talk that way!" I raised myself up on my elbows. "*White* people made the world this way. Not God. White people want to keep Negroes down. Louise probably had to bite her tongue the whole time she was saying 'yes, ma'am' and 'whatever you say, ma'am' to you."

She slapped me. It wasn't hard. It wasn't much. But she had never so much as laid a hand on me before and I thought we were both in shock. For a moment, neither of us spoke, and I lay back on my pillow again, turning my face away from her.

"Louise knew her place," she said finally. "That's all I'm saying. And you should know yours." She smoothed the hair back from my forehead. My cheek—and my heart—still hurt from where she'd slapped me.

"Does this have something to do with little Mattie?" Mama asked me now.

"What do you mean?" I asked, although I knew.

"Well, she and Louise were the only Negroes you've ever really known, and Mattie was your little friend and their story was certainly tragic, so I just thought, maybe you—"

"Mama, don't be ridiculous," I said. "UNC is integrated. My *dorm* is integrated."

"Your dorm is . . . ?" Her eyes widened.

"Yes. It is."

She shook her head as though she couldn't believe the state of the world. "Well, I just thought . . . you know . . . how bad you felt about Mattie. That maybe you're thinking this is something you should do. A way to honor her or something. You never seemed to get it through your head that you were a hero that day." She smoothed my hair behind my ear. I resented her touch after that slap. "An eleven-year-old hero," she continued. "Why don't you hold on to that? To what you did that day. Let it be your legacy. Your contribution to—"

"Mama, stop it!" I sat up, nearly knocking her off the edge of the bed. I couldn't bear to listen to her go on about Mattie for another minute. Mattie had drowned in the lake at the end of Hockley Street and I hadn't been able to save her. The newspaper wrote me up as a hero, though, and for years afterward, people would stop me on the street to tell me how brave I was to try to save "the little colored girl."

My mother stood up abruptly, surprised by my outburst. I thought she might slap me again but she held her knotted fists at her sides.

"I want to do this, all right?" I said. "Why does it have to be such a big deal? I'm nearly twenty-one years old. I have straight As. I'm not stupid or foolish or . . . I'm going to do it."

"Your father said no and he's right," she said firmly. "So we talked about it and we think a good idea is to get you out of Round Hill for the summer. Dorothy Rogers would love to have you come stay with her in Myrtle Beach. You love it down there and she said Reed is welcome to visit anytime. What do you think?"

Any other summer I would have jumped at this chance. Dorothy Rogers, an old friend of my mother's, was easy to be around and she had a great pool. I thought of Myrtle Beach with its beach music and dance competitions. It was tempting, but it was not what I wanted. I wasn't looking for fun this summer.

"I want to work for SCOPE, Mama," I said.

She looked down at me. "The answer is no," she said. "Discussion over."

I watched her leave the room, her spine straight with determination, but I was equally as determined. I hadn't mentioned the permission form. I crossed my room to my desk, picked up a pen from my blotter, and for the first time in my life, I forged my father's signature.

Chapter 10

≈

KAYLA

2010

I've never felt so alone.

I'm in the great room of the new Shadow Ridge house, by myself. Daddy's waiting for Rainie's sitter to show up at his house so he can come over to help me deal with the movers and I can't wait for him to get here. Three trucks are in front of the house. The moving van from the storage facility is in the driveway, while out on the street, there's the truck with the new furniture for Rainie's room and the guest room, and behind that one is the truck with the furniture for our two offices, one of which we no longer need. I hadn't thought of that—canceling the new furniture for Jackson's office. Now his office will only remind me of the fact that he is missing. And yet, I let them bring in the desk he selected, along with the filing cabinet and bookcase, because I feel too numb to tell them to take them back to the store. I'm exhausted and we are only half an hour into this move.

Daddy shows up at ten thirty, just as I'm trying to explain to the movers how I want the bedroom furniture arranged. He senses my tension and stands back quietly to let me work it out with the two men doing the heavy lifting. Once the bedroom is finished and the men leave the room, Daddy gives me a hug.

"How are you holding up, sweetheart?" he asks.

"Hey, ma'am!" someone calls from downstairs. I smile gamely at my father. "I'm okay," I say, "but I'll be very glad when this day is over."

The move-in passes by me in a blur. By two o'clock, all the furniture is in place, nearly a dozen burly men have come and gone, and I'm glad I paid extra to have most of the boxes unpacked, even if I'm certain nothing in the kitchen is where I'll ultimately want it to be. The only rooms that are still full of boxes are the two offices, and I have a feeling Jackson's office will stay boxed up for a good long time.

"It's a beautiful house, honey," Daddy says. He sits down on the new sectional and looks around him, a small smile on his face. "I like this wall color you picked out. Very soothing."

I lower myself to the other end of the sectional. It's soft but not too soft, and I settle into it. Finally, something that's just right. All the furniture I selected is designed for comfort, with rounded corners and nubby fabric, a counter to the sleek lines of the house.

My father touches the quilt I've tossed over the back of the sectional. "I recognize this," he says.

"I thought you might." I smile. My mother had made the beautiful quilt for me when I went away to college. "I designed the room around it," I tell him, choking up a little. "See how the blues and greens are picked up in the sectional and the chairs and the area rugs?"

Daddy takes this in. His smile is sad now, but he nods. "I *do* see it." He looks directly at me. "I love that you did that, honey."

I have a sudden brainstorm. "I have too much space for one woman and one little girl, now, Daddy. I think you should forget about the condo and move in with us." I'm completely serious, but also selfish. I want another adult with me in this huge house that might look sparkly fresh and new but feels tainted. A terrible accident happened here, and now that red-haired woman knows that this is where I live. It feels like too much.

Daddy shakes his head. "Thanks, but I think you and Rainie need a fresh start here, without me hanging around. And besides, I'm looking forward to my new little abode."

For a moment, we're both quiet and the house fills with the distant sound of hammers and saws as work on the newer Shadow Ridge houses continues. "You'll be living with that noise for a few more weeks, I'd guess," Daddy says. "But then, peace. I think this will ultimately be a lovely, peaceful neighborhood. I like how they left so much space between the houses. Rare these days. And the trees . . . while you know I think you have too many . . . they'll buffer any noise. The construction racket would be worse without them." I hear his encouragement. He wants me to feel okay.

I nod. I frankly like the idea that there are people nearby right now, even if they're noisy construction guys.

"I should get Rainie's room ready for her," I say, but I don't budge from the sofa. I'm bone-tired.

"Leave it till tomorrow," Daddy says. "And look, honey, if you and Rainie want to stay with me tonight, you know you're welcome."

Oh, that's so tempting, but I won't give in to it. I look toward the lock on the front door. The security system is ready for me to arm, if I can remember how to do it. I've never felt the need for one before, but I'm glad Jackson insisted we have one in this house. I hope it never needs to be put to the test.

A short time later, Daddy goes back to his house to pick up Rainie and bring her "home." He walks her into the house, but then leaves, telling me it's time for Rainie and me to explore our new home together. He looks tired and I hug him gently as I thank him for his help.

Rainie and I spend the next hour checking out all the newly furnished rooms. We end up in her bedroom, where I make her full-size canopy bed with her new Dora the Explorer sheets. "What would you like for dinner?"

I ask, tucking in the top sheet. "We have to go out. We have zero food in the house."

"Taco Bell!" she shouts, and claps her hands.

So strange. Before the accident, it was always McDonald's. Now this Taco Bell kick. "Taco Bell it is," I say. "And then a quick run to the grocery store so we have food for breakfast. Need to go potty before we leave?"

"No," she says, but I take her anyway. She'd been such an easy little kid to toilet train but that, like everything else, has occasionally slipped backward since the accident.

Downstairs, I try to set the alarm before we leave the house, but I can't get it to work. Either a door or window is open, the touchpad tells me. Number thirteen, whatever that is. I check the back door, but it's locked. Has to be a window. Rainie is starting to lose her patience, so I give up. It's not until I'm in the car that I feel shaken by the number. *Thirteen.* I roll my eyes at my silliness. I'm being paranoid.

The construction guys are only working on a few of the houses this late. It's after five and the short street is much quieter as I turn off Shadow Ridge Lane onto Round Hill Road. Rainie and I eat at Taco Bell and she tells me about building block towers with the babysitter at my father's house while I was with the movers. "Tiffany said I should be an architreck like you and Daddy," she says.

I smile. "An architect," I say.

"Architect," she repeats.

"I think you'd make a good one if that's what you decide you'd like to do."

It's nearly seven when we get home. She doesn't want a bath until I explain that she's a big girl now who has her very own tub in her very own bathroom. That seems to satisfy her. She chatters about her friends from preschool as I wash her back. After her bath, we curl up together in her new bed and as I read to her, I wonder how she will fare this night. I've shown her several times how to get from her bedroom to mine, and I promise to leave the hall light on. I'm most worried about her making a wrong turn in the hall and falling down the stairs. Every time I think of that possibility, my body gives a little jerk.

Rainie is exhausted, though. She's already asleep by the time I finish the book. I get out of her bed, turn off the light, tiptoe out the door, and pad quietly downstairs. I'm uncomfortably aware that every window I pass has no blinds or curtains. The wall of windows in the rear of the house, so spectacular in the daytime, makes me feel exposed and vulnerable now. Jackson and I planned to leave those windows uncovered, but that's not going to do. I'll order coverings for all the windows this week.

The front windows, though, already have beautiful Roman shades, and after I close them all, I sit on the sofa and dive into the information the security system guy left with me to figure out what number thirteen might be. It turns out to be an unlocked kitchen window. I lock it, scurrying quickly through the kitchen with its sliding glass doors, and hurry back to the living room, where I successfully set the alarm and my heart stops its ridiculous gallop.

Upstairs again, I make the king-size bed—we'd sold our queen for the king and right now, I regret it. I don't want all that empty space to remind me how alone I am. I sit on the edge of the bed and before I know it, I'm sobbing. Big gut-wrenching sobs that hurt my chest and throat. I'm tired of trying to be strong. I miss my husband. My best friend for the last ten years. It's so unfair. We were supposed to have more children together. Design more houses together. Grow *old* together. We had it all planned out. *Damn it!* I pound my fist on the bed. It doesn't even make a sound.

I finally pull myself together. Turning off the bedside lamp, I cross the room to look out the window at our new street. The darkness takes my breath away and I shudder. There are no lights in any of the unfinished houses and the streetlights are not yet working on Shadow Ridge Lane. There is only one light I can see and it burns in the window of the old Hockley house. I drag the one chair in the bedroom close to the window, and I spend the better part of an hour staring at that light as if it's shining from a lighthouse and I am lost at sea.

Chapter 11

ELLIE

1965

Two days before school ended, I went to the doctor at the student health center to get the physical I needed for SCOPE.

The doctor, who looked about a hundred years old, gave me a vision test, took my blood pressure, listened to my heart, asked me if my periods were regular, and then pronounced me fit.

"I admire you for doing this," he said, signing the form and handing it to me. I was still sitting on the examination table in the paper gown. "If I were forty years younger, I'd join you." He smiled warmly.

"Thank you," I said, grateful for the support. "You're the only person who's had anything positive to say about it."

He rested his hands on his thighs and looked at me with crinkly hazel eyes. "It's much easier to put our heads in the sand and let someone else do the hard work, isn't it," he said. "But somebody has to do it. It's the only way to bring about change. I like the way your generation has picked up the torch and run with it."

"Thank you," I said again.

He left me alone to get dressed and when I caught a glimpse of my reflection in the mirror above the sink, I was smiling. I felt strong and capable and sure of my decision. I was ready to carry that torch.

≈

The final document I needed to return to Reverend Filburn was the scariest. It was the release form that held the Southern Christian Leadership Conference—Martin Luther King's organization that was behind the SCOPE project—free of liability if I was injured or killed. My signature had to be notarized, which meant I needed to go to the bank.

Reed looked up in surprise when I walked in. He was working with a customer at his desk. I smiled and gave him a little wave, then went over to Lucy Baker's desk. She looked surprised to see me.

"Well hello, Ellie," she said, as I neared her. "So good to see you."

"Hi, Miss Lucy," I said. "You have a minute to notarize something for me?"

"Of course, dear. Have a seat."

I'd known Miss Lucy my whole life. She babysat for Buddy and me when we were little, then taught me piano until both she and my parents realized I had no talent. Then she became the leader of my Fireside Girls troop, and then I had her as a substitute teacher in nearly every class in my high school. Now in her fifties, she had finally settled into this desk job at the bank.

I handed her the form. She had no need to read it—as a matter of fact, I thought she had no *right* to read it—but the bold letters at the top caught her eye. "SCOPE," she said. "What is SCOPE?"

"It's an organization to help people register to vote," I said. I'd decided that was the way I'd describe it from now on. I didn't have to be any more specific than that. But Miss Lucy had apparently been keeping up with the news and her eyes widened.

"That group coming down from the North to register the coloreds?" she asked.

I nodded. "Yes. I'm going to work with them."

"Sounds like something your aunt Carol would have done."

I smiled. "It does," I agreed.

"That woman never met a cause she didn't want to take on."

"So true," I said, even though I knew Miss Lucy hadn't meant it as a compliment. Aunt Carol had been no great fan of hers, either.

"Does Reed know about this?" Miss Lucy asked, glancing across the room to where Reed was still busy with a customer.

None of your business, I thought, but I kept the smile on my face. "Of course," I said, as though Reed didn't have a concern in the world about it.

I could tell that Miss Lucy wanted to say more, but she clamped her lips together. As she pulled out her stamp pad, pressed it neatly to the page, and signed her name, I could imagine her brain feverishly processing the information she'd just learned. When I stood up and reached for the form, she held it just out of reach, looking up at me with the sincerest blue eyes, eyes I'd known nearly my entire life.

"You don't want to do this, dear," she said quietly. "Give it a little more thought."

"I *do* want to do it," I said, leaning over to take the form from her. "Thank you." I bristled as I walked away. It was none of her business.

Reed was alone at his desk and I stopped to say an awkward hello. I didn't sit down, just stood across the desk from him, clutching the form in my hand.

"When do you leave?" he asked.

"Saturday." I wanted to add that I felt a little nervous, but it would hardly be fair to ask for comfort from Reed when he didn't want me to go.

He simply nodded, his face serious. "Be safe, Ellie," he said. "I hope it turns out to be exactly what you're looking for."

I shouldn't have been surprised by his kindness. That's who Reed was.

But I found he'd stolen my voice, so I just nodded with a tight smile, and by the time I reached my car, my eyes burned with tears.

≈

It never seemed to occur to my parents that they should have to give their official okay for me to be able to participate in SCOPE. They knew I planned to go and they'd stopped arguing with me about it. I thought my mother must have talked my father into letting me do it. I could imagine the conversation. *If we put up a fuss,* my mother would say, *she'll be even more determined to stick it out. If we willingly let her go, she'll be home in less than a week. You'll see.*

Three days before those New York students were to pick me up for the long drive to the Atlanta orientation, Sheriff Parks showed up at our front door to talk to me. Byron Parks was a childhood friend of my father's, and he was no stranger in our house. He was also my godfather, and Buddy and I had called him "Uncle Byron" from the time we were small. He and his family came to our barbecues and we'd go to his house for their annual New Year's Eve party. In spite of the fact that I'd known him all my life and in spite of the fact that he was soft-spoken, kind, handsome, and rather charismatic, I was never really comfortable around him. He'd been the one to pull Mattie Jenkins out of the lake, his pale hair covered in stringy green muck. He'd been the one to tell the newspaper I was a hero. I always, to this day, felt embarrassed around him.

"Let's sit on the porch," he said to me now, with his straight-toothed smile. He could sound so gentle, but I knew he could be tough when he needed to be. Everyone knew he beat the hell out of a guy who'd robbed the jewelry store downtown, for example. Sitting with him in our white rockers, my bare feet on the warm gray wood of the porch, it was hard to picture him beating up anyone. Across the dirt road from our house, the emerald-green kudzu looked like a pack of wild animals against a pale blue sky.

"Your daddy asked me to have a chat with you." He sounded almost apologetic.

I rolled my eyes. "I'm sure he did," I said.

"Just because he loves you," Uncle Byron said. "He's worried about you. Beside himself with worry, actually, and it's not unreasonable."

"I know," I said.

"Sweetheart, do you have any real idea what you're getting into?" he asked. "You're used to living in this pretty house with pretty things." He swept an arm through the air to take in our house. "Your daddy works hard to provide all this for you."

"I know," I said, feeling ever so slightly guilty at that. Daddy provided "all this" for me, and I was choosing to spend my summer living in poverty.

"It can be dangerous," Uncle Byron said. "You know about those three civil rights workers who were killed last year? Not pretty deaths, either."

"In Mississippi. Not North Carolina." I was tired of that particular argument. "I know there might be some slight danger, Uncle Byron. I know all that. I still want to do this."

"It'll just make it worse for those folks if y'all shake things up," he said. "You might do more harm than good."

I turned my head so he wouldn't see me roll my eyes again. Then I looked at him once more. "How are Ruthie and Jimmy doing?" I asked abruptly, hoping we could change the subject to his children.

He stared at me for a moment as if trying to decide if he should let me get away with it. "They're fine," he said finally. "You were always their favorite babysitter."

"They're wonderful kids," I said.

"They are," he agreed. With a sigh, he pulled his card from his pocket, leaning over to hand it to me. "Any time," he said. "Doesn't matter where you are, even if you're not in my jurisdiction. You find yourself in trouble, you get to a phone and call me, hear?"

I nodded. "Thank you," I said, palming the card. "That makes me feel safer," I added, and I meant it.

≈

The night before I was to leave, my mother received a phone call as we were cleaning the kitchen. She said nothing after "hello," and I watched her face go pale. She hung up without another word, then turned to look at me where I was drying the dishes.

"It was a man," she said. "He said, 'Tell your commie bleeding-heart daughter she'd better watch her step this summer. You never know what might happen in those darkie neighborhoods.'"

I shivered. Who would make a call like that? Who even knew what I was up to? Aside from telling Uncle Byron, my parents had kept my plans to themselves, and I doubted Buddy or Reed or Garner or Brenda would have told anyone. I thought of Lucy Baker at the bank. Would she have spread the word? I felt a stab of guilt that, because of me, my mother'd had to receive such a phone call.

"I'm sorry, Mama," I said. "I wish I could control the outside world, but I can't."

"You can still back out," she said.

I set the dish towel on the counter and walked across the room to wrap her in my arms. "I hope that's the only call like that you have to get," I said. I doubted it would be, though. Lucy Baker had a very big mouth, and Round Hill was a very small town.

Chapter 12

Buddy stood in the doorway of my bedroom as I finished packing my suitcase. I was aware of him there in his blue coveralls, BUDDY HOCKLEY stitched above his pocket. I felt disapproval running like a thread from him to me.

I snapped my suitcase closed and looked across the room at him. His expression was sad but resigned.

"I'll miss you," I said. It would be my first summer without my brother. Without my parents. Without Reed and Brenda and Garner.

"You can still change your mind," he said. "Even once you're . . . wherever they stick you, you can change your mind. I'll come get you. You need me, call me here or at the car shop. Day or night. All right?"

He was such a sweetheart. "You're the best big brother." I crossed the room to where he leaned against my doorjamb and wrapped my arms around him. "Don't worry about me," I said. "And don't let Mama and Daddy worry, either, okay? It's not like I'm going a million miles away.

Hopefully they'll assign me right back here in Derby County after the orientation in Atlanta."

"It's a big county," he said dryly, not returning my embrace.

I let go of him. Gave him an annoyed look. "Stop it," I said. "You're being silly."

"I wish I was," he said. "You've led sort of a protected life, you know? The world out there ain't as kind as you seem to think it is."

I lifted my suitcase off my bed. "You better get going," I said. "You'll be late for work."

"I love you, little sis." It wasn't like Buddy to say those three words, and his cheeks were pink. I never doubted for a minute that he loved me, but I didn't think he'd ever actually told me before.

"I love you, too," I said. "Now, skedaddle."

He hesitated a moment longer as if he had more to say, but then he turned and I listened to him clump down the stairs.

I'd already said goodbye to my parents that morning. Mama only mumbled a goodbye before she left for her job at the library. Daddy had barely been talking to me ever since I'd told them I was definitely going, and he was gruff when he hugged me goodbye. I didn't think he'd really expected me to go through with it. He said pretty much what Buddy'd just said. "You can come home any time. If you find this is a mistake, don't feel like you have to stay there just to save face."

I was frankly glad when all three of them were out of the house. Now all I had to do was wait for the New York students to come pick me up. I was told they'd arrive between nine and ten that morning and I had my suitcase, a backpack with the recommended books and my camera, and the sleeping bag we'd been told to bring "just in case" on our front porch by eight. I assumed the students would be tired from driving all night, so I'd made some lemonade and a pound cake. I was as nervous about meeting them as if they were some sort of alien creatures instead of college students just like me. UNC had plenty of Northerners, I reminded myself, though I couldn't say any of them were among my close friends.

The blue and white Volkswagen van didn't pull into my driveway until just after eleven. I'd worried they'd forgotten about me. I stood at the front door in my skirt and blouse and watched as the two guys and one girl climbed out of the van. The girl wore shorts and it occurred to me that, for the long drive to the orientation in Atlanta at least, I could have done the same. Too late now.

"Hey!" I waved as they crossed the yard toward the house. "I'm Ellie!"

"We got all turned around," the girl called. She tried unsuccessfully to smooth her short auburn hair away from her face. The air was sticky as tar.

"You live out in the boonies," one of the guys said.

"I guess," I said with a shrug and a smile. "Probably compared to where y'all live. New York, right?"

"I'm from Connecticut," the blond boy said. "But these guys are from the city."

"Oh." I knew "the city" meant New York, as if there were only one "city" in the world. Aunt Carol used to refer to it that way, too. I'd never been there. New York was like a foreign country to me, and I had the feeling Round Hill seemed that way to these students, too.

"You live in the middle of nowhere," the girl said, looking around. "Oh man, check it out!" She pointed toward the kudzu across the street and the guys followed her gaze. "I've never seen anything like that. What is it?"

"Kudzu," I said. "You don't have that up north?"

"No, thank goodness." She wrinkled her nose.

"I think it's really cool," said the dark-haired boy.

"It's going to give me nightmares," the girl said. "And it's everywhere! How come you don't have it in *your* yard?" she asked, frowning toward our mowed side yard.

"My father hires a neighbor's goats a couple of times over the summer," I said. "They take care of it."

All three of them stared at me. "You're kidding, right?" the dark-haired boy asked.

I laughed. "No, really. You'd be amazed how much kudzu a goat can eat

in a day." They went back to staring across the dirt road and I had the feeling they saw me as the hick they'd expected. The girl finally turned to me.

"Can we use your bathroom?" she asked. Her damp hair was sticking
to her forehead.

"Oh, of course! I'm sorry. Come on in! Y'all must be exhausted and fam-
ished. When did you leave New York?" I asked.

"Last night around eight," the blond guy said as they climbed the steps
and followed me into the house. "We took turns sleeping and driving.
Stopped at a truck stop for burgers in the middle of the night."

My hostess skills were severely lacking. "Have you had any breakfast?"
I asked.

"Nothing," the girl said.

I pointed her in the direction of the bathroom and she was already
unsnapping her shorts as she headed down the hall.

I had to reorganize my thinking. I'd figured we'd have a little cake and
lemonade and then we'd be on the road, but these three needed a break
and some real food. "I can make you sandwiches," I said to the boys. "And
coffee? Do you want coffee or lemonade?"

"Both," the guys said in unison, and I laughed.

I fed them tomato-and-mayonnaise sandwiches and lemonade. I was
too nervous to eat, myself; I felt like an outsider in my own home. The
three of them seemed to know each other well from the ride down. The
boys were from Columbia University and the girl from Drew University,
a school in New Jersey. They were already telling inside jokes about
things that had happened so far on their trip, and they made no effort to
include me in their conversation. I thought back to what Reverend Filburn
had said about me not being trusted. I felt shy, the way I often did in a new
situation, and I wasn't sure how to break into their tight little circle.

I gradually got their names. The girl was Peggy Greenberg, which I
knew was a Jewish name. I'd never met a Jew before, nor an Italian, which
David DeSimone turned out to be, despite his blond hair. The dark-haired

boy with a sort of Beatles haircut was Chip Stein. Another Jewish name. Two Jews, an Italian, and me. I felt pretty plain vanilla sitting with them at my kitchen table. I was also annoyed with myself for automatically categorizing them. I was certain, though, that they were doing the same with me. They kept laughing about my father hiring goats to do our gardening and I had the feeling that would be the running joke for the ride to Atlanta.

"This is one of the counties SCOPE'll be working in, right?" Chip asked, finally directing a question to me. He looked around the kitchen as though it represented all of Derby County.

"Yes," I said, "though not here in Round Hill. It's a really big county. I'm hoping I'll be assigned back here after the orientation."

"I think you're the only Southerner in the whole program," David said as he finished his sandwich.

"The only *white* Southerner," Chip corrected him.

"Right," David said. "I guess there'll be lots of locals working with us, wherever we land."

"What's this little town like? Round Hill?" Peggy asked. "It looked cute when we drove through it, with all the little shops. Very quaint. Looks like it's from another era. But it's mostly farms out here, right?"

Round Hill looked like it was from another era? "It's just . . . a regular place," I said. "To be honest, I've never been out of the Carolinas, so I don't know any different. And you're right—there's a lot of farming—but my father owns the pharmacy, so we're not farmers."

"Your accent," Peggy said. "That's going to take some getting used to."

"Yours is pretty familiar to me," I said. "My favorite aunt grew up in New York."

"Why'd you want to do this?" Chip asked as we moved on from the sandwiches to the pound cake.

"Probably for the same reason you do." I shrugged. "To help people vote."

"Most Southerners couldn't care less if Negroes get the vote," he said.

"Most would just as soon they *never* get the vote," Peggy said. She looked at me as if for validation.

"A lot do feel that way," I said. "But I care, which is why I'm doing something about it."

"Where do you go to school?" Chip asked. "You're in college, right?"

"Carolina," I said.

"Where's that?" David asked. "Never heard of it."

"The University of North Carolina. In Chapel Hill? We just call it 'Carolina.'"

"Oh, Chapel Hill I've heard of," Peggy said. "That's a really great school."

"Yeah," said Chip, wide-eyed, and I had the feeling their impression of me finally jumped up a few notches.

"I'm a pharmacology major there."

"Really." Peggy eyed me like she wasn't quite sure what to make of me now.

Chip looked at his watch. "We should go," he said. "We've got another eleven hours ahead of us." He looked at me. "You know how to drive?"

I nodded.

"You're a lot fresher than we are," he said. "Can you take the first shift behind the wheel?"

I hadn't realized I'd be expected to drive someone else's car, but of course it made sense.

"Sure," I said.

"Can you drive a van?" Drew asked.

I laughed. "I can drive my brother's old pickup," I said, "so I guess I can drive just about anything."

We carried our plates to the sink, where I washed and dried them quickly. I didn't want to leave them for my mother.

"We have to remember to be careful once we get to Atlanta," David said as we walked out the front door onto the porch. "They said to stay in the Negro neighborhoods if we can."

That seemed backward to me. "Why?" I slung the bag of books over my shoulder, then picked up my suitcase and sleeping bag. Most people I knew *avoided* Negro neighborhoods.

Chip took the suitcase from my hand in a gentlemanly gesture. "White people'll be watching for us," he said. "For the SCOPE workers. They don't want us there. We're a threat to them."

"To their way of life," David said.

"They'll be out to get us," Chip added.

"Oh," I said, remembering the murdered civil rights workers. "Well, let's be careful then." I did not plan to become a victim.

≈

For the first four long hours, I drove while the three of them slept. Chip was stretched out on the long middle seat, and Peggy and David, who I now realized were a couple, slept tangled up together in the back row. The only person awake, I felt alone and a little scared. Were all the students going to be like these three chilly know-it-alls? Most of them would know other students, since they were coming from the same universities. They'd have school, home states, and their very Northernness in common. I would try to win them over, and if I couldn't, well, it didn't matter, I told myself. I wasn't in SCOPE to make friends. I'd keep my goal in mind: getting folks registered to vote.

Around five o'clock, I saw Peggy get to her feet in the rearview mirror and make her hunched-over way toward the front of the van, where she perched on the edge of the long middle seat. "I need a bathroom break," she said.

"Me too." I smiled at her in the mirror and pulled off at the next exit with a restaurant.

It turned out that the three of them were twenty-one, so they were able to drink rum-and-Cokes while I nursed a beer as we ate burgers and fries, surrounded mostly by truckers. I wasn't tired when Peggy started driving, so I sat in the other front seat. I thought I'd try to get to know her better, but found it hard to make conversation with her. I asked her about her family. Her father was a rabbi. That sounded so exotic to me. Her mother was a librarian, like mine, which finally gave us one thing in common, though that didn't seem to impress her. Her mother probably worked at some huge New York library, while my mother worked at our little Round Hill library in a converted old house.

"Have you ever done anything like this before?" I asked.

She sighed, as if deciding whether or not to continue our conversation. "I worked with inner-city kids last year in this program that's part of the War on Poverty, and that was okay," she said finally. "But my father kind of talked me into this one. Though he wasn't happy when David joined up, too." She glanced in the rearview mirror, I assumed to see David.

I was stuck on the term "inner city," which I'd never heard before. I guessed it meant the poor parts of New York, and I tried to picture my father actually *pushing* me into a program to register Negro voters.

She hadn't asked me if *I'd* done anything like this before, but I answered the question anyway. "This is my first time doing something like this, myself," I said. "I've done absolutely nothing. And now I plan to change that."

Chapter 13

KAYLA

2010

I drive to the office Monday feeling even more anxious than I did last week. I actually case the main level of the parking lot for the red-haired woman before slipping into my usual spot and getting out of my car. I barely slept over the weekend, still trying to figure out what the woman wanted with me. Does she regret confiding in me? If she'll murder one person, she could just as easily murder two. If the woman knows where my new house is—and she obviously does—does she also know that Rainie spends her mornings at preschool? Does she know where that preschool is? How the hell does she know anything about me?

I spend half an hour on the phone, trying to find a fencing company willing to run a fence between my thickly wooded backyard and the lake. It turns out, fencing companies are not crazy about installing fences through a wooded lot. I hear about copperheads and yellow jackets and the sheer misery of clear cutting a straight line for the posts. The one company that is willing has no openings for a month. I make an appointment with them to come out and take a look. Give me an estimate. Then I get off the phone and stare out the window for a while. I have never even seen the lake, it's so deep in the woods. Do I really need to worry about it?

After work, I visit my favorite shop for window treatments in Carlisle, the county seat of Derby County, where all the good stores are. Amanda, an interior designer I've worked with often on my projects, gives me a bunch of catalogs and a stack of samples to bring home. Now I have an hour or so to myself before I have to pick Rainie up and I can't wait to get to the new house and figure out how to cover all those big gaping windows.

I turn onto Shadow Ridge Lane to the familiar sight of white construction vans. Straight ahead, at the end of the road, I see our perfect house in its cave of green trees, but what catches my eye is that white sedan in the driveway of the Hockley house. A woman with short gray hair is lifting fabric grocery bags out of the trunk. I remember the welcome light in that house from the night before. On a whim, I pull in behind her car. She looks up, the bags weighing her down. I get out of my SUV and wave.

"Looks like you can use some help!" I call, walking toward her.

She smiles. "I can't argue with that!"

I slip one of the bags from her arm and pick up the remaining two from her trunk, then follow her up the driveway, past Buddy Hockley's blue truck and through the side door of the house.

I feel like I've stepped back in time. We're in a kitchen, the wallpaper covered with faded images of rolling pins and sacks of flour. There's a small white four-burner stove and an out-of-place stainless-steel refrigerator. The porcelain sink is huge. White cabinetry covers two walls and looks as though it's been repainted a dozen times over the years. On the wall next to the door is a key rack that was probably made in a long-ago shop class. Three key chains dangle from it, the wallpaper worn away where the keys hit the wall. The kitchen is the antithesis of my shiny modern kitchen and it feels comforting to me. Something smells amazing in this room. There's a slow cooker on the counter and whatever is in it makes my mouth water.

"You can set the bags right there." The woman nods toward the table, which is covered in a blue-and-white-checked tablecloth.

I lower the bags to the table. "Can I help you unload the groceries?" I ask.

"No, but you can sit and have a cup of tea with me," she says, as she begins pulling produce from one of the bags. "You must be the new neighbor. You bought that gorgeous house at the end of the street, right?" I can't place her accent. Not Southern, but not Northern, either.

"That's right," I say, sitting down at the table. "And you must be Mr. Hockley's . . . aide, or . . . ?"

She laughs. "I'm his sister, Ellie. Do you know my brother?"

"No. I mean, I've seen him around, so I know who he is. Everyone sort of knows everyone around here."

"Oh, don't I know it," she says.

I wonder how old she is. Her hair is very short and is not exactly gray, as I'd first thought. More of a blond-gray. She's an inch or two shorter than me, around five four. She's slender and appears to be in great shape in her jeans and green T-shirt. Even her arms look toned. Her eyes are a clear pale blue behind silver wire-rimmed glasses and she wears dangly silver earrings. There are very few lines in her fair skin. I think she's probably in her late fifties.

"I heard Mr. Buddy is ill," I say. "I was sorry to hear that."

She nods. "That's why I'm here. He and my mother both need some-one to look after them and I was able to make the time."

"That's great you could come. My name's Kayla, by the way."

She looks up from her task to smile at me. "Happy to meet you, Kayla." She pulls a can of loose tea from the shopping bag, opens it, raises it to her nose, and takes a deep breath. "Ahh, beautiful," she says. "Would you like to join me for a cup of tea?" She turns the can to show me the label. ROOIBOS.

"I've never had that. How do you pronounce it?"

"Roy-boss," she says. "Full of antioxidants. It's delicious and good for you."

"I'd love a cup," I say. I'm a coffee drinker, but I'm so ridiculously excited to meet a neighbor that I'll drink anything she offers. She seems equally pleased to have company as well.

"Are your brother and mother home?" I'm being nosy. I'm certain her brother is home; the truck is here. I'm just curious to know what's wrong with him.

"Yes. They're both sleeping right now, which is what they do most of the time these days. My mother's eighty-eight and she doesn't walk well and she's just worn out. She's been in an assisted-living place for the last three years, but she despises it—even though it's supposed to be one of the best—so I figured I'd bring her home as long as I'm here. I've set up the downstairs bedroom for her. My brother has congestive heart failure." She fills the kettle and sets it on the stove. "There just isn't anything they can do for him now. He still has some good days and usually comes downstairs and has dinner with Mama and me."

"I'm sorry," I say. "Is he your older brother?"

"Older and only."

"You grew up in this house?"

She shuts her eyes and I swear I see pain in her face. But it's as though she quickly catches herself. Doesn't want me to see it. "Until I was twenty," she says. "I moved away then. Moved to California. And although Buddy used to come out to visit me every few years, I haven't been back here since I left. Forty-five years."

"Wow," I say. I realize she must be sixty-five. "It must have been a shock to see Shadow Ridge Lane with all the houses going up."

She groans. "I can't get used to that big sign at the entrance. 'Shadow Ridge Estates.' Estates!" She laughs. "Shadow Ridge this and Shadow Ridge that. This street will always be Hockley Street to me. I mean, can you tell me where the ridge is that makes your new neighborhood Shadow Ridge?"

I laugh myself. Jackson and I had joked about that. "There's no ridge that I know of," I say. "Just like there's no hill in Round Hill."

"Exactly," she says. "Do you know what's happening with these houses?" She gestures toward the street. "Are they sold or what?"

"Our house was completed first," I say. I don't want to get into an explanation of why our house was finished so far ahead of the others. "Some of the others are sold. Maybe half of them. But I think it'll be a while before anyone else moves in. I'm your only neighbor for now."

She'd opened one of the cabinets and had been reaching for the cups, but she stops. Lowers her arm. Her expression is serious as she looks directly into my eyes with her clear blue ones. "I heard there was an accident," she says softly. "I heard that the husband—your husband—died. I'm very sorry. That's a tragedy."

"Thank you." I feel touched. I think of the red-haired woman. She could have simply heard about Jackson through the grapevine, too, and that gives me a few seconds of comfort until I remember that the red-haired woman was in Greenville, thirty miles from Round Hill, too far away for the rumor mill to reach her. I don't want to think about her and I focus on Ellie again. "So it's just my daughter and me now." I glance at my watch. I have plenty of time before I need to pick Rainie up from my father's, and I'm in no rush to leave. I like Ellie—her energy and friendliness. I like knowing I have a neighbor.

Ellie takes down the cups and sets them on the counter. "Your daughter's only three, right?" She scoops the loose tea into a teapot. "That's got to be so hard on her. And you."

I nod. "She'll be four in a couple of months. How did you know her age?"

She looks thoughtful. "I don't know. I must have heard it somewhere."

I don't like that Rainie and Jackson and I have been the topic of so much conversation. "Will you be staying in Round Hill?" I ask, changing the subject.

She sighs and pours hot water into the teapot. "I can't leave Buddy and my mother," she says. "I've thought of taking them back to San Francisco with me, but I live in a little cottage and all their doctors are here and I'm not sure either of them would survive the trip. So I think I'll be here until . . ." She gives a little shrug.

"I understand," I say. "It's got to be hard to be uprooted and not know when you can go home."

Ellie leans back against the counter, her arms folded across her chest. "The hard part is that I have a yoga studio and one of my friends is taking over my classes, but I've left things a little topsy-turvy, you could say."

"You teach yoga?" I can't keep the surprise from my voice, and she smiles.

"For thirty-five years."

"No wonder you're in such amazing shape."

She laughs. "Thank you."

"There's a really good studio on Main Street," I say. "Have you been?"

"I've heard about it, but haven't found the time to stop in yet. I've just been using a room upstairs. Do you practice yoga?" She pours our tea, catching the tea leaves with a small strainer.

"I used to, off and on, though I wasn't very good at sticking with it." An understatement. "I did it in my early twenties and then pregnancy yoga when I was expecting Rainie and then a little before I went back to school. And then the accident happened and—" I shrug my shoulders and Ellie nods.

"Life intervened," she says, setting the two cups on the table and sitting down across from me.

"Right. And now I'm back at work. I took off a few months after the accident, so yoga is not the first thing on my mind." I taste the tea. It's far too hot to drink, but the flavor is woodsy, as if I'm drinking my backyard.

"What sort of work do you do?" she asks.

"I'm an architect. My husband and I both were. We designed the house." I nod toward the end of the street. "We both worked for the same design firm in Greenville."

She frowns. "Has to be hard, going back to work without him there," she says, and I nod.

"Extremely," I say.

"Who's watching your little girl while you're working?"

"She's in preschool in the morning and then my father takes care of her in the afternoon." I look at the time on my phone again. "Which reminds me that I'd better go pick her up soon." I nod at the cup of tea in my hand. "This is . . . interesting." I smile.

"It'll grow on you," she says.

I take another sip. She's right. It's not bad. "What are you making in that slow cooker?" I ask. "It smells delicious."

"Doesn't it?" she said. "It's a Middle Eastern stew. I eat mostly vegetarian and a bit of seafood, so I cook a little chicken separately and toss it into my mother's and Buddy's bowls. But I have to say I'm frustrated with the stores in Round Hill."

"How come?"

"No za'atar in any of them. No Middle Eastern or kosher groceries in Round Hill. I'm spoiled by living in California. Have you ever had it?"

"I think so," I say. "Kind of a combination of herbs and spices?" There's a great Middle Eastern restaurant in Greenville and I'm pretty sure I know what she's talking about.

"I'm going to have to send away for it. For a man raised on chicken and dumplings, Buddy loves my Middle Eastern cooking."

"How did you end up in San Francisco?" I ask.

"Oh, that's a long story." She waves away the question. "But it suits me there. I have lots of good friends whom I miss dearly."

"I know what that's like," I say. I lost friends by becoming a widow. They rallied around me in the beginning, but every one of my close friends is part of a couple and sometimes I wonder if they think widowhood is catching.

I glance at the clock on Ellie's range. "I'd better go." I drink the rest of the tea and get to my feet.

"I'll walk out with you," she says.

Outside, we walk down her driveway past Buddy Hockley's truck and her car. When we reach the street, I look straight down Shadow Ridge Lane and see my house, surrounded by trees. I turn to face her. "It was so nice meeting you, Miss Ellie," I say sincerely.

"Oh, none of that 'Miss Ellie' stuff." She laughs. "I've been away from the South for so long, I won't answer to that anymore. Just 'Ellie,' please."

I smile. "Okay, Ellie. I'm happy we're neighbors, even if we're at opposite ends of the street." I look toward my house again. Hesitate for a second before I speak. "Last night"—I nod toward her old white house—"I looked out my front window and the neighborhood was pitch black except for a light in this house. Your house. It made me feel . . ." I'm suddenly embarrassed, baring my soul to this near stranger.

"Less alone?" Ellie offers.

"Exactly," I said.

"I'm glad," she said. "You let me know if you ever want to practice some yoga. No charge, of course. It's always nice to have a partner."

"I will," I say, wondering if I could fit that in.

"I hope I haven't made you late picking up your daughter."

"Oh no. My father just lives over on Painter Lane."

Her smile grows uncertain. "What's his name?" she asks. "Your father?"

I suddenly remember Daddy saying something about hanging out with the Hockley kids in a tree house. "I think you knew him," I say. "Reed Miller."

She hesitates a moment. I can't read her expression. It's flat, but there's something brewing behind it. "Ah," she says finally. Then she turns away from me, abruptly. Over her shoulder she calls, "Have a nice afternoon, now."

I stare after her, confused by such an awkward ending to a comfortable visit. One thing I know for sure, though: she knew my father.

Chapter 14

ELLIE

1965

I'd been dozing on the van's long middle seat for a couple of hours when Chip called out, "We're here, you guys! Wake up."

I sat up as we bounced along a potholed driveway onto the campus of Morris Brown College in Atlanta, where our orientation would be held. The buildings looked old and weather-beaten, some of them brick, some wood. We checked in in one of the main buildings, where a woman handed each of us a folder, a black and white SCOPE button, and our dorm room assignment. Peggy was ahead of me in line and I could tell that she was not at all happy to discover that, of the hundreds of students at the orientation, I'd been assigned as her roommate. I heard her actually groan at the news. I didn't like her any more than she liked me. My attempts at conversation with her and David in the van were often left hanging in the air. Chip, while not exactly warm, had at least made some small talk with me, but I had a bad feeling. If four white students couldn't connect any better than this, how could we expect white and Negro to get along?

Together, Peggy and I lugged our belongings out the door and across the campus to the ancient girls' dorm, Gaines Hall, where a sign on the door read NO SMOKING, NO DRINKING, NO MEN.

"Oh, this mattress!" Peggy said, once she'd dropped her suitcase on the floor of our tiny room and sat down on the squeaky bed.

I sat on my own mattress and felt the springs give way under my weight. "I think these mattresses have been here since the place was built," I said.

I set my suitcase on the bed and began hanging up my skirts and blouses, while Peggy headed for the door. "Where are you going?" I asked.

"To find David," she said without a glance in my direction.

She left and I stared at the door as it closed behind her. I felt very alone. Here I was, on a campus where I knew no one, with a roommate who didn't like me. Would all the students treat me so coolly? There wasn't much I could do about my accent or my heritage. I missed Brenda, whom I knew I was losing to Garner and a baby. I missed Aunt Carol, who would have cheered me on. And I missed Reed, who loved me more than I deserved. In that moment I would have given just about anything to feel his arms around me.

I wanted to go outside to explore a bit but thought I'd better read over the orientation material instead. Tonight was a welcoming session. Monday through Friday looked like very long days filled with speeches and training sessions and workshops. We'd learn about the history of Negroes in America and there would be a lot of sessions about the South with a capital "S." I wondered what I had yet to learn about the land I'd lived in my whole life. The words began to swim in my vision and before I knew it, Peggy was waking me up to go to dinner and the welcoming session.

≈

We filled the metal folding chairs in the sweltering gymnasium and listened to a number of speakers warn us of the danger in the weeks ahead. The head of SCOPE, Reverend Hosea Williams, whose name was familiar to me after all the reading I'd been doing, introduced what felt like dozens of other folks who had various roles in the program. Everyone who spoke gave us the same message: our work was important but dangerous. We needed to keep our wits about us, be sure to let someone know where we were at all times, and always be mature representatives of the program. And we had to *produce*. I knew that meant we needed to persuade people to register to vote. I looked around me at the serious faces—all those white students from up north and out west, as well as a good number of Negro volunteers who would help us connect with distrustful residents. I listened to the speakers and thought to myself, *What am I doing here?* I'd never felt so out of place in my entire life.

At the end of the evening, a gray-haired woman named Mrs. Clark taught us "freedom songs." "You'll know 'em all by heart by the end of the week," she promised, handing out the mimeographed lyrics. I liked singing, but in that cavernous space, with unfamiliar melodies, my voice sounded as small and inconsequential as I felt. When we sang "We Shall Overcome," our last song of the night and the only one slightly familiar to me, I felt so false. I had nothing to overcome. It wasn't until I was lying, hot and exhausted, on my sagging mattress later that night, that I realized I carried a huge burden of my own creation—a burden it would take a miracle for me to overcome.

≈

Monday afternoon, Hosea Williams announced that he wanted to speak with two students and I was surprised and unnerved when he spoke my name into the microphone. "Those two students, please meet me in the back of the gym," he said.

Oh, great, I thought. This could not be good. I felt hundreds of eyes on me as I walked from my seat near the front of the gym to the rear. I waited my turn as Reverend Williams spoke to the other student, a boy, who looked angry by the end of their conversation. The boy stomped past me without making eye contact, and Reverend Williams waved me over.

"How are you doing?" he asked when I reached him. This close to him, I could see his neatly trimmed mustache and serious brown eyes.

"Fine." I tried gamely to smile. "Though I'm wondering why you wanted to see me." I glanced in the direction the angry boy had gone.

Reverend Williams nodded. "We have some concerns about you," he said, getting right to the point. "First, you're from North Carolina, and second, you haven't been vetted by any of the universities that are working with SCOPE, nor have you been through the campus briefings on field-work. All the other students have gone through a thorough educational process to be sure they know what they're getting into and to assure us of their . . . stability. The fact that you're a Southerner'll make it hard for you to gain anyone's trust."

"Reverend Filburn mentioned that," I said. "But he thought it would be okay." I didn't know if I should address his concern about my stability. I wasn't feeling very stable at that moment.

He nodded. "Yes, Greg Filburn persuaded me to give you a chance," he said. "But I warn you, it's going to be tough." His dark eyes were unsmiling. "I'm going to make sure you're assigned to Greg's county. What is it? Derby?"

"Yes, sir."

"He'll be able to keep an eye on you. Assuming you make it through orientation," he added. "If you decide you want to back out after this week, we'll understand."

"Okay," I said. "Thank you." I walked back to my seat, ignoring the curious looks from other students who were no doubt wondering what I'd done to merit Hosea Williams's attention. I felt unsettled but determined as I took my seat again. I hadn't realized that Reverend Filburn had gone out on a limb for me. I didn't want to let him down.

≈

It was a challenge to sit on those hard chairs for speech after speech, but I grew more alert with each one. Every speaker mentioned that President Johnson would be signing the Voting Rights Act in early July, making it easy—or at least *easier*—for us to register voters. The act would get rid of literacy tests and other obstacles to registering. I kept thinking of our former maid, Louise, and that dirt road through Turner's Bend and all those run-down houses. I imagined myself going up to one of those houses by myself, knocking on the door, trying to persuade whoever answered to register to vote. The thought was outlandish, and I understood for the first time why we'd have Negro canvassing partners. No one would trust us otherwise.

During the breaks, I struggled to connect with people and I felt my old childhood shyness returning. It seemed that everyone already had his or her own little group of friends, which made sense, since nearly all of them had come from a college with their fellow students. I seemed to be the only loner, or at least that's how I felt. It was like being in junior high school all over again.

Late into the night, Mrs. Clark taught us more freedom songs. There was one that I really liked—"I'll Fly Away"—which I knew from church but which touched me in a new way all of a sudden, especially when all the harmonies kicked in in that big open space.

Mrs. Clark was a wonderful teacher. "Now you young folks from the North," she said, "y'all need to learn how to sing Southern! There ain't no 'g' in 'i-n-g.' It's 'singin',' not 'singing.' " Finally, a skill that came easily to me.

She introduced us to a song called "I Love Everybody."

"People who have nothin'—no runnin' water, not hardly a thin' to eat— still sing this song about lovin' everybody," she said. Then she led us in the song, which included, by name, people in power who'd beaten or killed civil rights workers. We even sang that we loved the racist governor of Alabama, George Wallace. I pictured Aunt Carol rolling over in her grave. She hated that man.

I began to really feel the emotion of the songs and by the time we ended with "We Shall Overcome," I was more awake and joy-filled than I'd been all day.

Once the events of the evening were over, I crossed the dark campus, hoping Peggy would still be up. I felt inspired to make a new start with her, hoping she had the same positive feelings about the day that I did. She wasn't in the room when I got there, though, and it was way past curfew. I climbed into bed, but was too fired up to sleep. Something had happened to me in the last twenty-four hours. I couldn't name it. Couldn't even understand it. I felt hope and fear, determination and cowardice, all mixed together. I wondered if that's what all those speakers had wanted us to feel.

≈

I was still awake when Peggy slipped quietly into the room an hour after I went to bed. I sat up.

"You don't need to be quiet," I said. "I'm awake. You can turn on the light."

She flipped the switch and I blinked at the brightness. Peggy's curly auburn hair glittered in the light. She dragged her suitcase onto the floor and ignored me as she rummaged in it for something.

"Today was really good, wasn't it?" I asked.

She didn't look up but I could feel her roll her eyes. "If you say so," she said.

"I learned so much."

She looked at me then. "They probably don't teach you much in your little segregated schools in Podunk, North Carolina."

I bristled. I was sick of tiptoeing around this girl. "First of all," I said, "my high school was *integrated*." Not by much, but it definitely had not been the lily-white school she was picturing. "And second of all, I got into the University of North Carolina, which was no easy feat, so I must have had a decent education. And third of all, can we please try to get along? Because that's why we're down here, right? To learn how to help people get along? And if you and I can't even do that, there's really no hope."

Whoa, it felt good to get all that out, and for a moment she just stared at me.

"You're probably right," she said, "but it doesn't matter. I'm leaving."

"You're . . . already?"

"David and I split up." I thought she was crying, but she turned her head away from me so I wouldn't see as she went back to digging in her suitcase. "And I was never so bored as I was this morning listening to those speeches. You sat through them all day? I couldn't stand it. So I know I'm in the wrong place for me. I'm leaving in the morning."

I was quiet for a moment, taking this in. "You were doing this because David was?" I asked.

"I thought I could get into it but it's just not how I want to spend my summer."

"Can I . . . can I help you with anything?" I asked.

"Just go back to sleep."

I lay down and rolled onto my side facing the wall. I heard her open the door to the closet as sleep finally found me, and when I woke up early in the morning, she was gone.

≈

Peggy was not the only student who left. Over breakfast, I heard whispers of at least two other students leaving. It was probably good they left now, before the hard work began. I was determined not to be one of them.

I was sitting across from a guy as I ate, and he smiled at me. "I love the food in the South," he said, nodding to the biscuits and sausage gravy on his plate. My own plate held scrambled eggs and grits. My usual breakfast.

"Where are you from?" I asked.

"New Jersey, where I'd be eating pork roll and eggs and hash browns." He grinned. He looked as though he wore a perpetual smile. "You're from down here, obviously. With that accent." He had a pretty significant accent of his own.

"You could tell from that one sentence?"

"Oh yeah," he said. "South Carolina?" he guessed.

"North," I said.

"Well, good for you." He took a forkful of his biscuit. Chewed and swallowed. "They told us Southern students wouldn't work out, though."

"I'm beginning to wonder," I said, thinking of my conversation with Hosea Williams.

"Maybe you can lose that accent." He looked doubtful.

"Is it really that strong?"

"Wow. Yeah."

"Wow. Yeah," I repeated, trying to imitate him. "How was that?"

He seemed to find it uproariously funny. "What's your name?" he asked, when he'd finished laughing.

"Eleanor. Ellie."

"Well, Ellie," he said. "You look like you're up for a challenge. What're you doing with SCOPE?"

"I want to help," I said simply. "Same as everyone else."

"Cool," he said. "I'm John. Happy to meet you."

"You too."

"Actually, this is my third trip South this past year. And to be honest, I've gotten to really crave biscuits and gravy."

I gave him a quizzical look. "Third?"

"I was in Mississippi last summer, doing civil rights work. And I was out here just a few months ago for the Selma march. The third march. The big one. The one where no one got killed," he added soberly.

This guy didn't just *talk* about doing the work, I thought. He actually did it. "It must have been . . . it must have felt so good, being in that Selma march. Knowing what it meant."

"It did indeed," he said.

"You're courageous," I said. "You didn't know how that march would turn out. That you'd be safe."

He smiled. "I'm *committed*," he said.

"Are you a student?" He looked too old, but how else would he have time to be a civil rights worker?

"Seminary," he said.

I nodded. I could picture him as a preacher.

We were quiet for a moment. I swallowed a mouthful of grits, looking around the cafeteria. "I think I'm the only Southern white person here," I said finally to break the silence.

"You may be right," he said. "Your accent's nice, but it does make you more . . . vulnerable. You'll have to work harder to let people know you're on their side."

"I'm nervous," I admitted.

"I understand," he said.

"Were you nervous? Last summer, knowing other workers had been killed? And in the march, knowing—"

"Yes, of course." He smiled at me with sympathy. "By the end of this week, you'll feel less jittery, but you need to keep some of those nerves. Don't let your guard down. There are people down here who'd just as soon kill a civil rights worker than look at one. The trick is to stay focused on the goal. Keep your eyes on the prize, like they say in the song. That's all you can do, Ellie May."

I hated when people called me "Ellie May," after the dumb-blonde character Elly May Clampett on *The Beverly Hillbillies*, but coming from John, who I liked a lot even though I'd known him mere minutes, the name made me smile.

≈

John sat next to me for that morning's session, which was about nonviolence. There was a lot of talk of Jesus and Gandhi and I imagined John was remembering that peaceful, powerful march from Selma to Montgomery. "Nonviolence is healing," the speaker said.

One young man in the audience raised his hand and the speaker called on him.

"I was in the march from Selma to Montgomery," he said, "and there wasn't nothin' those troopers in Selma could've done to me that would make me act as ugly as they did."

I found myself shivering although the air in the gym was hot and thick and sticky. How did you do it? How did you not fight back when you were being attacked? How did you not want to kill someone when they were killing you? How did you sing that "I Love Everybody" song when someone was pouring ammonia over your face?

During a break, I told John about the protests in Chapel Hill. "I was covering them for the campus newspaper," I explained. "First I thought they were kind of stupid and then . . . I began to understand why they were doing it. And one day, I joined a protest. The police came and I didn't fight them but I didn't go limp, like a lot of the protesters did. I couldn't make myself be so vulnerable."

"It's more than just 'going limp,' Ellie May," John said. "It's more about focusing on that feeling of love for everybody. Like the song." He winked at me. He made it sound so easy. John had a little Gandhi in him, I thought. I was glad to be sitting next to him. He made me feel safe and strong. I knew, though, that I was going to have to learn to find those feelings inside myself.

John became my buddy for the rest of the week. The long days and evenings were exhausting in the most wonderful way, with each day ending the same way as we broke into our enormous circle, crossing arms, holding hands with our neighbors, and singing our hearts out. I was glad I no longer had a roommate and I'd walk back to my dorm room, brush my teeth, strip off my clothes, fall onto my bed, and be unconscious before I had the chance to notice the lumps in the mattress.

On Thursday evening, Martin Luther King, Jr., came to speak to us. Oh, how I wished Aunt Carol could have been with me! I'd seen grainy images of Dr. King on the TV news and recent pictures of him in the paper after the Selma march, but to see him in person, close up—I was in the fifth row of that huge space—was truly thrilling. We'd had good speakers that week, but this was different. Dr. King seemed to speak in waves, almost chanting at times. I stopped taking notes and just listened to him. I didn't need to write down his words to remember them. He was frustrated that President Johnson hadn't yet signed the Voting Rights Act. "A state that has denied opportunity for quality education for Negroes has no right to demand literacy as a prerequisite for voting," he said in that mesmerizing voice that touched my soul. "The fact that the Voting Rights Act is not yet the law of the land will make your work harder," he said, turning his head left and right to take us all in, "but I know you're not here because the work is easy." I glanced up at John and saw tears in his eyes. Only then did I realize I had tears in my own.

That night, I dreamed about Mattie Jenkins. We were together, deep in the frigid water of the lake at the end of Hockley Road, and I was trying to pull her to the surface. I struggled to grip her in my frozen fingers, but she kept slipping through them.

I woke up choking, gasping for air. I needed to walk outside in the thick, dark Georgia humidity before I could shake the dream from my mind. It wasn't the first time I was tortured by that dream. I only wished it could be the last.

On Friday night, we were split into two groups: male and female. A handsome man named Andrew Young talked to us—the white girls—and he was kind but very firm.

"Avoid being seen in integrated cars or walking in integrated groups whenever possible," he said. I'm sure I wasn't the only girl in the group who wondered how we'd be able to follow that rule, since most of us white canvassers would be working side by side with our Negro partners.

"Be aware of your surroundings at all times," he continued. "If you see white men in a truck while you're canvassing with a Negro partner, get to safety immediately."

I thought of Reed and "Mildred," his white and blue 1955 Ford truck. It was weird to think that I should be afraid of a guy like Reed.

"Dress conservatively," Reverend Young said. "Don't drink and don't date. Don't fall in love with anybody." His eyes grew wide with the warning. "You fall in love, you'll be tempted to put the welfare of that person ahead of the good of the team," he said. "Don't go to parties, and absolutely don't get involved with Negro boys."

I nodded along with the other girls as he issued his warnings, knowing I had no intention of going to parties or falling in love. That was not why I was there.

≈

When we sang our freedom songs that night, I realized that I knew every word of every song, and when we sang "We Shall Overcome," I broke into tears, unable to sing as I clutched the hands of John on my left and a girl I didn't know on my right. She nodded at me, gripping my hand harder. That song—all the songs really—felt so different to me now than they had earlier in the week. I felt the history behind them. The emotion. I felt full of love for everyone in that huge space.

John squeezed my hand and when I looked at him, tears running down my cheeks, he smiled at me through the words of the song. When the singing was over, he hugged me tight.

"You're going to do fine, Ellie May," he said.

I hoped he was right.

Chapter 15

KAYLA

2010

For the first time, I don't think about the red-haired woman as I walk into Bader and Duke Design, but my peace of mind doesn't last long. I Skype with a contractor, then meet with a woman who wants to add a mother-in-law suite onto her split-level. Her mother-in-law is with her and I find myself scrutinizing her to see if she might be Ann Smith out of her disguise. I feel guilty because I can barely pay attention to what the two of them are saying. Once I'm sure the woman is not Ann Smith, though, I snap out of my fog and focus on their needs one hundred percent, or at least, close to it.

After work, I stop in the Middle Eastern restaurant that I always pass on my walk to the parking garage. It has a little market attached to it, where I buy a good-sized bag of za'atar, smiling to myself at the thought of surprising Ellie with it. I might ask her about a yoga session someday soon, too. I can use a de-stressor.

I drive to Carlisle to drop off the samples for the window coverings. I've already faxed Amanda my selections and I have to cut her short when she tries to engage me in conversation. I'm running late.

Once in Round Hill, I pick up Rainie from her preschool. As soon as she's in the car, she hands me a painting she made of something unrecognizable but which she tells me is two giraffes. *This is good*, I think. *This is encouraging.* Her early artwork at the school was just as unrecognizable, but when I'd ask her to tell me about what she'd drawn, her answers always upset me. A dead puppy—that was one of them. A lady with no eyes was another. Strange things that made me weep for my little girl who was having to face grown-up pain well before she should have to.

"I can't wait to show Gramps the painting!" she says now from her car seat.

"Gramps has an appointment this afternoon," I say, "but you'll be able to show him tomorrow."

"No!" she says. "I want to show him right now!"

I feel a meltdown coming on. "You know what we can do this afternoon, Rainie?" I ask, warding off the wail I know is coming.

"What?" She sounds suspicious.

"We can explore our new yard! There are some trails through the woods, and someone told me there's a lake back there." Of course, it was Jackson who told me about the trails and the lake, but I don't want to bring him up when she already sounds so fragile. "Won't that be cool?" I ask her. "Finding new things right in our own backyard?"

"Are there ducks? Can I feed them?"

"I don't know, but we should go find out."

I think back to the afternoon before, when I picked her up at my father's house. She'd had a tumble off the jungle gym, a fall that had clearly terrified my father. Daddy and I had been so wrapped up in talking about that fall that I forgot to tell him about meeting my neighbor until I was ready to get in the car.

"Oh," I said to him as I slipped behind the steering wheel, "I met the Hockley daughter yesterday."

He looked at me blankly, as if he didn't quite understand what I said. "Ellie?" he finally asked.

I nodded. "She seems really nice. She's out here from California taking care of her mother and brother, who's very ill. She teaches yoga."

The slightest smile crossed his face. "Does she, now," he said. It wasn't really a question.

"I don't think she remembers you," I said. "She didn't seem to recognize your name."

He frowned at that. "Does she have some . . . a cognitive problem?" he asked. "Some dementia?"

I shook my head. "She didn't seem to," I said. "Not at all."

"Then she remembers me," he said, his expression oddly grim. "You can trust me on that." He turned and started walking away. "Have a good night," he said over his shoulder.

I didn't shut my car door. "What do you mean, Daddy?" I called after him, but he just raised his hand as if saying *goodbye* or *I'll tell you later* or *it's of no consequence,* and I remembered that Ellie's response to learning *his* name had been just as baffling.

≈

Our back deck is huge and beautiful, the composite faux wood the same color as the gray-brown bark of the trees that surround it. There are a dozen planters built into the railings, but they are empty. Filling them was to be my job and I fear it's going to take me a long time to find the enthusiasm to bother with them.

Last night, after I put Rainie to bed, I sat out here with a glass of wine. I heard the hum of cicadas. *This is so nice,* I told myself. *So peaceful.* Then I heard what must have been an owl, the sound eerie and echoey in the darkness. It was followed a moment or two later by an unidentifiable animal sound. It was almost a scream. It sent a chill up my spine. The woods were invisible, just a flat, black screen in front of me that my vision had no chance of penetrating. I heard footsteps off to my right, but could see nothing. Heart thumping, I reached for my wine, ready to go back in the house. Suddenly, the deck lights illuminated the tawny coat of a deer at the edge of the woods. One doe, then another and another. I laughed at my nerves.

"Hi, beautiful," I said aloud. "Have we taken over some of your land? Can we share?"

The doe stared at me a while longer before slipping back into the darkness with her followers. I listened to them retreat, the human-sounding footsteps on the forest floor making me smile this time. I'd have to get used to living in the woods, I thought. What a wonderful playground they could be for Rainie.

Now I study our harmless-looking backyard in the daylight. There is no grass at all in this yard, only moss and wood chips. I look at the circular trail that begins at either end of the deck before disappearing into the woods. Although Jackson had wanted to walk the trail with me, I hadn't gotten around to going with him, one of the many things I wish I could have a second chance to do.

"Which way do you want to go?" I ask Rainie, pointing from one end of the deck to the other. "Both paths lead right back here."

She looks back and forth, then points to the left. "That one," she says, walking across the deck toward it.

"Perfect!" I say. "Let's go!"

We set out on the trail that runs west from the house. It begins with large slate stepping-stones, but once inside the forest, the floor of the trail is the packed carpet of leaves and earth, and the trees instantly create a tunnel around us. I should really embrace these trees Jackson was so drawn to. While I can tell an oak from a maple and a pine, that's about as far as my tree knowledge goes. I'll get a book on tree identification and teach Rainie how to tell one from the other.

We've gone a short distance when Rainie runs ahead of me and trips over a huge root, falling to her hands and knees. I wait for the howl I know is coming, but it's more of a whimper of surprise. I catch up to her and squat down.

"That must have really surprised you," I say.

She looks at the dirt on her palms. Rubs her hands together to get it off. "I tripped." She gives me a wounded look. Tears are in her eyes but she's in control of them.

I touch the root that stretches across the width of the path. "Do you know what this is, Rainie?" I ask, pointing to the root.

"A pretend snake?" she asks, and I smile. The root does look snakelike. "I like that funny answer," I say, "but it's actually a tree root. The water in the earth goes up through these roots and feeds the tree. So we have to be very careful on this path because there are probably a lot of these big roots."

"And we don't want to hurt the trees," Rainie says, as though proud of herself for making that leap in understanding, and I just want to hug her to pieces, but I keep my hands at my sides as I help her to her feet.

"Well, it would be really hard to hurt the tree because it's very, very sturdy," I say, "but it could hurt *us* if we trip over the root, as you just found out. So we need to walk instead of run. Okay?"

"Okay," she says. "Let's go find the lake, Mama!" She reaches for my hand and we begin walking again.

I've always considered myself more of a beach girl than the woodsy type, and now I remember why. Woods are spooky. The trees are on our right, our left, ahead of us, above us, and when I turn to look behind us, they are there as well. Without this narrow trail—a trail that will soon be swallowed up if I do nothing to maintain it—we would be quickly lost out here, just yards from our new house. I feel a weird chill, a draft of cold air slipping over my shoulders. I look up at the sun-stealing canopy of green above us and sigh to myself.

"Mama, I see water!" Rainie points ahead of us and I see what's caught her attention: the dark murk of a lake through the trees. I sense her energy.

She wants to dart ahead of me and find a way to that water, but she knows better than to run now. We can't get to the lake, anyway. The trail we're on is about ten yards from the lake and the brush is so thick it would take a person—or at least it would take *me*—half an hour to work my way through it, assuming I didn't get bitten by a snake along the way.

"How do we get to the ducks?" Rainie asks, her shoulders drooping in disappointment.

The oval-shaped lake is about twice the width of our new house and three times as long. A few skinny trees grow straight out of the water, which is an impenetrable dark brown. Whether the color is from silt or muck or simply the lack of sunlight reflecting off it, I can't tell. It's not an inviting body of water, that's for sure. There is something truly creepy about it. I hold on to Rainie's shoulder as though the lake might somehow pull her in. At the very least, it's most certainly a breeding ground for mosquitoes and I feel more sure than ever that there are snakes close to our ankles, waiting to chomp on us. I'm also certain there are no ducks. I doubt a duck has ever gotten within half a mile of this nasty body of water.

"Oh, honey," I say. "This is very disappointing, I know, but there are no ducks at this lake. We can't even get to it."

I'm afraid she's going to cry, but instead she gives a heavy sigh and says, "*Very* disappointing," and I laugh and lean over to hug her. *What would I do without you?* I think, holding her so tightly that she squirms. I straighten up, glad she doesn't look up at me and see the tears in my eyes.

"Let's keep going," I say, taking her hand again, anxious to leave the lake behind us. I wonder if we've reached the halfway point of the trail yet. I look back over my shoulder at the lake and the tangle of vines between it and the trail. Do I really need to worry about putting a fence back here? It would cost a mint to fence in our entire property all the way back to this lake. The window coverings are going to take a big chunk of my savings, and I can't picture Rainie—I can't picture *anyone*—working their way back that far. Still, I like the idea of cutting my property off from that nasty body of water.

We keep going, watching for tree roots and—now that they're on my mind—snakes. Then, suddenly, we come to a large opening in the woods. It's almost a perfect circle, about the size, if not the shape, of our great room. It's the strangest space. It looks as though nothing has ever grown here. The ground is mostly a carpet of brown pine needles. Nature didn't make this circle, I think, and I feel that cool chill around my shoulders again despite the sticky heat of the day. I look up at the mix of pine trees and massive oaks, one of them almost certainly that huge oak I can see from our deck. I catch my breath when I see a tree house nestled between its enormous branches.

"Look, Rainie," I say, pointing up. She follows my finger.

"A little house!" she says. "Can we go in it?"

We walk around the massive trunk of the oak to find a zigzagged series of steps and a railing made of fresh, clean wood, built, no doubt, by my husband. The house is high in the tree, at least twice my height.

"Okay," I say. "You go ahead of me and just be really careful. Hold on to the railing Daddy made. I'll be right behind you."

It's slow going. The steps are narrow and steep and Rainie can barely reach from one to the next. I hold my left hand close to her back as we climb, my right clutching the railing. Soon we find ourselves in a musty-smelling empty wooden shell. The wood is very old except for one corner where Jackson must have repaired some damage. I suddenly recall Daddy telling me that the Hockley kids had a tree house in the forest at the end of the street. Could this house possibly be that old? I laugh to myself. I wonder if Ellie would like to see this? If this is where she spent some of her childhood?

"I love this little house!" Rainie spins a circle in the middle of the room, arms outstretched. "I can bring my stuffed animals up here!"

I stop her spinning and put my hands on her shoulders. "Rainie, until you're older, you may not come up here alone, okay? It's way too high and those stairs are too dangerous."

She wrinkles her nose. "How old?"

"Eight," I say, and she stomps her foot.

"That's too old!"

"That's the rule. Promise me you won't try to come up here by yourself."

She pouts. "I promise," she says.

"Okay. Good."

There is a deck attached to the tree house. I crawl through the low rear doorway, but the opening is high enough for Rainie to walk through. The deck itself is clearly old, but it looks like Jackson built a railing around it, the wood new and sweet smelling. The clearing is far below us. From this height it's even more obvious that it's a large, man-made circle. So strange.

Rainie giggles. "I'm pretending I'm a squirrel."

"I'm pretending I'm a bird," I say. We chat a while longer, then make our cautious way down the steps to the ground. For a moment, I can't find where the trail picks up. I can't even see the part of the trail we arrived on, and I turn around in a disoriented circle before I notice a few small cuts on the trees where branches have been removed to create the entrance to the trail. I breathe a sigh of relief and Rainie and I start walking in that direction.

Rainie chatters about the "little house" the whole way home. "I can't wait till I'm eight!" she says. "But I can go up in it with you, right?"

"Right," I say cheerfully, but I hope she'll soon forget about the tree house. It's going to be a good long while before I want to walk this trail again.

Chapter 16

————— ≈ —————

ELLIE

1965

It was nearly nine o'clock on Saturday night by the time all the students were packed up and ready to leave Morris Brown College for their field assignments. I'd hoped John—the only real friend I'd made during the week—might miraculously be joining me in Derby County, but he was assigned to a county in Mississippi, which I knew was what he wanted. There would be ten of us "freedom fighters" in Derby—eight guys and two girls. The only person whose name was familiar to me was Chip Stein, one of the boys I'd ridden down to Atlanta with.

Several vans showed up at the college to transport all of us to our assignments, but Paul Golden, an older graduate student from Columbia who was assigned to Derby, had a car he was letting SCOPE use for the summer. Before I knew it, I found myself in his silver Plymouth with him and two other students, ready to head back to Derby County. We agreed we'd take turns driving on the eleven-hour trip, and Paul got in behind the steering wheel to start us off. Jocelyn, the only other girl heading to

Derby County, was in the front seat. She had a delicate look about her. Her pink glasses nearly blended into her fair skin, and she was slender, almost skinny. She wore her long dark hair in an ivory barrette at the back of her neck. She was twenty, like me, and even though we hadn't met before we got into the car, she turned to me, instantly chatty and friendly—even after she heard my accent—as we waited for one of the SCOPE leaders to send us on our way. I liked her immediately. I was in the back seat with a student named Winston Madison, who didn't say a word to any of us.

Before we took off, one of the SCOPE leaders, Dan, leaned in the car window to wish us a safe journey. When he saw me sitting next to Winston, he rearranged us, putting Winston up front with Paul, and Jocelyn in the back seat with me, so we wouldn't have a Negro guy sitting next to a white girl in case anyone noticed us while we were on the road.

"You're just asking for trouble if you get stopped with you next to Winston," Dan said, once he was satisfied with the new seating arrangement. He told Winston to duck down if we passed too close to other cars until we were on the highway. Winston nodded, but looked unconcerned. He was tall and lanky, with dark eyes behind horn-rimmed glasses. I'd noticed him over the course of the week, as he seemed to like to sit near the front of the packed gym, like John and I did. He was hard to miss. While most of the boys wore tan chinos and plaid shirts, Winston always looked freshly pressed in dark slacks, a white shirt, and an occasional tie. He wore his hair close-cropped as if he'd just stepped out of a barber shop. The only time I saw him smile was when Reverend King took the microphone. He was there to work, not play. Not that the rest of us were playing, exactly, but we were energized and enthused, while Winston seemed to hold everything in, a tight spring. Only when we sang at the end of the night did he seem to relax.

"So," Paul said, once we were underway, "I'm from New York State. Poli-sci major. What about you guys?"

"Tucson, Arizona," Jocelyn said. "I go to UCLA. Majoring in library science."

"I'm from Derby County, as y'all know," I said. "I go to the University of North Carolina in Chapel Hill, majoring in pharmacology."

"Wow!" Jocelyn said. "You must be a brainiac."

I wasn't a brainiac, but I was definitely starting to like Jocelyn.

"And you, Winston?" I leaned forward to look at him.

"Call me Win. I'm a junior at Shaw University in Raleigh, and I'm also from Derby County," he said, surprising me. "They're sending me up there because I know it. I know the people. I can help y'all to get a foot in the door."

"I'm from Round Hill," I said.

He nodded. "I know," he said. "I saw it in the roster. I live in Darville, the other end of the county."

I didn't know a soul in Darville. "What are you studying?" I asked him.

"Education," he said. "I want to teach."

"So what's Derby County like?" Paul asked, and Winston—Win—and I spent the next hour or so attempting to educate Paul and Jocelyn about Derby. It was quickly apparent that we were talking about two different counties: my lily-white Round Hill and Win's mixed-sounding Darville. I knew nothing about the parts of the county we'd be working in. Nothing about the inequities, the farming communities, the sharecroppers. All I knew about those aspects of the South was what I'd learned this past week, which had been all theory and no reality. Listening to Win talk about how the sharecroppers suffered, how they were afraid to even attempt to register to vote because they might lose their income and their homes, I felt a blush creep up my neck at my ignorance. Win struck me as bright but humorless. There was a tense feeling about him, like if you scratched his calm, almost intellectual surface, you'd find a very angry man.

"I live in a little white vacuum," I said, surprising myself when those words came out of my mouth.

"You had Black kids in Round Hill High School, though, right?" Win said, turning his head to look at me. I was jarred by his use of the word "black."

"Yeah, sure," I said, though I didn't think I'd said two words to the few Negro students in my high school. They came in from other communities in the morning and returned to those communities in the afternoon. We had nothing in common. I was disappointed in myself for never reaching out to them.

"Hey!" Jocelyn said. "Paul looks like he's falling asleep at the wheel already and we're only an hour into our trip. We should sing!"

I laughed at her enthusiasm. "Are you a cheerleader at UCLA?" I asked.

"Do I look like a cheerleader?" she asked. It was too dark to see, but I imagined she was rolling her eyes. She looked nothing like a cheerleader.

"What song should we start with?" I asked.

Both of the boys grumbled with their lack of enthusiasm as I started singing my favorite, "I'll Fly Away," and Jocelyn quickly joined me. Paul, too, a moment later. I thought Win—serious, zipped-up-tight Win—was going to skip the singing, but he surprised me, and soon the four of us were swaying and clapping—except for Paul, who kept his hands on the wheel—and singing at the top of our lungs as we drove along Georgia's dark highways.

We drove nearly straight through, Atlanta to Derby County, eleven long dark hazy hours with only a few stops for food and bathroom breaks. We picked up sandwiches for Win, who had to stay in the sweltering heat of the car, since he wouldn't be welcome in the restaurants. And we had to pull over a few times to find a place wooded and isolated enough for him to relieve himself. We were very careful. We knew that the sort of people who were on the road in the middle of the night in Georgia and the Carolinas would not take kindly to seeing an interracial group traveling together and we didn't want our SCOPE summer to end before it even began. Win accepted all of this as though it was nothing unusual, but it really bothered me. He was one of us. It was so wrong that he had to endure the humiliation of being treated like a third-rate citizen. *This is what it's all about,* I thought to myself. *This will never change without Negroes being able to vote.* Everything made so much more sense to me now. I thought that was why Win seemed so serious. That was why the students in Chapel Hill had endured the ammonia poured over their heads and why, even though I hadn't completely understood my motivation at the time, those of us kneeling on Franklin Street hadn't budged when angry people drove their cars close enough to us to touch. As John had said, we had our eyes on the prize.

≈

Our destination was a small special education school that was closed for the summer. The school was in Flint, a Derby County town I'd never even heard of, although it was no more than twenty miles from Round Hill. We got lost, but finally saw the beige SCOPE van in a small parking lot, and Win, who was driving at that time, pulled in next to it. Exhausted from very little sleep, we dragged ourselves and our meager belongings toward the building. I felt desperate for a shower.

I was just a few feet from the school's double doors when I saw the bullet hole, unmistakable for anything else, in one of the door's windows. The window of the second door had been completely blown out. We all stopped short, staring.

"Damn!" Paul said, the first blasphemy I'd heard from any of us. I had to agree with him.

"Welcome to Derby County," Win said, almost under his breath.

Inside the building, though, the atmosphere was almost partylike—or as partylike as it could be with a bunch of young people who'd had very little sleep in the past twenty-four hours. The other students assigned to Derby County had arrived less than an hour before and they applauded when we walked in. We found ourselves in a large room with a couple of tattered sofas, a bunch of wooden chairs, and several small desks—the kind with attached seats. Two large metal desks topped with typewriters and stacks of paper were at one end of the room. Near the door was a table with an ancient-looking mimeograph machine next to platters of baked goods, a huge urn of coffee, and pitchers of orange juice and water. The beige cinder-block walls were covered with children's drawings.

We helped ourselves to a late breakfast and Reverend Filburn walked into the room as I sat down on one of the wooden chairs to eat.

"Ah." He smiled at us, taking a seat on the corner of one of the metal desks. "Looks like all of our freedom fighters are here now and accounted for." The chatter in the room ceased. "I'm Greg Filburn, your SCOPE field director here in Derby County." He had the same deep voice, the same horn-rimmed glasses, but he seemed different from the distrustful minister I'd met in the AME church. He was relaxed now, dressed in casual slacks and a pale blue shirt with the sleeves rolled up. "Let's have some introductions," he said.

We went around the room, introducing ourselves. There were twelve of us, ten from the Atlanta orientation and two local residents who would canvass with us. I recognized one of them—Rosemary—but couldn't place where I'd seen her before. She was the only one among us who looked well-rested, since she hadn't just made the overnight trip from Atlanta. I was glad to have another girl in the group with all that testosterone floating around. Rosemary had an engaging smile and it took me all of two seconds to see that she was aiming it at Win, who didn't seem to notice.

The other local person was Curry. He looked older than the rest of us, late twenties at least, and Greg said he'd be our primary driver. Curry looked like he didn't have a care in the world. He gave us a wave and a smile, and he chain-smoked cigarettes throughout the meeting.

When I introduced myself, Reverend Filburn—Greg—said, "Glad to see you, Eleanor," and I was relieved to feel his acceptance, even though I knew he probably still had reservations about my participation.

"This school will be our headquarters," Greg told us as we sipped our coffee. "Since it's Sunday, we don't want to disturb the folks you'll be staying with, so you'll spend tonight here and tomorrow you'll move in with your families. Do you all have sleeping bags?"

I nodded. A few of the guys groaned, but we all had them.

"Good." Greg's expression sobered. "Tonight, you men will sleep in this room. Rosemary and Curry will be staying with their own families here in Flint. Jocelyn and Eleanor—we'll put you in an interior room." He glanced at the double doors, then looked back at us. "You probably noticed the bullet holes when you came in," he said. "That happened last night. Our welcoming committee. I'm sure they were disappointed to realize that no one was here yet, so don't be surprised if we have a repeat performance tonight. I'm going to ask some of you fellas to board up the broken windows."

"Was that the Klan?" one of the guys asked. I'd already forgotten his name.

"Most likely just a few disgruntled Flint residents," Greg said. "They're known more for intimidation than actual physical violence, but it's happened, so be careful. More dangerous are the lone white men who want to take matters into their own hands," he said, repeating the warning we'd heard all week. "Be aware of your surroundings at all times. Stay out of white neighborhoods. You see a car or truck with a white driver, you hide. There's nothing cowardly about saving your life. And don't get caught white and Negro acting like equals by any white folk. That's how James Chaney and the other two men got themselves killed last summer. Especially be careful, male and female together." He looked at me, then Jocelyn, then Rosemary, who nodded in a way that said she understood what he meant. Understood it better than Jocelyn or I ever could.

"You might've been led to believe the Klan is farther south," Greg said, "but the United Klan of America has a stronghold here in North Carolina. Nearly twelve thousand members in two hundred Klaverns led by Bob Jones, their racist, bigoted, dangerous so-called Grand Dragon. He holds rallies just about every night. It's like a county fair for these people. Thousands of them. Mothers, fathers, children. Food and fun for all." Greg had a rhythm going. He reminded me of Dr. King in that moment. "They listen to speeches designed to fuel hatred. And for a finale, they burn a massive cross to symbolize their unity against people who aren't just like them. People like us."

I was perspiring in the airless room and the conversation wasn't making it any better. I lifted my hair off the back of my neck, my fingers grazing my slick skin. Someone had passed around a sign-up sheet for the two showers in the school's locker room. I was seventh on the list and couldn't wait to stand under a spray of water.

"I'll be here for you most of the time except Saturday nights when I go home to see my family, and Sunday morning, when I'm usually ministering to my AME congregation in a little town called Turner's Bend."

I turned at the sound of a sudden thud to see that Chip had fallen asleep and slid off his chair. He laughed. We all laughed. Except Win, who only smiled.

"Back in the chair, Chip," Greg said, but he was laughing, too. I liked him much better than I had when I'd met him in his Turner's Bend church. Of course, then he worried that I might plant a bomb in the pews.

"I do have a major bit of unfortunate news, though," Greg said, as Chip got into his chair, and we all fell silent. "Looks like we aren't going to be able to register voters in Derby County right away, folks. Probably not for a few weeks."

I thought every one of us gasped. If we didn't help people register, what were we going to do here?

"They closed the registrar's office," Greg said. "Shut it down. They're waiting until LBJ gets around to signing the voting rights bill into law. Then they'll have to open. So for now, we'll still canvass, educating folks, getting their commitment to register when the time comes. And we'll focus on political education and the other parts of our job as SCOPE workers."

I was disappointed. I'd pictured lines of people at the courthouse, finally getting their turn to add their names to the voting rolls. But in a way, this might be better. If people tried to register now, before we had the Voting Rights Act in place, they might have to pass the trumped-up literacy test or get turned away just because the clerk got out of bed on the wrong side that morning.

When the meeting was over, Rosemary showed Jocelyn and me to the very small windowless art room where we would sleep. The room smelled of paint and library paste. We pushed the handful of desks against the wall and dumped our rolled-up sleeping bags in the middle of the wood floor.

"You look so familiar," I said to Rosemary as I slid my camera case from my shoulder.

She nodded. "You're Buddy Hockley's sister," she said.

"How do you know Buddy?" I asked, surprised.

"My cousin Ronnie works at the car shop with him. I've seen you there a time or two."

"Oh, right!" I said. Ronnie'd been working at the car shop since Buddy opened it four years ago. "Buddy couldn't run that place without Ronnie," I added.

Rosemary smiled. "I'll tell him to ask for a raise," she said, and I laughed.

Rosemary left us, and Jocelyn and I rolled out our sleeping bags. It was nearly one in the afternoon. I lay down on top of my sleeping bag, trying to stay awake so I didn't miss my turn in the shower, but the pull of sleep was too great. My turn came and went while I slept.

≈

When we all met over blueberry muffins and coffee on Monday morning, I was wide awake, hungry, and nervous about meeting the family I'd be living with. Once we were dropped off with our families, we'd have no transportation and few of the families would have a phone. We'd really be on our own.

The boards the guys had hammered into place over the broken windows were still in place and intact.

"Nothin' happened," Paul said, brushing his blond hair out of his eyes. I thought he looked relieved.

"We were ready for them!" Chip laughed, holding a baseball bat in the air. I bit my lip, trying to imagine a baseball bat against a shotgun. I remembered not liking Chip on our long drive from Round Hill to Atlanta, but he really seemed to be a nice guy. In retrospect, I knew my own prejudices and my own fears had influenced my feelings about him on that drive.

When we'd had our fill of muffins and coffee, Greg gave us our canvassing assignments. I'd be partnered with Win, and we'd canvass in a rural area on the outskirts of Flint. We'd go door to door, educating people about the voting rights bill and telling them about a "peaceful protest" we planned to hold Friday evening in front of the courthouse in Carlisle, the county seat.

I was disappointed that I wasn't assigned to Turner's Bend. I'd pictured myself working in that little community, where people seemed to know Daddy and his pharmacy, and where Louise Jenkins used to live—and maybe still did. I thought I might be able to make some connections to people through knowing her.

But I would go wherever I was needed. Do what I'd been taught to do this past week. As I climbed into the van with Win and Curry for the drive to my assigned family, I felt brave and excited. I felt as though I was a part of something righteous.

Chapter 17

─────≈─────

KAYLA

2010

"This is so thoughtful of you." Ellie holds the bag of za'atar in her hand. I stand on her front porch watching as she raises the bag to her nose to breathe in the scent. I think she's genuinely happy to have the spice blend, but she doesn't seem particularly happy to see me.

"Who is it?" A man's voice comes from the dim living room behind her. Ellie says nothing. Hesitates a moment. Then offers me a small smile. "Please come in," she says, stepping back to clear the doorway for me. "You can meet Buddy and Mama."

"Thanks." I walk into the living room. It's a gloomy room, the sunlight outside not quite making it in, the walls an indeterminate color, the floor covered by a large braided rug. It takes my eyes a moment to adjust. A woman with fuzzy gray hair sits in a rocking chair close to the television. I see her in profile, but she doesn't seem to notice me, her gaze riveted on the game show she's watching. The room smells like lavender, and I guess the scent comes from an oval-shaped essential-oil diffuser sitting on the mantel. A man sits on the couch, attached by a tube to one of those boxy oxygen concentrators like my mother needed to use toward the end of her life. He wears a plaid shirt, denim overalls, and dark socks. No shoes. His belly looks bloated. Even lying there, hooked up to the machine, he's familiar. Buddy Hockley. I've seen him here and there in Round Hill all my life.

"This is my brother, Buddy," Ellie says, as Buddy struggles to get to his feet.

"Oh, don't get up!" I raise a hand to stop him, but he's determined. He grins at me. Holds out a hand, and I step forward to shake it. His hand feels spongy in mine.

"Reed's little girl." He smiles, as I step back. "I've seen you around town since you were a little thing. Had no idea Reed's girl is the new neighbor." He looks at Ellie with an expression I can't read. Ellie's own face remains flat, her lips a thin line. "Sure are a beauty," Buddy adds.

I'm not a beauty, just your average twenty-eight-year-old grieving widow scared to death about her future, but he's a sweet old guy and I can't help but return his smile. "Thanks," I say.

"Look more like your mama than Reed, though, don't she, Ellie?" Buddy asked.

Ellie gives me a patient smile as if she's only tolerating this conversation, waiting for me to leave. "I never knew your mother," she says. "I left before Reed . . . before she and your father . . . got involved."

"Well, Mr. Buddy's right," I say. "I do look like her." I want to tell Buddy to sit down again. I'm worried about him. He's starting to huff and puff a bit. Ellie picks up on it, too, and she walks over to the couch and gives him a tap on the shoulder to inspire him to sit again, which he does.

"And this is Mama," she says, guiding me a few steps to the left so I can look down at the old woman. "Mama, this is Reed Miller's daughter, Kayla. Do you remember Reed?"

The woman has her daughter's clear blue eyes. She nods to me. "Hello," she says. "Ellie, make her some of your tea," and with that she returns her attention to the game show. I remember Ellie saying that she's been in an assisted-living place for several years.

I look at Ellie. "I don't need any tea, thanks," I say with a quiet smile. I'm sure I've interrupted something. Ellie has her hands full and doesn't want my company today. She's not exactly throwing me out, but her body language seems to be moving me toward the door.

"How you likin' that fancy new house of yours?" Buddy asks.

"Oh, I'm just getting used to it," I say. "My daughter and I were exploring and I found an old tree house out in the woods behind the house. My father mentioned something about it being a place you used to—"

"That ol' thing still up there?" Buddy asks. "Don't you go climbin' it, sweetheart. Do you know how old that thing is? I haven't seen it in . . . I don't know . . . prob'ly forty years, you think, Ellie?" He looks at his sister, who has completely lost whatever smile she had.

"It should come down," she says. "Seriously." She looks at me. "You should have someone take it down."

"I think it's totally safe and solid," I say. "My husband replaced some of the old boards and built new steps going up to it."

"Don't know why anyone'd want to build a house in them woods anyhow," Buddy mutters. I have the feeling he's not talking about the tree house any longer. He means my house.

Ellie looks down at the bag of za'atar in her hand and for a moment the only sound in the room is the voice of the game show host. The silence isn't benign, though. There's something going on in this room I don't understand. Awkwardly, I speak up.

"I've been thinking about your offer to practice yoga with me," I say to Ellie. "I'd really like that. I think I can use it."

She doesn't answer. She stares at me and I see the wheels turning in her head; I just don't know why. "Do you have time with your work and your daughter and fixing up your house?" she asks. She doesn't sound enthusiastic. As a matter of fact, all in all, she is a different woman than she was the first time I met her when she'd warmly invited me into her kitchen for tea and conversation.

"I can make time," I say. "I need to do something physical. And peaceful. But I understand if you're too busy," I add. I soften my voice. "I know you have your hands full."

"She ain't too busy," Buddy says from the couch. "And she needs someone to talk to besides me and Mama, don't you, Ellie?"

Ellie's lips form a tight line. "Let's go out front," she says to me, walking toward the door.

I nod. "Goodbye, Mrs. Hockley," I call, but the old woman doesn't seem to hear me. I smile down at Buddy. "Bye-bye."

"You tell your daddy 'hey' from me," Buddy says. "He was a good mayor. Not like that girl we got now."

"I'll tell him," I say, and I follow Ellie outside.

On the porch, she turns to face me. "I'm afraid I might have spoken too soon about the yoga," she says. She looks through the screen door as if she can see her brother and mother in the living room, but all I can see is the square light of the TV. "Mama is in worse shape than I thought . . . mentally, and my brother's going downhill faster than I anticipated," she says. "Hospice is involved now, but I worry about leaving them alone for too long. And I've gotten busy with some other projects. Doing a bit of writing and keeping in touch with a couple of organizations back in San Francisco. Helping them out."

"Oh, I understand," I say, but there's something weird going on here. Maybe she's already grieving her brother and mother. Her only family. I remember how I felt that last month of my mother's life as Daddy and I journeyed with her toward the inevitable. I didn't know night from day back then. The faraway look I see now in Ellie's eyes had been in my own during those last few weeks. I was never quite in the present, but rather in that place that hovered between hope and reality. "I'm sorry for what you're going through," I say. "Please let me know if there's any way I can help."

"Well"—she holds the za'atar in the air—"you already have. Mama won't eat it but Buddy and I will both enjoy this." She looks down Shadow Ridge Lane toward my house. "Is the lake still back there?" Her tone is casual, but something in her face tells me the question is loaded.

"Ugh, yes," I say. "Jackson—my husband—and some of his friends cleared a trail that goes in a big loop through the woods behind our house. It doesn't quite reach the lake, but you can see the water from the trail. There's all these vines and probably poison ivy and snakes you'd have to go through to get to the lake, and the water doesn't look . . . It looks gross, at least from where I was standing."

Ellie is looking down the road as though she can see straight through my house and the forest behind it to the lake. "Once upon a time, it was a pretty little lake," she says. "There was a path that went right by it and I would walk that way to school every day."

"What school?" I frown. There is no school in that area that I know of.

"There used to be a school a quarter mile or so past the lake," she says. "Grade school. They tore it down when they built the new one when I was twelve or thirteen."

"Wow," I say, trying to picture how different my backyard must have looked then. "It's got to be strange for you to be back here after so long."

She turns and looks squarely at me as if she's coming back from wherever her memories had taken her. "Stranger than you can imagine," she says. "And if I could control my own life, I wouldn't be here at all. But here I am." She holds up the bag of za'atar. "Thanks again." She reaches for the door, my cue to leave.

"Enjoy it," I say as I start down the porch steps. Ellie doesn't go into the house right away and I feel her eyes on me.

When I reach the sidewalk, she calls out, "Kayla?"

I turn to look at her. She has one hand on the door handle, the other clutching the bag of herbs. "Take the tree house down," she says, and then she adds, "Please," and I know there is more that concerns her about that tree house than just a few old rotting boards.

Chapter 18

———— ≈ ————

ELLIE

Dear Brenda,

    I've thought about you every day since I left, hoping you're feeling better and that you and Garner are as happy as you were on your wedding day. I miss you so much already!

    I'm only about twenty miles from home but I might as well be on another planet. I also don't feel quite like Ellie Hockley any longer. During my week in Atlanta, I think I went through a sort of metamorphosis, one that I'm still experiencing. It was phenomenal! Martin Luther King actually spoke to us! I was so close to him. I know you don't share my excitement about that sort of thing; I wouldn't have been all that excited about it a month ago myself, but it's part of the change in me I'm talking about. I understand now how important it is for Negroes to be able to vote. I won't go on about all that. I just wish I could sit down and talk to you about it.

So, I arrived in Flint Sunday morning. We spent the night in a run-down special education school. Then today we were driven to the homes we'll be staying in while we're working in the area. I'm the only white girl working "in the field," as the other one, Jocelyn, decided to stay in the school building and do office work. I'll be canvassing out in the boonies. Remember when we went to Turner's Bend to meet Reverend Filburn? Well, that was like New York City compared to where I am now. It's very rural. The houses are mostly spread out from one another, some a half mile apart! I will definitely be getting my exercise as I walk from house to house. Only one of the students has a car here, but he's not allowed to use it in his assignment. He has to walk like the rest of us. Most of the people in this part of Derby County are sharecroppers. They are so poor and they live in terrible conditions. Honestly, it's so much worse than I imagined.

Curry Barnes is a local man who is helping our leader, Greg (Reverend Filburn), drive us around. He's twenty-five or so and a serious chain-smoker. He's the one who drove me to my assignment today, taking me way out into the country. He turned onto this "road" that is more of a path, full of ruts from the last rain. I was certain we were going to get stuck or blow a tire. Then he just dropped me off in front of this tiny old shack, winked at me, and said "Take care of yourself," and I can tell you, I never felt so alone. There wasn't another house anywhere that I could see, though there were tobacco barns and fields all around me. I took pictures and I'll send some when I get them developed. You won't believe what it's like.

The whole house is about the size of your bedroom. I went up the rickety steps and knocked on the door. An old dog laid there on the porch and it was so hot, he didn't even bother getting up to see who I was. All of a sudden, four little girls ran out the door and onto the porch and they were all over me! They knocked me down with their exuberance. I didn't bother getting up. I just sat there, a sweaty mess, with these kids laughing and climbing on me and running their hands

over my hair and my face and then the littlest one—GiGi—settled herself in my arms. She smiled up at me and I felt—it's hard to describe—I
wanted to cry. The children were so cute and so happy, but they live in
such a sad place.

Then their mother, Mrs. Dawes, came to the door and yelled at them
to leave me alone and soon I was back on my feet, the spell broken.

"You late," she said to me. No hello, just that. This woman has so
much work to keep up with. She can't waste any of her energy on extra
words.

Anyhow, I introduced myself to her but she'd already been told my
name. Her family will get a few dollars a week for having me stay
with them. I felt shy, but Mrs. Dawes was even shyer. I'm not sure how
happy she is about having me here. Not only does she have these four
little girls but she has two older boys who work with her husband in
the fields. I'm just another mouth to feed. She showed me where I'll be
sleeping: I'll share a twin bed with two of the little girls in a room where
all six of the children usually sleep, but while I'm here, the older boys,
eleven and twelve, will sleep in the living room. I apologized for putting
them out, but she said, "What you're doin's important." It was the first
positive thing she said to me, and I was touched.

Then she showed me the outhouse and the outside pump for water
and the oil lamps they use at night! Can you imagine? I thought of all
that we grew up with, you and me. Our pretty houses with our big bedrooms and hot water and electricity. I feel so bad for this family and
others like them, though Greg said pity won't move us forward. I know
I'm going to have to get tougher to deal with this.

I'm writing this letter sitting on the porch steps while Mr. Dawes falls
asleep in the rickety old rocker next to the rickety old dog. He didn't say
a word to me at dinner, but he didn't say a word to anyone. He was bone-
tired, I could tell. He might even be sick. To say this family has a hard
life is putting it mildly. Neither Mr. nor Mrs. Dawes is registered to vote
and I couldn't bring myself to talk to them about it, at least not yet. I

feel so intrusive and so WHITE and so rich, at least compared to them. Not being able to vote is part of what keeps them living in these terrible conditions, but I don't feel like I have a right to say anything to them about it. I have to learn how to do this work. It's so important.

After I wrote that last sentence, the kids came onto the porch from the yard where they were chasing lightning bugs. They joined me on the steps while I taught them a freedom song. They were quick learners and soon we were all singing "I Love Everybody," little GiGi cuddled in my arms while the six-year-old, Gail, stood behind me, braiding my hair. I almost started to cry, sitting there with them, their faces so happy and their voices so joyous. In a few more years, I worry that they'll be worn down by life like their older brothers and their parents.

I miss you and Garner—and Reed—and home and the easy life, but I know I'm where I'm meant to be right now. You can write to me at the return address on the envelope. That's our headquarters.

Love, Ellie

Chapter 19

———— ≈ ————

KAYLA

I head back toward Round Hill after work, worrying that my father might forget to pick up Rainie since her preschool is closing half an hour early today. I picture my little girl waiting alone and scared in the schoolyard. I catastrophize a lot these days.

Ever since Jackson's death, I see the world as freakish, ready to attack. At a stoplight, I call my father. He's in the car and I hear Rainie chattering to him in the background. I'm embarrassed to let him know that I doubted him.

"Just calling to say hi," I say cheerfully. "I'll see you two later. Light's changed. Love you!"

That is the confusing up-and-down spirit I'm in as I turn onto Shadow Ridge Lane. I notice that Ellie's car is gone from the Hockleys' driveway, and something draws my eye toward the rear of the house as I pass. Smoke? Probably just something cooking on their grill. But Ellie is out. Would Buddy be able to grill something? And then I see a flame shoot skyward from the corner of the screened back porch and I slam on my brakes. I turn off my car right there in the middle of all the construction vans and fly out of it, calling to the nearest workers.

"Fire!" I shout, pointing, and two of them race after me as I run toward the Hockleys' driveway. By the time we reach the backyard, the side of the porch is in flames, the screens a fluorescent red as they curl out of their frames. I can see that Buddy Hockley is inside, struggling to open the porch door. He collapses against it and I try to pull it open, but the door appears to be locked. I kick at the screen with all my might, once, twice. The third time the screen gives. My eyes burn, but I'm able to reach through the broken screen and fumble around for the lock, finally finding it, giving it a turn. The door opens, and Buddy staggers out of the building, collapsing on top of me on the ragged lawn.

I hear the sizzle of water against the flames. One of the construction workers managed to find a hose. The two of them shout in Spanish, and water is everywhere. I'm soaked and trapped beneath a very large, very ill man, but all I feel is relief at seeing that fire die. In the distance, I hear sirens, already growing close, the benefit of living in a small town.

"Mr. Hockley?" I say. "Mr. Buddy?" He struggles to roll off me, hacking and wheezing.

"Sorry," he says. The one word seems to take a lot of effort.

"It's okay," I say. "Is your mother all right?" I wonder if I should go into the house to find her.

Buddy rolls onto his back on the wet lawn. "I turned . . . it off," he says. The four words seem to exhaust him. Another coughing attack. "It won't explode."

"What do you mean?" I ask, sitting up. "What won't explode?"

"The oxygen concentrator," he says. I try to see inside the porch from where I'm sitting, my eyes burning from the smoke and my wet hair stuck to my cheeks. One of the construction workers has gone inside and is spraying the interior of the porch down with the hose. I can't see more than vague shapes.

Mr. Hockley is trying to sit up and I help him. Then I notice that the long sleeve of his plaid shirt is blackened as well as wet, and that beneath it, the skin of his arm is red and swollen. I also see a pack of cigarettes in his shirt pocket.

"Were you smoking while you were using oxygen?" I ask, incredulous.

"The tube was . . . I tossed it away from me. It wasn't near me, but I guess . . ."

"Oh my God," I say, my hand on his shoulder. "You're so lucky you weren't killed."

One of the construction workers squats down next to us. "He okay?" He nods toward Buddy.

"He has a burn on his arm." I point to Buddy's arm. I don't want to touch the blackened fabric. I don't want to make his injury worse.

"Help come." The young man points toward the street and I nod.

"Thank you so much for your quick thinking. You and your friend." I nod to the other man, who now stands near us, the hose still in his hand, his fingers off the nozzle. "Thank you for finding the hose."

I don't think they understand all of what I've said, but they understand "thank you," and they nod.

The man with the hose takes a few steps toward us, reaches into Buddy's pocket, pulls out the pack of cigarettes, and slips them in the pocket of his T-shirt. He grins down at Buddy. "No good for you," he says. "I save you from them."

I can't help but laugh.

In a moment, the yard is filled with firemen and medics, with Ellie literally at their heels, her arm around her mother, who is walking with a cane. "What happened?" Ellie yells. "Oh my God, Buddy! Are you all right?" She lets go of her mother and is quickly on her knees next to her brother, along with the medic who is examining the flesh of Buddy's forearm. The burn is second-degree, the medic says. I think I smell the burned skin, but it's probably only the wooden frame of the porch. I feel a little dizzy.

"She saved my life." Buddy nods toward me between coughing attacks.

"I had help from those two—" I look around, but the construction workers have disappeared, gone back to their jobs. Just another day's work. Mrs. Hockley leans against the side of the house, watching us with a frown. I tell Ellie and the firefighters what happened, how I saw the fire, how the construction workers saved the Hockley house. Ellie hugs Buddy the same time she's chewing him out. "This is not the way I plan to lose you, you fool!" she says, with such affection that I'm touched. She hugs him again, then leans over to hug the medic treating him. She stands to hug the two firefighters, a man and a woman, who are closest. By then, I'm standing up myself, and I'm not surprised when she hugs me, too.

"You tell me when you want to practice yoga," she says. "Any time you want."

Chapter 20

―――≈―――

ELLIE

In the morning, I helped dress the four youngest Dawes children. I was determined to help out, however I could. GiGi and Sally, the two youngest, were still in diapers, but Gail and May—six and four—were proud to show me that they could dress themselves and use the outhouse on their own. They were better at using it than I was. I kept thinking, *I can't believe people have to live this way in the United States of America,* but I knew that sort of thinking wasn't helpful. Getting people engaged in politics to make their lives better; that's what would help.

Mr. Dawes and the boys had eaten and left the house by the time I helped Mrs. Dawes make grits and eggs for the younger children. She wore a flour-sack apron over a faded yellow housedress and a blue scarf tied over her hair. Aside from giving me a few instructions, she was her usual quiet self, while the children giggled and bickered with one another across the wobbly wooden table.

"Do you know that you'll be able to register to vote soon?" I asked as we cleaned up after breakfast. I felt ridiculously awkward, asking her out of the blue like that. I seemed to have forgotten all the icebreaking tips I'd learned during the role-playing workshops in Atlanta, and Mrs. Dawes didn't look up from the basin where she was starting to wash the dishes. "Once President Johnson signs the voting rights bill, you can register," I said.

"So I hear." She glanced up from her task, her eyes tired. "And when's that gonna be? The twelve of never, I s'pose?"

I couldn't blame her for doubting that something good might be on the horizon. "I know," I said. "It should have happened by now. It should have happened long before now. But it's going to happen very soon." I told her about the peaceful protest we were planning to hold in front of the courthouse Friday evening, but I could tell that there was no way Mrs. Dawes, with her six children, was going to make it to that protest.

"Maybe my husband can go," she said.

"I'll arrange a ride for him," I said, as though the decision had been made.

I cleaned GiGi's face with a cloth, then lifted her from her high chair. She immediately climbed into my lap and started playing with my hair, which seemed to be a draw for the little girls.

Mrs. Dawes glanced at me. "They ain't never seen hair like yours," she said. A few of GiGi's little braids were coming loose from colored barrettes, and I began to rebraid them as she gently stroked my own hair.

"They tol' us all you kids was from the North," Mrs. Dawes said as she dried a bowl. "New York or someplace up there. You ain't from New York, though."

"I'm from Round Hill," I admitted.

Our conversation, such as it was, was interrupted by a knock at the front door and I knew it was probably Win, ready to start canvassing with me. Mrs. Dawes left the kitchen to go to the door and by the time she returned to the room with Win, they were laughing. Mrs. Dawes lit up in the first big, genuine smile I'd seen from her.

"Oh, yes," she said to Win. "He was the funniest preacher I done ever seen! And don't you know he kept that camel in his mama's yard?"

"No!" Win laughed like this was the most amusing thing he'd ever heard. The laughter seemed out of character for him, but I liked hearing it. I liked knowing that he had that side to him.

"You two know each other?" I said. I lowered GiGi gently to the floor as I got to my feet.

"Uh-uh," Mrs. Dawes said. "Never laid eyes on this child before."

"Did Ellie tell you we gonna have a protest at the courthouse in Carlisle Friday night?" Win asked her. "And then soon we'll have a mass gatherin' outside the school in Flint? They'll be food and games for the kids and we'll talk about the changes y'all need here in Flint."

"She made mention of that protest," Mrs. Dawes said. They both looked at me.

"I told her we could provide transportation Friday night," I said, for something to say.

"That's right, Miz Dawes," Win said. "We can get you there and back, so you talk to Mr. Dawes about it. I want to meet him. I wanna know if that camel story is true."

Mrs. Dawes laughed again. "Oh, it's true, all right," she said.

Win looked at me. "Got your walkin' shoes on?" He looked down at my sandals. "You gonna have some mighty dirty feet by the end of the day."

I shrugged. "I know how to wash them," I said with a smile. I'd walked all over campus in these sandals. I'd be fine.

≈

"Okay," I said, when Win and I were out of hearing range of the Daweses' house, "you *do* know her, right? Mrs. Dawes?"

"Never met her before in my life."

"Then how did you have her laughing and talking in the two seconds between when she opened the door and you walked in the kitchen with her? I haven't been able to get more than a couple of words out of her or her husband."

"That's why we're doing it this way. White and Black together," he said, his gaze up ahead on the nasty rutted road. "I know how to break the ice and I know the preacher at their church and everybody knows the rumor about their old preacher having a camel. So they trust me. They won't trust you, not right off." He glanced at me. "It's not your fault. They just won't. Some of these folks have never met a white person who cared a lick about them. A lot of them have never met a white person, period. Once they see you and I are okay with each other, they'll let you in."

"Why do you say 'black' instead of 'Negro'?" I asked.

He squinted against the sunlight. "It's a strong word," he said after a moment, as if that was all the explanation that was needed.

I tried to imagine referring to Louise as "black." I didn't think she'd like it. "Couldn't it be seen as insulting?" I asked.

He surprised me by nodding. "Yes," he said. "So I'm careful with it. I won't use it with most of the folks we see. But I personally like the feel of it. The strength of it."

We walked in silence for a while. I carried the packet with our canvassing paperwork and voting rights pamphlets, and I kept my gaze cast down on the road, not wanting to step in one of the ruts and twist an ankle. After a while, I spotted a small cluster of houses up ahead, maybe an eighth of a mile or so. Finally. A goal.

"I thought I knew how to do this, after all the role-playing and everything we did during orientation," I admitted, "but it felt so awkward, talking to Mrs. Dawes about registering. They're working so hard and it's got to be the last thing on their minds. Plus, I just kind of popped the conversation on her. No buildup. No camel stories."

He didn't crack a smile. So serious, this guy. "We have to help them see that it needs to be the *first* thing on their minds to make their lives easier," he said. "Think about the Dawes family. How would being able to vote help them?"

"This road," I said. "This road is a mess."

"That's for sure," Win said. "This doesn't even qualify as a road. What else?"

"Electricity?"

"That would surely help. And you're on the right track. You and I know that the right to vote will mean a better life for their kids in the future, but people need to see the concrete ways it can change their lives right now. Roads. Electricity. Plumbing. A decent minimum wage, that's an important one. Huge."

"They could vote Negroes . . . Black people . . . into office," I said, trying out the word. "They could have better schools."

"Now you're cookin' with gas," he said. "You can see why white folks are afraid of Black folks getting the vote. They think they'll lose power. Right now Blacks are dependent on the white man and that's the way the white man wants it." I heard anger behind the words.

"It shouldn't be an 'us versus them' thing," I said.

"Tell that to your white neighbors."

For a moment, neither of us spoke. "You had a whole different way of talking to her than you do right now," I said finally. I was awestruck by Win, the way he had two sides to him. He was like a chameleon, able to match whatever environment he was in.

He almost smiled, but not quite. Except for when he was talking to Mrs. Dawes about the camel, and occasionally when we sang freedom songs, I didn't think I'd seen a smile out of him. "It helps to connect to people, talking their language," he said.

"I don't know how to do that," I said.

"It'd be weird coming out of your mouth. You just be you—a well-intentioned rich white girl—and let me be me."

I stopped walking. "That's not fair," I said, surprised and suddenly angry.

He stopped, too. Looked me in the eye from behind his horn-rimmed glasses. "No, I guess it wasn't," he said finally.

"That's how you really feel, though?"

"Look, I'm part of SCOPE because of Dr. King," he said, starting to walk again. "I met him through some friends and he said I was needed here. When Dr. King says he needs you, well, you do it. Whatever he says. But the longer I'm in this fight . . . this battle . . . the more I think it's got to be a *Black* battle. So . . . there's noble intentions here, I know that, and I know you're here out of a good heart, right?"

I nodded.

"A good heart and wanting to do the right thing and make a difference and I've got to . . . I have to put my own . . . values . . . aside and do what I promised Dr. King I'd do. 'Just give Hosea and me this summer,' he said to me. So . . . Ellie . . ." My name came out of him slowly. "I apologize. It doesn't matter if you're white or Black or rich or poor or in between, we're here to do the same work."

"Yes," I said. "We are."

≈

Win turned out to be an amazing teacher. I was awed by the way he switched his way of talking—his whole personality, really—as soon as we were greeted at the door. The way he picked up everyone's language and their accents and the cadence in their sentences, from the first words out of their mouths. Some people were nervous, their eyes darting past us as if they were looking for their landlords who'd be angry to find them talking to us. Others invited us right into the house. Sat us down and gave us welcome lemonade or sweet tea to drink. I watched how Win connected to them. There was no way I could imitate him, but I found that if I asked questions about what problems they were dealing with without judgment or putting words in their mouths, people opened up. I knew it was only because I had Win at my side that they trusted me. His smile was genuine and it was clear that every woman we saw sort of melted when he spoke to them. That didn't mean they agreed to register. Not at all. But by the time we stopped to eat—me, a fried chicken leg and hunk of corn bread Mrs. Dawes packed for me, and Win, a peanut butter sandwich—we had three yeses on our canvass sheet and a whole lot of maybes that Win told me meant no.

We sat in the shade of an old shed, batting away the gnats as we ate.

"They're afraid of losing their jobs if their employers find out," I said, parroting what I'd learned during orientation. I was anxious to show Win that I knew *something*.

"Exactly," he said. "But a good many said they'd come to the protest, so that's positive."

My legs were stretched out in front of me and my feet were appallingly filthy. I knew that I was beginning to get a blister on my heel, but I would say nothing. Tomorrow, though, I'd wear my sneakers.

≈

Our second day together found us surrounded by children—little ones who wanted to hold my hand as we walked and older kids who were drawn to Win's transistor radio and the music on the Negro station. "My Girl" and "Shotgun," and "I Can't Help Myself." The children turned out to be a real boon to our canvassing. They told us who lived where, how many kids in each family, what type of work the parents did, and often, what sort of problems were dragging them down.

By the time Win and I sat down in the shade of a tobacco barn to eat our lunch, we already had eight commitments to register on our canvass sheet.

"So how's it going at the Daweses' house?" Win asked as he freed his tomato sandwich from its wax paper wrapping.

I wasn't sure how to answer. I could say "fine," but I opted for the truth. "It's hard to get used to," I said. "The outhouse. No electric light at night. I'm sleeping in a bed with two little girls climbing all over me." I had to admit that I'd slept incredibly well the night before, though, kids or no kids, after covering so much of Flint by foot.

"It's the same at the house I'm in." He took a long drink from the thermos he wore attached to his belt.

"It hurts me to see it," I said.

"Me too," he agreed. "Though none of it's a surprise to me." Suddenly, he jumped up and grabbed my arm. "Back here!" he said, tugging me to my feet and pulling me behind the barn.

"*What?*" He'd nearly yanked my arm out of my shoulder.

He pointed to our left and I saw what had caught his attention: a beat-up white pickup truck, a white man at the wheel.

"I don't think he saw us," Win said, "but did you notice the empty gun rack?"

"No." I was trembling. After having "watch out for white men in trucks" drummed into me fifty times, I still hadn't thought to react when I spotted the truck in the distance.

"Generally means he's got the gun on the seat with him," Win said. "And he'd probably be happy to find a reason to use it."

"Yikes." I thought of the gun-shot windows at our headquarters. "Our second day and we almost got ourselves killed."

He actually smiled. "We did pretty well, almost getting killed only once," he said.

I thought it was the first time he'd directed his smile to me, and I felt a little of what those housewives must be feeling when they couldn't seem to take their eyes off him. I looked away from him, shaken.

"Well, we're on our feet now," I said. "I guess we should get back to work."

Chapter 21

KAYLA

2010

Once Rainie is asleep the night after the fire at the Hockleys' house, I stand in the doorway of the room that was to be Jackson's office. It's stacked nearly wall to wall with boxes, some of which I'm sure contain bills or other important papers. I dread the disorganization I'll find once I open the boxes, though. Jackson was a stickler for detail as an architect, but he was a scattered mess when it came to his office, papers on the floor as well as every other flat surface. He promised me he'd change his sloppy ways in the new house. I wish he'd had a chance to prove to me that he could do it.

Daddy had taken care of getting rid of Jackson's clothing for me in our old house, but he hadn't touched his office, and it had been one of the last things on my mind. I remember standing in the doorway of Jackson's office in the old house, Daddy's arm around me, as we stared, glassy eyed, at the sea of papers on the floor and desk and pouring out of open file cabinet drawers. "Let's just throw it all in boxes," Daddy said. "You'll just have to go through everything when you have time at the new house."

I'd been all too eager to agree. I'll do one box a night, I tell myself now. That should be manageable.

I get a trash bag for recycling, planning to get rid of absolutely everything I can. The evening is cool and remarkably dry for June and I open the windows, surprised when the scent of the Hockleys' fire drifts into the room even though my house and theirs are at opposite ends of the street. I think of that burn on Buddy Hockley's arm and hope he's not in too much pain.

I clear the top of the desk so I have plenty of space to work. Opening one of the boxes, I pull out a handful of old bills and other paperwork. I make a "keep" pile on the desk and begin sorting through the papers. I'm halfway through the box, having trashed nearly all of it, when I'm stunned to find a typewritten letter from my father.

Dear Jackson,

I've watched as you and Kayla plan your new home. I'm proud of how the two of you have made names for yourselves as architects and how you can now afford to build the beautiful home you've dreamed of. It's a real honor to be your father-in-law, Jackson.

I've kept quiet as you two searched for the perfect site for the new house and I was pleased when you said you were looking to build just two miles from me; I love having Rainie be a big part of my life. If I didn't sound thrilled when you told me your exact choice of location at dinner tonight, I'm sorry. I know my reaction disappointed both of you and I think I need to explain. I didn't want to go into it all with Kayla there and poison her feelings about the site, if it does turn out to be where you decide to build.

The Hockleys, who, as you know, own the only property on Hockley Street, will never sell their house as long as either Buddy or Eleanor, who

lives in California, are alive. They are the stubborn types who will probably put something in their wills to turn that place into a halfway house
for drug addicts or some such thing after they die. If you go through with
building your home on Hockley Street, just know you'll most likely have
that old house in your neighborhood for as long as you live there.

One other thing, and of course I feel like a fool writing this, but . . .
when I was young, everyone thought the woods where you plan to build
were haunted. I don't believe in spirits, of course, but I can't help it; I've
always had an uncomfortable feeling about that area. But who knows?
If you and Kayla decide to build there, maybe it will be your beautiful new
home that puts my discomfort to rest.

I felt like I needed to share my thoughts with you, but I trust your
judgment and I know you always have Kayla and Rainie's best interest at
heart.

With love and admiration,

Reed, a.k.a. Dad

What the hell?

Jackson never mentioned the letter to me, but I do remember the
dinner Daddy referred to. He came over on a weeknight, as he often did.
He was lonely since Mom died and I loved the way he interacted with
Rainie. Even then, when she was barely two, he was so attentive to her and
she lit up when he was around. That evening, as we ate tuna noodle casserole made from my mother's recipe, one Daddy loved, we told him that
we were in negotiations with the developer who planned to put twenty-
one houses on Hockley Street, turning it into an upscale neighborhood
they'd call Shadow Ridge. Jackson and I were about to put our deposit
down on the prime lot; the one with all the trees at the end of the street.
I expected my father to congratulate us. He knew we'd been looking
for the right piece of land for over a year. But he pushed his casserole
around on his plate, not looking at either of us. I remember exchanging
a glance across the table with Jackson.

"You know where we mean?" I finally asked my father.

Of course he knew. It wasn't like Hockley Street was tucked away out in the boonies.

Daddy finally looked up. "Sure," he said. "I'm just trying to picture it. All those houses on that little road. All that kudzu."

Jackson had laughed. "Yeah, that'll be a mess to get rid of all right, but not my problem. The developers are responsible for clearing the land. I just want to be sure they leave the most trees possible."

"Uh-huh." Daddy stared at his wineglass. Finally, he looked up and smiled at me, then Jackson. He nodded his head. "Well, you're sure that's the lot you want?" he asked.

I can't remember what Jackson and I said after that. Something like, *we think this is the perfect lot* or *we've made up our minds*. Now I wonder if my father'd had a sixth sense about us building here. Something he couldn't adequately express. There is no doubt in my mind that if we hadn't chosen to build this house on this spot, Jackson would still be alive and I'd feel joy every time I walked in the front door. But there is no way my father could have predicted what happened. And the bit about the area being haunted? I'd felt it, hadn't I? At night, when the world outside the house was dark as pitch? Or even in the daylight, when Rainie and I walked around the trail and I felt the wave of cool air that had made me shiver, despite the warmth of the day.

I wish I hadn't found the letter. I crumple it up and put it in the recycling bag, then take it out again. Flatten it on the desk. I don't know why, but I think I should keep it. Then I look around the room at the dozens of other boxes, and I hope there will be no more surprises.

Chapter 22

---≈---

ELLIE

The past four days had been some of the longest—and most education-al—of my life. I finally felt like Win and I had become friends. He gave me small peeks into his life: He had a younger sister, handicapped from having polio. She took all his parents' energy, he said. "Someday when they're gone, she'll be my responsibility," he told me. I could tell that he loved his sister, that she broke his heart, and that his family was close. He missed them. I envied him for that. I did miss Buddy, but not my parents. To be honest, I was glad to be away from them. As for Reed, I wasn't sure how I felt about him after the past couple of weeks. I hadn't written to him. He didn't fit very neatly into my life right now. I felt like it had been years instead of two weeks since I'd last seen him and my family. No one other than my fellow field-workers could understand what I was experiencing.

I felt safe most of the time as I canvassed with Win. No white people lived in this part of Flint and we hardly ever saw anyone on the rutted roads other than curious neighborhood children, much less white men ready to kill us. The children loved the novelty of us. We were new people to talk to and sing with and walk with. Many of them were particularly interested in me. They didn't see white people very often, if ever, and they held my hand, swinging my arm as I taught them "I'll Fly Away" and "I Love Everybody," inserting the names of people they loved and—at my insistence—the people they hated, and they taught me their favorite songs and took us to see their parents, giving us exactly the introduction we needed.

We fell into a rhythm, Win and me. When an adult would answer the door Win would either begin with his "camel connection" if he thought the family would know what he was talking about, or else he'd mention Martin Luther King.

"Dr. King sent us to talk to you about your right to vote," he'd say. He'd play up his connection to the beloved man, and except for the truly frightened folks—those who were afraid they'd lose their home or their job if caught talking to us—we'd get an invitation inside.

What happened next seemed to come more and more naturally to me. If a housewife was shucking corn, I'd sit down and start shucking with her while we talked. If she was feeding a toddler, I'd offer to take over to give her a chance to sit and chat. If there were children—and there were always children—I'd engage them in a game or a song. In every house, I found something to love—hand-stitched quilts or a child's painting hanging unframed on a wall—and I'd ask about it. I was sincere in my questions and my compliments. It was my favorite part of canvassing, really. Getting to know people. Letting them open my eyes to their lives. I tried not to let it show that my heart ached over the poverty in front of me. My pity would help no one.

Win and I would do a back-and-forth exchange about the voting rights bill.

"A new law is coming real soon to help you vote," he'd say.

"Have you ever tried to register before?" I'd ask.

That's when we'd hear the horror stories. The embarrassment of failing the impossible-to-pass literacy test. The shocking beatings outside the courthouse. The threats over being kicked out of their homes.

"Once the law is passed, federal officers will protect you as you register," Win would say.

"And no more tests," I'd add. "They have to let you register. Then you'll be able to vote for people who can help you."

"Negro candidates will stand a real chance of winning," Win would say.

We'd go on like that, talking about how the law could change their lives. Then we'd try to get their commitment to register once LBJ signed the bill into law and we'd promise them a ride to the registrar's office.

Win said he was good at getting us in the door and I was good at keeping us there. I liked that. We were a team.

After we finished canvassing on Friday afternoon, we waited at the edge of a cotton field for Curry to pick us up. I felt exposed, standing there. We'd seen no white people in that area, yet I felt a sort of premonition and wished that Curry would hurry up.

I thought about how strange it was that, in less than a week's time, I'd gone from feeling nervous about living in a Negro neighborhood—a Black neighborhood—to feeling nervous about seeing white people. After that first time, when Win and I saw the guy in a truck and hid behind a tobacco barn, we'd had no trouble at all.

I saw a black truck in the distance, though, and I knew our luck was about to change.

Win picked up my anxiety. "Hold on," he said. "It might just be . . . Oh shit! Let's get out of here!"

I saw the two white faces in the truck's cab before I turned and began running with Win through the green leaves of the cotton field. I looked behind me only long enough to see that the men had gotten out of their truck, one of them with a shotgun in his hands. I heard the echoing crack of his gun. Two shots. Three. Four. I never ran so fast in my life, expecting to feel a bullet in my back at any moment. The men shouted and laughed, but they didn't chase us down, and Win and I both collapsed on the other side of the field under the shade of a tree, gasping for air. My bare legs were scraped and my blue shirt was stuck to my skin with sweat, but I was happy to be alive.

When we'd caught our breath, Win smiled at me. He smiled more often now. He seemed more relaxed than he'd been the first couple of days of our canvass. "Damn," he said. "I thought we were goners there for a minute." He took off his fogged glasses and cleaned them with a handkerchief, then wiped the perspiration from his glistening forehead, and I noticed the perfect symmetry of his face. I hadn't thought of him as handsome before that moment. Nice looking, yes. But right now, all I could see in front of me was a beautiful young man.

≈

That evening, all of us field-workers took turns using the van and Paul's car to ferry people from their homes to the courthouse in Carlisle to protest the registrar's office being closed. It was strange to be downtown with all the cars and people—white people—on the sidewalks. In just a few days' time, I'd lost the sense of being part of that "small town" world. Before the protest, Greg told us that, for the past two nights, some "troublemakers" had shot off guns and revved their truck engines outside the school. "Nothing more than that," he said calmly, "but y'all should be aware that people definitely know we're in the county and what we're about, and they don't like it." We all let that news sink in. "Now as for the protest today," Greg continued, "you, Paul, you'll lead a prayer."

"Me?" Paul laughed. "But I'm Jewish."

"Don't Jews pray?" Greg asked. "Anyway, you're a Christian today. Win, you make a short speech on the importance of registering once the bill gets signed and the office opens up. And Ellie, you lead the singing." That made me instantly nervous and I began running through all our songs in my head.

≈

I was worried that no one would show up for the protest, but the court-house green slowly began filling up. Once everyone—except for the late stragglers, of which there were plenty—was in front of the building, we formed a big circle on the lawn. I took some pictures as Paul said a prayer that seemed warm and heartfelt, and Win talked about the changes voting would bring to the Negro families of Derby County.

After Win finished talking, I made a little speech about songs being a kind of prayer, and I talked about how I hadn't known many of the freedom songs a few weeks ago, and how they now filled me with joy and hope. My voice shook when I first started speaking but by the time I began singing "This Little Light of Mine," it was so strong that it surprised me. Everyone knew that song and pretty soon we were all singing, our arms crossed, our hands linked, and I got the same warm feeling I'd had that last day of orientation in Atlanta. I looked around the circle at the sweaty faces, Black and white, and felt lifted up by the fact that, even if what we were doing made no difference at all, we were bonded, all of us, and we wouldn't give up the fight. Across the circle, I caught Win looking at me and he smiled, nodded his head. I knew he was saying, *Good job, Ellie.*

While we were singing, three policemen appeared on the sidewalk by the courthouse, their hands on their clubs, their eyes on us. They were part of a growing crowd of white people, none of whom was there to cheer us on. A few of the men jeered, but we ignored them. I was surprised that I felt no danger. Only happiness.

~

After we drove those who needed rides home, we met back at the school to discuss the protest. Win sat next to me in the heavy wooden chairs, intentionally. I saw him seek me out. And I saw Rosemary's face as he sat down. She gave a small shake of her head I could only read as disapproval. Or maybe I was imagining things.

"You did great," Win whispered to me as Greg started our meeting.

"You too," I whispered back.

"Good job, folks," Greg said from his usual perch, sitting on the corner of one of the metal desks. "You probably didn't notice, but there was a reporter standing on the sidewalk, watching us. Taking notes. Snapping some pictures. We'll be in the paper. We'll gain the support of the good-hearted people in Derby County . . . as well as the wrath of those who don't want us here." He went on for a while in his deep voice, but I wasn't really listening. I was so aware of Win sitting in the chair next to me. I felt an almost uncontrollable need to reach over and give him a hug. Just a happy, contented hug.

"And Ellie," Greg said, jolting me back to the room. "You have a beautiful voice. You can be our official song leader from now on."

≈

I lay in bed back at the Daweses' house that night, cuddling with GiGi and Sally, thinking about the crazy turn my life had taken. I wanted to tell Win what had driven me here. I wanted to tell him about Aunt Carol and how my eyes had been opened by the Chapel Hill protests. Most of all, I wanted to tell him about the terrible day Mattie drowned in the lake. I wanted him to know who I truly was. To see past the brave veneer of a do-gooder girl. I wanted to tell him about the real me. The me that still shamed me. I thought of what words I could use to tell him, but I fell asleep before I could figure out how to string them together.

I was dead asleep when the shouting began. I sat up in the darkness, disoriented, my brain still wired from the singing at the protest. The little bodies around me were heavy with slumber. It took me a minute to realize that someone was pounding on the bedroom door. Suddenly, it flew open.

"Get up! Get up!" Mrs. Dawes shouted. She carried a lantern that illuminated the fear in her dark eyes. "Keep the children with you!"

"What's going on?" I asked, but she was already gone. From the corner of my eye, I saw a flicker of light. I leaped out of the bed and pulled aside the thin curtain at the front window, then caught my breath. A cross was ablaze in front of the house, no more than a few yards from the bedroom where I stood in my nightgown and bare feet.

"Kids!" I shouted to the four of them. "Wake up!" I jostled them. Shook them. Yelled at them. They were like dead children, their bodies too heavy with sleep to respond. I finally got the two older girls up and I grabbed the little ones in my arms as I ran from the bedroom to the front porch.

Outside, Mr. and Mrs. Dawes and the two older boys ran back and forth from the pump to the fiery cross, buckets of water sloshing. Embers flew through the air from the cross and I was terrified one of them would land on the roof and set the house ablaze. I thought I should help, but Mrs. Dawes yelled at me. "Just keep the children on the porch!"

So I stayed in the rocker, GiGi asleep on my lap, Sally on the splintery porch floor sucking her thumb. The two older girls stood next to me, clinging to my shoulder, my neck, staring at the flames. I could see the fire and fear reflected in their eyes. And I knew I was the person who put it there.

Chapter 23

KAYLA

2010

Although I invited her to hold our yoga practice in my new house, Ellie insisted we have it in her home, where she could be at the beck and call of her mother and brother. She's cleared one of the big upstairs bedrooms of most furniture and there is plenty of space. The room is empty except for her purple mat and a huge purple exercise ball. A table in the corner holds a CD player and another essential-oil diffuser, and the air smells like lemons.

The windows are open, and I realize there is no air-conditioning in this house, or at least not in this room. But there is a ceiling fan and the window lets in a light breeze. It also lets in the sounds of construction, both of the Shadow Ridge houses and the back porch repair that's underway.

"I'm not going to bother with my usual yoga music," Ellie says, motioning toward the CD player. "Instead, we'll let the construction sounds be part of our practice. Rather than be annoyed by them," she says, "let them simply wash over you."

I find the noise a challenge at first as I sit on my pink mat, which I'd managed to unearth from one of the larger moving boxes in the spare bedroom. The shouts of the workers and the buzz of their saws and staccato banging of their nail guns are a distraction, but Ellie sets an example of a woman at peace and I soon have the feeling of being completely in the room with her. Nothing outside can touch me.

I let her guide me through the asanas. It's hard not to gawk at her incredible flexibility and strength. I'm not clumsy, and after the last few rough months, I'm certainly not overweight, but I'm not *lithe*. That's the word that keeps running through my mind as I watch Ellie move smoothly from one long-held pose to the next. She is sixty-five years old and she is still lithe.

This is just what I need, I think, before reminding myself not to think. Just to be. Moments of peace come and go. It's been a long time since I've felt any peace at all, so I'm grateful. Ellie's breathing seems to become my own, or perhaps it's the other way around. We end, of course, with Savasana, and I shut my eyes and feel the hot lemony air against my skin as I try to calm my mind instead of thinking of all I need to do for the rest of the day. I've almost managed to clear the thoughts away when I'm brought back to the room by the slamming of a car door.

We both stretch and sit up slowly. She looks at me. "All the noise was a real test," she says. "Were you able to cope with the distractions?"

"I was," I say, smiling. "That was incredible, Ellie." I stretch my arms over my head. "Really, it was just what I needed. And you're amazing."

"I could tell you found it soothing," she says. "I think you'd benefit from making this a regular—"

"Ellie!" She's interrupted by a woman's voice calling from the yard. Ellie gets to her feet, graceful as a gazelle, and looks out the window. "Up here," she calls, then turns to me. "It's a friend," she says. "I told her you'd be here and not to come till later, but no one listens to me, it seems." Her smile looks distracted now, and I think it's time for me to leave.

"Oh, I'll go," I say, scrambling to the end of my mat.

I hear someone on the stairs and a slender woman about Ellie's age appears in the doorway as I begin rolling up my mat. She wears black jeans and a peach-colored blouse. Her white hair is stylish, very short on one side, grazing her chin on the other. I imagine she was a real beauty when she was younger. Her smile is instantly engaging and I smile back at her as I roll the mat. She's vaguely familiar, as is nearly everyone in Round Hill.

She grins at me. "Reed Miller's daughter!" she says. "Ellie told me you'd be here today. I've seen you around over the years but didn't know who you were."

"This is Brenda Cleveland," Ellie says. She's on her feet now, doing something with the essential-oil diffuser. She glances at me over her shoulder as she adds, "She's my oldest friend."

"Oldest, as in we've known each other a very long time," Brenda says. "I'm actually two months younger than she is." She looks around the empty room. "You really need some chairs in here, Ellie," she says. She sits down cautiously on the purple exercise ball.

I get to my feet and slip the carrying strap of my mat over my shoulder. "I'm Kayla." I hold out my hand, which she shakes. "You know my father personally?" I ask. Everyone knows Reed Miller, the former mayor. Not everyone knows him as a friend.

Brenda sends Ellie an odd look, almost quizzical, and Ellie seems to avoid eye contact with her as she pours more oil into the diffuser.

"Of course I know your father," Brenda says. "Everybody knows everybody, especially those of us from the old days when Round Hill was tiny. I knew your mom, too. But Ellie knew your father best."

"We're not talking about that," Ellie says firmly. She screws on the top of the bottle of oil.

Brenda winks at me. "I guess we're not talking about that," she says.

"Okay." I smile, but I'm curious. I remember how both Ellie and my father acted strangely when I mentioned one to the other. A long-ago romance that ended badly? I'm going to have to have a chat with Daddy.

"I hope you didn't stop the class on my account," Brenda says to Ellie.

"I can visit with Buddy and Mama downstairs if you want to keep going for a while."

"We're finished," I say. "It was wonderful. Have you seen Ellie do yoga?"

"Actually, I haven't," Brenda says. "Until she showed up back here a month ago, I hadn't seen hide nor hair of her since we were girls, even though we were once best friends."

"I invited you to San Francisco several times," Ellie says.

"I don't fly," Brenda says. "And she would never come home."

"Well, I'm here now," Ellie says, an edge to her voice. I don't know if she likes this old friend or not.

"So tell me all about you," Brenda says to me.

"I really should go," I say, although I don't want to. I'd like to know what went on between Ellie and my father.

"No, stay awhile," Brenda insists. "I want to hear how your daddy's doing these days. I know you lost your mother a few years ago. I was sorry to hear that."

"Thanks," I say. "And my father's doing really well." I look at Ellie. She moves back to her mat, sits down, and stretches over her legs. I can't tell if she wants me to stay or not. I know she only spent the last hour with me out of gratitude for possibly saving her brother's life. I stand awkwardly in the middle of the room, my arms around my rolled-up mat.

"Do you live nearby?" Brenda asks.

"Actually, yes. I live in the house at the end of the street." I nod in the direction of our new house.

Brenda's eyes widen and she laughs. "I didn't realize anyone had actually moved into 'Shadow Ridge Estates' yet." She puts air quotes around "Shadow Ridge Estates." I have the feeling my little neighborhood has become the object of derision.

"It's going to be really nice when the other houses are finished," I say.

"Well maybe change is good in this case," she says, rocking back and forth a bit on the exercise ball. "This area was always a little weird, what with the kudzu and woods and all."

"It wasn't 'weird.'" Ellie lifts her head from her stretch over her legs. She sounds defensive, and Brenda smiles.

"Ellie and Buddy and Mama are thrilled about Shadow Ridge Estates, aren't y'all?" Brenda looks at her old friend, who shrugs. I think Brenda might be a bit of a bitch.

"We've accepted it," Ellie says. She crosses her legs, hands on her knees. "It couldn't stay the way it used to be forever. Plus, I live three thousand miles away, so what does it matter to me if there's a development here?"

I remember my father's letter to Jackson. How the Hockleys would never let go of their property, even after their deaths.

"What will you do with your house after . . . once you go back to San Francisco?" I ask, the question awkward as it comes out of my mouth.

"You mean once Buddy and Mama are gone?" She looks at me, getting to the point. "I guess I'll sell it, then. I'm not attached to it any longer."

So, Daddy was wrong about the Hockleys hanging on to the property forever and ever.

"Where did you live before?" Brenda asks me.

"On Fletcher Road," I say. The air from the ceiling fan feels good on my face. "Over by—"

"Oh yeah," Brenda says. "Cute little houses over there."

"Our house *was* cute," I agree, "but way too tiny. And no trees at all."

Brenda laughs. "Well, you've got trees now, don't you? I've never seen a developer leave so many trees."

"Actually, they freak me out a little," I admit. It feels good to say it out loud to someone. "We have fifty windows and I feel pretty exposed. I ordered window treatments but they won't be in for a while."

"Well, I'm sure no one's ever back in those woods," she says reassuringly.

"I'm talking to fencing companies to—"

"Oh no, honey," Brenda says. "You don't want a fence! So ugly."

"Well, I'd make sure it's attractive from the street," I say, a bit annoyed, "and I really think I should have a fence. There's that lake behind my house that worries me, since I have a little girl. But other than that, I love the house." Maybe if I say it enough times it will come true. "My husband and I are architects and we designed it ourselves. He died recently, so the house is full of so many of his ideas and makes me feel—"

"Your husband died?" Brenda interrupts me, her face suddenly pained. "How terrible! He must have been awfully young."

"Just twenty-nine," I say. "It was an accident. So now it's just me and my little girl."

All three of us are quiet for a moment. Ellie's eyes are shut as though she's not quite in the room with us. The silence feels weird. Sort of charged. I hear the sliding of van doors outside. The voices of the construction workers. I think it's time for me to leave.

I open my mouth to say goodbye, but Brenda breaks the silence first. "I lost my husband young, too," she says quietly.

"Oh, I'm sorry." I feel an instant kinship to her. There's grief in her eyes, even after all these years. "How old was he?"

"Only twenty-two. We were getting the nursery ready for the baby I was expecting. He was repairing the ceiling and lost his balance. Fell off the ladder."

"Oh," I say, a hand to my throat. I'm startled by the coincidence. "My husband was working in our new house, too. He was climbing the stairs— the house was only half built then—and he didn't notice a pile of screws on one of the top steps. The railing wasn't up yet. He fell off and broke his neck."

Brenda nods as if my story makes sense to her. "Garner didn't die right away like that," she says. "I lost him in the emergency room."

Ellie suddenly opens her eyes. "I'll never understand why you called Uncle Byron for help instead of an ambulance," she says.

"You don't think rationally at a time like that, Ellie." Brenda speaks quietly, but I see the muscles in her throat contract. She looks at me and I nod. I know what she means. You become a different person in a moment of panic, if only for a few seconds.

"Did you ever remarry?" I ask.

She shakes her head. "Garner was the love of my life," she says. "And I . . ." She licks her lips. "The stress was too much. I lost the baby I was carrying. So, I've been alone since. All my adult life. No husband. No children."

I feel sympathy for her, but I know I won't let her future be mine. I still have Rainie. And I'll meet someone, someday. It's hard to imagine falling in love with anyone but Jackson, but I'm hopeful that it will happen.

"I can't believe you moved into the house where your husband died," Brenda says. "I could never do that."

Her words hurt, they're so abrupt. "Well, we designed it together so it's very special to me," I said. "There's so much of Jackson . . . my husband . . . in it. We were living with my dad for a while, but once the house was finished, I—"

"You should go back to your father's," Brenda says. "Take it from me, sweetie. You need that support. You may not realize it now, but if I were you, I'd sell that pretty new house and let Reed take care of you. It'd be good for both of you."

"I'm not leaving," I say, with more strength in the words than I feel. "And anyhow, my father's moving into a condo, so I no longer have that option." I think of my father's letter to Jackson, warning us about the location, and the crazy lady in my office who said the trees would suck the breath out of us, and Ellie telling me to take the tree house down. It seems like nobody thinks I should live in Shadow Ridge.

"Well, enough of this," Ellie says. She gets to her feet and crosses the room to shut the windows. She sounds bored, as though she thinks her friend should have moved on long ago. I think she's tired of Brenda's story. Maybe she's heard it one too many times over the decades in letters and phone calls and thinks that Brenda has wallowed long enough in her grief. There's something between these two women besides friendship, I think. Something old and prickly.

Right now, though, I feel responsible for bringing the conversation down. "I need to run." I touch Ellie's arm. "I'll let myself out," I say. "This was wonderful."

"We'll do it again," Ellie offers, surprising me. Despite how well our session went, I still don't get the feeling that she likes me all that much.

"I'd love that," I say. I head to the door, but Brenda speaks up again.

"My Garner was your father's best friend," she says.

I turn to her. "Your husband?"

She nods. "They were best friends. We used to double-date all the time. Ellie and Reed, Garner and me."

I look at Ellie, almost accusingly. Why hadn't she said anything?

She shrugs. "It was a very long time ago," she says in a way that immediately closes the subject. Suddenly, she looks exhausted, the vibrant yoga teacher gone, and I know it's truly time for me to go.

Chapter 24

ELLIE

1965

By the time I sat down to breakfast the morning after the cross burning, Mr. Dawes and his two sons were ready to leave for the field. He looked at me with tired eyes, red from the smoke.

"You can't stay here no longer," he said.

"I know," I answered. "I'm so sorry." I'd apologized over and over the night before for bringing danger to them and their home. I'd barely slept, holding GiGi and Sally tightly against me, thinking of how much worse it could have been. All the "what-if"s terrified me.

I had no way to let anyone know what had happened until Curry and Win came to pick me up to take me to the school for our Saturday meeting. I watched the two of them rush out of the beige SCOPE van, Curry stopping to examine the smoldering cross, while Win leaped up the steps to me.

"Is everyone all right?" He looked past me into the house as if he could see Mrs. Dawes and the children inside.

"Yes." I nodded. "But I can't stay here."

He went inside to speak with Mrs. Dawes, while I carried my things to the van. I tossed them on the back seat, then got into the front seat to wait for Win and Curry. That's when I thought to myself, *You automatically got into the front seat, even though Win was in the front seat when he and Curry arrived. You automatically expect him to ride in the back.* Yes, I did. The South had raised me. It was time for the South to let me go. I got out of the van and moved to the long middle seat.

Curry and Win returned to the van, Win getting into the front seat without batting an eye. "Greg has to find you a new place to stay," he said to me over his shoulder.

"Did any of the other SCOPE workers have a problem last night?" I asked.

"I don't think so," Curry said, lighting a cigarette. "You're the only girl stayin' in the community, and the only Southerner. Might be the reason."

"Or maybe just coincidence," Win said.

I wondered which of them was right.

≈

The cross burning at the Daweses' had not been the only trouble the night before. That was obvious as soon as Curry pulled the van into the small parking lot at the school. Every window we could see either bore bullet holes or had been completely shot out.

"Oh no." I gathered my things from the back seat, hoping Greg, Paul, Chip, and Jocelyn, all of whom spent their nights at the school, were okay.

"We're fine," Greg said when we walked into the building. "Nothing serious. We just have a few windows to repair."

Jocelyn looked up at me from the desk where she was using the typewriter. "I just locked myself in the art room," she said. "It's like a bunker in there." Jocelyn always looked a little pale, a little fragile, but this morning she was positively ghostly.

I took Greg aside and told him what had happened at the Daweses' house in the middle of the night. He'd made light of the mayhem outside the school building, but I could tell he was truly upset by my news. We'd put an innocent family at risk.

The other SCOPE workers gradually filled the room, all of us automatically taking the same seats we'd been in at our first meeting the week before. One week! It was hard to believe we'd only been in Flint that long. It felt like at least a month.

Greg led us in a short prayer, then sat on the edge of the metal desk, folding his hands on his thigh.

"Last night, some folks with nothing better to do decided to shoot up the school," he said. "I called the police department and they said they'd send someone right over, but no one ever arrived, so now we know we can't count on the police for help. It's my belief the mayhem is the result of just a few local fellows with too much beer in their bellies and time on their hands. They'd like us to leave Flint, but we're not going to do that."

I looked at Win. He wore that expression I hadn't seen on his face in several days. Eyes straight forward. Jaw tight. Chin set.

"Of more concern to me is what happened at the home where Ellie's been staying," Greg continued. "A cross was burned in the front yard last night. It could easily have taken that house down and the family with it. That feels like Klan activity and we have to take it seriously." Everyone turned to look at me as though I'd passed some sort of test, one no one else wanted to take. "Ellie, I'll find another home for you," Greg said, "but we'll need to move you every couple of nights. The fewer people who know where you are, the better."

When the meeting broke up and most of the "freedom fighters" headed out into the community to canvass, I stayed at the school helping Jocelyn with paperwork. Greg left to visit some of the other ministers in the area, trying to find a new home for me. Chip and Paul took off for the hardware store to get wood to board up the windows.

After a week of spending every day with Win, it felt strange not to be with him. I knew Rosemary was canvassing with him in my place, and as I mimeographed song sheets, it took me a little while to recognize my discomfort as jealousy. I wasn't interested in Win as anything other than my canvassing partner, I told myself, but we'd worked well together this week and it just felt wrong that Rosemary was with him now.

What does it matter? I scolded myself. Developing a relationship—especially an interracial relationship—was completely against the rules, even if I *were* interested in him that way.

I was almost done with the mimeograph machine when Jocelyn looked up at me from the desk where she was typing something.

"I just want to say that I admire you, Ellie," she said, breaking into my thoughts.

"You do?" I asked, surprised.

"I do. I feel like such a coward." She wrinkled her nose. "I came into this . . . into SCOPE, totally expecting to, you know, stay in the community and canvass, like you're doing, but . . ." Her voice trailed off.

I sat down in the chair next to her desk. "But . . . ?" I prompted.

"It was the bullet holes in the doors that first night. They scared the daylights out of me."

"I know. They scared me, too."

"Yes, but you went ahead with what you said you'd do. Work in the community."

"Someone needs to do the office work, Jocelyn. It's not like you're doing nothing."

"I know. I guess I'm just disappointed in myself. And anyway"—she laughed—"here I am, staying in the one place that's getting shot up."

"Must have been scary last night."

"Not as scary as that burning cross," she said.

"I was mostly afraid for the children in the house," I said. "I felt like I would be responsible for any of them getting hurt." I got to my feet. "Do you have some more work for me to do?"

She handed me a stack of mail. "You can put these in the cubbyholes," she said.

I sorted through the pile of mail, most of it for Greg. Then I put the few letters into the appropriate cubbyholes for the SCOPE workers. The very last letter in the stack was for me from Brenda. I sat on one of the small wooden chairs to read it.

Dear Ellie,

I was glad to hear from you. To answer your questions first, I'm a very happy girl. Garner is as wonderful a husband as I imagined he'd be, bringing me flowers every few days and pampering me constantly. I finally stopped throwing up all the time, and the doctor says I'll be able to feel the baby move any day now. I'm already madly in love with him or her. We are working on the nursery and thinking about names. I like Lisa or Amy for a girl and I want to name the baby Garner Jr. if it's a boy, but Garner won't hear of it. Too confusing, he says. Anyway, we have plenty of time to figure all that out.

Now to you, dear Ellie. What the hell are you doing??? Your living conditions are horrendous. Sleeping with other people's children? No lights? Using an outhouse? I will never understand why you're doing this, for heaven's sake! As soon as that voting rights bill gets signed or whatever needs to happen, all the Negroes can just go on their own to register, and if they don't, well then it's their loss. I miss you. And Reed misses you like crazy. He's moping around like a sad puppy, though he won't tell you that. He said he hasn't heard from you and I think he's too proud to be the first one to write. Do you have any idea how much that boy loves you? He says he admires you for your courage, but that doesn't make him any less sad. He's not going out with anyone, in case you were wondering. At least not yet. Garner and I are taking care of him for you but I'm secretly hoping you'll see the light and come home. We promise not to say "I told you so." Please, please come home!

Brenda and Garner

I thought about Reed while I swept up the broken glass on the school's second story. He hadn't been much on my mind over the last couple of weeks. I should write to him, but I didn't really know what to say. I was surprised he said anything about my courage, since I knew he didn't want me to be here. It was good for us to have this break, I thought. It would give us both some time to figure out what we really wanted. The one thing I was absolutely certain I *didn't* want was Brenda's life. I was nowhere near ready to be a mother. I'd loved those little Dawes kids—truly loved them and I already missed them. But it was one thing to cuddle some adorable little kids and then give them back to their mother. It was another thing to be tied to them all day and all night. Maybe someday, but not now. And Brenda had signed her letter "Brenda and Garner," as though she was no longer an individual. As though they had become one person. I guessed there was something sweet about that, but honestly, I found it nauseating.

≈

Greg returned to the school around one o'clock and began slipping papers from his desk into his briefcase. I was back on the first floor and I walked over to his desk and spoke quietly, not really wanting Jocelyn to hear me.

"I'm sorry, Greg," I said. "I don't know if the cross happened because—"

"You have nothing to apologize for." He interrupted me. "You're an asset, Ellie, and as long as we can keep you safe, I'm glad you're here." He pulled his mail from his cubbyhole and put it in his briefcase. "I'm still looking for a home for you," he said. "A few possibilities, but for tonight, at least, you'll stay here at the school."

"That's fine," I said. Tonight I could have a real shower and real toilet tissue instead of the hay and dried corn cobs in the Daweses' wretched outhouse. It would be bliss.

"As for me," he said, closing the clasp on his briefcase, "I'm headed home for some family time and to tend my flock in the morning." He smiled at me, then looked over at Jocelyn to include her in our conversation. "Y'all and the boys have a safe night, now."

Once Greg had left, Jocelyn pulled a few sheets of paper from the typewriter and separated them from the carbon paper. "He's so nice," she said, nodding toward the door through which Greg had disappeared.

"He is," I agreed, and I told her how I'd practically begged him to let me work with SCOPE.

"See what I mean about admiring you?" Jocelyn said. "You really fought to be here."

I felt embarrassed, undeserving of her admiration, and I was glad when Paul and Chip showed up carrying several sheets of plywood.

"Look what we found," Chip said. He and Paul rested the wood they were carrying against the wall, and Chip pulled a folded sheet of paper from his pants pocket. "Stole it from a telephone pole." He unfolded the paper and held it out for Jocelyn and me to see.

In big black letters on a tan background, it read *United Klans of America* and below that, *Come hear the truth from the Grand Dragon of North Carolina.* Below that, *OPEN TO THE WHITE PUBLIC ONLY!* Then came the date and a Round Hill address.

"Round Hill's where I live!" I pointed to the address. "I know where they're talking about. It's a big old cow pasture just outside the town. Nobody uses it anymore." I hated that the Klan was meeting so close to my home. Was this the first time or had I been ignorant of all the other times a gang of racists had gathered practically in my backyard?

"It's tonight." Jocelyn pointed to the poster.

"And we're the white public," Chip said. "I think we should go. I want to see what they do at these rallies. What we're up against." He glanced at Paul, who gave a noncommittal shrug.

"Could be educational," he said.

"Are y'all crazy?" I asked. "They're a bunch of hateful bigots. That's all you need to know. And they'll kill us if they figure out who we are. They just burned a cross outside my bedroom window."

"It's not like we'll stand out," Chip said. "Those rallies are packed, aren't they? We'll just look like four more racist white assholes. Aren't you curious?"

Jocelyn looked at me. "Do women go?" she asked.

"Uh-huh." I nodded. "Even kids, from what I've been told."

"Then let's do it," Jocelyn said, her eyes on me.

Greg would be disgusted with us. Probably furious, too, for putting ourselves at unnecessary risk. I thought of the cross outside my bedroom window with the Dawes children sleeping next to me. Danger so close. But Paul was right. No one would know we were any different from anyone else. And the fact that it was so close to where I lived made me curious.

"All right." I removed the black and white SCOPE pin from my collar so I didn't forget to do it later. "We can go for a little while," I said. "Just to see what it's like."

Chapter 25

———≈———

We left the school a little before eight in Paul's car. It was still light out, and I sat up front to give directions once we neared Round Hill. It felt so strange to drive past my old high school, and Painter Lane—Reed's street—and the turnoff that would take us to Hockley Street and my house. I had to bite my tongue to keep from asking Paul to take a quick jog down Hockley. I'd only been gone a couple of weeks and driving through Round Hill already made me a little homesick. I felt like I'd been away for a lifetime.

But soon we were out in the country on the other side of Round Hill. We came to a bend in the road and I knew the old cow pasture would come into view soon. I caught my breath when it did. The huge empty field had turned into a sea of cars. They were arranged in neat lines in the middle of the field, but helter-skelter around the border, as though tossed by a tornado. In the distance I could see the throng of people. There had to be a thousand of them. Maybe two thousand.

"Well, that's damn depressing," Chip said. He leaned forward from the back seat and tapped my shoulder. "Your town is full of haters," he said, and I felt a lump form in my throat.

"Who knows where all these people came from?" I felt defensive. "Don't blame it all on Round Hill." I knew the truth, though. I knew there were plenty of haters in my hometown. Plenty who complained about letting Black students into my old high school. Plenty of shops and restaurants where they weren't welcome. I just avoided the haters. They weren't part of my circle. They weren't part of my parents' circle either. Some people hadn't been happy when my father opened his pharmacy doors to Black customers, but he stood his ground and I'd been proud of him. I hoped that, deep down inside, he was proud of me now for being in SCOPE, and that the only reason he hadn't supported my decision was because he was worried about me.

We had to park a good distance from the rally itself, Paul jostling the car into a muddy spot between a couple of other Plymouths. We could barely squeeze out of the car doors, but we managed, and soon we were walking on the old country road toward the rally.

"It just looks like a big fair or something," Jocelyn said.

It did. It reminded me of our annual Derby County Fair. There was even a Ferris wheel on the far side of the field. The crowd was thick, people packed in tightly, the men in white shirts and dark trousers and the women in their everyday dresses. The air smelled of hot dogs and the people stood around talking and laughing, paper cups in their hands. Children ran between them, chasing each other, waving miniature Confederate flags. There was a stage at one end of the field where a man spoke into a microphone, his voice echoing from huge speakers set up along the edges of the field. We headed toward the stage and it wasn't until we'd gotten closer that I saw what made this gathering different from a county fair. In front of the long stage stood a line of a hundred—at *least* a hundred—people in white satin robes and pointed hoods. They applauded whatever the man on the stage was saying. His robe and hood were green, shimmering in the waning sunlight. We jostled closer to one of the enormous speakers so we'd be able to hear him.

Paul nudged the man next to him. "Who is that guy?" he asked, pointing to the dark-haired, round-faced man on the stage.

The man looked at Paul as though he'd dropped down from another planet. "Bob Jones, of course," he said, a hint of pride in his voice. "Our Grand Dragon."

"Oh, right," Paul said. "I didn't recognize him in person." Paul turned to the rest of us and rolled his eyes, mouthing, *The Grand Dragon*.

I snapped a few pictures of Bob Jones and listened to what he had to say. It seemed important to know what we were up against. I felt embarrassed that my new Northern friends were witnessing this—that they would think every Southerner bought into the message of white supremacy. I had to admit that from the size of the crowd, it certainly looked like it.

"Do you know, we're now ten thousand members strong in North Carolina?" Bob Jones shouted. Cheers and applause erupted from the crowd. "We have Klaverns in every corner of the state, more than in *all* the other Southern states combined!" His face was shiny with sweat. "We travel across the Old North State every night, sharing our message with good, honest, hardworking folks like you, working to preserve our precious way of life!" Another cheer went up from the crowd. I wondered if we should cheer, too, just to protect ourselves. We mustn't stand out. But not a soul seemed to be paying attention to us.

"I ain't got nothin' against the colored man," Bob Jones shouted. "I'm all for equal rights, but *separate* rights." More cheering. "Integration is a threat to your jobs, folks, you know that," Jones said. "A threat to your very way of life. And if Lyndon Baines Johnson bends to the communists and the Jewish cabal behind the civil rights movement, well he can go straight to hell!"

The crowd loved that, apparently, shouting and cheering and waving Confederate flags. I felt sick. Sort of helpless. How did our little band

of freedom fighters stand a chance against so many thousands of hateful
people? I thought of the sweet Dawes family, struggling just to survive, and
my eyes filled with tears.

"Holy mackerel!" Jocelyn grabbed my arm. "Look at how big that
cross is!"

I'd been so focused on Bob Jones and the crowd that I hadn't realized
the towering structure behind the stage was a cross. It had to be at least
eight times the height of Bob Jones himself and I knew—everybody who
lived in the South knew—that its bulk was formed by gasoline-soaked bur-
lap. The blaze would be enormous. I thought of how terrifying the small
cross had been at the Daweses' house and I hoped we didn't stick around
long enough to see this one burn.

As Bob Jones continued spewing his hateful talk, I glanced around us
at all the excited, open faces, glad they were unfamiliar to me. But then my
eyes lit on one man. He was maybe twenty feet away from me, off to
my left, and for a moment I was absolutely certain he was Garner. The
man turned away to speak to someone and I lost sight of him, but I felt a
shiver run up my spine. I stopped examining the crowd and told myself I
was crazy. Garner wouldn't come to something like this.

But then, neither would I.

Jones stepped aside from the microphone and a white-robed woman
took his place. "We have our raffle winners!" she shouted, her voice so
high-pitched and piercing through the speaker that I winced. The woman
called out a few numbers and people squealed or shouted from different
parts of the crowd. She told the winners to make their way up front when
the rally was over. Then the Grand Dragon stepped behind the microphone again.

"So what should we do about LBJ?" he shouted, and the crowd went
wild with derisive jeers. I was no fan of President Johnson at that moment
myself, but for different reasons. Was he ever going to sign the voting
rights bill?

A woman pushed her way in front of us, holding out a large bucket, and it took me a moment to realize that she was collecting money for the cause. Paul had a clear head, dropping a few coins into the bucket and giving the woman a conspiratorial *we're one of you* wink. The woman smiled her thanks at him, then glanced at Jocelyn and her expression suddenly darkened. She turned away from us and continued on through the crowd. I looked quizzically at Jocelyn. What had she seen in Jocelyn's face? Then I realized it wasn't Jocelyn's face that gave her away. Her SCOPE pin was still on her collar, the black and white circle looking like a target against her pink blouse.

"Your pin!" I shouted into her ear.

She felt her collar. "Oh! I'm an idiot!" She unfastened it and slipped it into her purse.

"The civil rights movement has got to be kept down!" Bob Jones shouted. "We've got to put our heel on its heart and squash the lifeblood clean out of it. Civil rights workers are the villains and must be stopped. Now we've got coloreds running for office. Gaining power. Any day now, they're gonna have the vote and they'll be sitting next to your daughters in their high school classroom. I tell you, I am not about to let my daughter sit next to no colored boy!"

There were whistles and applause and cheering, a palpable, mounting hysteria that frightened me. This was always the hot-button issue; every Southerner knew that. Black boys and white girls. *Danger!* Bob Jones knew just what he was doing, planting that image in the eyes of every scared white parent in the field. Making them crazy with fear and anger.

Darkness had fallen around us without me even knowing it and giant floodlights flickered to life. Paul turned to look at the rest of us. "Let's beat the rush outta here," he shouted against the din.

We followed him toward the road, keeping up with each other, afraid to lose one another in the growing darkness. Suddenly, I spotted the woman who had been carrying the bucket working her way through the crowd, pointing at us. Shouting something. People turned to look at us. Above Bob Jones's ranting I heard someone shout, "Them SCOPE kids!"

"Sons of bitches!"

"Commie lovers!"

And then I saw who was with the woman. She was dragging the man by the arm, pointing at me and my friends. Sheriff Byron Parks, the man I thought of as my father's best friend. The man I called "Uncle Byron." He locked eyes with me and I froze. In a moment he was next to me, nudging me and my coworkers in the direction of the road.

"I'm just here to keep order!" he shouted in my ear, and I wanted to shout back, *Then why aren't you in uniform?* But maybe he had to be in street clothes. Maybe that was the way he handled a crowd like this one.

"You need to get out of here!" he shouted. "Keep going!" He waved us forward. "Just head for the exit! Get out of here before anyone else realizes—"

It was too late. A mob was after us. I heard the shouts and felt the surge of people who knew we didn't belong. They were worked up enough to beat us to a pulp without a second thought. I grabbed on to Paul's shirt to keep from losing sight of him, my hand clutching the fabric in my fist. Then suddenly, the floodlights went out and we were in darkness for a few seconds before the gigantic cross flared to life behind the stage, the flames cutting through the black sky. People applauded and shouted and whistled and I hoped the spectacle stopped whoever was after us. Everyone began singing "The Old Rugged Cross" as we continued our way through the crowd, twisting and turning until we were finally free. We ran for the road. With my eyes glued to the white of Paul's shirt in the darkness, I didn't see the ditch between the field and the road. I was down in an instant, the world a blank.

Chapter 26

≈

KAYLA

2010

It's time for me to have a serious talk with my father. I remember the way he'd acted when I first told him I'd met Ellie, the way he blew me off with a wave of his hand as if he hardly knew her name. Now to learn that they had once been a couple? And that letter he sent to Jackson! I still have no idea what to make of that.

I invite him over to dinner for that night, fairly late in the evening so Rainie will go to bed before he leaves and we can talk. When he arrives, he plays with Rainie and her Legos in the great room while I grill hot dogs on my new range and bake French fries in my wall oven. I've barely noticed the new top-of-the-line appliances I should be appreciating. Over dinner, he tells me he's sold most of the furniture he'll no longer need when he's in the new condo and he has a firm move-in date a couple of weeks away. He doesn't seem the least bit sad or nostalgic. He's ready for a change and probably would have made it months ago if Rainie and I hadn't landed on his doorstep. I feel sad about losing the safe haven of my childhood home. I loved knowing it was there for us if we ever needed it again, but I'm glad for my father. He already has friends in that condo complex. It'll be a good change for him.

I can't focus on his move right now, though. I'm too caught up in thinking about his letter to Jackson. I can't figure out if I'm angry at him or not. If he had misgivings about Shadow Ridge, why didn't he share them with me, too, instead of just writing to Jackson? And not telling me about his relationship with Ellie . . . that just seems weird to me, but who knows? He must have his reasons. I intend to find out what they are.

After dinner, I get Rainie ready for bed and Daddy reads her a story while I straighten the kitchen. Then I pour myself a glass of wine and sit down in the great room, Daddy's letter to Jackson in my lap.

"Want a glass of wine, Dad?" I ask when he walks into the room. He's smiling, no doubt from his time with his granddaughter.

"Sure," he says. "Don't get up. I'll get it."

I hear him in the kitchen as I think about how to begin this conversation. I feel almost like a snoop, having read the letter that was not meant for me. Daddy's still smiling when he returns to the room with a glass of white wine.

"This house is gorgeous, sweetheart," he says as he sits down on the other end of the sectional from me. "And Rainie loves her new room, doesn't she? What do you call that wall color? Fuchsia?"

"She just calls it purple. Her favorite color."

"It suits her."

"Dad, I need to talk to you." I set my wine on the table next to me. His smile disappears.

"Are you okay?"

"I'm fine, but there are a few things bugging me," I say. "You haven't been honest with me, and I don't understand why."

His frown deepens. "What are you talking about?"

"First of all, I found this letter you wrote to Jackson." I hold up the letter.

He raises his eyebrows as though he doesn't quite know what I'm holding in my hand. Then it sinks in. "Oh," he says. "My trying-to-dissuade-you-two-from-building-here letter."

"Yes. You said the Hockleys will make sure their house is never demolished even after they're dead, and—"

"I was exaggerating," he says. "But I knew that the Hockley house could be an eyesore in this neighborhood for another twenty years. That's before I learned that Buddy Hockley was so sick, of course."

"And what were you talking about when you said the woods are haunted?" I have to laugh. My father is so grounded in reality. "Since when do you believe in ghosts?"

He takes a sip of his wine, then looks away from me for a moment. "Well," he says finally, "I didn't want you to build here and maybe I was grasping at straws, but I wasn't lying exactly." He looks at me. "When we were kids, we all thought this area was haunted. All the kudzu. And the woods . . . You could hear the strangest noises coming from those woods, and—"

"You still can," I say.

"Look, honey." He sets down his glass and leans forward, elbows resting on his knees. "I didn't want to get into this, so I guess I was beating around the bush in the letter. I'd hoped you and Jackson had some other option and if you were weighing one against the other, maybe I could sway both of you by writing to him. When he decided he wasn't afraid of the Hockleys' house and he wasn't afraid of ghosts, I just let it go and said no more. But there used to be an area back there—" He nods toward the rear of the house. Toward the woods. "—a circular area where there weren't any trees, and—"

"It's still there," I say.

"It is? After all this time?"

"Well, I think so. I mean, there's like . . . a clearing. And it's roughly circular. Nothing much growing in it. It's kind of weird." I remember feeling a chill in that circle. I feel another now.

Daddy sits back, clearly a bit stunned that the circle is still there. "Well," he says finally, "the Klan would meet there."

"The KKK met in my backyard?"

He nods. "A very long time ago, yes. There was a dirt road back then . . . Hockley Street itself was a dirt road . . . but this was more of a skinny, muddy trail, just wide enough for a single vehicle to get down. And it led all the way from the end of Hockley Street through where this house is now and back to that clearing. And it became—"

"When was this? I mean, like, what years?"

"When I was a young man. The sixties. The Klan was active then because of all the civil rights legislation. The Civil Rights Act, the Voting Rights Act, et cetera. The Klan would have big rallies in much bigger venues than your little circle in the woods, but some of the local Klavern held secret meetings there. Here." He points toward the rear of my house. "At the end of Hockley Street."

"But Daddy," I say, still perplexed as to why this would disturb him decades later. "That's ancient history. Yes, it's creepy. But someone could find fault with any place we chose to build. Don't you think?"

He nods. "You're right, of course. It's just that I was . . . so aware of this. I mean, I knew some of those Klansmen."

"You *knew* them? Like, as friends?"

"It wasn't the way you think of the Klan today. Back then, a lot of otherwise upstanding people in town belonged. I guess I felt like, if it was up to me, I wouldn't want that sort of history in the backyard where my kids were going to play."

"Well, that's—" I hunt for a word. "—*unsavory*, I guess," I say. "But it's not like they lynched anybody back there, right?"

He doesn't answer as quickly as I would have liked. "Right," he says finally.

"They didn't, did they?" I ask, thinking of those eerie animal screams I'd hear at night.

"No honey," he says. "No one was lynched in your backyard."

"If that's what you were worried about, why didn't you just tell us?" I ask. "Let us decide if it bothered us enough that we didn't want to build here?"

He looks at the ceiling. "In retrospect, that's what I should have done," he says.

"That wouldn't have stopped us." Actually, I think it might have, but it's too late now. "But on another note, Daddy, here's my bigger question." I kick off my sandals and tuck my legs under me on the sectional. "I practiced yoga with Ellie Hockley today and I learned that you and she were once an item."

His eyes widen. "She told you that?" he asks.

"Not directly. Her friend came over. Brenda. *She* told me."

"*Brenda* was there?" he asks. "That surprises me. She and Ellie had some sort of falling-out decades ago, after her husband died."

"Garner," I say. "Brenda said you were good friends with him and he died in a fall. Sort of like Jackson."

He lets out his breath as though he'd been holding it in. Sets his wineglass on the side table. "Garner. Yeah," he says. "We *were* good friends back then. It was awful. Brenda lost her baby. I tried to comfort her after it happened, but she withdrew from everyone. I almost never see her around town; she became sort of reclusive, I guess."

"And what was with you and Ellie?"

"What did she say?"

"Ellie said nothing, but Brenda said you were a couple."

"We were very young. It was all . . . you know, typical. She was my first serious girlfriend. We started dating my senior year of high school. She was a couple of years behind me. We doubled a lot with Garner and Brenda. We'd go to dances. She loved to dance." For a moment he looks lost in memory and he nearly smiles, but not quite. "Then we eventually went to different colleges, had different experiences, and drifted apart," he says. "Garner and I went to ECU in Greenville. Brenda and Ellie went to UNC. Brenda and Garner dropped out to get married. Ellie dropped out and moved to California."

"Who broke up with whom?" I ask.

He looks away again. I'm not used to my father's discomfort when he talks to me. "I don't remember the specifics, it was so long ago." He lets out a long sigh. I think I'm tiring him. "She got involved with a political group called SCOPE. It was the sixties, you know? Everything was about civil rights back then. She met someone there. Fell in love with him and that was that. I was . . . hurt." He gives me an embarrassed smile. "Jealous and angry. We were all very young," he says again. "That's when she moved to California. She lost touch with everyone, as far as I know."

I can easily picture the Ellie I was with today being a radical in her youth. "Were you hippies?" I grin. I doubt it. I've seen pictures of my father during his college years. His hair was never much longer than his collar.

"We broke up before the hippies really came along." He shuts his eyes for a moment. I *am* tiring him. "You know, honey, it was a long time ago. We were kids. It's hard for you to imagine what the times were like. Vietnam. Assassinations left and right. Racial problems. A President Obama would have been unthinkable back then. I don't like to go back there in my memory, and I'm betting Ellie doesn't like to either."

I get up. Walk over and lean down to hug him. "I love you," I say. "And I'm sorry if I brought up bad memories. You don't have to worry. I'm done badgering you for tonight."

We talk about Rainie then, always a safe topic. I tell him how disappointed she was about the ugly lake and how she loved the old tree house. We have a second glass of wine and when I walk him to the door and step out on the front porch, he turns to me. The porch light glitters in his thick white hair, but his blue eyes look tired.

"Don't let Rainie play in those woods, Kayla," he says, his voice serious. "Not till she's older. All right? Maybe not even then."

"Daddy?" I wrinkle my nose at him. "What—"

"Just humor me," he says, leaning over to kiss my cheek. "I love you, honey. Good night."

I watch him walk to his car, and although the night is warm, almost hot, I rub my arms as though I'm chilled. I feel a wave of sadness wash over me. I wish Jackson had heeded my father's letter, no matter how silly or misguided his reasons for writing it. I wish he'd told me about it.

I wish we had found us a different place to build our home.

Chapter 27

ELLIE

I woke up in darkness not knowing where I was. My head felt as though it had been cracked open. I heard myself groan, and someone leaned over me. Brushed a hand over my forehead. Made me wince.

"Oh, thank God! She's waking up, guys!"

"Where are we?" I asked. "Are we moving?"

"We're looking for the hospital. You fell. Do you remember falling?"

"I tripped." My body jerked at the memory of flying through the air. I was beginning to make sense of where I was. What was around me. My head rested on Jocelyn's lap. We were in the back seat of Paul's car. "Am I bleeding?" I asked.

"No, but you were knocked out."

I shut my eyes. All I wanted to do was go to sleep.

"Don't sleep!" she said, pinching my shoulder through my blouse.

"Ouch. Stop it." I knew there was no energy at all in my voice. I wasn't even sure Jocelyn heard me. When I shut my eyes again, I saw the giant cross on fire. "I hated the . . ." I hunted for the right word. Couldn't find it.

"The rally?" she prompted.

"Yes. I hated it."

"We all hated it," Paul said from somewhere to my right. I turned my head and could just make out his profile in the darkness. He was driving, focused on the road.

"I see the hospital," the other boy said. I couldn't remember his name. But I saw lights from the hospital through the window above my head. Round Hill Hospital, where I'd had my tonsils out and my hand stitched up after I cut it carving a boat out of balsa wood. I closed my eyes. The hospital would take care of me. I could sleep.

≈

The next thing I knew, Jocelyn was squeezing my shoulder, telling me to wake up. "Open your eyes," she said. "Don't sleep."

Everything was the same. The same jut of her chin above me. The same dark car ceiling. The same stop-and-go motion that was making me nauseous.

"Why are we leaving?" I asked. "Did they . . . fix me already?"

"No, honey," Jocelyn said, and I thought, *"Honey"? Why is she calling me honey? Why did she bite off the words like she was angry?* "Once they found out you're one of 'those SCOPE kids' they said you have to go to the Negro hospital. 'The colored hospital,' they called it."

"I don't know where that is," I muttered. That seemed so wrong. "I'm from Round Hill. I had my hand taken out there."

"Your hand taken out?" Jocelyn asked, then she spoke across me to the boys. "She's delirious or something," she said.

"I'm driving as fast as I can," Paul said.

"It's in Carlisle," the other boy said, loudly, so I could hear him. Chip. His name was Chip.

Carlisle? Carlisle was a million miles away. I shut my eyes. I wouldn't let Jocelyn wake me up again.

≈

At the hospital, they kept me awake when all I wanted to do was sleep. They shined lights in my eyes and put ice on my head and gave me pills to lessen the pain. A nurse sat next to me, smiling and talking. I tried to tune her out and sleep, but gave up after a while. I got my words mixed up when I spoke to her. I wanted to tell her about SCOPE but couldn't remember the name of it. She knew, though. She said her auntie had been one of the protesters in front of the courthouse. She was proud of her.

I had no way of reaching my SCOPE team, but I assumed they knew where I was, since Paul, Jocelyn, and Chip had brought me here. "Just you don't worry 'bout it," the nurse said. So I didn't.

≈

Sunday was a blur, but when I woke up Monday morning, I felt almost fine. I sat up in the narrow hospital bed and ate eggs and grits and talked to my roommate, who was there for a broken leg. "You white, ain't ya," she said. "Why you here?"

"Yes, ma'am, I am," I said, and I explained about the white hospital turning me away. The more my head cleared, the angrier I got about that.

The nurse told me someone from SCOPE would pick me up that afternoon. She said she was "truly honored" to have me as her patient and thanked me for the work we were doing. I was suddenly glad the white hospital had turned me away then. Nobody there would be thanking me.

≈

Win walked into my room right after lunch. I lit up, seeing him, but he didn't smile.

"You're a fool, girl," he said, pulling a chair next to my bed and sitting down. He spoke quietly, with a glance at the curtain pulled around my roommate's bed. "What were y'all thinking, going to a Klan rally? That mob could've killed you. You're lucky you got away with just a lump on your head."

"Nobody did this to me," I said. I touched the tender spot on my forehead and tried not to let the pain show in my face. "I did it to myself. I tripped."

"So I heard. Running to get away from the mob. Greg lit into Paul and the others. He'll probably go easy on you since you're hurt, but you'd best have some remorse."

It all came back to me. The woman collecting money in the pail. How she lost her smile when she saw Jocelyn's SCOPE button. The angry spectators. The enormous flaming cross. *Uncle Byron.* I looked at Win. "It was nasty," I said.

"Mm. Not surprised to hear it."

"The sheriff from Round Hill was there. Byron Parks. He's my father's lifelong best friend. He's my *god*father!" I shook my head, still distressed at seeing Uncle Byron in that ugly crowd. I thought I should write to Daddy to tell him Uncle Byron had been there, but then I'd have to admit that *I'd* been there and he'd come to get me. Assuming he could find me.

"Maybe your father was there, too," Win suggested.

I rolled my eyes in annoyance. The movement made my head throb. "My father would never be a part of the Klan," I said.

"You're naïve."

"You're jaded," I countered. "My father's not like that."

"You told me he didn't want you in SCOPE," he said.

"He didn't want me in SCOPE because he was afraid I'd get hurt, not because he's a racist."

"If you say so."

I frowned at him. "You're so—" I struggled for a word. "—*distrustful*," I said. "Of whites, I mean."

He smiled. "It's just been my experience that white folk can put on a nice, happy-to-meet-you mask, but underneath it they're the same as the worst racist on the block."

"Is that what you think about me?"

He studied me from behind his glasses, then shook his head. "No, El-lie. Uh-uh. I believe you're the real deal. You and the other freedom fighters . . . nobody stays in a house with a damn outhouse unless they're serious about this work."

I felt relieved that he believed in me. I respected him and wanted his approval.

"How'd you get here?" I asked.

"Borrowed Paul's car. I'm taking you back to the school as soon as they say you can go. Greg's got a new house for you to stay at, but he wants you to move around every couple of days, like he said. You're a target. Those Derby County honkies thought you were a true North Carolina girl, but you turned out to be a rebel and now they're out to get you."

I wondered if I should just stay at the school, like Jocelyn. I thought of the four little girls in my room at the Dawes house, how they'd slept in their innocence while the cross burned outside the bedroom window. "I'm putting my host families in danger," I said quietly.

"Greg'll move you so fast from one house to another that no one'll know where you are," he said. He looked toward the window. Chewed his lower lip. "Another subject," he said. "We decided we're going to have one of those courthouse protests every week. Every Friday. The one we had was pretty good. At least it brought people together. We'll have more folks next time, and more the time after that."

"I love that idea," I said, though I'd thought the protest had been bet-ter than just "pretty good." I thought of the singing and how people really got into it. How Greg told me I had a good voice. "They're still not going to open registration before the bill gets signed," I said. "They won't open up no matter what we do."

"You're right, they won't. But we'll make a point and we'll get folks excited about it. Get them jazzed. So when the time comes to actually register, they're ready."

"It's so frustrating, encouraging them when they can't register."

"And we'll need more than just songs," he said, looking toward the window again. His mind wasn't here in my room. He was already at that protest in his head. "We need signs," he said. "And a little self-righteous anger."

"But peaceful anger," I said, and he laughed. I loved it when he laughed. It was so rare.

And then he quickly sobered, as I expected he would. "What good did we do, Ellie? Nice colored people singing freedom songs while white people walk all over them?"

"Dr. King would say we did some good," I said.

Win looked away from me again, his gaze toward the window. I couldn't read his face. "I'm not sure his way is the best way anymore," he said.

Even to me, that sounded blasphemous, but we had no time to debate, as the nurse came back in my room with a bottle of painkillers and a bag with my clothes. Win got to his feet. "I'll wait for you in the lobby," he said, and the nurse looked at him, then me, then him again. She shook her head.

"You two be careful out there," she said.

Chapter 28

———≈———

KAYLA

I'm standing on the trail through the woods behind my house, staring across the sea of tangled vines, small trees, and grisly-looking under-growth to the sick-looking lake. Next to me a blond-haired guy wearing a forest-green LET US FENCE YOU IN! T-shirt says, "I'm sorry, ma'am, but there ain't no amount of money you can pay us to do this job."

"You're kidding," I say. "Don't you have to do this sort of thing all the time? Clear away undergrowth to build a fence?"

"Not like this." He shakes his head. "If this was my place, I'd forget about it. You might could put the fence closer to the trail. You know"—he points to the edge of the trail near where we stand—"right about here in-stead of closer to the lake. You decide to do that, you call us."

"All right," I say with a sigh. "Thanks for coming out."

We walk back along the trail to the house. I make small talk with him. Where's he from? Carlisle. How long has he been in the fencing business?

Five years. He asks me questions about the Shadow Ridge houses. Are all the yards as spooky as mine? My yard reminds him of the woods near his childhood home where an old witch was rumored to live. Honestly, I've just about had it with people giving me a hard time about my home. I've decided to consciously change my feelings about the property, focusing on how much Jackson loved the trees and all the wonderful elements we built into our house design. Daddy said it was "gorgeous" the other night and it is. It's a breathtaking house and I'm not going to let small-minded people ruin it for me.

The fence guy and I reach the circular clearing and begin crossing it to pick up the trail on the other side.

"My father told me the Klan used to meet right here in the old days," I say.

"Oh, I think the Klan used to meet just about everywhere back then," the young man says. "Prob'ly still do. We just don't hear about it so much."

I can't help it: I shudder at the thought of my yard still being a gathering place for the Klan. I want that fence more than ever now.

In my driveway, I thank him for his time and wave as he drives off. When I turn back to the house, I remember that tomorrow is trash day. They missed us last week, the trash guys not yet used to anyone living at the end of Shadow Ridge Lane. I wheel the can to the end of my driveway even though it's only midafternoon. I don't want to forget to put it out. Even with the lid closed on the can, the trash reeks after two weeks in the summer sun.

≈

Rainie is chatty as I help her get dressed for school the following morning.

"I want to play with the carrot-net, Mama," she says, checking her shirt before she puts it on to make sure she'll have the label in the back.

"What's the carrot-net, honey?" I ask, helping her pull the shirt over her head.

"A horn thing," she says.

"Oh, a clarinet?" I smile. "You're learning about musical instruments at school?"

"Yes, a girl played that one and I like it." Her brown eyes, huge, deer-like, sparkle. I want to hug her to pieces and if we had more time, I just might, but we're running late.

"In a couple of years, I'll get you clarinet lessons if you still want them."

"Promise?"

"Promise."

"Yay!" She claps her hands together, and she's still talking about the clarinet as we eat our oatmeal and I fill my travel cup with coffee for the drive to my office.

In the garage, I buckle her into her car seat, thinking that I should do more to nurture her interest in the arts. I'm still thinking about that as I open the garage doors and begin backing down the driveway toward the street. In my rearview mirror I see that my large brown trash can is on its side and I silently curse the trash collectors for their sloppy job—until I realize that someone has strewn my two weeks of rotting trash from one side of my front lawn to the other.

"Oh no," I say.

"Oh, no," Rainie repeats. "Did it 'splode, Mama?"

"I don't think it exploded," I say, horrified by the smell that cuts straight through the car windows. "I'm not sure what happened." It's pretty clear to me that someone intentionally dumped my trash all over my lawn, but I don't want to scare her. I'll let her think it was nature, not man, that caused this revolting mess.

≈

After dropping Rainie off at school, I call the office to let them know I'll be late. I have a meeting later this morning, but fortunately no client appointments. Back home again, I park my car in the driveway, get out, and look with dismay at the field of filth in front of me. Someone had to work hard to spread the trash out like this. I set the trash can upright and that's when I see the typed note taped to the lid: *your woods are a source of evil that touches all our lives.*

I suddenly feel as though I'm being watched. I look around me. The construction workers are arriving now, the air filling with the sound of van doors sliding open and slamming shut. None of the workers pays any attention to me. I feel torn between crying and screaming. I do neither. Instead, I pull my phone from my purse and call the police.

≈

I'm making Rainie's bed upstairs half an hour later when I hear a car door slam in the driveway. I look out the window to see a police car behind my SUV. An officer stands at the edge of my driveway, hands on her hips, taking in the trash heap that is my yard.

I walk out through the garage to avoid crossing the revolting lawn and before I even reach the officer, everything begins to pour out of me. "My husband died in February," I say. "We designed this house—I'm an architect—we were both architects. We were just in the middle of building it when he died, and people warned me not to move into it. I didn't even *want* to move in without my husband. I'm trying to love it, I *do* love it, but I hate it!" I say those three words out loud for the first time. "I hate it, but we put everything into it. Our hearts. Our savings. Everything! I hate the woods. People keep telling me I should leave." I thrust the note that had been attached to the trash can toward her and she takes it gingerly. "This weird woman came to my office in Greenville and said she wanted to kill someone and she knew all sorts of things about me. I spoke to the police in Greenville, so there's a record of it. And now I get this note." I gesture toward the slip of paper. "And I have to clean the trash off my yard!" My voice shakes. I'm somewhere between fury and tears.

The officer looks up from the note, waiting patiently to be sure I'm finished.

"Have you or your daughter been physically threatened?" she asks.

I try to remember. "It *feels* like we have been," I say, "but no. No one has said 'I'm going to kill you' to me. Not specifically. But even my *father* tried to warn us not to live here. He said the Klan used to meet in the woods behind the house." I point toward the house as though we can see through it to the forest.

The officer is Black and her eyebrows rise at the mention of the Klan. "You're not aware of anyone meeting back there now, though, are you?" she asks. "Have you seen any sign of people being in the woods or—"

"No." I take in a long breath. I suddenly feel ridiculous. It was cathartic, spilling all my woes out to a stranger. "I'm sorry I called you," I say. "I mean, there's nothing for you to go on here, and there's really been no crime other than . . . this." I gesture to the trash on my lawn. "Just . . . various people telling me I picked the wrong place to live." I shake my head.

"Do you own a gun?" she asks.

I shake my head. "I don't want a gun."

"How about a dog? Maybe time to get one. A big one."

I shake my head again. I'd love to have a dog, but how would I fit one into my life right now?

The woman surveys my yard again. "Let me help you clean up the mess," she says.

"Oh no!" I say. "I'm sure you have a lot more important—"

"If I get a call, I'll have to leave," she admits. "Until then, I have gloves. Do you have a pair for yourself? And a rake?"

We each take a trash bag and work our way through the yard, raking up paper towels and wrappers and bits of food already crawling with ants. I keep choking back tears over her kindness. It's been a while since I've felt that from anyone: genuine kindness. By the time we have every scrap of trash back in the can, though, I'm smiling. We pull off our gloves and toss them in the can. Shut the lid.

"I seriously can't thank you enough . . ." I say, reaching out to shake her hand. I see the name plate on her shirt: s. JOHNS. ". . . Officer Johns."

"Sam," she says.

"What?"

"My name's Samantha Johns." Putting her hands on her hips again, she looks over the lawn, clean now, though ragged from our work. The stench of garbage is still in the air. "This was probably just kids messin' around," she says. "Maybe you built your house where they used to play ball." She reaches in her pocket and pulls out her card. "But you call me if anything else happens," she says. She looks past me toward the house. "It's one of the coolest houses I've ever seen," she says. "Try to enjoy it."

≈

That night, I find a printout of a newspaper article in one of the boxes in Jackson's office. It's a poor-quality photograph of several children, bundled up in heavy coats, standing in strange positions on what appears to be white sand. Beneath the photograph, this caption: *Children enjoy pretending to skate on Little Heaven Lake on their way to Lingman Elementary School.* The date of the paper is January 23, 1956. I remember Ellie telling me that when she was young, a path ran next to the lake, leading to an elementary school. I look harder at the photograph. I suppose what I think is sand is actually ice, and the children are trying to keep their balance.

Little Heaven Lake.

More like "Little Hell Lake," I think.

That will be my new name for it.

Chapter 29

ELLIE

Win drove me from the hospital to the school in Paul's car. I sat in the passenger seat, ready to duck if we saw any cars or trucks with whites in them. I wanted to talk to him about what he'd said about Dr. King back at the hospital, but I knew that would be a long conversation, one not to have in a hot car with a throbbing head and uncertain stomach. Instead, I kept my head very still, not even turning to look at Win when he spoke.

"Are you okay?" he asked. "You seem pretty out of it."

"I feel like I'm either going to fall asleep or throw up," I said.

"I vote for the former," he said. "And I think this isn't the day for you to canvass or move to a new house."

I shut my eyes again. Much as I enjoyed meeting new people and walking the countryside with him, he was right. I didn't have it in me today.

"I'll ask Greg if I can stay at the school another night." I glanced over at him, wincing when I turned my head. "I'm sorry to desert you one more time. I'm sure you can canvass with Rosemary again."

"Oh no!" he said. "That girl is too intense."

"What do you mean?" It was pretty clear that whatever he meant, he wasn't crazy about Rosemary, and that pleased me. I didn't like it when she looked at him with those hungry eyes of hers.

"She thinks she knows all the answers," he said. "People don't like that. They don't like some know-it-all coming in and telling them what they should think and how they should feel." He glanced at me. "You do it right, Ellie," he said. "The way you get to know people, who they are, what their story is. You take the time to do that before you get into the important stuff."

I felt my cheeks heat up. "Well, she knows a whole lot more than I do," I said, defending Rosemary against my will. "Maybe you're just seeing my ignorance coming out."

"Why're you putting yourself down?" He frowned. "I see your *human-ness* coming out. That's what people respond to, whether they're white, black, or green. You've got the gift. You get people to trust you."

I was so moved by his words that for a moment, I forgot the throbbing in my head. "Thank you," I said. I admired him. That he thought I was skilled at canvassing really moved me, and I carried that feeling inside me for the rest of the drive.

≈

Inside the school, Greg chewed me out for going to the rally, but he wasn't as harsh as I'd expected. Paul, Chip, and Jocelyn had probably gotten the brunt of his lecture and he'd run out of steam by the time he got to me. Or maybe he felt sorry for me. I was sure I looked pretty bad with my bruised head and heavy eyelids.

I went to the little art room, where my sleeping bag was still stretched out on the floor next to Jocelyn's. I lay down, feeling the medication catch up to me, and I slept straight through the night.

In the morning, I felt one thousand percent better. My bruised head was tender to the touch but had lost the debilitating achiness, and I decided not to risk taking a pain pill and ending up sick and groggy again. I ate breakfast, then loaded my things in the van, and Curry drove me deep into the countryside to find my next temporary home.

We were in the middle of nowhere when I spotted a small, neat white-washed house and I was happy when Curry came to a stop in front of it. A woman sat on the porch and it looked like she was shelling peas. Behind the house was a barn and a small pasture where two brown cows grazed. I already wished I could stay in that house for the rest of the summer instead of a couple of nights.

"This looks positively luxurious," I said.

"Don't get too comfortable." Curry tossed his cigarette butt out the window. "You know Greg's gonna move you sooner than later. And see that house down there?" He pointed a short distance down the road to a small, unpainted house with a patched roof.

"Yeah. What about it?"

"That's where Win's stayin'. You're next-door neighbors, practically."

I smiled. I liked that idea.

"He said he'd come by after lunch so y'all can do your canvassing," Curry said. He offered to carry my things up to the house, but I told him I was fine. I pulled my suitcase, book bag, and sleeping bag from the rear of the van and headed across the dirt yard to the house.

The woman was already on her feet and smiling by the time I climbed the three steps to the porch. She wore a pink apron over a pink-and-white-checked dress. "I'm Georgia Hunt," she said, taking my book bag from me and setting it on the painted porch floor. "And you must be Eleanor Hockley."

"Ellie," I said, "and I'm happy to meet you. Your house is so pretty. It looked like a painting when we were driving up."

Georgia Hunt laughed. "Did it, now," she said. She tilted her head as if examining me. "Well, how're you feelin', Miss Ellie? I saw Mr. Win this morning and he told me you fell in a ditch and hurt your head."

I was one hundred percent certain "Mr. Win" hadn't told her I'd been running from the Klan when I fell.

"I did," I said, gingerly touching the lump at my hairline. "But I feel much better now. Ready to get back to work."

"Not before I feed you somethin'," she said.

Two children, a boy and a girl, suddenly appeared around the corner of the house and raced onto the porch.

"Is this her?" the boy asked, looking up at me. "I'm Benny!" He was about seven years old with reddish-brown hair and a smattering of freckles across his nose.

"Don't be rude," Mrs. Hunt said to the boy. She said something else, but I barely heard her. My gaze was riveted on the girl. She was a couple of years older than her brother. Her hair was straightened, like her mama's, and she wore a pink bow just above her temple. She was, at least to my mind, the spitting image of Mattie Jenkins, right down to that pink bow. Her name, though, was DeeDee and she leaned against her mother's hip, staring up at me with big dark Mattie eyes.

"You gonna stay in my room with me," she said. She had small white pearls for teeth. "You gonna sleep in my closet!"

"Oh, I am?" I laughed, though I was still shaken by the resemblance. "Well, I can't wait to see your closet."

Mrs. Hunt chuckled. "We put a mattress in her closet," she explained. "That Reverend Filburn said to keep you safe, after what happened . . ." She let her voice drift off, nodding toward the children, obviously not wanting them to know about the burning cross.

"That sounds perfect," I said.

While Miss Georgia made lunch, DeeDee led me to her tiny room, which she presented as if it were a palace. Her narrow bed was neatly made, several stuffed animals resting on the pillow. She showed me everything, from her white doll to the box where she kept the bows for her hair.

DeeDee's closet was exactly the size of the twin mattress, which had been made up with sheets and a light quilt—and a ragged stuffed dog on the pillow. "In case you be scared in the dark," she said. "And this mornin', Daddy put these wood things in the window for fresh air," she said, running to one of her windows to show me the wooden dowel in the frame. I knew the dowel had been placed there because of me: DeeDee and I could enjoy some air, but no one could open the window wide enough to get into the room. That was the only sign I saw that the Hunts had any apprehension about having me there.

≈

Win and I canvassed together for the rest of the week, and the Hunts asked Greg if I could stay a few days longer. They saw no need for me to move again, and since everything had been quiet since the burning cross incident, Greg finally agreed. I was thrilled. First, there were the creature comforts of indoor plumbing and electricity, but my pleasure extended far beyond that. I loved my little closet bedroom and how Benny and DeeDee climbed onto the mattress with me so I could read to them. They were already good readers themselves and had a nice little library of books, but they loved my attention and I loved giving it to them. At night, I'd fall asleep knowing that my attachment to DeeDee wasn't exactly healthy. I had her all twisted up in my mind and my heart with Mattie and that couldn't be good, but still, I relished the comfort I felt in that house.

I felt more at ease canvassing every day, reaching out to people, talking to them about their lives, listening to their stories. I ate their pies and drank their lemonade and let their children crawl into my lap and play with my "golden hair." At different moments I felt touched or angry or amused or sad. More than anything, I felt honored when people told me the truth about their lives. Honored that they trusted me. I knew a lot of that trust had to do with the fact that I had Win by my side, but it didn't matter. It was an honor, anyway.

Thursday night, all of us freedom fighters went back to the school to make posters for the protesters to use the following night. Miss Georgia and her children joined us along with a few other families. The Hunts had been registered to vote for years, and they were every bit as invested in helping others to register as we were. We all sat at the cafeteria tables with our markers and pencils and dozens of sheets of poster board, and we wrote LET US REGISTER NOW! and LET MY PEOPLE VOTE and OPEN THE REGISTRAR'S OFFICE! and LBJ! SIGN THE BILL TODAY!

DeeDee sat next to me, coloring in the big block letters that I drew, and we were nearly finished when Greg called my name. I looked up to see him in the doorway of the cafeteria, and he was not alone. Standing next to him was my father. My whole body froze.

I forced myself to stand up, smiling at Miss Georgia across the table as if to say, *This is no problem. I'll be right back.* My fellow SCOPE workers watched me as I crossed the cafeteria, and Win caught my eye, his face blank of all expression.

"Hi, Daddy," I said, when I was close enough to speak without being overheard by anyone other than my father and Greg.

He looked at Greg without greeting me. "Where can we speak privately?" he asked. I knew he was holding in his anger. I could see it in the tight line of his jaw. I pressed my hands together. My palms were sweaty.

"Take him to the storage room," Greg said. He glanced at my father, then back at me. "Let me know if I can help."

Daddy followed me to the storage room, which held a few chairs and desks and gym equipment. Mats and basketballs and baseball bats were helter-skelter on the floor. I closed the door behind us and motioned to the chairs, but my father didn't sit down, so neither did I. I didn't want him to have all the power by standing over me.

"You need to come home," he said. "You haven't written or called or told us a thing about what you're doing. I wouldn't even know where to find you if Brenda hadn't told me. She's the only person who's heard from you. You left Reed high and dry. He's been so good to you. Treated you so well." It was a lecture, quietly delivered. I heard hurt behind the words and almost wished he'd yell at me.

"I'm sorry I haven't written," I said. "I've been so busy here and—"

"Eleanor," he interrupted me. "I don't pretend to understand why this is so important to you, but whatever the reason, it has to end. Now. Tonight."

Oh no, I thought. There was no way I was leaving, not tonight or any other night.

"Daddy, you don't under—"

"Byron saw you at a *Klan* rally," he said. "What the hell were you doing there, Ellie? What does that have to do with getting people to vote? He said everyone there knew you were with this"—he waved his hand in the vague direction of the cafeteria—"radical group. Do you know what could have happened to you?"

"We were fine, Daddy. And doesn't it bother you that Uncle Byron was with a bunch of racists?"

"Byron is a *sheriff*. He was exactly where he should have been, keeping law and order. You, on the other hand, were not thinking." His voice was getting louder. He looked around the small room as if seeing our surroundings for the first time. The old gym mats. Puckered footballs. "Look," he said firmly. "You need to just get your things. Then we can talk about this on the way—"

"I have a commitment here," I interrupted him. "I need to honor it. I'm working hard and we're making progress."

"Progress at *what*? When Johnson signs the damn bill, people can register. There's nothing you can do before then."

"Yes, there is actually," I argued. "We're educating people. Getting them to commit to registering. I'd be letting everyone down if I left."

"You're letting your mother and me down if you stay."

That hurt to hear and I bit my lip to keep from crying. "You don't understand," I said.

"Where are you sleeping?" he asked, catching me off guard. "Brenda said you're staying in a Negro home."

"I'm staying with a family on their farm," I said. It sounded idyllic, coming out of my mouth like that.

"A colored family?"

"What does it matter? What are you so afraid of, Daddy?"

I saw his nostrils flare. He moved toward me abruptly, scaring me, and for the first time in my life, I thought he might hit me. But he kept his hands at his sides, even if they were knotted in fists.

"I'm quite serious when I tell you this, Eleanor," he said. "I'm not going to physically drag you out of here, humiliating both of us, but if you don't come home with me now, *willingly*, don't bother coming home at all."

"You don't mean that," I said.

"Get your things."

I swallowed. Stiffened my spine. "Tell Mama I love her," I said. "And I love you, too." Then I walked past him, intending to return to the cafeteria, but instead I went to the little room I'd shared with Jocelyn, shut the door behind me, and stood there shaking, tears running down my cheeks. And I stayed there until I was sure my father was gone.

Chapter 30

On Friday night, Curry and Paul picked up people from the countryside and brought them to the courthouse green, and families with their own trucks and cars drove themselves. It had to be intimidating, I thought, driving into the lily-white county seat of Carlisle, but they did it. Word had gotten out, and soon we had a group of about fifty people that swelled slowly to a hundred, maybe more, and my excitement grew along with the crowd. I felt so proud of them all for coming, and so proud of us for making it happen.

Rosemary, Jocelyn, and I gave out the protest signs, but many of the people brought their own handmade signs and they seemed to know exactly what to do. We all walked in a huge circle on the courthouse green, chanting, "Open the doors; give us the vote!" Greg held a microphone attached to a finicky speaker to talk about equality and nonviolence and with every other sentence, more people joined the line of protesters.

I'd spent the afternoon canvassing with Win, but I'd spent the morning crying at Miss Georgia's kitchen table. I was still stinging from my father's visit. Miss Georgia said she saw the look in his eyes before I left the cafeteria with him and she knew he was going to try to take me home.

"You got to think what this is costin' you, honey," she said. "It's somethin' my people learned early on. We learned to weigh and measure the cost of everything. You got to decide what's worth fightin' for. When your daddy left alone, I knew you'd made your choice. I was proud of you. But it's a decision you'll have to make over and over again, not just once, and nobody's gonna blame you if you change your mind."

I thought about her words now as I marched around the courthouse green, snapping pictures with my camera and shouting for voting rights. What I was fighting for had changed in a few weeks' time. I'd joined SCOPE to honor Aunt Carol's memory as well as to ease my guilt over what happened with Mattie. Now my reasons were a whole lot bigger than just myself, and as I watched so many determined people walking around the courthouse green—some of the folks familiar from my canvassing, some of them strangers to me—my heart felt full.

A few people shouted ugly things from cars as they passed by, and a couple of hecklers paced on the sidewalk without saying a word. I found their behavior even more disturbing, but did my best to tune them out.

Greg talked about the importance of SCOPE being in Derby County and how we'd let everyone know the second the voting rights bill was signed. We'd pick them up and drive them to the courthouse, and we'd stand in line with them in solidarity, and we'd celebrate with them when they were handed their registration card. I felt happy and excited and anticipatory.

As dusk started to fall, we made a huge circle in the courtyard. Curry turned on a spotlight, but the moon was full and I could see everyone's face nearly as clear as day. We laid down our signs and held hands as we began to sing. I stood between little DeeDee and Ben. The children in the circle knew the words to many of the songs. A few nights ago, I'd taught

DeeDee and Ben the couple of songs unfamiliar to them, so that on this night, their high voices rang out loud on either side of me, touching me, making me smile with the joy I always felt in a song circle.

But the darkness seemed to give the hecklers courage. More came, as if word had spread about the protest. Although I kept my focus on our song circle, I felt the energy mounting in the street and on the sidewalk.

"Which one is the Round Hill girl?" someone shouted.

"Hey, Blondie!"

I knew they were shouting at me. I was the only blond in the courtyard. My palms started to sweat. Would they turn their shouts into action? I thought of Chaney, Goodman, and Schwerner.

I spotted a couple of policemen on the sidewalk, each with a hand wrapped around the billy club at his waist, and I hoped they were eyeing the hecklers and not us. You never could tell. We kept singing. Just kept right on going. But I was scared, for myself and for the people we'd encouraged to join us here. I wanted to escape, but there was nowhere to go. I thought of the protest on Franklin Street in Chapel Hill. How we stood our ground. I clutched DeeDee and Ben's hands. Along with everyone else, they were singing "I Love Everybody" at the top of their lungs.

An object suddenly whizzed past my head. I heard a yelp from somewhere in the circle. Then another. Then a rock broke the front window of the courthouse. The sons of bitches in the street were throwing things at us! Bottles. Rocks. Stones from the gutter. Whatever they could get their hands on, they threw. People in the circle stopped singing, let go of one another's hands, covered their heads, and the circle turned into a sea of confusion, with people running this way and that, shouting, panicked, and I thought, *Guns. What if someone has a gun?* Still clutching DeeDee and Ben's hands, I went rigid, as if I could make my skin tough enough to fight off a bullet.

"Hey Blondie," someone shouted. "Look over here!" Like a fool, I turned to look. Something whizzed past me, and DeeDee suddenly let out a scream. I looked down to see blood running over the front of her ruffled white blouse and she pressed her hand to her cheek. I let go of Ben.

"Let me see, DeeDee!" I shouted, bending close to her. "What happened?"

She was sobbing. Miss Georgia grabbed her to examine her face. There was a deep gash on her cheek below her eye, gushing blood. Completely on impulse I pulled my white sleeveless top over my head and pressed it to the little girl's cheek to try to stop the bleeding.

"Oh, sweetie," I said above the din. "I'm so sorry!" I heard the wolf whistles. Turned my back to the street as I continued pressing my bloody shirt to DeeDee's cheek.

"Here, put this on." I turned to see Win next to me in his undershirt, holding the green shirt he'd been wearing out to me. Miss Georgia took over pressing my bloody white shell to DeeDee's cheek and I slipped into Win's shirt, only taking the time to fasten two of the buttons.

I looked at Win. "We need to get her to the hospital," I said.

"Leland ran to get the truck," Miss Georgia said. She looked out at the street. It was too dark now to see how many people were out there but the bottles and missiles and shouting seemed to have stopped, or at least slowed down, and our group was dispersing, some of the people running, others calm, and a few holding steadfast with Greg, who stood by the courthouse steps singing "We Shall Overcome" over and over in his deep and steady bass. "Don't know how we gonna find him in this mess." Miss Georgia looked worriedly toward the street.

"Which way did you park?" Win asked, and she pointed to the right.

"Not more than a block," she said.

Win looked at me. "You don't see him in a few minutes, come find me."

We waited, huddled together, DeeDee crying in her mother's arms, Ben holding my hand, leaning against my leg. I glanced toward the street where darkness had descended in the last few moments, and the white men, as best as I could see, had evaporated into the night. The few people who remained in the courtyard stood close to Greg, singing with him, and the words to "We Shall Overcome" filled this little patch of downtown Carlisle. I wasn't singing. I wasn't listening. At that moment, I was only thinking about DeeDee, hit by the rock that I knew had been meant for me.

Chapter 31

─────── ≈ ───────

KAYLA

2010

I'm in my bedroom, putting on my walking shoes, when my phone rings. The number on the screen is unfamiliar, and against my better judgment, I answer it.

"Is this Kayla Carter?" the caller asks.

"Who's calling, please?" I respond, already annoyed. I left Rainie on the deck playing with one of her dolls as she waits for me to get my act together and take her for a walk through the trail behind the house. I'm trying to inoculate myself against the eerie feeling I get in the woods by spending time on that trail.

"You ordered window shades and things from us," the woman says, "and I'm afraid we've lost the order. The paperwork with all your choices and the measurements? We need you to fax your copy to us."

I sit down on the edge of the bed. "What do you mean, you lost the order?" I think of all the energy that went into figuring out how to cover my fifty windows. All the time I spent with Amanda, the designer who has always been right on top of things when I've worked with her in the past. "Are you saying my window treatments haven't even been ordered yet?" I ask, my voice rising. "You're supposed to *install* them in a couple of weeks."

"It's entirely our fault and I'm going to knock five percent off your order," she says. "So could you fax your paperwork over to us right now and I'll get it taken care of?"

I'm not sure if I'm speaking to a woman or a man. A woman, I think. She has one of those deep, androgynous voices and she sounds sort of breathless.

"I placed the order with Amanda," I say. "Can you put her on the phone?"

"Amanda's not here right now. It's not her fault, but somehow your order didn't get transferred over. I'm so sorry. Do you have your copy of the order so you can fax it to us again?"

"Somewhere," I say. "But I want to be moved up in your queue. You owe me that."

"Oh, of course," the woman agrees. "And that five percent discount, too. Fax the information over to us right now. We're putting together our order for this week and we don't want to hold yours up any longer."

"I'll have to find it," I say, getting to my feet and heading for the hallway and my office.

"That's fine. I'll keep an eye out for it." And with that, she hangs up.

I shake my head in annoyance as I walk into my office. My desk is piled high with dozens of receipts related to the house. I peek out the window to check on Rainie, but I can't see the part of the deck where she's playing. Sitting down at the desk, I start working my way through the stack of receipts.

It takes me forever to find the information. There are pages of it— measurements and prices and treatment choices for nearly every window in the house. Who am I supposed to fax the information to? I pick up the phone again and tap the woman's number, but it only rings and rings and rings. I roll my eyes. I should go tell Rainie I'll be a little while longer, but

I just want to get this done, so I sort through the pages of information until I find the shop's fax number. I jot a handwritten note to Amanda, asking
her to be sure my order goes out today. Then I set the stack of papers in
my multi-use printer and hit fax.

When I'm finished, I'm in a grisly mood—not at all in the mood for a
walk through the woods past "Little Hell Lake." I shut my eyes. Fold my
hands in my lap. *You are incredibly lucky to live in a beautiful house with enough
money to buy window coverings for fifty windows,* I remind myself. In a moment,
I feel better. Not exactly peaceful, but I'm pretty sure my blood pressure's
back in the normal range. I take the papers from the machine, set them on
the desk, and head downstairs and out to the deck.

Rainie's not there.

"Rainie?" I call. Her doll is gone too. Could she have headed down the
trail without me?

I take off at a jog, calling her name. I trip over one of the roots and
scrape my knee and my palms. Getting to my feet again, I brush my
stinging hands together to get rid of the dirt. I call her again and listen,
but hear nothing other than birdsong. I jog back to the house and head
up the south side of the trail, but there's no sign of her there either, and
I start to cry, panic mounting, as I pull my phone from the pocket of my
shorts.

I call my father, who says he'll be right over. Before he hangs up, he tells
me to call the police. "Better to overreact than not," he says, and for the
second time this week, I dial 911.

Chapter 32

———— ≈ ————

ELLIE

The doctor in the emergency room was the same man who'd been on duty when I came to the ER after the Klan rally. He remembered me. Mr. Hunt and little Benny stayed in the waiting room, while Miss Georgia and I each held one of DeeDee's hands as the doctor stitched her cheek. She was a little trouper, holding still, eyes squeezed shut. She would have a scar on her pretty face. That broke my heart and when I looked up at Miss Georgia's tear-filled eyes, I knew it broke hers as well.

We rode home in the Hunts' truck, DeeDee and her parents in the cab, Benny and me cuddled together between bales of hay in the bed. We stared up at the full silver moon and the blanket of stars above us. Benny fell asleep against me, wiped out from the events of the night.

The doctor had given DeeDee something to help her sleep, and she was already conked out by the time Miss Georgia tucked her into bed, while I read to Benny in his room. I left him asleep and was about to go to bed myself when I heard the light tap on the screen door and found Win on the front porch.

"How is she?" he whispered.

I stepped onto the porch, shutting the screen door behind me. "She's going to have a reminder of tonight for the rest of her life, I'm afraid," I said, running my finger down my own cheek.

He looked at me grimly. "In more ways than one, most likely." He nodded toward the steps. "Wanna sit?" he asked. "You can see the moon from here."

I sat down near him on the top step. "Have you ever been through anything like this?" I asked. "What happened tonight?"

He shrugged. "A few times. This was just a skirmish in comparison to some others I've been through," he said. "This was nothing really. Poor DeeDee got the brunt of it."

"I think they were aiming at me."

He nodded. "They don't like seeing white and Black together, uh-uh. That taps into something primal in them. Sets them off."

I sighed. Looked over at him. "Are we . . . the white students . . . are we just making things worse?"

"What do you think?"

I looked down the road toward the raggedy little house where he was staying. The way the moonlight settled on the roof made it look almost pretty, like old silver. "Maybe," I said. "Maybe in some ways. But . . . I think Black people need to know that a lot of us are on their side."

For the longest time, he said nothing. The sound of the cicadas rose and fell in the fields and trees.

"Why are you doing this, Ellie?" he asked finally. "It's got to be costing you. Your father last night . . ." He shook his head. "That was one angry man. I mean, he was holding it all in, I could tell, but I could still see the sparks flying off him."

"He's a really good person," I said. "He's just worried about me, that's all."

"So why?" he pressed. "Why are you here?"

I thought of Aunt Carol and how she influenced me with her passion and commitment, but I knew my love and admiration for her was not the complete answer to Win's question, and tears started running down my cheeks before I even knew they were coming. I turned my head away from Win, but he knew. The moonlight wouldn't let me hide anything tonight.

He let me cry for a while before he asked, "You going to tell me what's got you like this?"

I'd never told a soul the truth about Mattie, but suddenly I knew I had to. I couldn't carry it around with me any longer, and I trusted Win. I swallowed hard. Brushed the tears away, then smoothed my hands over the hem of my skirt, my fingers trembling.

"When I was little, we had a maid," I said, glancing at him before focusing on the way the moonlight played on the cornfield across the road. "Her name was Louise. I didn't have many friends back then. I was extremely shy and we lived—still live—on this country road not close to the other kids in my school. I wanted to fit in with the popular girls, but I just didn't. So, whenever school was closed for a holiday, Louise would bring her daughter, Mattie, with her to our house. I knew Mattie was . . . well, I was old enough to understand she was slow. Later I realized she was mildly mentally retarded, but all I knew then was that I loved playing with her. She was fun. So inventive—she didn't seem to see limitations, you know?" I looked at him and he nodded as if he understood. "And she was always so positive. It was like she didn't know she was different." My throat tightened, but I smiled at the memory of Mattie trying to learn to ride my bike on our dirt road. Mattie trying to run through the kudzu. "I really loved her." I glanced at Win again. His face was unreadable. "There was a lake by our house," I said. "Little Heaven Lake. Mattie and I would fish in it and catch absolutely nothing." I chuckled to myself. "I don't think there was anything in that lake to catch. But it was just fun, being with her. She didn't care that I was shy." I knotted my hands together in my lap until they hurt. "So, sometimes in winter, the lake would freeze. Not often. I haven't seen it frozen in years, but that year—I was eleven—it froze, and some kids would skate on it. Just on their shoes. Nobody had skates in Round Hill. This was during the Christmas holiday, so Mattie came to our house with Louise, and she and I went to the lake to play, and these two very popular girls from my school were there. They looked down their noses at Mattie and me but then they called me over to skate with them. To hold hands and spin around, that sort of thing. I was so thrilled they asked me. I wanted to ask Mattie to join us, but one of them said flat out, 'Don't call that . . . colored retard over here.' " Of course, she hadn't said "colored" and I was sure Win knew I was cleaning up the language for his sake. "I hate myself for this, Win," I said. "I hate myself for every part of it. And I've never told anyone before and I don't know why I'm telling you. I just—"

"Go on," he said.

"The girls . . . the popular girls wanted to go to one of their houses and they asked me to come. I couldn't believe they were actually inviting me. But I looked over at Mattie and she was skating toward the thin ice and I called to her to say I was leaving for a little while and to stay on the thicker ice, and she nodded, and then I just left with the girls. We walked toward one of their houses, but I really couldn't hear a thing they were saying because my mind was back on Mattie. I kept picturing how she must've felt, watching me walk off with other friends when I'd come to the lake with her. And I wasn't sure she understood what I meant about stay- ing off the thin ice. So finally I stopped walking and I told the girls I had to go home. I ran back down the path to the lake and Mattie had fallen in the water. She was struggling to get out. She was already too exhausted to even call to me, and she grabbed on to the ice but it kept breaking. I laid down on the ice to try to pull her out. She was crying . . . I'd never seen her cry before . . . and her wet clothes were dragging her deeper.

Then the ice gave out under me, too. I fell in. I grabbed on to Mattie and tried to get both of us to the bank. There was this old farmer who lived near the lake and he heard me shouting and came running. He saw me in the water, trying to pull Mattie to safety. He had a hoe and I was able to grab on and he pulled me out, but Mattie was under the water by then. She was gone." My breath caught in my throat. Win was quiet. Waiting. "And the worst part," I said, twisting my hands together in my lap, "was that the farmer told everyone how I risked my life trying to save this little colored girl. And it was written up in the paper. My mother still has the article. They called me the 'heroic Round Hill girl.'"

I looked up at the sky, remembering how my mother cried when they gave Louise the news. "Louise left us soon after," I said. "She was destroyed. She hugged me and kissed me and thanked me for trying to save her daughter."

My tears started again and I rubbed them away with my hands. I wished Win would say something. Touch me. Rest a hand on my shoulder. Absolve me. But he was still as stone next to me. I looked over at him, wiping my eyes with my fingers. "It wasn't really a conscious decision," I said, "SCOPE. I wasn't sitting around looking for an opportunity to do something good, but when I heard about it, I . . . it felt like a way to . . ."

"Atone." He finished my sentence for me.

"Yes, though it's become much more than that to me," she said. "I see the . . . *injustice*. I want to be part of fixing it."

"Got to be hard to live with that guilt," he said.

I nodded. I liked that he didn't try to take that guilt away.

"You've never told anyone?"

I shook my head. "No."

"Why're you telling me?" he asked.

Why was I? "I don't know. I'm sorry. I just burdened you with a—"

"No. Hush." He knocked my shoulder lightly with his. "If I can't handle that burden then I'm not much of a man. Or a friend."

I looked at him. He wasn't going to touch me. He wouldn't make that move himself. I reached over to lay my hand on his where it rested on his knee.

He lifted my hand and moved it back to my own thigh. I felt my cheeks grow hot.

"Listen, Ellie," he said with a sigh. "I care about you. And I think . . . I know . . . you care about me. But we can't let it be any more than that."

"Oh, I know," I said, locking my hands together in my lap. I felt my cheeks color and was glad the moon was no brighter than it was. "I don't think of you as more than a friend." Did I? Was I lying?

"I think you're really pretty," he said. "I think you're beautiful, actually. You're smart and you have a big heart. I watch you when we canvass, how you're genuinely interested in the people and their problems. And you don't give up on SCOPE even when you're scared or have to sleep in a bed with a dozen little kids or your father tries to drag you away. I admire you." He looked away as though he might have said too much. After a moment, he turned back to me. "I don't have a problem with Black and white mixing in general, but it's not right for me," he said. "Not how I feel about this . . . *path* . . . this *Black* path . . . I have to be on right now. My people have to stick together. Do you understand what I'm saying?"

Honestly, he was overwhelming me with so many words. I could barely sort one word from another. He thought I was beautiful? He admired me? I did understand, though. What he said fit who he was. I realized in that moment that I'd been hoping, deep down where I didn't understand my own feelings, for something more from him. I should have known better.

"Yes, I understand," I said.

For a moment, neither of us spoke. We sat facing the cornfield. The man in the moon seemed like a benevolent third person, sprinkling the tops of the cornstalks with light.

"I'm glad you told me about Mattie," Win said finally. "Glad you felt like you could. It helps me understand that . . . darkness I see in you sometimes."

"I didn't know I had a darkness," I said.

He smiled. "Yes, you do. It's a mile wide and a mile long." He got to his feet, readying to leave. "What happened with your friend Mattie might have been your first reason for joining SCOPE," he said, "but you've done enough work now. You've repaid that debt. Now you're staying because you're a good person. Give yourself some credit, Ellie, okay? I'll see you tomorrow."

I sat on the steps, watching him walk down the road to the small, run-down cabin where I could see a kerosene lantern flickering in the window, maybe to guide him home. Then I got to my feet and tiptoed my way through the dark house to DeeDee's bedroom, where the little girl remained in her deep, drugged, sleep.

I didn't realize I was still wearing Win's shirt until I began to undress for bed. It was green and short-sleeved. Soft. It smelled of soap and sweat. I decided to sleep in it. I slipped off my skirt. My loafers. I made sure the wooden dowels were in place at the windows. Then I lay down on the mattress in the closet and the evening came back to me in a rush. I'd felt such joy at the beginning of the protest. So many people showed up. So much enthusiasm. Such passion. The song circle was wonderful. When the heckling started, it had seemed so mild at first . . . until it wasn't.

But what I would remember best about the night was talking to Win on the porch. Telling him everything I'd carried around with me for the past nine years.

Two hours later, I was still awake. I barely knew what I was doing when I got up. I put my skirt back on. My shoes. I left the house half in a daze. The full moon lit up the rutted road. The cornstalks on my left, the whis-kery weeds on my right. I walked like I knew the path well, like I'd made this walk a dozen times before. I arrived at the little unpainted house, the old wood silver in the moonlight. I knew which window was his, but I had no intention of knocking on the glass. No intention of waking him. I low-ered myself into the spiky weeds beneath his window, my back pressed against the side of the house, my arms wrapped around my shins. I leaned my head against the old wood and felt his nearness. When I shut my eyes, a sense of longing filled my chest. I let it come, let it go. This was enough, I thought. This closeness. I didn't dare want anything more.

Chapter 33

―――― ≈ ――――

KAYLA

My daughter is missing.

Samantha Johns shows up at the same time as my father, this time with siren blaring. I can't remember her name to introduce her, even though it's been barely a week since she helped me clean the trash off my lawn. We stand in the driveway next to that lawn now. On the street behind us, the sound of hammers and saws fills the air.

Daddy goes into the house to check every nook and cranny, and Officer Johns—Sam—asks me questions. Where was she? How long was she out of my sight? I feel like we need to be moving. We need to *do* something.

I see Ellie and Brenda coming quickly up Shadow Ridge Lane toward us. Ellie's at a jog, Brenda trailing a few feet behind. "What's wrong?" Ellie calls out before she reaches us.

"Rainie's missing," I say. "My daughter."

"Oh no," Brenda says. She's winded from rushing up the street, her face

flushed and glistening with sweat. The longer side of her angled haircut
is pasted to her damp cheek.

"What happened?" Ellie asks.

"We need to start looking for her!" I say. All the questions make me
feel like a terrible mother. I *am* a terrible mother. I left her out there alone
because I was more worried about my damn window treatments.

"What happened to your hands?" Sam asks.

I look down at my hands. My palms are dirty and beaded with blood.
"I ran up the trail to try to find her and tripped."

Sam lifts her phone and makes a call, relaying information about her
location and Rainie's disappearance. Daddy comes out of the house then.
I look at him hopefully, although I know he couldn't have found her inside, and he shakes his head. Then he notices Ellie, and his steps slow.

"I didn't know your father was here," Ellie says in a whisper.

"Hi, Brenda, Ellie," my father says formally when he reaches us. "Good
to see you."

"Hey, Reed," Brenda says, but Ellie looks away without a word.

"Let's go check out that trail," Sam says, hooking her phone back to
her belt. She looks toward the vans that line the street and the unfinished
houses full of carpenters and handymen. "We need to speak to some of
these guys, too."

"A lot of them only speak Spanish," Ellie says. "I'm fluent. Want me to
see if they know anything?"

"Great." Sam and Ellie quickly exchange names and phone numbers,
then Sam looks at me as Ellie heads back down the street. "Where is the
trail?" she asks.

"This way," Daddy says. He's already walking toward the side of the
house, heading for the deck and the trail. "We should split up," he calls to
us over his shoulder. "I'll take the path on the right."

"It's a circular trail," I explain to Sam.

She nods toward Brenda. "You go with him," she says, pointing to where my father disappeared around the corner of the house. She looks at me. "You come with me."

Sam walks the trail much more slowly than I think we should, but I can tell that she's searching the woods and undergrowth with an eagle eye. "She might have gotten lost out here," she says. "Woods are disorienting, and this trail has some spots that might be confusing to a small child."

"You're right," I say, and I begin doing what she's doing—searching the woods as we walk, not just the trail itself. In the distance I hear my father and Brenda calling for Rainie, an echo to my own calls.

We finally reach "Little Hell Lake" and I change my call to a shout, my panic growing as I look across the tangled brush toward that murky water. But there's no sign of Rainie. My phone rings. I stop walking and quickly pull it from my pocket, answering it without even looking at who the call is from.

"Kayla?" a woman asks.

"Yes?"

"This is Amanda from the Curtain Shop. I just—"

"I can't talk right now, Amanda. I'll—"

"I'm just confused about these faxes we got from you," she says. "Why did you send them?"

"Someone there said you lost my orders and I had to resend them. But I can't talk—"

"I'm the only person who makes customer calls," she says, "and your order is well underway. There was no need to—"

"You're kidding." I stand stock-still. "Are you sure?"

"Yes. Who did you speak with?"

"I'll call you later," I say, hanging up. I look at Sam. "I think someone called me earlier just to keep me doing busywork so she had time to take Rainie." I hear the fear in my voice. I feel so helpless.

Sam's phone rings before I even finish my sentence. She looks at the screen. "Your friend," she says, pressing the speaker button so I'll be able to hear. "Anything?" she asks Ellie.

"One of the workers saw a woman walking through the woods near the side of the house a while ago," Ellie says. "He said it wasn't the woman who lives there. It wasn't Kayla. He wasn't very close to her, but he's pretty sure she was talking on a phone."

I lean close to the Sam's phone. "Did he say what she looked like?" I ask.

"Yes," Ellie says. "He said that's why he noticed her. She had long bright red hair."

"Oh no," I say, but at that very moment I hear my father's voice.

"She's here!" he shouts.

"We've got her!" Brenda calls.

"They have her!" I shout toward the phone, then start running down the rest of the trail, through the creepy circle, to the tree house, Sam close on my heels. I can see motion inside the tree house and I hear the distinctive crying of my little girl. I circle the tree to find my father carefully lowering himself down the steps, Rainie in his arms. I step forward, reaching for my daughter, a wide smile on my face. I don't want Rainie to see me looking as frantic as I feel.

"The lady went away," Rainie whimpers, once she's in my arms. Her lower lip trembles. Her face is dirty and tear-streaked.

"What lady, honey?" I ask.

"She had funny glasses." She rests her head against my shoulder. She's too big for me to hold this way, but I'm not ready to let her go.

"Could you see yourself in her glasses?" I ask, and I feel her nod against my shoulder. I look at Sam. She's writing something on a pad.

I set Rainie down and squat in front of her. She takes a fistful of my hair in her hand as if to keep me there.

"Did the lady help you climb up into the tree house?" I ask.

She nods. "I wanted to go up there and look at the whole world. Like we did that day," she says. "But then she walked away." She points down the trail. "I yelled for her to come back but she didn't even turn around. I tried to get down but I couldn't." That trembling lip again, and I stand up, leaning forward to hug her. *Did I nearly lose someone else I love in a fall? I really want to get my hands on that bitch.*

"You were right to just stay put, sweetheart," Daddy says. "You knew we'd find you."

Sam has been taking this all in. Now she crouches in front of Rainie. "Hi, Rainie," she says. "My name is Sam and I've been helping your family look for you. Can you tell me something? What did the lady say to you when you first saw her? You were on the deck, right?"

She nods. "She said she was Mama's friend." She looks up at me. "She said you were busy and you asked her to take me for a walk and soon you'd come to be with us."

Bitch bitch bitch. And how many zillions of times had I talked to Rainie about not going anyplace with a stranger? Not enough times, obviously. I catch my father's eye. His brows are raised in a question. *Did you actually ask someone to take her for a walk?* I give him an *are you crazy* look in response.

Sam wants to question her a little longer, but Rainie has to go potty and we head back to the house. She clutches my hand, and I don't want to let go of her any more than she wants to let go of me.

"It's so damn spooky back here," Brenda says, and I want to slug her. I don't want Rainie to fear these woods. Her backyard. Brenda's right, though. It's undeniable. You'd never know it's July when you're deep in these woods. It's sticky hot, true, but so dark. So creepily dark.

Yet at that moment, I don't care. The only thing in the world that matters to me right now is that my daughter is safe.

Chapter 34

ELLIE

1965

In the morning, the Hunts told me they'd decided I'd better move to another house. "We love having you here and the kids love you," Miss Georgia said, "but we just can't take the risk. DeeDee's gonna need a lot of time for healing and we think it's best—"

"I agree," I said quickly. "I don't want to put any of y'all at more of a risk than I already have."

DeeDee was still asleep and I wished I could see her one more time before I left. I wanted to give her a hug and tell her what a brave girl she was, but there was no time. I packed my things, and Curry and Win pulled up out front as soon as I walked onto the porch. We were supposed to canvass an area about five miles west of where we were today. Instead, Curry was going to drive us back to the school so I could store my things and let Greg find me a new home.

I sat in the back of the van, my gaze on Win's profile. I felt different being so close to him after telling him everything the night before. He seemed to be his usual serious self, reserved and unflustered by the change in our plans. He kept his eyes straight ahead on the road as if he were doing the driving himself.

"Y'all have a meeting tonight," Curry said as we headed to the school. "Greg wants to talk about the protest. How y'all can change it up for next week."

"He thinks we should have another one?" I asked, surprised.

"Oh yeah." Curry caught my eye in the rearview mirror. "You ain't gonna let 'em win, are you?"

"Curry's right," Win finally turned to look at me. "He—"

"Truck!" Curry said, and I dropped to the floor behind the front seats. It was second nature now, hiding from white people, and I'd come to understand why it was best for me to ride in the back seat.

I practically held my breath until Win said, "He's gone," and I returned to my seat with a sigh.

"So what were you saying about a protest?" I asked.

"If we stop now, we're just telling them that they can scare us off with violence," Win said.

Well, maybe they can, I thought. "I don't want to see anyone else get hurt," I said.

"Nobody does," Win said, as Curry pulled into the parking lot of the school.

The guys helped me carry my things inside. Jocelyn looked up from the desk where she was typing.

"My occasional roommate!" she said with a smile. "You back again?"

"Looks like it," I said.

"Well, toss your stuff in 'our' room," she said, with air quotes around the word "our."

I was starting toward the little art room when Greg walked in from the cafeteria. He stopped short when he saw me. "You need a new place," he guessed, and I nodded. "How's the little girl doing?"

"She was still sleeping when I left. I think she'll be fine, but I know whoever threw that rock was aiming at me and I don't want her or anyone else to get hurt because they're around me. So"—I shrugged—"time to move on."

Greg looked toward the ceiling, thinking. "I know of a couple of possibilities for you," he said. "For now, drop your things off and head on back out. It's Saturday. You can catch some of the men at home. Did Curry tell you we'll have a meeting tonight before I leave for Turner's Bend?"

I nodded. "I'll be here," I said.

≈

Curry drove Win and me out to a dirt road lined with small unpainted shacks. Children were everywhere, clustered in the yards and tossing a ball in the road. They rushed Win and me when we got out of the van. For the children in this part of Derby County—*any* part of Derby County—it was a shock to see a Black man and white woman together, and they knew we were there for something important. We let them tag along with us. They knew everyone on the road and I got a kick out of their sense of self-importance as they introduced us to their parents and aunts and uncles and neighbors. They were a big help, getting us in a lot of doors that would have been closed to us otherwise.

Neither Win nor I mentioned our conversation from the night before. I didn't know if it had changed his feelings about me, but it had definitely changed mine about him. I could barely take my eyes off him, stealing glances at him when we walked down the rutted road. Trying to make him laugh when we talked to people we hoped to register. By the end of the day, we had fifteen solid commitments, and twenty people said they'd come to the protest on Friday night. Many of the folks we talked to, though, nodded toward their children when they turned us down about the protest. "Who gonna look after them when we in jail, huh?" they asked. A very reasonable argument.

≈

We returned to the school at four and Jocelyn handed me my mail: two big Kodak envelopes containing my developed pictures and two letters from Round Hill. I went to the art room and sat on my sleeping bag, my back against the wall. I smiled as I looked through the pictures, then put them in a cigar box I'd found in the art room closet for safekeeping.

The first letter was from my mother, telling me that I'd humiliated my father by not coming home with him and that they were both very hurt by my behavior. *I believe you intentionally misrepresented what you're doing and how you're living,* she wrote. *Right now when I think of you, it's not with love. It's with disgust.*

"I don't care," I muttered to myself as I folded her letter and stuck it back in the envelope. The twisty feeling in my chest, though, told me otherwise. How could I *not* care? Who wouldn't be hurt by such hateful words from her own mother? I tried to shake off the sadness as I opened Brenda's letter.

Brenda began with her usual happy talk about the baby and Garner, but then she got to the subject of me. *I hoped you'd get tired of whatever it is you're doing in Flint and come home,* she wrote. *Byron Parks told us he saw you at a KKK rally. I told him he had to be wrong, but he swore up and down he saw you there. Did you go? Are you that crazy? Garner says what you're doing is ridiculous, that the register's office or whatever it's called isn't even open and you're wasting your time and trashing your good name by spending the summer with a bunch of Negroes for no good reason. Please come home. I need you and Reed sure as heck needs you. It's so mean that you haven't written to him.*

It *was* mean. Why hadn't I written to him? Of course, he hadn't written to me either, but I was the one who'd made the decision to go away. I was the one who owed an explanation. But I didn't know what to say to him. We'd been close for so long. Why was I throwing it all away? I thought of Win in the other room, reading one of his political books. Nothing could ever happen between Win and me, for a million reasons. He could only be my friend. But Reed . . . Reed could be my husband. The father of my children. If that was what I wanted. Right now, though, it wasn't.

Right now, I wanted to discuss those political books with Win. I wanted to stand shoulder-to-shoulder with him, fighting for voting rights. For fair and equal treatment of everyone. Right now, I couldn't see a place in my life for drive-in dates and ice-cream sundaes and long phone calls about nothing of consequence.

I heard the hum of voices coming from the main room and knew that Greg would soon start the meeting. I felt pretty down. The bitter letters from two people I loved had taken a toll on me. But once I walked into the large room filled with my new friends, my spirits lifted. Greg sat on the edge of his desk. He smiled at me. Nodded toward an empty chair. I sat down, and as Greg talked about the protest and what we could do differently next time, I looked around the room. There were twelve of us SCOPE freedom fighters and several local teenagers who were now canvassing with us. My white friends' skin had grown darker from the sun in the past couple of weeks. Had mine? I looked down at my forearms. Yes, definitely. Walking five or ten miles a day in the North Carolina sun could do that to you. And we were all so grungy! We'd started out looking neat and scrubbed and now everyone's legs and feet were filthy in their broken sandals or sneakers.

After the meeting, Greg packed up to go home to Turner's Bend. Before he left, he reminded us we were representatives of SCOPE and suggested we spend the evening reading from our books about racial justice. A few of the SCOPE workers left as well, heading to the store for cigarettes and snacks, but many of us stayed, wanting each other's company. We talked about how the week had been, how we were being received in our neighborhoods, that sort of thing. Finally, around nine o'clock when people who were staying in the neighborhoods stood up and stretched, ready to figure out how to get home, Curry got to his feet.

"Y'all wanna have some fun tonight?" he asked, an impish expression on his face.

The next thing I knew, six of us had piled into the van and Curry was driving us who-knew-where. It took about half an hour and we drove through pouring rain, the night black outside the van windows. It was hard to believe that only the night before, the moon had lit up the earth like daylight.

Curry pulled into a tiny lot in front of a small brick building we could barely see because of the rain, but in spite of the pounding on the van's roof, I could hear music. A couple was necking under the building's awning. We darted from the van and ran for the front door and by the time we got inside we were soaking wet and laughing. All of us. Even Win. Seeing him laugh was such a rarity. I wished he would do it more often.

My wet hair dripped down my face and I brushed it back with my hands, catching the surprised look of a girl standing near the jukebox. That's when it hit me: This was a Black club. Jocelyn, Paul, Chip, and myself were the only white people in the place. I felt momentarily uneasy, but I knew Curry wouldn't have brought us here if it wasn't okay. We were also probably the youngest people. This felt like a very adult club. It smelled of beer and sweat. The music was loud. At that moment, a song I'd heard a couple of times on Win's transistor—"Shotgun"—was playing on the jukebox. Couples danced to the driving beat, grinding against each other in a way that seemed shocking, a little dangerous. I wanted to stare at them. My whole body felt hot, watching them. I wanted to feel what they were feeling.

Before I'd even caught my breath from running inside, two men asked me to dance. Both times, Win stopped them with "They're with me," encompassing both Jocelyn and myself and clearly meaning *Hands off.* I was grateful. I really didn't know how to behave in a club like this, white or Black. I rarely went to the bars in Chapel Hill. I had no interest in the frat parties. All I did at school was study or hang out with Brenda, looking forward to our time with Reed and Garner.

Curry had disappeared but he soon returned with bottles of beer for Jocelyn and me. The air in the club was steaming hot and the chill of the beer felt good in my throat. It was better than any beer I'd tasted before. I felt as though, somehow, this club was heightening all my senses.

Paul started dancing with a girl, and while I drank the last of my beer, Jocelyn tugged Chip onto the cramped dance floor. Curry disappeared with a woman he obviously knew. Win gave me his usual serious look and nodded toward the dance floor as the Four Tops started singing "I Can't Help Myself." He took off his glasses and slipped them in his shirt pocket as I set my bottle on a windowsill and followed him onto the floor. We danced without touching. I kept my eyes on his face and danced the way we did at Carolina—the jerk, the mashed potato, the twist. I could already feel the beer loosening me up. Win had his own style. He never once looked at me. More at the floor, the windows, the ceiling. Never looked into my eyes. The song stopped, but another started right away and we kept on dancing. Then a slow one, very familiar to me, Dionne Warwick's haunting "Walk On By." I didn't have the chance to wonder if he was going to lead me off the dance floor so he wouldn't have to touch me. I remembered what he said the night before about interracial relationships, how it was wrong for him. But he reached for my hand, drew me against him. Held me close, closer than he had to, his chin against my temple. He sang a few lines of the song and I felt his lips move against my skin. I remembered the night before, sitting outside the house where he was staying, feeling that closeness. Needing it. I needed it now, and I tightened my own arm around his back to let him know. He drew his head away, but not his body. Looking down at me, finally really looking at me, I thought he had a question in his eyes. I didn't know what he was asking but it almost didn't matter. I knew my answer was yes.

We didn't let go of each other all evening. I was in love, yes, but I wasn't a fool. I was a virgin with no intention of ruining my life with a pregnancy. But there were other ways I could ruin my life. I had to keep reminding myself that the man I had my arms around would not be welcome anywhere in my world. Not anywhere.

We didn't talk. Sometimes words weren't needed, though I still craved them. I drank another beer as we danced. What was going through his head? Did he feel what I felt—the connection that had built between us the last couple of weeks, the intensifying of it last night on the Hunts' porch? And now this physical connection. This *sensuous* connection. He touched me even during the fast songs now. His hand slipping around my waist, over my hip, over my belly. And I touched him back, feeling brazen, ignoring everyone else in the club. If people were watching us, I didn't know or care. Sweat poured down my neck and slipped between my breasts. For the first time in my life, I felt more animal than woman and I relished the feeling.

"Baby, I Need Your Loving" was playing when he pressed his lips close to my ear and said, "We need to get out of here."

I nodded as I pulled away from him, and then I saw, clear as day across the room, Rosemary. Her gaze was on us. Her eyes locked with mine and I quickly looked away. "Let's go," I said, turning my back to her.

We left the building and I thought we would become like the couple we'd seen out front, necking beneath the awning. But Win held my hand as we ran through the rain across the small, jammed parking lot to the van. He pulled open the side door, helped me onto the rear bench seat, then followed me once he'd shut the door behind him.

I expected to be ravished. I *wanted* to be ravished. But I should have known that was not Win's style. He was too cautious. For a moment, I worried the magic I'd felt inside the steamy little club would disappear. But no. He put his hand on my throat, his touch gentle yet assertive, and leaned over to kiss me, his other hand buried deep in my wet hair. He unbuttoned the top button on my blouse. Then the next. I felt the heat of his fingers against my skin. I wanted to lie back on the seat and have him undress me in a way Reed never had. Reed, always considerate. Always cautious. But Win abruptly drew away from me.

"We can't do this," he said. "Not here. Not now. It's a mistake. A mistake in too many ways."

"I love you," I said.

He stared at me. Kissed me, lightly. "I love you, too, Ellie," he said, "but it's no good. I promised myself I'd never let this happen. It's impossible. It's too dangerous. You know that."

"No," I said stubbornly. "Please don't let it be impossible."

"Sit up," he said, and I did.

He buttoned the top buttons of my blouse. "Don't cry," he said.

I touched my cheeks. I hadn't realized I was crying.

"Win," I said. "Rosemary was in there."

He stared at me without speaking. The shadow of the raindrops on the van windows created streaks down his cheeks. I traced one of them with my fingertip.

"Did she see us?" he asked.

"Yes."

"Shit!" he said, and I thought he was reacting to Rosemary seeing us, but then the rain on the van windows bloomed red, and the whole world outside swirled with the color. I knew what caused the light before I turned to look: two police cars.

"Duck down!" Win said. "I don't think they're here for us. They can't be."

But they were. Not just for Win and me, but for all us freedom fighters. We watched as two officers, billy clubs at the ready, stormed through the front door.

"Go, Win!" I said. "Get out of here before they find you with me!"

He seemed frozen, but after a moment he opened one of the doors and ran through the parking lot into the road. I knew we were far from the house where he was staying and I had no idea how he would be able to get there—most likely, he didn't even know what direction to head in—but at least he was safe.

In a moment the front door of the club banged open and I watched as my friends—Curry, Paul, Chip, and Jocelyn—were marched toward one of the police cars. Another officer walked toward the van and pulled open the door.

"Who you with in here?" he asked.

"No one," I said. "I didn't feel well. Just came in here to take a nap."

"Yeah, right," he said. He stepped into the van and checked any place someone might be hiding. Looked at me again. "Think you're a smarty-pants, don'cha," he said.

"No, sir. I'm just—"

"Shut up and follow me."

I thought of going limp, but I didn't have the heart for it. I didn't feel militant in that moment. I felt frightened. For myself. For my friends. And especially for Win. I followed the officer to the cars.

Chapter 35

KAYLA

2010

Daddy agrees to keep Rainie a couple of hours longer on Wednesday so I can do Ellie a favor: drive her mother to the doctor. Ellie has to take Buddy to his doctor at the same time, and Brenda has a dental emergency. I'm so grateful for Ellie's help in finding Rainie yesterday that I would do anything for her.

Mrs. Hockley is not the dementia-addled woman I'd thought her to be. Yes, I have to help her down the porch steps and the walkway and into my car, and I have to buckle her seat belt for her, but she proceeds to give me accurate directions to her doctor's office. She seems to have her wits about her.

"And call me Miss Pat," she says, after the third time I call her Mrs. Hockley. It's not exactly a friendly invitation. More of a command. I think Miss Pat had been a force to be reckoned with in her youth.

"Your hair looks very nice today," I say, remembering how it looked—wispy and tired—when I first met her in the living room of the Hockley house. Today it's smoother and a bit fuller.

"It's my going-out wig," she says, startling me with how easily she admits to wearing faux hair.

"Seriously? I wouldn't have known." I'm being honest.

"Brenda got it for me. She got me another one but I look like a dandelion in it."

"Well, this one is really nice."

"So you're Reed's daughter?" she asks after a pause.

"I am."

She shakes her head. "Ellie missed the boat there." She brushes a bit of lint from her navy-blue skirt. "Your daddy was a fine boy and she was a stupid girl to let him get away."

"Oh, well," I say lightly. "It's hard to know what someone's relationship is like from the outside." I don't bother to mention that I wouldn't be here if Ellie and my father had stayed together.

"I don't even know that girl." She turns her head away from me to stare out the window.

"You mean Ellie?" I ask.

"Who else?" she says. "I don't know her. She left at twenty and came back at sixty-five. What loving daughter does that?"

Oh boy, I think. I have a therapy session on my hands here.

"I guess it was hard to have her so far away for so long," I say.

"It was like not having a daughter at all," she says. "But frankly, there were many days I was glad of it."

"Why is that?" I feel nosy, but I'm curious.

"That girl," she says with disdain, as though those two words alone answer my question.

We're both quiet for a moment. I'm waiting for more. And it comes.

"She brought us nothing but trouble and shame," she says. "She put other people—perfect strangers—ahead of her own family."

"She told me she was—and still is—a civil rights worker," I say.

Miss Pat makes a dismissive motion with her arm. "She turned her back on us," she says. "Cost us our friends. It wasn't like it is today. You couldn't imagine a Black president back then. Hard to imagine it *now*, frankly. No one approved of what she did. I could never get back my standing in Round Hill. She didn't care who she hurt. I don't know how she turned out so selfish."

I'm having a bit of trouble following her. "Do you love her?" I ask the question, flat out.

"I love *Brenda*," she says with great certainty and a nod of her head. "Brenda's been a daughter to me. She visited me at least once a week while I was in that assisted-living cesspool Buddy stuck me in. And I do love my son," she adds hurriedly, turning toward me. "Let me assure you of that. He had no choice but to put me someplace, what with his own illness. But Brenda is a real saint. She's my true daughter."

"I'm glad she's been there for you," I say.

We fall silent for a moment. She tells me to turn right, then left. It's a shortcut, she says. I think about the night before, when I found some newspaper articles in a file marked "Hockley Street" in Jackson's office. There was a lighthearted article about Hockley Street's invasive kudzu, including a photograph of what looked like an almost perfect topiary of a dinosaur. There was an article about nineteen-year-old Buddy Hockley opening his car shop. There was one about Brenda's husband's death, how he was brought to the hospital by Brenda, Sheriff Byron Parks, and Danny Hockley, who must have been Ellie's father.

The final article was about Ellie joining the civil rights organization SCOPE. It's the last few lines of that article that stick in my mind as I listen to Miss Pat malign her daughter. *Eleanor Hockley had a long history of good deeds in Round Hill*, the article said. *When she was eleven, she nearly lost her own life when she tried unsuccessfully to save a Negro girl who'd fallen into Little Heaven Lake.*

The imagery was horrible. I pictured the little girl being sucked under that murky black water. I'm going to get my property fenced off from that lake if it's the last thing I do.

"Last night, I came across some newspaper articles my husband must have found as he researched Hockley Street," I say. "I saw—"

"Why would your husband do that?" she asks. "Research Hockley Street?"

"Because we were moving there," I say. Maybe she hasn't made the connection that I'm her new neighbor. "I live in that house at the end of—"

"Oh, right." She shakes her head. "I hoped I'd be dead by the time all that building nonsense started."

"It's very noisy, I know."

"Tell your husband to come talk to me," she says. "I can tell him anything he wants to know about Hockley Street, as well as some things he'd probably rather *not* know."

My chest squeezes tight. How I wish I could send Jackson down the street to talk to her! "I'm afraid I lost my husband in an accident earlier this year," I say.

"Oh. Right. Sorry." She scratches her temple. "Ellie said something about that. How old was he?"

"Twenty-nine."

"Mine made it to forty-five," she says.

"Oh, that's still young," I say. "I'm sorry."

"I blame that on Eleanor, too," she says, and I have the feeling Ellie couldn't win with this woman, no matter what she did. "She dragged our family down," she says, smacking her palm on her thigh. "You don't put other people first. You put your *family* first. It's her fault Brenda got widowed at twenty years old and lost her baby. It's her fault her father—my Danny—killed himself. That's not a girl who loves her family. That's a girl who loves herself."

I'm completely in the dark. "I didn't know that's how your husband died," I say.

"Went out in those woods right where your house is now and shot himself in the head. Took us two days to find him."

Oh no. My hands grow damp on the steering wheel. Why hadn't anyone told me? Had Jackson known? Did he keep that from me, too? That, and the little girl who drowned in the lake?

"My daughter never cared about me," Miss Pat prattles on. "Why should I care about her?" She points to the small parking lot in front of a brick medical building. "This is it," she says. "Just turn in here."

≈

When I bring Miss Pat home an hour and a half later, Brenda greets us on the porch.

"Thank you, thank you!" she calls to me as I help Miss Pat up the porch steps. "You saved us."

"It was no trouble," I say as the old woman and I reach the top step. I raise my voice as Mrs. Hockley reaches for the handle of the screen door. "It was nice chatting with you, Miss Pat!"

She waves without turning around, and Brenda helps her open the door. "You go on in, Mama, and I'll be in in a minute," she says. Once she sees the old woman safely inside, she turns to me.

"Did she talk to you?" she asks. It seems like an odd question.

"A bit," I say. "She told me how much she adores you. I guess you've been the daughter to her that Ellie couldn't be, since she lived so far away."

"Well, I adore her, too," she says. "My mother died when I was thirty and Miss Pat moved right in to fill that spot for me."

"How did you make out at the dentist?" I ask, to be polite. Her tooth is not what's on my mind.

"Need a crown, but at least my tooth's no longer killing me." She smooths the shorter side of her white hair behind her ear. "Is your little girl doing okay?" she asks. "I hope she's not too traumatized by the other day. That was so weird."

"*I'm* the one who's traumatized by the other day," I say. "I'm still mad at myself for not keeping a better eye on her."

"Well, you don't expect strangers to be wandering around a neighborhood like this one, do you."

"Miss Pat mentioned something disturbing," I say, changing the subject. "Did Ellie's father kill himself in the woods by my house?"

"Yeah, he did." She looks down the street where my house waits for me. I have the unnerving sense that it's alive. That it's mocking me. "That was a horrible time," Brenda continues. "And Ellie didn't even come home for the funeral."

"Wow." I try to imagine not caring enough about my father to stay away from his funeral. It's impossible. "That's so sad," I say. "He must have been horribly depressed."

Brenda looks toward my house again, then turns back to me. "Do you believe in ghosts?" she asks, head cocked as if she's truly curious about my answer.

"Not at all."

"Well, that's good," she says. "Because that lot your house is on . . ." She shakes her head. "Between Mr. Danny shooting his head off, and that little Black girl who drowned . . . and I'm guessing the Klan killed some people back there . . . and now someone tried to take your daughter . . . well, it's just good you don't believe in ghosts. At least one generation of kids grew up thinking that little girl haunted those woods. There used to be a path that led to a school back there"—she points toward my house—"and no one would walk on it any longer. They'd rather walk an extra quarter mile to school than go by that lake."

Thanks a heap for telling me that, I think to myself. But I make myself smile. "Well, fortunately I think that's all just silly."

She smiles at me. Gives me a wink. "Then you're the perfect person to live there," she says.

Chapter 36

—≋—

ELLIE

1965

Jocelyn and I had a cell to ourselves in the county jail. It was exactly as I'd imagined a jail cell to be: disgusting. But after putting up with the Daweses' outhouse, I figured I could handle the filthy exposed toilet and brown-stained sink. And after sleeping in my sleeping bag on the hard floor at the school, I could handle the wretched bare mattress—as long as it wasn't infested. That thought kept me sitting up most of the night, my back against the hard, concrete wall.

They'd divided us up, Jocelyn and me in one car. The boys, including Curry, in the other. The officer didn't answer when Jocelyn and I asked him what the charges were against us, but we knew it didn't matter. We were headed to jail, no matter what.

When we were finally alone in the cell, we sat next to each other so we could whisper without any other prisoners overhearing us. The cell across from us was empty, but we could hear women's voices coming from somewhere nearby. Yelling, mostly. *Let me outta here!* and *Fuck y'all!*

So it wasn't until we were sitting side by side on the cool, filthy floor, our backs against the concrete wall, that Jocelyn whispered to me. "Where's Win?"

"I got him out of the van when we saw the police go into the building to get y'all," I said.

"Good," she said. "I was worried. I hope the boys aren't getting beaten up or anything."

"Hope not," I said, but I was thinking about Win out there in the pouring rain, not knowing which direction to head. At least he was safer out there than he would have been if he'd been found with me.

She smiled. "You're in love with him," she said. "Win."

Oh God. We'd been way too careless tonight. Yet hearing those words warmed me and I couldn't help my smile. I knew I could trust Jocelyn. "You could tell?" I asked.

"Uh-huh. Not just tonight, either," she said, as if reading my mind.

I gave her a puzzled look. "How could you know?"

"You never take your eyes off him," she said.

"Yes, I do too!" I felt the heat rise in my cheeks. There was no way she could know how I felt about Win. I hadn't even realized my own feelings until the night before when I told him about Mattie.

"Don't worry," she said. "It's mutual. He never takes his eyes off you either."

How could I have missed that? For a moment, I basked in that thought, but then my throat tightened. "Jocelyn," I said quietly. "It's not good."

She was shaking her head before the words were out of my mouth. "I know," she said. "And listen, Ellie. If I noticed, you can bet Greg has, too. He's got his eye on you two. You need to be careful."

"Rosemary was there tonight," I said.

Jocelyn frowned. "Where?"

"At that club."

"You're kidding. Are you sure it was her?"

"Yes. And she saw Win and me leave together."

A female voice suddenly ricocheted off the walls and metal bars, making us both jump. "What y'all whisperin' about in there?"

Jocelyn and I looked at each other, then started giggling. "Nothing!" I hollered back. We waited a moment for her to speak again, but the woman was apparently done with us.

"Do you know where we are?" I whispered. "I mean, what town?"

"I have no idea. Carlisle, probably."

"The van is still back at that crazy juke joint. Greg is going to be furious," I said. "Do you think they'll make us pay bail to get out of here?"

"I hope not. I have no money and SCOPE sure has no money."

We were quiet for a while, sitting there. I was sure we were both dreading the moment we had to use that toilet. Finally I drew in a long, tired breath. "Wanna sing?" I asked.

"Why not?" she said.

I started singing "I'll Fly Away" and pretty soon the woman with the booming voice joined in with us, and then another, and another. Finally, a woman way in the distance hollered for us to shut up. But we didn't. We sat up singing our freedom songs for most of the night.

Chapter 37

KAYLA

"What's on that tree, Mama?" Rainie asks as I back the car out of our garage.

I look over at the small redbud tree in our front yard. It looks strange. It's a distance from us and appears as though it's suddenly hung with Spanish moss. I press the brake and squint. It's not Spanish moss at all. It's squirrels. Dead squirrels. Maybe twenty of them. Maybe more. From where I sit, it looks as though they've fallen from the sky.

I feel sick to my stomach, and I press the gas before Rainie has the chance to figure it out for herself. "I think it's a kind of moss," I say, my voice sounding like it belongs to someone else. "I'll ask someone to take it down. Okay?"

"Okay," she says from behind me. From the sound of her voice, I know she is unbothered. Ready to move on to the next topic. But I'm frankly terrified. What the hell is going on?

When I get to her school, I go inside to explain to her teacher and principal that I'm worried about Rainie's safety. They look alarmed as I tell them about the kidnapping. The squirrels in the tree. I ask them to please, *please* keep a careful eye on my daughter. Her teacher says she won't let Rainie out of her sight.

Then, on the drive home, I call Samantha Johns and my father.

An hour later, Samantha, Daddy, and I are in my front yard, looking up at the desecrated redbud tree. The sight is both nauseating and frightening. I welcome my father's protective hand on my back.

"Looks like they used a pellet gun," Daddy says.

"Right," says Sam. "They killed the squirrels someplace else, then came over here during the night and just tossed them in your tree."

"Why is someone *doing* this to me?" I ask, as if she might have the answer.

She looks at me with steady dark eyes behind her glasses. "Let's go inside," she says. "I want you to take a look at some pictures."

Inside, I make coffee for the three of us. It's my fourth cup since I took Rainie to school and my nerves are a wreck. We sit in the kitchen, Daddy and me on one side of the quartzite-topped island, Sam on the other. She produces a loose-leaf notebook filled with mug shots of women. She's made a little cutout of mirrored sunglasses that she holds over the face of each woman as I study the photographs, but we don't get very far. I just don't remember the woman's face from when I saw her in my office. I can remember the things that stood out about her: the bright red hair, the sloppy acrylics, the glasses—all the things that were temporary. The features of her face are lost to me.

"There *is* one thing," I say, "though I don't think it's going to be much help."

"What's that, hon?" Daddy asks.

"She had a mark on the inside of her right arm. I caught just a flash of it and at first I thought it might be a scar. Like, maybe she'd tried to slit her wrist at some point. But it was too short . . . or the wrong shape. Not like a clean slice." I draw my finger horizontally across my wrist to demonstrate.

"A burn?" Sam suggests.

"Possibly. Or maybe a birthmark. I only got a quick look at it."

She jots something down on her notepad. "How is Rainie doing?" she asks as she writes.

"She's a tough little cookie," my father says with a smile.

"He's right," I say. "She's so resilient. I couldn't sleep the night after she was taken, and I kept checking on her, but she was sleeping soundly every time. *I'm terrified, though, like I shouldn't let her out of my sight.*"

Sam nods as though she understands. She pulls a sheet of paper from the back of the notebook. "You need to see this," she says, setting the paper in front of me on the island. "These are calls that your husband made to us while he was working on the house."

I frown. "He called the police?"

"I assume he didn't tell you?"

"Well, no. I don't remember him saying anything." *Damn it, Jackson,* I think. *Why did you keep so much from me?* "What did he call about?"

Sam turns the paper so she can read from it. "Stolen power tools from the work site. Stolen tile. Stolen hardwood flooring. Stolen paint." She looks up at me. "These are all on different dates," she says.

"That's crazy," I say. "He never told me things were taken." I look at my father. "Did he say anything to you?"

"Not a word."

"There's more," Sam says.

"Why didn't they lock everything up?" I ask.

"Apparently they did," she says. "They had a trailer they stored the material in."

I nod. "I remember the trailer."

"It was broken into. Repeatedly."

"Could it have been one of the guys working with him?" my father asks.

"They were all questioned and ruled out."

"What do you mean, 'There's more'?" I ask.

She looks at the paper again. "Dead animals were found in the house as it was going up," she says. "Mostly squirrels." She nods toward the front yard, where dead squirrels are baking in my redbud tree. "And in one instance, a cat."

"Oh God." I press my hand to my mouth.

She turns the paper over and I'm glad to see the back side is blank. "That's it," she says. "You didn't know about any of that?"

I shake my head. "Do you think . . . Is it possible Jackson's accident wasn't an accident?"

"That was investigated," she says. "The guy who left the screws on the steps freely admitted to it and was, according to the report, devastated."

I look past her at my sparkly new white and gray kitchen and the glass walls of the great room beyond. "Someone doesn't want us here." I suddenly remember my father's letter to Jackson. I turn to him. "Is all this connected somehow to your letter—"

"No, of course not," he says. "I'm as in the dark as you are."

"What letter?" Sam asks.

"I wrote Jackson a letter when he and Kayla were considering this lot," Daddy says. "I grew up close by and I always had a bad feeling about this area."

"Oh right," Sam says. She looks at me. "You told me the Klan used to meet in your backyard."

My father and I both nod.

"Well," Sam says. "I'm sure this Shadow Ridge development has had a lot of opposition from the old-timers in the area. But I've talked to some of the foremen and crews on the street to see if they've had problems with things being stolen, et cetera, and it seems like all the issues have been with your house, Kayla. Maybe because it was the first to go up. Who knows."

I let out a long sigh, sitting back, my arms folded across my chest. "I have a love/hate feeling about this house," I say. "Jackson and I were so excited about it and everywhere I look, I see an idea we talked about and couldn't wait to bring to life. I feel his presence here." I shake my head. "But it's brought me nothing but trouble. And other weird things happened here, too. Not just the Klan meetings." I tell her about the girl who drowned in Little Heaven Lake and Mr. Hockley shooting his head off. "Maybe he did it right here," I add, stomping my foot on the floor. "Right beneath where we're sitting."

"Honey . . ." My father pats my knee.

"Well, that's . . . pretty horrible," Sam says, "but it's ancient history. You've got a real nice house on a real pretty piece of land with a—" She searches for a word. "—colorful history. Soon you'll have a bunch of new neighbors to share the ghost stories with."

"Mm." I'm not convinced.

"I'd say someone's trying to scare you, not hurt you," she says. "But you might want to get that big dog, for your own peace of mind."

Chapter 38

ELLIE

1965

Jocelyn and I were released from jail late the next afternoon, the Fourth of July, without fanfare or discussion of any charges against us. We didn't ask questions or protest our treatment. We just wanted to get out of there. When we left the building, blinking against the blinding sunlight, Curry was waiting in the van, smoking a cigarette, as though nothing had happened. We climbed in and the first thing he said to me was "Win made it back to his house." He knew that was all I cared about. Jocelyn squeezed my hand.

"What happened to everyone else?" I asked.

"We all spent the night in lovely accommodations at the expense of the state," he said. "This mornin', I hitched a ride to get the van. I picked up the boys in front of the jailhouse and carried them to the school, then drove to the house Win's stayin' at and found him there eatin' breakfast like he'd never been gone. Don't know how he got there, but don't care either.

Now I'm here to carry y'all to the school and I can tell you, the Rev ain't happy. I told him it's all my doin', so go along with that."

It *was* all his doing, but we didn't argue with him. I was just so happy that Win was all right and that Jocelyn and I were out of that miserable jail cell.

Curry took us to the school, where Jocelyn slipped quietly into her desk chair and began typing as though she'd been there all along, but Greg called me into the storage room. He shut the door and pointed to one of the chairs.

"How'd you like jail?" he asked as I lowered myself to the chair. He didn't bother to sit, but stood opposite me, arms folded across his chest.

"I didn't. And I'm really sorry," I said. "We shouldn't have gone out last night, but it seemed harmless at the time, and I still don't really understand why the police—"

"I'm aware you have a close relationship with Win," he interrupted me. "I blame myself. My plan was to alternate you and Rosemary with him, but you and Win were working well together, getting a lot of folks committed to register and showing up at the protests, and I didn't see—I didn't *want* to see—the warning signs. I'm tempted to send you to another SCOPE site, Ellie. I want you—"

"No!" I felt panicky at the thought of leaving. My friends were here. My work was here. My *heart* was here. "I belong here," I said. "I love what I'm doing."

"If you think it's important work, then you need to treat it as such," he said. "No horsing around. For both your sakes—and SCOPE's sake—I'm splitting the two of you up. You'll be canvassing with Rosemary from now on and Win with Chip."

The emotion that ran through me felt almost like panic. I wouldn't be able to see Win until our weekly protest on Friday night, and then we'd be working, surrounded by a hundred or more people. Greg would no doubt keep an eye on us the whole time. Maybe I could see him on Saturday night, when Greg went home to be with his family? But after what happened last night, I doubted either of us would—or should—take the risk.

≈

I spent that night in the school. Paul had figured out a way to get up on the roof and all of us—Jocelyn, Paul, Chip, and I—sat up there watching fireworks in the distance. In the morning, Curry drove me to the next house where Greg said I'd be staying for three nights. It wasn't far from the Hunts' house. Better yet, it wasn't far—maybe a quarter mile—from where Win was staying. I was never the sort of person who disobeyed her parents. I never sneaked out of the house in the middle of the night or lied about where I was going. I wouldn't do it now, at the age of twenty, either, but knowing that Win was close by gave me comfort.

Even though my new residence had some electricity—though intermittent—and running cold water and a decent shower attached to the side of the house, in some ways it was the worst of the three houses I'd stayed in. The family was painfully quiet. The Hunts, and even to a certain extent the Dawes family, had seemed to want me there. They seemed to believe in what SCOPE was trying to do. But I had the feeling that this family—the Charles family—had heard about the bad luck the other families had had because of me, and they were only taking me in because they desperately needed the few dollars they'd get from sharing their house with me. They responded to anything I said, any attempt at friendliness, with a stare or a shrug. No one smiled in this house. The two bedrooms were crammed with mattresses and people—mostly teenagers—who came and went, while Mrs. Charles cooked, struggling to make beans and salt pork and corn bread stretch far enough to feed us all. The teenagers hardly gave me more than a glance. I wasn't introduced to them and I didn't ask about them because I didn't want to put anyone on the spot. There was no man in the house and I didn't know who belonged to whom. I simply tried my best to blend into the woodwork, eating barely enough to stay alive, thinking they all needed that food more than I did.

The room I slept in had two mattresses on the floor. A couple of teen-aged boys, maybe thirteen and fourteen, slept on one, while I slept with an eighteen-year-old girl and her two-year-old son. I tried to talk to the girl in the evenings, to connect to her, but she'd been working all day at a chicken plant and was exhausted. Although I knew she'd taken a long shower—the outdoor shower was right outside the bedroom and I heard it run and run and run—she still carried the scent of the plant into the room with her.

"I can't get rid of it," she said apologetically, as I moved over on the bed to make room for her. "The chicken smell. But we need the money."

They were the first words anyone in the house had spoken directly to me.

"It's good you have a job," I said, because I didn't know what else to say. I hurt for her.

She let me use the only pillow. She didn't need it, she said, and she was right: she fell asleep the second she laid her head on the mattress. As I lay there, with her little boy's arm snug around my waist, tears stung my eyes. I felt wealthy. Spoiled. I'd never truly suffered a day in my life. *Dear God*, I prayed. *Please let something good happen for this family.*

≈

It was a long week. I ended up staying at the Charleses' house every night because a cross was burned outside the house Chip was staying in and the school was shot up again, which I was sure had terrified Jocelyn. So Greg had to find a new place for Chip and since nothing terrible had happened to me at the Charleses' place, he figured I could safely stay there. By the third day of canvassing with Rosemary, she told me I was "gettin' ripe." I explained about the house I was in and my bedmate's situation. We'd been walking down the road and she stopped short and stared at me. "It's gonna take three hundred years of havin' the vote to turn this mess around," she said.

"I know," I agreed.

While I missed Win with an almost physical pain, canvassing with Rosemary was not as bad as I'd expected. She was intense, like Win had said, but some people liked that about her. They took her seriously and her passion got us in a few doors for a few glasses of sweet tea and good conversation. We still did our best to hide if we saw a white man driving down the road, but it wasn't nearly as dangerous canvassing with another girl, even if she was Black, and my heart didn't climb into my throat every time we had to make a run for it.

But she was nosy about Win and me. "Must be hard not seein' him all this week, huh?" she asked, her tone nonchalant.

"Oh, it's not so bad," I said, refusing to rise to the bait. "It's probably good to mix up who we canvass with. Helps us build our skills."

"You know I saw you at the Jinx Club," she said.

"Yeah, I know. Do you go there often?"

"In the summer. Me and my cousins, we hang out there a lot."

I remembered with a jolt that her cousin Ronnie worked with Buddy. "Your cousin Ronnie?" I tried and probably failed to sound casual.

"Yeah, he was there." She sounded just as casual. She nodded toward the clipboard I was carrying, which had our canvassing data on it. "Did you mark down that last house?" she asked, and I checked the clipboard as though I could actually see what I'd written through my fear. Had Ronnie seen me with Win? Very, very doubtful, I thought. If he had, he would have told my brother, and Buddy would have shown up by now to drag me home.

≈

Friday evening, Curry made the rounds of the houses where SCOPE students were staying, picking us up to drive us to the courthouse in Carlisle for the weekly protest. Chip, Jocelyn, and Win were already in the van, and the back seat was piled high with the protest placards. My heart felt like it would explode at seeing Win after a week. He turned from the front seat to smile at me as I slid into the middle bench seat next to Chip and Jocelyn. I wondered if he noticed I was wearing his green shirt.

"Is Paul picking up the others?" I asked, mostly for something to say that would keep me from shouting, "I love you!" I'd showered like mad and hoped I hadn't brought any of the chicken plant stench into the van with me.

"Paul's gettin' a couple and Greg the rest," Curry said.

I spoke only to Chip and Jocelyn on the drive to Carlisle, acting as though I felt nothing for the man sitting in front of me. *Six days*, I thought. *I haven't seen him in six days.*

We parked down the street from the courthouse. Curry, Chip, and Jocelyn each left with an armful of placards, but Win and I dawdled so we'd have a few minutes alone. He moved next to me on the middle seat and I was reaching behind me for a placard when he rested his hand on mine. "Hold on," he said. "Let's just sit for a minute."

I was relieved by the suggestion. I sat close to him and he glanced through the window before putting his arm around me.

"I missed you this week," he said.

I hadn't imagined his feelings for me. I nuzzled my cheek against his shoulder. Felt him kiss my temple. "It's felt more like five weeks," I said.

"It goes against everything I believe, though," he said.

I lifted my head to look at him. "You really believe it's wrong?" I asked. "Us?"

He drew in a long breath, momentarily shutting his eyes. "I always thought it was wrong for *me*," he said. "I think Black folks have to stick together to get anywhere. To get power. Falling for you wasn't in my plan." He drew away and looked hard into my eyes. "Don't frown." He touched my cheek, and I was reassured by his smile. "I didn't count on you," he said. "On your dedication. And your goodness. On how you let yourself be so . . . vulnerable with me." He looked away from me then. Let out a long breath. "You can't help who you fall in love with, can you." It wasn't a question.

"I love you," I said.

He nodded slowly, his gaze on me again. "We have to be so, so careful," he said.

I looked past him to see Curry walking toward the van.

"Curry," I said, and we both immediately turned, getting to our knees to grab the placards.

Curry opened the van door. "Need some more signs," he said, looking from me to Win and back again. "You two just lookin' for trouble, ain't you?"

"Here," I said, handing him three of the placards. "Have some signs."

Curry took the signs from me, shaking his head like he couldn't believe we could be so stupid. Or so obvious. Then Win and I got out of the van and started walking toward the gathering, our own arms weighed down with placards.

"I like your shirt," he said as we walked.

"Not as much as I do." I felt giddy with the joy of being with him. Giddy with the joy of walking next to him again, our bare arms brushing against each other.

≈

There was a good crowd at the protest. I'd worried about that after what happened last week with the rock-and-bottle-throwing melee that had ended with little DeeDee getting that cut on her cheek. I saw only Mr. Hunt in the crowd tonight; he wasn't going to risk his family by bringing them here again. Still, he waved to me across the green with his usual friendly smile.

So the whole Hunt family might not have been there, but many others came, even more than the week before despite the threat of violence, and they held our placards or ones they'd made themselves and marched around the courtyard, calling for their right to vote.

There were a few policemen in the street and some hecklers, but no one threw anything that I was aware of, and after an hour or so, we fell into a circle as naturally as if we did it every night. We crossed our arms, held hands, and began to sing "This Little Light of Mine." It was then that I saw my brother. Buddy walked around the circumference of the circle, searching faces for, I assumed, mine. When he reached me, he grabbed my shoulders and pulled me from the circle.

I turned to him. "What are you doing here?" I asked, as calmly as I could.

"I'm here to talk sense into you!" he shouted over the singing. Grabbing my arm, he drew me another few yards from the circle so he didn't have to shout to be heard. "You need to know what you're doing to your family."

His eyes were bloodshot and I smelled beer on his breath. "What do you mean?" I asked.

"We love you, Ellie," he said, his voice thick with emotion and booze. "We love you more than anything." Was he going to cry?

I grabbed his hand. "What's wrong, Bud?" I asked. "Is everyone okay?"

"Ronnie told me he saw you with a colored boy," he said, "and you weren't just holdin' hands. His cousin Rosemary said you're in love with him."

I swallowed, my nerves on fire. "I care about him," I admitted. I dared to hope that my brother, who I knew loved me more than anyone, would understand.

"Are you crazy?" he asked, his arms flailing about. "What are you *thinkin'*? This whole . . . I knew this whole SCOPE thing was a bad idea, but I don't think you know how hard you've made it for your family. And when people find out you been . . . you're hangin' around with that boy, it's only gonna get worse." His voice was rising. I'd seen Buddy drunk more than a few times and I recognized those red eyes. The sputter when he talked.

"Settle down," I said.

"No white man's ever gonna want you, Ellie. You think Reed'll take you back once you been with one of them?" He nodded toward the circle.

"I'm doing really important work here," I said, ignoring his question. "I tried to explain it to Daddy but—"

"Do you know the FBI has your name? They have the names of all you SCOPE people. All the . . . Martin Luther King fanatics."

"I don't believe that," I said. "And so what, anyway? Are you crying?" There were tears in Buddy's eyes and I stepped forward to wrap him in my arms. "You're worrying too much," I said softly, my lips close to his ear. "I'm fine and healthy and happy and—"

He pushed me away so hard I nearly fell. "I got a friend down at the police station in Carlisle," he said. "I know you spent a night in a jail cell. I didn't tell Mama and Daddy because holy hell'd come down on you, Ellie, but you *got* to come home. Whatever you're up to here is no good and you're gonna get hurt. I mean, *physically* hurt."

"No I'm not," I said. "I'm not worried about it so you shouldn't be either."

"Has that boy touched you? Tried anything with you?"

I remembered Win's arm around my shoulders only an hour before. "It's none of your damn business!"

"You got to come *home*, Ellie."

"Daddy told me I can't come home again," I said.

"You know he didn't mean it. And there's somethin' he ain't tellin' you."

"What?"

"He's lost customers 'cause of you doin' this."

"Lost customers? Why?"

"Everybody knows you're out here, doin' what you're doin'. Tryin' to change things when they're just fine the way they are. Some of Daddy's longtime customers are taking their business to the Dellaire Pharmacy. I've lost a few folks, myself, and Mr. Cleveland—Garner's daddy—raised my rent by five percent on account of what you're doin'. Mama's friends are givin' her a rough time of it, too. Plenty of gossip she's gotta deal with. So it ain't all just about you, Ellie."

His words upset me, I couldn't deny it. I didn't want my actions to hurt my family, yet I had to do what I thought was right, didn't I? *Keep my eyes on the prize.* "You don't understand," I said. "You haven't seen what I've seen these past few weeks. You don't understand the political situation. You've never met the real people who suffer every single day because of the way things are." I started to choke up with the truth of what I was saying. "You don't know what it's like for the people I'm trying to help."

Blotches of color had formed on Buddy's cheeks and neck, a telltale sign he was having trouble holding his anger in. Even as a little girl, I knew to run and hide when his cheeks turned red like that. He stood in front of me with his hands on his hips. "Right now I don't give a *shit* what it's like for those 'real people'!" he shouted. "This has nothin' to do with them. It has to do with how you're hurtin' your own kin. I'm only tryin' to protect you against yourself, 'cause you ain't thinkin' right, little sister."

"I'm not going home, Buddy," I said.

"His name is Winston, right?" he asked, startling me. "Goes by Win?"

He knew his name. That scared me. "I don't know what you're talking about."

"Which one is Win, huh? Your spook boyfriend? Which is he?"

It was all I could do to keep from smacking him. He turned to look at the circle of people. They were singing a lively "I'll Fly Away."

"He's not here," I said.

Buddy grabbed the shoulder of one of the older men in the circle. "Do you know which one of these boys is Winston?" he asked.

"Ain't no idea," the man said, and returned to his singing.

Buddy cupped his hands around his mouth in a megaphone. "Hey, Win!" he shouted toward the circle. "*Win!*"

I spotted Win, way too close to us. If only he'd been on the other side of the circle, he would stand a chance, but hearing his name, he stopped singing. Looked toward us.

"Ha!" Buddy shouted. "Son of a bitch!" He raced toward Win, who was cornered between the crowd and the brick building. Before Win had a chance to run, Buddy was on him, pulling him out of the circle, pummeling him, punching his stomach, his face, knocking off his glasses. I was next to them in a heartbeat, trying to grab Buddy's arms, pull him away, but my brother was enraged. Rather than fight back, Win dropped to the ground. He didn't dare try to defend himself. The do-nothing cops were just waiting for a Black person to get out of line. Buddy kicked him. "You ever come near my sister again, I'll make sure she's the last girl you ever touch!" He angrily grabbed my arm. I thought he was going to twist it. Break it. But he let me go, fury still in his face, and took off, disappearing around the side of the building.

I dropped to the ground next to Win. He was dazed, his chin, his nose, his forehead bleeding. Blood was in his eyes, and he reached blindly for my hand. I thought of what Buddy had said about my father losing customers and my mother losing friends. That was not my fault. Not my business. My business was the bruised and beautiful man in front of me, hurt by my own kin.

≈

I thought Greg should take Win to the hospital. The wound on his forehead was bleeding badly and he seemed dazed, looking through me instead of at me. I worried his cheekbone might be broken. Maybe his nose, too, the way it was gushing blood. But Greg wanted to take him back to the school. He and Chip and I managed to get him to Greg's car and lay him across the back seat. Chip got in with him and pressed a handkerchief to the worst of his wounds. I tried to get in the front seat to go with them, but Greg barked at me.

"No! If you want to help, get Curry to take you back to the school," he said. "Get the first-aid supplies ready. If you want to help, that's what you can do."

So I rode back to the school with Curry, thinking, *At least Greg isn't sending me back to the Charleses' house. At least he's letting me help.*

Greg beat us to the school and by the time Curry and I rushed in, he and Chip were settling Win on the couch in the lounge. I ran to where Greg kept the first-aid supplies and soon he and Chip were dressing the wounds while I sat on a chair next to Win. He squeezed my hand and winced in pain. Greg made him some concoction to drink, and Win drank it down quickly, wincing at the taste or the burn, I didn't know which.

"Don't you think he should go to the hospital?" I asked Greg quietly as Win's eyelids fell shut.

Greg shook his head. He sat back in his chair, hands on his knees. "Once, a few years ago," he said quietly, his eyes on Win, "a civil rights worker I knew was beaten like this at a protest. We took him to the hospital and his attackers were waiting for him in the bushes outside the hospital doors. They jumped all of us. That fella didn't make it."

"My brother wouldn't—"

"Your brother wouldn't *what*, Ellie?" Greg said, anger in his voice now. "Hurt a fly? Well look what he did here." He nodded at Win. "I don't want him calling his friends to meet him at the hospital to finish what he started. All right? Win'll be safer here."

I didn't know what Greg gave Win in that drink, but whatever it was knocked him out and I was glad he was no longer in pain. I started to get to my feet, but Greg reached over, his hand on my arm to keep me seated.

"You're going to have to leave Flint, Ellie," he said.

"No. *Please,* Greg! Let me stay."

"I might be able to find you a place in one of the other counties outside North Carolina. I know they lost a few volunteers in Virginia, so maybe—"

"*No,*" I said again. "Don't make me leave."

Greg gazed at me, his face serious. He nodded toward Win. "I know you love him," he said. "And I know he loves you. He told me as much. But all you can bring him is trouble. He has a good head on his shoulders, but he's human. We're all human. We fall in love, we lose all sense of reason."

"I'll end it with him," I promised, wondering if the words were a lie even as I said them.

"You'll tell him it's over and he'll talk you out of it," Greg said. "I was young once. I know how this plays out."

I didn't know what to say. How to fix this. How to get what I wanted without hurting anyone.

"Curry can take you back to the Charleses' house now and then drive you home to Round Hill in the morning," Greg said. When I didn't respond, he added, "If you love him, Ellie, you'll leave him."

I felt my eyes burn. I looked down at Win again. The face I loved, bandaged and battered. Blood was seeping through the gauze taped to his chin. I knew in my heart Greg was right. How many more beatings would he have to endure to be with me?

I looked up at Greg. "I'll go," I said.

Chapter 39

Curry and I barely spoke on the drive from Flint to Round Hill in the morning. He suggested I ride in the back, but I refused. I smoked one of his cigarettes, exhaling with a vengeance. I couldn't remember ever feeling so despondent. I felt as though I was losing everything that mattered. Win, yes, of course. But all my new friends, too. The power of the protests. The song circles. The people who invited me into their homes for lemonade and conversation. The children who held my hand on the dirt road as Win and I canvassed. I wasn't just moving from one town to another. I was moving from one *world* to another, and I wasn't ready to make that move. Not at all.

"Truck," Curry said as a black pickup headed toward us.

I crouched down, thinking, *This is the last time I'll ever have to do this.* Even that made me sad.

I stayed low in the seat as we drove through Round Hill. It was late Saturday morning and people were out and about downtown. It was best that Curry and I weren't seen together.

Curry turned onto Hockley Street.

"That's my house," I said.

"I guessed that," he said, "seein' as it's the only one."

Both our car and Buddy's truck were gone and I was relieved. Wherever Buddy was, I hoped he was repenting for his behavior last night. I still couldn't believe his rage. I'd seen him angry before, yes, but brutal? Never.

I dared to give Curry a quick hug, then gathered my things out of the middle seat and headed for the house.

Inside, I breathed in the familiar scent. Our house always smelled like a mix of citrus and mildew to me. It wasn't unpleasant at all. It was home. The house seemed so big and we were so *wealthy*. I hadn't known how well we lived. How we wanted for nothing. How much of our comfort came from generations of having control over our lives? From being able to vote people who would help us into office? I dropped my things on the floor of my bedroom, flopped down on my bed, and looked up at the ceiling. I had to find a way to keep this part of me alive—the part that had been awakened to another side of America.

And then I thought of Win, waking up this morning in pain, his face swollen. How did he feel when Greg told him I was gone for good? I started to cry. I wept and wept and wept, giving myself permission to finally break down. *Get it all out now,* I thought. Once my family was home, I intended to be dry-eyed. I'd help out at the pharmacy. I'd help Mama with the house. I'd forgive my brother for stupidly trying to protect me when I'd needed no protection. If I had to be home, I was going to truly be home. But I'd hold on to the new part of myself, too. I would never lose the Ellie I'd become this summer.

I worried my father would make good on his threat to kick me out of the house, but I couldn't have been more wrong. When he got home from the pharmacy late that afternoon, he wrapped me in his arms. He seemed close to tears. I'd never seen him like that. When he said "Welcome home," his voice was husky.

My mother, though, stopped short when she walked in the kitchen and saw me there with my father, and what I saw in her face wasn't surprise, or love, or even anger. It was disgust. "Go take a shower," she said. "Then set the table for supper."

"Yes, Mama." I would do whatever she asked of me.

After I saw my brother. Through the kitchen window, I could see Buddy's truck pull into the driveway. I watched him get out of the truck, pop the hood, and begin tinkering with one thing or another. I walked out the back door and through the porch. When the porch door slammed shut he looked up, one hand on his hip.

"Hey!" he called. "You home for good?"

A thousand emotions ran through me as I neared him. I loved him more than anyone in the world. Even more than Win. But my anger from the night before was still coursing through me, more so with every step, and by the time I reached him, I drew my hand back and slapped him hard across the face.

He was stunned. I thought we both were. But then he pulled me to him and we wrapped our arms around each other. I felt his breath catch. He was sorry. Whether he said it or not, I knew he was. "Please tell me you're home for good," he said, his breath against my ear.

"I am."

He pulled back from me. "That's what I prayed for last night," he said. "That, and that I didn't kill that boy. I hate him, but I don't want to kill nobody."

"You didn't," I said. "But you could have. And I love him, and if you love me you should've put your damn bigotry aside and let me have him. I've left him behind for his sake, not for mine." I felt my voice start to crack. "I don't want him in danger from people like you."

≈

I called Brenda that evening, but got no answer. I couldn't forget that letter she sent me—the one where she sounded appalled by the work I was doing.

I'd written back but hadn't heard from her again and I was dying for a real heart-to-heart. She and Garner were probably having dinner at his family's house. More like a mansion, that house. I guessed Brenda was getting what she always wanted: a man she loved, a baby on the way, and money. I just wanted one particular man. I didn't care about the other things.

I thought of calling Reed, but it was too soon. I didn't know what to say to him. Monday morning, though, I had to figure out what to say to him in a hurry when he showed up while I was working at the pharmacy. I figured Buddy had told him I was home. I wondered what else Buddy had said.

I smiled awkwardly at him as he walked to the counter where I was working. He didn't return my smile. "Can you take a break?" he asked.

I looked toward my father, who was stocking boxes of aspirin on one of the shelves. "Hey, Reed," Daddy said. He moved toward us, and they shook hands. "Good to see you."

"You too, Mr. Hockley."

"Can I take a quick break, Daddy?" I asked.

"Of course." He smiled widely, no doubt wanting to do all he could to bring Reed and me together again.

We walked out front and sat down on the retaining wall in front of the pharmacy windows. We'd only been apart a few weeks, but it felt more like a year. "How've you been?" I asked. "How are things at the bank?"

"How are things at the *bank*?" he asked. "Do you really think that's what I want to talk about right now?"

"You're angry," I said.

"I'm just . . . confused. It was too much, Ellie. You put yourself in harm's way out there in Flint. You had no need to do that. No need at all. Those civil rights workers might as well have targets on their backs these days, and for what—"

"*I'm* a civil rights worker," I interrupted him.

"What the hell got into you?" He ran a hand through his hair. "You had a perfectly good life and you went and upended it."

I thought of how I'd told Win about Mattie Jenkins and me, and how my guilt was one of the things that started me on the path to SCOPE. I could tell Reed the same story and compare his reaction to Win's, but I didn't want to. I'd explained it once to the person who mattered most and he'd accepted me for it. I didn't really care what Reed thought.

Yet I knew I still cared about Reed. I studied his beautiful blue eyes, cloudy now with anger. The way his thick dark hair fell over his forehead, forever annoying him. The lips I'd loved to kiss over the past four years. Of course I still loved him—there was no on/off switch for that emotion. But I didn't love him the way I once did. Not the way I did before this summer.

"Are you going out with anyone?" I asked, not sure how I'd feel about his answer.

"No one special," he said. "I was hoping you'd come back sooner rather than later."

"I'm back, but I'm different."

"I figured you would be," he said. He looked across the street toward the hardware store. "Buddy told me about the colored guy," he said. "He heard about it from someone and came right to my house to tell me. Hoped he could rile me up."

"So, did you get riled up?"

"I'd be lying if I said it didn't bother me. I just hope that you're done with whoever it is . . . and that you didn't let it go too far."

"I'm done." I couldn't leave it at that. That made it sound as though I'd willingly split up with Win. "I'm done with him because I don't want him to get hurt again. Buddy beat him up and if he's with me, I'm afraid that'll be his life. Getting beaten up."

"Do you love him?"

I hesitated a moment too long.

"There's my answer," he said, getting to his feet. When he looked down at me, his cheeks were blotched with red. "I still love you, Ellie. You know we had something good. We had the real thing for four years. The real thing isn't always sunshine and roses and it's not always . . . exciting or thrilling, but it's solid. That's the kind of thing that lasts. That's what we had, you and me."

I looked up at the blue sky, trying to pick apart my emotions. "I know," I admitted. "I know it was good . . ." I almost called him "honey," the way I used to. "But I don't know how I feel anymore," I said, looking squarely at him. He was as familiar to me as my family. "The one thing I know is that I can't just pick up where we left off."

"You're damn straight about that," he said.

Three women walked past us and into the pharmacy, the bell on the pharmacy door jingling. "I'd better get back," I said. "I'm trying to keep on Daddy's good side."

In spite of his anger, he held out his hand to help me to my feet, his touch a strange mixture of familiar and foreign.

"Thank you," I said. Looking past him, I saw his distinctive white and blue Ford truck parked at the curb. How many hours had I spent in that truck? Now the sight of a truck driven by a white man made me run in the other direction. "How's Mildred doing?" I asked, nodding toward the truck.

He looked confused for a moment by my out-of-context question, then glanced at the Ford. His beloved Mildred. "She spent a lot of time in Buddy's shop this month," he said. "Showing her age. Right now, left side of her rear bumper's dented. I need to take her in again. Don't even know how it happened."

"I learned to fear white men in trucks," I said bluntly, then winced. Why had I said that?

He stared at me. Shook his head. "I don't know who you are anymore," he said. He turned and headed toward his truck, while I walked back to the store, wondering how Win was healing today after the beating my brother had given him.

I was surprised that Brenda didn't stop by the store to see me. I was sure Reed would have told her—or at least told Garner—that I was there. Uncle Byron came in and looked surprised to find me behind the counter.

"You're home?" he asked. "For good?"

I tried to smile. "Daddy needs me here in the store," I said. That was going to be my party line, I'd decided. I'd tell only Brenda the truth about why I'd come home a month early.

"Well, sweetheart, I'm glad you're back. That voting program was the wrong place for you. It's too soon for the sort of change they're after, can you see that now? The time will eventually come, but it has to come naturally. Can't be forced. Things are fine the way they are."

"What were you doing at that rally, Uncle Byron?" I nearly whispered the question, not wanting customers to overhear us.

"I could ask you the same thing," he said. "I was there to keep the peace. What was your excuse?"

"Curiosity," I said.

"You kids weren't wanted there."

"We figured that out."

"I think maybe you played with fire a bit too much this summer," he said, and I wondered exactly how much he knew about my life in Flint. I was glad when a customer came up to me to ask a question, and Uncle Byron walked over to talk to my father.

I finally reached Brenda on the phone that night and knew instantly that something was wrong. Not with her. Not with the baby or Garner. Something was wrong between *us*.

"I'm home!" I said, trying to sound chipper. "Do you have time to get together this week?"

"I don't think so," she said, her voice flat.

"Oh please," I said. "I've missed you so much. I want to catch up."

She was as quiet as if the line had gone dead.

"Brenda? Are you okay?" I asked.

"I'm fine," she said. "The baby's fine. Garner's fine. But I think my best friend has gone off the deep end."

I stiffened. "What are you talking about?"

"Everyone knows about you and that Negro boy or man or whatever he is, Ellie. What the hell are you thinking?"

I was dumbfounded, first, that "everyone" could possibly know, and second, that my dearest friend was talking to me so coldly. "Who is 'everyone'?" I asked.

"What does that matter? The thing is they know, and if you think I'm going to meet you *in public* for lunch, you're out of your ever-lovin' mind. Garner and I are going to raise a family in this town and . . . Everything's different now, Ellie. I have our reputation to protect."

"Brenda!" I could barely believe what I was hearing. "You think having lunch with me will sully your reputation?"

"Garner says—"

"I saw Garner at a Klan rally," I interrupted her, suddenly very sure it *had* been Garner in the crowd. I wanted to shock her. Hurt her. "Is that where your husband spends his evenings now?"

For a moment, Brenda said nothing. "You know, I really missed you," she said finally, dodging my question. "But I feel like you died. Like the Ellie I've known since I was twelve years old has died a quick, horrible death."

"Well, I guess I feel the same way. My best friend has turned into a bigot right before my eyes!"

"I haven't turned into anything. I just never . . . we just never really talked about it before. Colored and white. We never had to. I didn't say anything when you did that ridiculous kneeling thing on Franklin Street, but now you've been sleeping in their beds and I have to tell you, Ellie, I almost threw up when you described some of the things you were doing. I tried to be understanding about it. Let you get it out of your system. But when Buddy told us you were involved with a boy out there in Flint, that was the final straw. Garner said we had to wash our hands of you. You're just lucky your family took you back. Your mother got kicked out of her bridge club, did she tell you?"

"Because of me?"

"Why else?"

"That's ridiculous."

"Maybe so, but it's the truth."

"I saw Reed," I said. "He didn't say anything about—"

"Reed adores you. Garner told him to forget you, but you can't do anything wrong in Reed's eyes, you know that. But I'm sorry, I just don't want to see you."

I started to speak again, to argue with her, but I realized she'd hung up. I stared at the phone in my hand, shocked. I thought I might lose Brenda . . . or at least a little part of Brenda . . . when she had her baby. When her priorities changed and we could no longer relate like two Carolina co-eds. But I never thought I would lose her over this.

Chapter 40

Loneliness felt like a disease with no cure. I remembered the feeling from my childhood. From the days before Brenda moved to Round Hill and we became inseparable. Now I'd lost her to Garner. To her need, one I'd never picked up on before, to protect some make-believe reputation the two of them didn't even have yet. The social status they were trying to earn.

I knew that what Buddy'd told me about the pharmacy was true. There were fewer customers coming through the front door than there used to be. Maybe because it was summer, I hoped. Surely it wasn't because I'd tried to help some people get the vote they deserved. And although my mother didn't say a word about her bridge club, she stayed home on Thursday afternoons now when for as long as I could remember, she'd meet up with her friends on Thursdays for girl talk and fun. Once I caught her crying, but she brushed aside my questions. Her anger at me was like a prickly ball rolling around the house, keeping me at arm's length. She would need time to get over it. We would both need time.

Buddy kept an eagle eye on me. He was the only person I thought I could talk to and even he didn't want to hear what I'd been doing in Flint . . . and he most definitely didn't want to hear a word about Win. He didn't want to know where I'd been staying. How I'd spent my days. I finally badgered him one too many times about why I'd become a pariah and he laid it all out for me: *Yes, Mama's friends shut her out because of you. Yes, it prob'ly was Garner you saw at the Klan rally; he's a closet bigot. You never knew that about him 'cause you didn't want to see it. Yes, everybody's lookin' at you sideways, wonderin' if you slept with a spook. Happy now?*

I missed doing something that felt important. I missed my friends in Flint, the like-minded people I'd quickly grown to care about. I missed some of the families I'd met while I was canvassing, the ones who'd invited me in and made me feel at home. I missed goofy Curry and delicate Jocelyn, who'd chosen office work over being in the field. And I missed Win so much that I'd cry into my pillow at night and wake up with puffy eyes that my family ignored in the morning.

I was tempted to call Reed, the only person in town who might be willing to give me the time of day despite his anger, but it would be wrong for me to give him any hope about us just because I was lonely. I asked myself if I truly still loved him and didn't know the answer. It wouldn't be fair for me to see him until I did.

Then one day, I came home from the pharmacy to find my mother, her back to me, going through the mail. I could see that she was studying one envelope, and when I said, "Hi, Mama," she quickly folded it and slipped it into her apron pocket before giving me one of the flat looks that were her new way of greeting me. Just that morning, she'd told me "I can't even look at you," words that cut me deeper than I could have imagined.

I was able to extract the envelope from her pocket after we'd finished the dishes that evening and she'd taken off her apron. It was addressed to me and had no return address, but I knew the handwriting. I'd seen it nearly every day on the canvassing sheet on our clipboard. I carried the envelope onto the screened porch and sat in one of the rockers. My fingers shook as I tore it open.

I miss you, Ellie. Is there any chance I can see you? I can use Paul's car. I'll understand if you say no.

No signature. None needed.

And I would not say no.

Chapter 41

KAYLA

"What animal sound is that, Mommy?" Rainie asks. She's cuddling with me on the big hammock on our deck, both of us slathered with mosquito repellent. The night is about as black as a night can get and the sound is haunting in the darkness. I feel a tremor run through Rainie's little body. But I can differentiate the sounds of the forest, now, having searched the internet for them, sharing them with Rainie. The different owls. The deer. The foxes with their multiple calls. None of them spell danger—at least not for us humans.

"That's one of the owls," I say. "Do you remember which one?"

"Umm," she says, "the barber owl!" She thinks she's being funny.

"You're close." I give her a squeeze.

"The barred one?" she tries.

"Bingo!" I say. "I think he's calling for his friend to come hang out with him."

"Really?"

"That's what I imagine."

It's so lovely on this wooded lot at night, I tell myself. I'm once again consciously trying to like Shadow Ridge. I'm trying to block the creepiness of the woods from my mind and put aside thoughts of the redbud tree covered with dead squirrels. I had to pay a guy two hundred dollars to clean up that mess. My father offered, but I refused to let him take on that job.

"Isn't it beautiful here?" I ask Rainie as I rub her back.

"It's sooo beautiful," she agrees, cuddling closer to me on the hammock. Above us we can see only trees, the leaves blackened by night, and beyond them a few dots of starlight.

I finally found a fencing company willing to work on my property. Anton, the young blond owner of the company, who looked like he just stepped off his surfboard, walked the proposed fence line with me and he didn't bat an eye when we got to the brush between the path and the lake. "Oh, we do this kind of thing practically every day," he said, and I felt like hugging him. The composite fence in the front yard will be a contemporary geometric pattern that will look great with the house. Back in the woods, out of sight from the street, it will be black chain link. They'll start clearing the brush and digging the holes for the posts tomorrow and I can't wait.

Rainie is asleep when I notice a distant light through the trees. It doesn't seem high enough to be a plane, but it must be. The height must be some sort of illusion. I leave Rainie in the hammock and cross the deck to the start of the trail. I take a few steps onto the path to get a little closer to the light. Then I freeze. It must be coming from the tree house! That's the only possibility. *Oh, God.* Could it be the redheaded woman? I race back to the deck, lift Rainie from the hammock, and rush into the house, locking the door behind me.

Then I call Samantha Johns.

Chapter 42

$\approx$

ELLIE

1965

I wrote back to Win immediately.

> Yes, please come! I live in the only house on Hockley Street in Round
> Hill. Park on Round Hill Rd after dark, not on Hockley where the car would
> stand out. Then walk to the end of Hockley Street. You'll need a flash-
> light, but try not to use it till you get to the woods at the end of the street.
> There's a narrow road into the woods. Walk down it a ways till you come
> to a circular area with no trees. You'll see my light. I'll be there at nine
> pm on August 2 and 3. Come whichever date you can. Be very careful.
> I love you.

I pictured Jocelyn getting the mail. Seeing that envelope with no re-
turn address and my handwriting disguised. I pictured her giving it to Win.
I imagined the scene obsessively as I stocked the shelves in the pharmacy.
It was the only thing that had made me smile in days.

On Monday night, I told Mama I had a headache and was going to bed early. It was just the two of us at home. Daddy and Buddy were both out. The men from Daddy's American Legion still got together to play poker, and I was glad they weren't giving my father the cold shoulder the way Mama's friends were doing to her. And who knew where Buddy was. He smelled of booze in the mornings and I was worried about him, but I knew that right now wasn't the time to confront him. I was tiptoeing around everyone. I'd caused my family pain and I was trying to go about my days quietly without making a fuss. None of us mentioned SCOPE, race, poverty, politics, bridge, poor sales at the pharmacy, or anything of any importance whatsoever. When we spoke at all, it was usually about the weather.

I arranged my pillows under my blankets so that my bed looked slept-in, then I left my bedroom and walked quietly to the stairs. Mama had the television on, and I could hear the drone of TV voices. I tiptoed down the stairs and out the back door, carrying my sleeping bag, a flashlight, and a paper bag containing two brownies I'd baked when I got home from the pharmacy. I'd given Win the choice of tonight or tomorrow night. If he didn't come tonight, I didn't know if I could survive another whole day like this one, waiting and hoping, my heart pounding nonstop all day long.

The moon was brighter than I'd anticipated, and my eyes adapted quickly to the darkness. In my imagination, the night had been far too dark for Win to be seen as he walked toward the woods at the end of the street. It was dark enough, I reassured myself. And besides, the only other person on Hockley Street tonight was my mother and she was parked in front of the TV, thinking her wayward daughter was safe upstairs.

The night was sticky hot and the kudzu rose like huge black monsters on either side of me. I felt a mosquito bite my shoulder. I was wearing a sundress I'd owned since I was sixteen. It was my favorite, a vibrant blue that looked black in the moonlight. I never wore a bra with this dress; the straps were too skinny and I was so small-breasted that a bra was unneeded. Quickening my pace as I neared the woods, I felt the fabric brush my nipples. I'd take this dress off for Win, if that's what he wanted. The thought was electrifying. I felt a yearning for him, a need I'd never experienced with Reed.

I turned on my flashlight when I reached the woods. I didn't need it, really. I knew the way to the circle and the tree house, plus the moonlight lit the narrow dirt road, but I wanted to experience the walk the way Win would. When I reached the circle, I walked around the oak tree and climbed the steps to the tree house. Opening my sleeping bag, I spread it out on the floor. Then I scooted on all fours onto the deck and sat down with my feet dangling over the edge, as I used to with Buddy, and I left my light burning, like a candle in a window.

I didn't know what time it was when I finally saw his light. It appeared through the trees, then disappeared, then appeared again. I knew it was him. It had to be. I wanted to call his name, but didn't dare, even though we were miles from anybody and too far from my house for my mother to hear me even if she stepped outside. Finally, he was in the circle, walking toward my tree.

He looked up at me. "I didn't expect to find you in a tree." He held the flashlight close to his face. I could see his rare smile. His white teeth.

"Come around the trunk," I said. "There are steps."

In a moment, he was with me on the sleeping bag. I'd imagined that we'd eat brownies, chat about everyone at SCOPE and how the canvassing was going, and then, finally, kiss. But—and it was entirely my doing—I wrapped my arms around him and pressed my lips to his.

Wherever he was staying now, it had a shower, because he smelled of soap. He kissed me with the same hunger I felt. Then I held him away from me.

"Want me to slow down?" he asked.

As an answer, I lifted my dress over my head. Tossed it to the side. In the dim light from the flashlight, I saw his eyes widen at my near naked-ness.

"Are you sure?" he asked. "You told me you didn't want to have sex un-less you were married."

I didn't want to think about the obstacles to us being able to marry. I wanted to think about right now. "Yes, I'm sure," I said, reaching for the buttons on his shirt.

We lay down and his kisses grew tender, his touch less hurried as he explored my body. The slowness only increased my hunger for him, and by the time he slipped inside me, I was more than ready for him. I expected pain, but there was little. Rather I felt only the relief of being so close to him.

I cried when it was over, the tears coming from some place I'd never known existed. He held me as I wept. He didn't utter false words of com-fort. Instead, as he stroked my hair, he said softly, "I know. I know." Because we both did know, didn't we? We knew this was impossible.

As we slowly came out of our reverie, we sat naked and ate brown-ies and talked about the work in Flint—he was canvassing with Paul now—and we chatted as though we had our own little world inside the tree house and nothing outside could hurt us.

"I miss everyone so much," I said after we lay down again, his arm around me once more. "I really miss being with a bunch of people, sing-ing freedom songs."

"What's your favorite?" he asked.

I didn't have to think about it. "I'll Fly Away," I said. "Even if it's talking about being, well, *dead*, it's got that joyous feeling to it."

"Death is nothing but a metaphor in that song," he said, and he sere-naded me with a couple of verses, making me smile and pull even closer to him.

Then, for a little while, we were quiet. Finally he spoke again.

"Listen, Ellie," he said. "I know we haven't known each other very long, but I'm not going to stop loving you."

"Me neither," I said. I'd never felt so sure of something.

He hesitated. Ran a hand up my arm. "You know I never planned on falling in love with a white girl," he said, touching my cheek, "but I've been looking at things from a different angle lately. I know you're as committed to civil rights as I am. That's what matters most to me."

"I am," I said.

He hesitated. "If we could figure out a way," he said slowly, "would you consider marrying me?"

I was both stunned and thrilled, but I felt the real world trying to work its way into the tree house. I wouldn't let it. "*Yes*," I said. "But I don't think we could stay here. In Derby County."

"I don't think we could stay in the South at all," he said. "Not safely. We'd have to go north. Or west."

"What about your family?" I felt so distant from mine, except for Buddy. It would take time, I thought, but Buddy would come around. He wouldn't want to lose me, no matter what I did—or who I married.

"I don't know about my parents," he said. "Not sure how they'd react. Most important, though, I'd have to find a way to take care of my sister."

"Yes," I agreed. I knew how much he adored his handicapped sister. "And I don't want to give up my dream of being a pharmacist. I love that mixture of magic and science."

That made him chuckle. "I love your brain," he said.

I laughed happily. "That's the most romantic thing you've ever said to me."

He squeezed my shoulder. "There's more where that came from." I knew he was smiling.

"And your dream of being a teacher," I said. "You can't lose that. So we'd have to go someplace where we could continue going to school."

"School part time," he said. "We'd have to work to keep a roof over our heads."

"Right." I couldn't believe we were talking about this. Maybe it could really happen. A tremor of joy passed through me at the possibility of a life with him.

It was nearly midnight when we walked together up Hockley Street toward Round Hill Road, where he'd left Paul's car. We held hands, our flashlights off, letting the moon guide us. I felt a little sore and wistful. I wondered if he was thinking what I was: The only place we could safely hold hands was in darkness. The only place we could be lovers was in hiding. Maybe we could have a future together, but it was distant and complicated. My joy at being so close to him was suddenly marred by my sadness.

As we passed the house, I saw that Buddy's black truck and our family car, which my father had taken to his poker game, were now in the driveway. I'd expected that, but I hadn't expected that the kitchen light would be on. Who was up and how would I get into the house and upstairs to my room? I said none of that to Win but he seemed to sense my anxiety, his hand tightening around mine.

"You live in a big ol' farmhouse," he said in a whisper.

"Mm." I knew he'd grown up in the heart of Darville. Different worlds, in too many ways to count. I walked him out to Paul's car. Round Hill Road was dark. No other cars. No people. I leaned against the sedan and he kissed me good night.

"Thursday night," he said.

"Thursday night," I agreed.

≈

Walking back to my house, I saw the kitchen light reflected off the side of Buddy's truck in the driveway. I hoped someone had left the light on accidentally. I decided to go in the front door. Maybe no one would notice me and I could slip up the stairs to my room unseen.

I opened the front door. I was so quiet, I couldn't imagine how anyone could hear me, but as soon as I stepped into the room and shut the door softly behind me, my father's voice boomed from the kitchen.

"Ellie, get in here."

I shut my eyes. Took in a breath. Made sure my dress was on right side out. Then I walked into the kitchen.

They were all waiting for me. My mother, father, brother. Mama sat at the table, crying, blotting her tears with a cloth napkin, and for a brief moment, I thought this midnight meeting had nothing to do with me. Had someone died?

"What's going on?" I asked, already feeling guilty that I hoped this was about some tragedy and not about me.

"Sit down," Daddy said. It was a command. This was about me, after all.

I sat down at my usual place at the table. I glanced at Buddy, sitting across from me. He just shook his head and looked away.

"You know," my father said, "we didn't talk to you about the toll your shenanigans have taken on our good name in this town and maybe we should have, because you don't seem to have figured out on your own what you've cost us."

"I was only gone for a month," I protested. "Your good name must have been pretty fragile if you could lose it over me trying to give poor people a say in their government."

"Eleanor!" my mother snapped, and I knew I'd stepped way over the line.

"You were with that boy tonight," Buddy accused me.

"What boy? What are you talking about? I was just outside to get some air. It's stifling in—"

"Don't lie to us!" my father shouted. "Mama thought she heard a sound and went to your room to check on you, and found your bed empty."

"What are you *doing*, Ellie?" Mama asked. "Who've you turned into?"

"I saw you with him," Buddy said, and the way he looked at me, I thought he knew I'd taken off my dress for Win. Let him touch me all over. Let him inside me.

"How could you see me with someone when I wasn't *with* anyone?" I asked.

"Two people comin' down Hockley Road in the moonlight? Could tell it was you plain as day, but couldn't make out the face of the boy. I assume he's the same one I beat up? Didn't learn his lesson?"

I felt frightened, not for myself, but for Win. Buddy's expression was serious and determined. He thought he was protecting me from someone—or something—but he was only hurting me.

"Look, everybody." My body trembled as I got to my feet. "I'm done with him. Tonight was just to tell him that. I'm done with him and I've left SCOPE and I'll start seeing Reed again and we can all put this month behind us, okay?"

I would do it, too. I'd do whatever I had to do to protect Win and get everyone off my back. I'd return to my old life. I'd work on getting Brenda's friendship back. That might take time. I'd get back in everyone's good graces, and then, when I got my pharmacist degree, I would move someplace far, far away where I could be my own person and not have to bend to the rules of anyone else.

"You're telling the truth?" My father looked suspicious. "You'll get back with Reed?"

"Yes. Not right this second. Not tomorrow. Let me ease into this, okay? I need to do this on my own time and I can't expect him to just pick up where we left off, either. But I ended it with Win . . . the guy you saw me with tonight." I looked at Buddy, acknowledging that he was right. "It's over." It hurt to say those words.

My mother was shaking her head. "I'm so ashamed of you," she said. "So disgusted! How could . . . ugh." She shuddered. "I just don't under—"

"It's all right, Pat," my father said, resting his hand on her shoulder. "She says it's over. Let's forget it happened. If Reed can forgive her, we can too."

"Thanks, Daddy," I said. I was amazed they seemed to believe me. I wasn't sure about my brother. His eyes were narrowed and suspicious and I had the feeling he would have liked to take another swipe at Win. But I seemed to have come out of this on top. "Good night," I said, and I turned and headed for the stairs wondering how I was going to get a message to Win to stay away on Thursday night.

We would have to work out another way to be together.

Chapter 43

———— ≈ ————

KAYLA

2010

The light still glows in the woods by the time the police officer shows up. He's very young and looks as though he spends all his free time at the gym. Although I'm disappointed that he's not Sam, I'm relieved to have him next to me as I point through the trees toward the small white light. I give him the short version of my disconcerting conversation with the woman in my office and the kidnapping of my daughter, who is now safely sleeping upstairs.

"The woman left my little girl in this old tree house," I say. "See that light in the distance? It's coming from the tree house."

"So you're thinking it's the redhead?" the officer asks quietly, as I guide him down the path from the deck. He lights the way with a flashlight.

"I don't know what to think."

We reach the trail that goes into the woods. Far ahead of us, the light glows. It looks like a star that fell into the trees.

"You go back on the deck," he says. "I'll check it out."

I return to the deck and sit at the glass-topped table. The song of the cicadas quickly swallows the sound of his footsteps and I fold my hands on the cool glass, waiting. My body's tense, fearing a gunshot. The longer I sit there, the more certain I feel that it's the red-haired woman in the tree house. The officer will arrest her for . . . what? Trespassing? I don't know. At the very least, he'll take her to the hospital and they'll give her a psychiatric evaluation and hopefully get her treatment in a nice, secure locked ward and I won't have to think about her any longer.

I hear footsteps and voices and get to my feet. Soon I see light bobbing through the trees, but when the officer emerges from the woods, it's Ellie walking next to him, not the redheaded woman. I hurry toward them.

"Ellie!" I say. "That was you up there? I had no idea!"

The light from my house is bright enough to let me know she's been crying. She's not wearing her glasses and her eyes are rimmed with red.

"I'm so sorry for trespassing, Kayla," she says. "And I didn't mean to scare you. I just remembered how lovely it is up there at night and I wanted to experience it again."

I still feel unsettled by the thought of someone wandering around my property uninvited. "Well, if anyone deserves to be in that tree house, it's you," I say sincerely, in spite of my discomfort. I look at the officer, whose expression is confused. "Ellie and her brother and father actually built that tree house many years ago," I say. "It's fine." Now I wish the officer would leave, but to his credit, he's not entirely comfortable with the situation and he takes me aside.

"You're sure you're okay with her being on your land?" he asks. "She's not the woman who threatened . . . who made a statement to you about killing someone?"

"Completely different person," I say. "Really. I'm sorry you had to come out here. It's okay."

Once the officer leaves, Ellie apologizes again. "I'll go home, now," she says. "And again, I'm sorry for wrecking your peaceful night."

He turned off his light and we were in complete darkness. I couldn't read his face, and I was glad he couldn't read mine. "My brother saw us walking back to your car the other night," I said. "He told my parents. I got the law laid down on me, but I couldn't figure out a way to get word to you. We really shouldn't be here."

He didn't respond right away and I took his silence to mean that he was unnerved. I was sure he didn't want to meet up with Buddy again. "Where do your parents think you are?" he asked.

"I told them I was going over my friend Brenda's. She and I had a falling-out and I said I was going to try to smooth things over with her. So I can't stay long. If for some reason they call Brenda and I'm not there, they'll—"

"Shh," he said. Wrapping his arms around me, he drew me down onto the sleeping bag. "Let's not . . . do anything tonight," he said. "Just stay like this for a little while. Then I'll leave and we'll have to figure out some other way to see each other in the future."

I rested my head against his chest, my arm across his waist. I clutched the fabric of his shirt. *What future?* I thought. *How can we ever make this work?*

For the next twenty minutes or so, we lay like that as he told me how everyone was doing in Flint. They'd brought in a new guy from Stanford University to take my place and he was experienced and good to canvass with, "but not nearly as much fun as you," he said. The plans were coming together for the next protest and I felt sad to realize I wouldn't be there.

"I've got a little gift for you," he said. He pulled something from his pants pocket and pressed it into my hand.

I sat up and turned on my light to reveal a silver bangle bracelet. When I saw the engraving, emotion flooded over me. *Ellie—We'll Fly Away—love, Win.* I was moved by the thought that went into the gift, the time it must have taken him to steal away from his SCOPE duties to buy it. I was moved by the obvious love behind it.

I turned out my light again, wrapped my arms around him. "I love it so much," I said, clutching the bracelet in my hand. I wished I could wear it, but I didn't dare. Not yet.

"Sh!" His body stiffened beneath my arms. I sat back and he pressed a finger to my lips. "Listen!" he whispered.

Footsteps. Deer or man? Sometimes at night it was hard to tell. I thought the sound was coming from the leaf-littered path that ran alongside the lake, a fair distance away.

"I'm leaving." Win turned my face toward him with his fingertips and kissed me lightly. He felt around on the sleeping bag, looking for his flashlight. I started to tell him I thought the sound was only deer. I didn't want him to go. But then there were more footsteps, and I knew they were human. My heart began to pound.

Win was already lowering himself down the steps.

"Try not to use your light," I whispered.

I heard the crunch of tires and crawled onto the deck just in time to see red taillights blink off on the narrow road that led from Hockley Street to the circle. It was a truck—I could tell that much in the gloomy light—and as it backed up near the circle in the darkness, I could see that something light colored was moving in the bed. Pigs? It was a moment before I realized there were *people* in the bed of the truck. People dressed in white robes and pointed hoods. *Oh God.* When the truck came to a stop, one of them opened the tailgate and they spilled into the clearing. All but one, who stayed behind, huddled in a corner of the bed. There were six or seven of them in the circle and they turned on their flashlights. Another few came from the woods. I knew Klan members met back here in the clearing. Was this coincidental or was it because someone knew I was meeting Win? I prayed for the former, but knew deep down it was the latter, and I knew it for certain when I heard a masculine voice, unrecognizable to me, call out, "Got him!"

I should have crawled from the deck back into the tree house and stayed silent, hoping no one knew I was up there, but there was no way I could do that. I couldn't see Win or his captor. Below me was nothing more than a sea of pale satin, roiling like whitewater. I heard a cry of pain and winced as though I'd been struck myself.

I shined my flashlight down on them just as one of them landed a punch to Win's jaw.

"Leave him alone!" I shouted. "He's with me! He's my friend!" A few of the hooded monsters looked up at me with their covered faces and round black eyes. They reminded me of maggots, all alike, all horrid and slimy in their satin robes. "Please!" I begged. "I'm Danny Hockley's daughter! Buddy's sister! Please! Just leave him alone!"

"Ellie!" I heard Win call, his voice strained. "Run!"

I didn't know what to do. If I went down to the clearing, was there any chance at all that I could calm them, or would they turn their wrath on me? I was afraid I knew the answer.

I could no longer see Win, but I knew he was on the ground being kicked and beaten. I heard grunts and groans, but couldn't tell if the sounds were coming from him or the mob, or both. We would have to wait this out—wait out the beating—until they grew tired of it and left. And then I'd put him back together again. Nurse him. *Screw my parents!* I'd go wherever Win needed to go to heal and I'd take care of him until he was whole again.

Suddenly, one of the maggots peeled away from the crowd and began walking toward me, toward my tree. I scrambled from the deck, through the tree house, to the doorway, turning off my flashlight on the way. I sat on the edge of the doorway and saw the white robe down below, the man feeling for the steps, for a way up to me. I held my breath, leaning back in the darkness, my knees bent, my legs coiled, and when that silk hood rose to the level of its empty-looking eyeholes, I shot my legs forward with all my might, my feet crashing into the hooded face, sending the man flying backward from the tree with a shout. I heard him crash below, and when I shined my flashlight toward the ground, he was lying still, a splash of shimmering white on the dead leaves. Almost instantly, another robed man appeared at his side and I quickly turned out my light. "Hey!" the man called toward the others. "Need some help here!"

I knew that voice. Uncle Byron? I couldn't swear to it, and I knew I wasn't thinking clearly, my brain swirling with fear and fury, but that voice was familiar. Another robed figure appeared below and the two of them grunted as they tried to help the man I'd pushed get to his feet. I watched just long enough to see them stumble away, dragging the man through the leaves and pine needles, then I crawled back to the deck. I could see Win, lying still, a couple of Klan members still kicking him. *Please don't let him be dead*, I prayed. I wanted everyone to clear out so I could go down and help him.

One of the Klan was kneeling near the back of the truck and it wasn't until he stood up that I could make out a rope tied around Win's ankles at one end, and the truck's bumper at the other.

"No!" I screamed. "Stop!" They were going to kill him. These Round Hill men I probably passed on the street every day. These *murderers*.

Someone's light passed over the rear of the truck and I saw the big white letters on the blue tailgate—FORD. *Mildred.*

Oh my God. Reed? It couldn't be! But in the glare of the flashlight, I saw the dented bumper and knew the truth. "Reed!" I shouted. "Stop! Please!"

That was it. It was too much. The fury inside me carried me through the tree house. I had the wherewithal to drop the bracelet in the space between the floorboards and wall of the house before clambering down the steps, leaping over the last few to the ground. I ran into the clearing just as the maggots were climbing back into the bed of the truck. Reed's truck.

"Reed!" I screamed running toward the truck. "Stop! Don't do this!"

Someone grabbed me from behind, arms pressed around me so tightly they pushed the air from my lungs. I kicked and screamed, lashing out with my elbows, reaching behind my head to try to pull the hood off the coward hanging on to me, but his arms were a steel trap. I could barely make out Win's still body on the ground behind the truck. Then the red taillights lit up and I watched helplessly as the truck took off, slowly at first, crunching along the narrow path to Hockley Street, dragging Win behind it.

"No!" I pleaded, though I knew no one was listening to me. No one cared. "No! Please!" I lost sight of him and the truck in the dark woods, but I heard it speed up when it reached the dirt road. Hockley Street. I screamed and screamed, fighting to get free from my silent captor to run after the truck of maggots and the man I loved. I screamed until I couldn't hear the sound of the truck any longer, and the man holding me threw me hard to the ground and took off into the woods with the other Klansmen who'd been left behind.

Chapter 45

---≈---

I was sobbing as I struggled to get to my feet, my ankle twisted beneath me. The pain was excruciating, but I knew it was nothing compared to what Win was enduring. I wanted to run after the truck, but couldn't put any weight on my foot at all. I felt around in the woods for a stick to use as a cane. I had no idea where my flashlight had landed. I threw up in the weeds, thinking of Win being dragged along the road that way. Thinking of what it would do to his body.

It took me forever to hobble through the woods and up Hockley Street to my house, and I was hysterical by the time I got there. Buddy'd just come in from seeing the girl he was dating, and he was making himself a sandwich in the kitchen. It must have been ten thirty by then. Maybe later. He knew the second I walked in that something was horribly wrong.

"Where's the car?" I shouted.

"Sh," he said. "You'll wake Mama. Daddy's got the car. He's at a poker game. What's wrong?"

"I need to use your truck!" I reached for his keys where they hung from the rack next to the back door, but he grabbed my arm.

"Whoa." He frowned. "What d'you need the truck for? What's going on?"

"I don't have time to explain everything!" But then I broke down, flopping into one of the chairs, my ankle unable to hold me up any longer. "The Klan's got Win, Buddy!" I said. "They beat him up—Uncle Byron was there—and now Reed's dragging him behind his truck." I leaned forward, pleading. "I need your *truck*, Buddy! I have to find Win."

"Reed?" Buddy said, as though that was the only word he'd heard out of all I said. "You know Reed better than that, honey. And Uncle Byron's playin' poker with Daddy, so he wasn't—"

"Who knew Win and I met at the tree house?" I asked.

"You were playin' with fire, meetin' him there," he said angrily. "Playin' with fire meetin' him anywhere! You know the Klan likes to get together back in them woods. One of them must have seen you. Seen that boy come to meet you and told the others."

"Let me take your truck!"

"C'mon, honey, settle down," he said. "You need to ice that ankle." He went to the refrigerator and pulled the ice tray from the freezer compartment. "Let's just sit tight tonight. We'll figure it all out in the morning."

"What do you mean, sit *tight*?" I shouted.

"Sh." He cracked open the ice tray over the sink. "Do you want to have to explain to Mama why you're upset?"

But I wasn't listening. The path was clear between me and the key rack. I jumped up and grabbed the key to his truck and took off out the back door, gritting my teeth against the pain in my ankle.

Behind me, I heard him drop the ice tray into the sink. "All right!" he shouted. "I'll go with you. You're gonna get yourself killed out there. Let me drive."

I let him get in behind the wheel. "Go to Reed's," I said from the passenger seat. "But slow. We have to look along the street for . . ." I couldn't finish the sentence, choking on the words. I imagined seeing Win, bloody and near dead, along the side of the road.

Buddy started driving, turning onto Round Hill Road, dark and empty this time of night. I sat on the edge of the seat, my gaze darting left and right, searching for Win in the cone of yellow light from the truck's headlights.

"Why'd you do it, Ellie?" Buddy pounded his fist on the steering wheel. "Why'd you let yourself get mixed up with him? You knew it'd come to no good."

It was too dark to see his face, but I heard the emotion in his voice: he was choked up. No matter how wrong he thought I was, no matter how stupid, he loved me. He didn't want me hurt.

Reed's house was dark. His parents' car was in the driveway but his truck was missing. That sent a fresh wave of terror through me. Where had he taken Win? Where were they now and what were they doing to him?

"He ain't here," Buddy said.

"Pull into the driveway," I commanded.

Buddy pulled into the driveway and I staggered out of the truck even before he came to a stop, nearly falling when I put weight on my ankle. He caught up to me and I leaned on him as I hobbled to the front door, where I pressed the bell over and over again.

Buddy grabbed my hand. "He ain't here, Ellie! You can see that. You're just gonna wake his parents."

A light came on in the living room and a moment later the front door opened. I was ready to bombard Reed's mother or father with questions, but it was Reed himself standing in front of us. He had on jeans with no belt and his plaid shirt was unbuttoned over his white undershirt. He wore a look of confusion. I wasn't buying it. I started screaming at him. Pounding on him.

"Where did you take him?" I shouted. "Where is he, you son of a bitch?"

"Hush, honey!" Buddy grabbed my arms. Held them at my sides.

"What the hell are you talking about?" Reed asked.

"Where's your truck?" Buddy asked him.

"What did you do with Win?" I shouted.

"My truck's at your car shop," he said to Buddy. "I dropped it off after work to get that bumper fixed and got a ride home." Then he looked at me. "And I didn't do anything with anybody," he said.

I looked at Buddy, feeling a slim bit of hope that it hadn't been Reed's truck after all. That Reed had no part in this mess. "Is that true? His truck's at your shop?"

Reed answered before Buddy could. "The shop was closed." He looked at Buddy again. "I left it there for you to take a look at in the morning. Dropped the keys through the slot in your door and put a note on the windshield. My left rear bumper's bashed in."

"What time did you leave it?" Buddy asked, loosening his hold on my arms.

"Right after I got out of work. Around six. Six thirty."

"Nobody else has a truck like yours around here, Reed," I said.

Reed looked from me to my brother and back again. "What the hell's going on?" he asked.

I started crying, suddenly exhausted. I leaned against Buddy; he was practically holding me up. "You couldn't handle it," I said to Reed. "You couldn't handle me being with someone else. I hope you suffer the way he suffered. What did you do with—"

"Is this about that guy you were—"

"We gotta go," Buddy interrupted him. He pulled me away from the door so hard I nearly fell off the step.

"Wait!" I said to him. "I need to know what happened to Win!" I called over my shoulder as Buddy dragged me away. "Where did you leave him?" I shouted. "Where is he?"

But Reed just wore a stupefied look, and Buddy told me to shut up. He opened the truck door for me and nearly had to lift me inside. "We have to go to the sheriff's office," I said. "Not Uncle Byron, though. I think he's part of the whole—"

He shut the door before I finished my sentence and walked around the front of the truck to get in. Reed still stood at his front door, trying to look innocent.

"Something ain't right," Buddy said, putting the truck in gear and backing out of the driveway.

"What do you mean?" I asked.

"I went back to the shop on my way to Jenny Ann's," he said, looking in his rearview mirror. "Had to be at least seven thirty. Eight, maybe. Reed's truck wasn't there."

I pounded the dashboard. "I hate him!" I said. "*Hate* him! Buddy, we have to find Win. Please help me. He's in a ditch somewhere. He's still alive. I can feel it!" I couldn't bear the thought of him lying alone somewhere, bleeding and helpless.

Buddy was heading into town but he missed the turn for the sheriff's office. "Where are you *going?*" I reached for the steering wheel, but he batted my hand away.

"My shop," he said. "I need to see where Reed put the truck. Maybe it was in the back lot and I didn't see it when I stopped in earlier." He wanted Reed to be innocent, I could tell. He wanted the truck to be there in the back lot and we could then imagine there was someone, some Klansman from the next county over, with a blue and white Ford pickup and a reason to hate Winston Madison.

We were a block away from the shop and we could already see it: Reed's truck, parked just about as close to the shop's front door as it could be. There was no way Buddy could have missed it earlier. Buddy pulled up to the curb and we both stared at the rear of the truck. My heart pounded in my throat.

There was no dented bumper.

Reed's truck had no bumper at all.

Chapter 46

———≈———

Buddy and I drove all over Round Hill. I got the flashlight from behind his seat and shined it in the roads and the woods and the fields. I kept saying, "He's still alive; I'm sure of it." Buddy said nothing at all except to tell me it couldn't have been Reed and the truth would come out eventually. We drove up and down every street in town. I made him take me back to his car shop to check the bed of Reed's truck, just in case the maggots had left Win in there. It took me so long to come up with that possibility that once I had it, I felt certain I'd hit on the answer, and I was angry at myself for not checking sooner. Maybe he'd been alive when we first saw the truck, but now it was too late. That was the way I was thinking, every horrid possibility running through my mind. But the bed of the truck was empty except for a nondescript cigarette lighter and an empty beer bottle.

I hobbled back into the truck. Buddy looked over at me. Touched my shoulder. "Honey," he said, "wherever they left him, we ain't gonna find him tonight."

≈

I turned on my radio the second I woke up the following morning, but there was no mention of the nighttime work of the Klan on the local station. There never was. I dressed and went downstairs, hoping I could use either Daddy's car or Buddy's truck to go to the police station, but my father and brother were both gone. Mama took one look at me when I limped into the room, then dropped her gaze to my swollen ankle. "What on earth happened to you?"

"I tripped on the back steps last night."

I could tell she didn't believe me. "You're a right royal mess," she said. "I'll make some eggs while you go clean yourself up and put on a dress. You can't work in the pharmacy looking like that. Your hair looks like a raccoon got at it."

"I don't have time to work in the pharmacy," I said. I planned to ride my old bicycle to the police station. Then I'd get one of the policemen to drive me all over Round Hill in the daylight, looking for Win.

"Sit down," Mama said. It sounded like a command.

"I'm not hungry. I—"

"Sit." I noticed that her eyes were red, and I sank onto one of the kitchen chairs. "You need to help your father today," she said. "He had a rough night. And I have some very bad news." She looked away from me. "I don't even know how to tell you."

I was instantly alert. "What?"

"Last night, Garner was trying to repair the ceiling in the room they're turning into a nursery and he lost his balance. Fell off the ladder and knocked himself out." She looked back at me. "Brenda called Byron, and Daddy was playing cards with him, so they both went over and drove Garner and Brenda to the hospital, but Garner was gone by the time they got there."

"Gone?" I said, like I'd never heard the word before. My mind was on fire, my thoughts so scattered. I was thinking of Win and how all the while we were driving around looking for him, Garner was dying. My eyes filled with tears as I thought of what Brenda was going through. Did we both lose the men we loved last night?

"And that's not all," Mama said. "Brenda was so beside herself that she lost the baby. She's still in the hospital."

Oh no. I stood up, wincing at the pain in my ankle. "I have to go to her," I said. Brenda and I had had a falling-out, yes, but I would always be her friend. And I *would* go to her . . . after I went to see Uncle Byron at the sheriff's office. If he was playing cards with my father the night before, then I was mistaken about hearing his voice in the clearing, and that was a relief. Maybe he could help me find Win.

≈

I gritted my teeth against the pain in my ankle as I rode my bike down our driveway. I pedaled up Hockley Street toward the woods, searching the sides of the road near the kudzu, both wanting and not wanting to find Win. My fantasy was finding him alive. Rushing to his side. Saving him before it was too late. But there was no sign of him, and I pedaled onto Round Hill Road toward the sheriff's office. Tears burned my eyes as I thought of Garner. Of Brenda. Of Win.

≈

"You heard about Garner?" Uncle Byron looked up from something he was writing as I walked into his small, cluttered office.

"Yes, it's so horrible," I said, my voice thick. "But that's not why I'm here." I sank into a heavy wooden chair across the desk from him and poured it all out, telling him I'd met Win in the tree house and how Reed—or at least Reed's truck—backed into the clearing and how the men in white robes beat Win and dragged him away. Uncle Byron tapped his pen against his chin the whole time I spoke.

"I haven't heard a word about any Klan disturbance last night," he said.

"It wasn't a 'disturbance'!" I shouted. "It was murder!" I'd meant to say *attempted* murder, and tears stung my eyes at my mistake. "He might still be alive, Uncle Byron." My voice broke. "Please help me find him."

Uncle Byron stood up and slammed his office door shut, then turned to me, angry blotches of color on his cheeks. "How do you suggest I do that, Ellie?" he asked. "This is a big county." He walked over to his desk again, but didn't sit down. "And to be honest, right now I'm thinkin' about Garner Cleveland. Your . . . *friend* Win is lost because the two of you were stupid enough to try to—"

"It's your job!" I shouted, getting to my feet myself. "What if he was white? Would you give a shit then?"

Uncle Byron folded his arms. The look on his face told me he didn't care one iota what happened to Win Madison. "Grow up, Ellie," he said. "He *wasn't* white. You knew you were asking for trouble when you started sneaking around with that boy."

If there was one thing I hated, it was being told to grow up. "You were at that Klan rally in the cow pasture," I said. "You know who's in the Klan in Round Hill. Talk to them! Somebody has to know what happened to Win. And talk to Reed! He lied about when he took his truck to Buddy's. He was jealous, and—"

"Reed Miller couldn't hurt a skeeter if it was biting the end of his nose." Uncle Byron sat down again. "Don't have it in him."

Something happened to my heart when he said that. Four years of caring about gentle, steadfast Reed Miller filled my chest and I lowered my face to my hands and cried, sinking into the chair again. I didn't know what to think. All I knew was that he lied about when he took his truck to Buddy's. And he hated Win.

"Meanwhile—" Uncle Byron leaned forward as I lifted my head from my hands. He folded his arms on his desk. "—don't you care that your best friend is grievin' her husband and child at this very minute? Or are you too busy moonin' over some colored boy you think got dragged to kingdom come last night?"

I hated him at that moment as much as I'd ever hated anyone. I left his office, trying unsuccessfully not to limp, not to appear weak in any way, and by the time I got outside to my bike, I wasn't sure if the tears running down my face were from grief or pain.

≈

Back on my bike, I didn't know where to go, but Uncle Byron's words were working their way into my brain. *Don't you care that your best friend is grieving?* I wasn't far from the hospital, so I pedaled there, parked my bike out front, and went in search of Brenda. She'd hurt me, the way she'd given me the cold shoulder after all our years as friends, but right now I knew she needed my friendship, and I sure as hell needed hers. When she saw me in the doorway of her hospital room, though, she rolled onto her side away from me. "Go away, you goddamn stupid bitch," she said.

For a moment, I froze in shocked silence. And then I did as she said. I went away. I left her, my once-upon-a-time best friend. She'd turned into someone I no longer recognized.

I knew my father was expecting me at the pharmacy, but I couldn't possibly work today. Instead, I rode my bike up and down nearly every damn road in Round Hill, all the roads Buddy and I had covered in the dark, and some of the roads outside the town as well. I didn't find Win, but I found the bumper of Reed's truck. I was on some nameless back road about half a mile past Round Hill Baptist when I saw the sunlight glinting silver in the weeds at the side of the road. I was a sweaty mess by then—it must have been a hundred degrees—and my ankle was as big as the moon. I got off my bike and walked over and sure enough, there it was, Mildred's bumper, all dinged up with a few yards of rope attached to it. I could see where they'd hacked the rope off. Where they'd cut Win loose. I stood alone in the middle of the road, not a soul in sight, scared of finding him and scared of not finding him. I called for him and listened hard, but heard nothing. Not even a bird. I rode my bike fast as a lightning bolt back to

Buddy's shop and made him close the shop and go back out there with me to search. I knew he felt the same way Uncle Byron did—that I brought this all on myself, as well as on Win, by getting mixed up with a Black man—but he never said it. He never rubbed my face in it. He just helped me look, walking into the weedy fields out there, getting chigger bites and hoping we weren't stepping on copperheads. And we found nothing besides the bumper. And finally Buddy put his arms around me.

"You have to let this go, little sis," he said.

I looked up at him. "He could still be alive," I said. My voice sounded childlike to my ears. I felt the tremor in my lower lip.

"Ellie, look how far we are from Hockley Street? From the woods where they tied him to the bumper? And it's pretty clear this is where they finally untied him. Way out here. I don't see how . . ."

He didn't have to finish the sentence. I pressed my forehead against his chest while he wrapped his arms around me and I sobbed. He said nothing, just let me grieve. *Please don't let him have suffered too much,* I prayed. *Please, God.*

I finally looked up at Buddy. "I've got to go to Flint," I said. "I've got to tell Greg and everyone what happened. I need to make sure his family knows. And then I've got to leave."

"Leave?" He frowned. "What are you talking about?"

"I can't stay here." I rubbed the tears from my cheeks. "I hate everyone here except you. And everyone here hates me back."

"You don't hate Mama and Daddy. You don't hate Brenda. And she needs you. She don't know it right now, but she'll figure it out eventually."

"Yes, I do," I said. "I hate everybody. Except you."

≈

I borrowed Buddy's truck and drove to Flint. Greg and Jocelyn were working at their desks in the school, but everyone else was out canvassing. Jocelyn sobbed, her face in her hands, when I told them, and for the first time, I saw real fury in Greg's face.

"You foolish kids!" he said, throwing the pen he was using across the room. "We have rules for a reason! You knew the jeopardy you were putting him in, Ellie!"

I broke down again and Jocelyn wrapped her arms around me. I couldn't speak. I was so wounded by Greg's words, and so deserving of them. I knew his anger masked his grief. He had the weight of the world on his shoulders, having to report what had happened under his watch to Hosea Williams and Dr. King. And he would have to be the one to tell Win's family.

"Please don't tell them exactly what happened," I begged through my tears. "Don't put that image in their minds. Please don't tell them how he died."

He stared at me, the whites of his eyes already red behind his glasses. "Doesn't matter what I tell them," he said. "There's no good way for your son to die."

Chapter 47

KAYLA

"Can you imagine what it would be like to be pulled behind a truck like that?" Ellie asks me. "Your skin coming off? The agony?" She's crying softly.

We're in my great room, Ellie on the sectional, me in an armchair, and the barely touched tea in our cups cold by now. I'm horrified. I have that feeling at the back of my throat that tells me I'm going to start crying any second. I had that feeling every day for the first couple of months after Jackson's death.

"I've tried my best to put it behind me," she says. "It's why I never came home before now. I knew it would just wake up the pain and no matter how many years—how many *decades*—have passed, I didn't want that pain back again. Losing someone I loved. Imagining what he went through."

"I'm so sorry," I say, not for the first time. I've said it over and over again as she told me her story. But I've also been biting my tongue. I'm certain my father had nothing to do with what happened to Win. I'm waiting for her to get to that part of the story—to the part where she tells me my father is innocent. Yet the way she acts toward Daddy . . . I have the feeling she still thinks he had something to do with it.

"Did you ever find out the truth about that whole thing with Daddy's truck?" I ask. "He'd never be in the Klan, Ellie, much less do something like that. You don't really still believe he had something to do with it, do you?"

"I don't know what to think," she says, wiping her eyes with the napkin I'd given her. "I don't think Byron ever questioned him . . . or anybody else, for that matter . . . but he had to know something, Kayla. He lied about when he left the truck at Buddy's shop. Why would he lie if he wasn't guilty of *something*?"

"You'll never convince me he had anything to do with it," I say. "Daddy's no bigot."

"Maybe he wasn't a bigot, but he was a jealous man." She gives me a small smile. "And you're a good daughter, defending him. And all I can do is hope that his conscience has punished him enough over the years. I wish he'd tell me the truth, though, whatever it is. One way or another, I could finally put that horrible time of my life to rest."

I will talk to my father about it. Ask him for the truth. For my own peace of mind, I need to know that he had no part in this horrific story.

"I guess you and Brenda became friends again over the years?" I ask, mostly to get the image of that poor guy tied to the truck out of my mind.

She presses her lips together, taking a moment to answer. "Not exactly," she says finally. "We hadn't talked since I left. Some forty-five years, not one word or letter. But Buddy and Mama were always close to her—Mama especially. Brenda's been the daughter to her I was never able to be. So when I knew I was coming back here, I wrote to her. I asked if we could let bygones be bygones. We've both lived long lives and I didn't want to hang on to ugly feelings about her. I was surprised when she wrote right back and said how much she wanted to see me and what it would mean to Mama for us to . . . reunite. We agreed to forget the past and start fresh. Pretend we were two sixty-five-year-old women meeting for the first time.

So that's what we've done. Or at least, what we've tried to do. It's not all that easy, with that history. There's tension between us, still."

I'd noticed that tension the day of my yoga class at Ellie's house. "She was so hurtful," I said.

"She probably felt the same way about me, though. Her husband had just died and I was too wrapped up in my own life to console her. But anyway, I made up my mind to judge her on the person she is now." She taps the rim of her teacup thoughtfully. "The truth is, if she and I were meeting today, I doubt we'd become friends," she says. "We're so different. But I'm glad she's here. She's a huge help with Mama. I'm sure Mama would rather have her as her daughter than me."

"I doubt that," I say, although remembering my conversation with Miss Pat the day I drove her to her doctor's office, I think Ellie might be right.

She shrugs with a resigned smile. "I left them. My parents. I sent the occasional letter and received the occasional letter in reply. Until now, that was the extent of my relationship with my mother. When my father died, I should have come home. I knew my mother blamed me—*I* blamed me—but I'd only left a few months earlier and the wounds were still deep. So deep. I couldn't bear to come back. I blamed everybody for what happened to Win."

"Did you ever check the internet to see if . . . maybe . . ."

"Win survived?" She finishes the sentence for me. "Of course I have. Many, many times. I think it would have been impossible, though. I think he might have been dead even before they tied him to the truck. I honestly hope he was, so he didn't feel any more pain."

I couldn't bear to picture it any longer. "So you went to California," I said. "As far from Round Hill as you could get."

She nodded. "Exactly," she said. "San Francisco. Earned my pharmacology degree, finally. But I quickly got involved doing community organization, which will always be my passion. My whole life was shaped by that summer with SCOPE."

"I think you mentioned that Buddy visited you out there. Did your mother?"

"Never, though you're right: Buddy came every couple of years. He understood why I couldn't come back."

"And you never married?"

She shook her head. "Never really had another serious relationship. I was married to my work. I took up yoga, which gave me some balance in my life . . . until Buddy got so sick and I knew I had to come back here. It woke everything up for me again. A lot of my anger got directed at your father in my mind because I had no place else to put it. When I met you and realized you were his daughter . . ." She let out a breath. "Well, you're not him," she said, then smiled. "I've tried to separate you from him in my mind."

"You mentioned 'Byron' a few times," I said. "He was the sheriff?"

"Byron Parks. Yes, and my father's best friend. I called him Uncle Byron all my life."

"Wait here," I said. I crossed the room and went upstairs to Jackson's office, where I dug through his files until I found the folder on the purchase of our house. I carried it downstairs.

"This is weird," I said, sitting down again. "The Realtor who handled the building sites out here emailed my husband to say there was another potential buyer for this lot." I leafed through the papers until I found the email printout I was looking for. I read it out loud. " 'Just wanted to let you know that you have some competition for that lot, Jackson, so you might want to act quickly. It's the best and biggest in Shadow Ridge. Your competitor is an old-timer who's lived in Round Hill all his life, a guy named Byron Parks. He's working on getting a mortgage, but between you and me, I don't think he stands a chance.' "

"*What?*" Ellie leans forward, reaching for the paper.

"I remember Jackson telling me about it," I said, handing the sheet of paper to her. "But Byron Parks died before he could go through with it."

Ellie scans the email. "This makes no sense. He would have been . . .

I don't know, at least ninety years old. What would he have wanted with this plot of land? This is bizarre."

I shake my head. "Ever since I moved into this house, my whole *life's* been bizarre," I say. Then I smile at her. "You know what, Ellie?" I ask.

She looks up from the email. "What?" Her blue eyes are expectant.

"I'm going to have someone take that tree house down this week," I say.

She returns my smile. Her face is finally relaxed. Her skin almost seems to glow. "A fine idea," she says, then adds, "Ask them to burn the wood to cinders."

Chapter 48

———— ≈ ————

I'm pleased when one of my appointments cancels the following morning, giving me a whole hour to dig around online for Winston Madison. I want him to be alive. I want to give Ellie that peace. After hearing about his horrific treatment, I could use that peace for myself. But I can't find him. I can't find a single person with that name. I even check the death records but it's as though Win Madison never existed.

After I leave Bader and Duke, I go to my father's to pick up Rainie. When I get out of my car, I can already hear giggling and squealing from the backyard. I walk around the corner of the house to find Daddy pushing her on the swing.

"Mommy!" she calls. "Come swing with me."

"Yeah, c'mon, Mommy!" my father calls. He's a handsome old guy, his smile so warm and love-filled. I want him to be innocent of doing anything wrong.

I sling my purse over my shoulder, then settle onto the second swing and begin pumping my legs.

We swing for a while, Rainie entertaining us with everything she did at school today, but I'm not really listening. Daddy can tell.

"What's up, kiddo?" he asks when I swing back in his direction.

"Tell you later," I say over my shoulder.

When Rainie grows tired of the swing, the three of us go inside, where I settle her in front of the TV. The living room is full of packed boxes and the walls are bare. My father is ready for the movers. I can't help but feel sad.

Daddy nods toward the kitchen and I follow.

"I had a long talk with Ellie last night," I say, sitting down at the kitchen table. "She told me about the night Win Madison was killed by the Klan."

He opens the refrigerator and pulls out a Diet Coke for me and a beer for himself. I've never seen him drink in the middle of the afternoon, and I think he must know what's coming.

"Does she still think I had something to do with it?" he asks.

"You can't blame her, Daddy. Can you explain how the Klan had your truck?"

He opens the beer. Takes a sip. "You sound like you doubt me too," he says.

"No. No, I know you wouldn't have been part of something like that."

"You're right. I wasn't." He glances toward the living room, where I'm sure Rainie is completely absorbed in the cartoon she's watching. "It was the thing to do in some circles, back then. Be a part of the Klan. To be honest, I sometimes felt"—he swirls his beer in the bottle—"left out, because I chose not to be involved." He looks at me, his blue eyes clear as seawater. "I didn't want anything to do with it. But most of the guys I knew were in it. Garner Cleveland. His father, Randy Cleveland, was a wealthy bigwig in town and a bigwig in the local Klan. My own father was in it."

"Really? Grandpa?

"Really. He got on my case for not joining. Said if I wanted to amount to anything in Round Hill, I had to belong. That I shouldn't hold myself above everyone else."

"Well, you showed him, Mr. Mayor." I smiled, but he didn't seem to hear me.

"Ellie's father was in it . . . I don't know if she knows that. I think Brenda even got caught up in it through Garner. There was a so-called auxiliary for the women. I don't know what they did. Baked cookies for the men. I don't know."

"Was Grandma part of it?" I'm repelled by the thought and relieved when Daddy shakes his head.

"What about Buddy?" I ask. "He had access to your truck, right? It was at his car shop and you told Ellie and Buddy that you'd put the keys through a slot in his shop door."

"That's right, I did. And while it's true that Buddy could have gotten my keys, he was no Klansman. Buddy wasn't a saint but he was basically a decent guy. I suppose he still is, but he's hardly spoken to me in forty-five years, so I wouldn't rightly know. I guess he still thinks I had something to do with it."

"Or else *he* did it and is worried you know it."

Daddy took a swig of beer and shook his head. "I can't picture it," he said.

"He would have thought he was protecting his sister. He beat Win up at a protest held by her SCOPE group."

Daddy shrugged. "I could see him throwing a punch. Can't see him killing a man, especially not like that." He grimaced. "I honestly don't know *anyone* who could do a thing like that. I think it had to be an outsider. I've thought a lot about it, believe me. The only other person I can think of who'd have the key to get into the car shop would have been Garner's father, Randy Cleveland, who owned the building. But he was supposedly out of town that night."

I sigh. I want answers and I'm sure my father's telling the truth when he says he doesn't have any.

"I think this is something we're never going to know," he says, looking across the counter at me. "I wish Ellie could let it go after all this time, for her own sake. Coming home to Round Hill must be torture for her."

I sit back on the stool with a sigh. "I know," I say. "But I don't know how you can ever let go of something like that."

≈

I have Friday off, and after I get home from taking Rainie to school, I'm pleased to see the fencing company's truck in front of my house. This will be their second day on the job, and I'm relieved to know that I'll soon have my fence.

I settle down on the sectional with my coffee and a new book on contemporary design. I'm halfway through chapter three when Anton, the owner of the fencing company, knocks on my sliding-glass door. Even before I open the door, I see that he's lost his surfer-boy tan. His face has no color in it at all.

I slide the door open. "Do you need water?" I ask.

"No, ma'am." He wipes his hand over his sweaty face, leaving a trail of dirt on his cheek. Is his hand trembling? "I don't know how to tell you this, Miz Carter," he says, "but we found some bones where we're digging back there by the lake. And they ain't from no animal, neither."

Chapter 49

An hour and a half later, Sam Johns arrives with a team of white-suited, blue-gloved men and women from Carlisle. When I called her, she said to tell the four workers to stop any digging but to remain for questioning, so they've been sitting on my deck, drinking lemonade and bottled water. They've told me about other things they've found during their fencing jobs—a wallet, a doll, a beer stein—but nothing like a skeleton. All of them are pale-faced and they speak quietly. They're shaken by the discov-ery, but not as shaken as I am.

Sam asks the fencing guys to lead the investigators to the "remains." I stay behind, alone on the deck, sad and a little nauseous. Should I walk over to the Hockleys' and tell Ellie? I have no number for her. Would she want to be here or should I wait until the . . . skeleton . . . has been taken away? I suppose there's a slim chance the bones are not Win's. Very slim.

As I sit there, other thoughts run through my mind. The red-haired woman tried to scare me away from my house . . . and my land. That Byron Parks guy—the ancient sheriff—tried to buy the property for no reason any of us could determine. I thought about the trash explosion on my lawn, the squirrels in my redbud tree, and all those weird things that Sam told me had happened while our house was being built. The stolen power tools. The dead animals. Someone who is still very much alive doesn't want me to find those bones. Someone doesn't want me to wake up the past.

It seems like a long time until one of the investigators, a petite blond woman accompanied by Sam, joins me on the deck and begins questioning me. That's when I know I need to get Ellie. She has more answers than I do and she needs to know what's going on. Sam checks her phone to see if Ellie's number is still on it from the day of Rainie's disappearance but she can't find it, so the two of us walk down Shadow Ridge Lane, past the white vans and the builders going on about their work, oblivious to what's happening at the end of the street.

"This is going to be so hard for her," I say.

"Want me to do the talking?" Sam asks, and I shake my head.

We climb onto the porch and ring the bell. I try to peer through the screen door to see if Miss Pat and Buddy are in the room; I don't want to have to explain everything to them as well as to Ellie. But Ellie comes to the door alone and steps onto the porch.

"Hey." She smiles at us, but quickly sobers at our flat expressions. She looks from me to Sam. "What's wrong? Is Rainie okay?"

"She's at school. She's fine," I say. "But Ellie . . . the fencing guys found . . . a grave in my yard." Not exactly a grave, I think.

"They found remains," Sam says, giving it to her straight.

Ellie's face blanches nearly to the color of her gray-blond hair, and for a moment I think she's going to pass out. I'm ready to grab her arm. Hold her up.

"Oh." She looks down the street toward my house. Her eyes close. She presses a hand to her face. "Is it Win?" she asks.

"We don't know the identity, but my investigator and I need to ask you some questions," Sam says. "Can you come with us?"

"All right," she says. "Let me grab my phone."

⁓

Once on my deck, Ellie tells Sam and the investigator everything she told me a few nights before, only this time without emotion. She keeps glancing toward the woods. She has amazing self-control. I'm the one struggling to hold it together. The blond investigator records the interview while Ellie describes finding the bumper of my father's truck with the rope attached, but no sign of Win. I realize Daddy will be questioned, too. And I suppose poor sickly Buddy as well, for his role in the story.

"Do you have an idea who took part in the beating?" Sam asks Ellie. It's got to be especially upsetting for Sam, hearing about the gruesome murder of a Black man, but her expression and voice remain professional.

Ellie looks down at the untouched glass of lemonade I gave her, as if thinking. As if she hasn't thought a million times about her answer. "Everyone was hooded, as I said," she says. "So I don't know. I thought I heard Byron Parks's voice, but everyone said he was at a poker game. And as I said, the truck belonged to my ex-boyfriend, Reed Miller." She doesn't look at me. "Kayla's father," she adds.

"I'm sure he had nothing to do with it." I can't stop myself from speaking up, and Sam gives me a small shake of her head.

"Kayla may be right." Ellie nods toward me. "I didn't think he was in the Klan and it's hard to picture, but it was definitely his truck. And he *was* very jealous."

I wish she hadn't added those last few words. I struggle to keep my mouth shut.

"We'll talk to him," the investigator says, "and we'll want to talk to your brother, too."

Ellie's expression is pained. "Please don't," she pleads. "He had nothing to do with it and he's terminally ill."

"I'm sorry," the woman says, "but—"

We suddenly hear voices coming from the path behind the deck and we all turn to see the investigators wheeling a gurney from the woods, a black body bag resting on top. Anton and his team of construction guys follow at a distance.

Ellie and I both turn our heads away. It seems like only yesterday that I watched as Jackson was carried from our unfinished house in a similar bag.

Sam and the investigator—whose name I can't recall—finally leave. Ellie and I walk them through the house and out the front door. Once they're gone, Ellie turns to me.

"I've got to get back to Buddy and Mama." She touches my arm and I know before she speaks that she's apologizing. "I'm sorry," she says. "I had to tell it the way it happened."

"I know. But he didn't do anything."

She looks toward the street to where the investigator's van had been parked. "Maybe we'll finally get some answers," she says, turning back to me.

And then she leaves me alone in my brand-new house that feels as haunted as any ancient mansion.

≈

I'm tucking Rainie in that night when my phone rings. The caller ID tells me it's Sam, and I give my daughter a rushed kiss on the forehead before leaving her room and answering the call in the hallway.

"I thought you'd want to know this," Sam says. "We had Winston Madison's dental records on file from the sixties when he first disappeared, so we were able to check the—"

"Is it him?" I interrupt her.

"It is," she says, and I shut my eyes. "The remains in your yard belonged to Winston Madison, without a doubt."

Chapter 50

I talk to my father from my car late the following morning as I drive home from work. He spent the early morning at the police station in Carlisle, where they questioned him for two hours. I'd barely slept last night as the reality of what had taken place in my backyard sank in. A man had been tortured to death there—a good man who hadn't de-served to die. Was there a chance my father might have to pay for his death?

"For a while there, I thought they were going to slap the handcuffs on me," Daddy says, and I hear anxiety in his voice. "They asked me five different ways how, if I dropped my truck off at Buddy's shop when I said I did, around six, it could possibly be gone when Buddy stopped by the shop an hour later. I said I don't know, that they need to look at the people who had access to the shop and who could have gotten my keys. I think they believed me about not being in the Klan, but they know I was the injured party in my relationship with Ellie, so I had a motive."

"I'm so sorry you have to go through this," I say. Then I hesitate before adding what's been on my mind. "Did you know before now that there was a . . . grave . . . in my yard?" I ask. "Is that why you didn't want Jackson and me to build—"

"No!" he says. "I had no idea. I only knew something terrible had gone down there."

I think of how Ellie must be feeling, knowing for sure now that it was Win in that grave. "Poor Ellie," I say.

"I know," he says. Then, "Listen, Kayla. I'm going to the Hockleys' to talk to Buddy. We haven't said more than 'hey' to each other in decades. He's the only person who could know how someone had access to my keys. Can you come with me? I'd like another set of ears on the conversation."

"Okay," I say. "When?"

"How about now? I have a couple of hours till I pick Rainie up at school."

I cringe at the thought of going to the Hockleys' to pepper that sick old man with questions, but my father needs answers and who knows how much longer Buddy will be able to provide them—assuming he has any.

"I can meet you there in half an hour," I say.

"Thanks, honey. See you then."

≈

I groan as I turn onto Shadow Ridge Lane. There's a police van in my driveway—the same van that was there before I left for work that morning. The investigators are digging through my yard, looking for forty-five-year-old clues. I park next to the van and run into the house to wolf down an apple and a slice of cheese. I look at my forested yard through the glass walls as I eat, hoping that if they do find any clues today, they have nothing to do with my father.

Chapter 51

Daddy's car is already in front of the Hockleys' house and he's sitting in the driver's seat, waiting for me. He gets out and gives me a quick hug. "Thanks for joining me," he says. I think this is the first time he's asked for my help since Mom died.

On the front porch, Daddy rings the bell. Through the screen, I hear the sound of a TV, then Buddy's voice. "Come on in," he says.

We walk into the living room, where Buddy's sitting in a recliner, hooked up to his oxygen, as usual. He wears blue pajama bottoms and a stained white T-shirt.

"Hi, Buddy." I stand just inside the front door, feeling intrusive.

"Hey, Bud," Daddy says, and while Buddy doesn't smile, he doesn't look particularly put out either.

"Hey, Reed." He nods toward the sofa. "Have a seat. Kayla, honey, the girls are in the kitchen. Why don't you go in and get your daddy and me . . . and you . . . some sweet tea from the icebox?"

"All right," I say as my father sits down on the sofa. "Be back in a minute."

In the kitchen, Ellie is cutting vegetables and putting them in the slow cooker, while her mother bends over the sink getting her hair washed by Brenda. The rims of Ellie's eyes are pink behind her glasses. I'm sure she had a terrible night.

"Hey, Kayla," Brenda says as she runs the spray head over Miss Pat's short thin hair. "You doin' okay after the brouhaha yesterday?"

"I'm all right," I say.

"Who's that?" Miss Pat says from her awkward stance as she leans over the sink.

"The girl from down the street," Brenda says. "You know. Kayla? The one where they found that skeleton yesterday?"

"Oh yeah," Miss Pat mutters.

I see the tightness in Ellie's jaw at the mention of the "skeleton." She looks at me and there's a question in her eyes: Why are we here? "My father wants to talk to Buddy," I say, "and Buddy asked me to get some iced tea."

Ellie wipes her hands on a towel, then opens the refrigerator and pulls out two bottles of iced tea. She hands them to me, then nods toward the living room. "I think I'd like to be part of that conversation, too," she says, taking a couple more bottles from the refrigerator.

I thank her for the tea. My gaze is on Brenda as she massages Miss Pat's scalp. Her sleeves are rolled up to her elbows, and it's only as I leave the kitchen that I register what I just saw: a pink birthmark on the inside of Brenda's right wrist. I've seen that birthmark before, and my mind is suddenly on fire as I follow Ellie into the living room.

Brenda is the red-haired woman.

I'm both furious and confused, my hands shaking as I sit down next to my father on the sofa. I set my bottle of tea on the coffee table without opening it. What the hell is going on?

"I'm sitting in on this conversation," Ellie says, handing one of the bottles to her brother. She doesn't greet my father and she takes a seat in an armchair across the room, as far from him as she can get. "Have the police talked to you yet?" she asks him.

Daddy nods. He says something, but it doesn't register in my brain. All I can think about is that the crazy woman who kidnapped my three-year-old daughter is in the kitchen. I sit on the edge of the sofa cushion as if ready to bolt. I should say something. Right now. But what?

As soon as I get out of here, I'll call Sam.

"So have you thought any more about it, Bud?" my father asks Buddy. "Who else could have gotten my keys after I put them through that slot in your shop door?"

I think Buddy says something about racking his brain, but I really don't know because Brenda is guiding Miss Pat into the room. Miss Pat, her thin curly hair in damp ringlets close to her scalp, seems frailer than the last time I saw her. She's shuffling more than walking. She looks small and vulnerable. She sits down in a wooden straight-backed chair and picks up a pencil and the folded newspaper from the table next to her. I can see the square of a crossword puzzle on the paper.

Brenda lowers herself into the upholstered chair next to her. I can't even look at her. Is she the one who littered my yard with trash? Did she toss dead squirrels into my redbud tree and steal things from Jackson's trailer? Is she the person who didn't want anyone to find Win's body in my backyard? *Oh no, honey, you don't want a fence!* That's what she said to me. Of course she didn't want me to get a fence! She didn't want anyone digging holes in my yard.

My father catches my eye. Gives me a quizzical look. I have no idea what he just said, or what Buddy just said, or how I should be responding. My body feels like it's buzzing.

"Are y'all still talking about that boy's grave?" Brenda asks. "Can't we put it to rest? I don't see why . . ."

She goes on, but I'm not listening. Her sleeves are still rolled up and my eyes are drawn like a magnet to the irregular pink pattern on the inside of her forearm. She stops speaking, following my gaze to her arm, then back to my face and our eyes meet. She hurriedly rolls her sleeves down, but I can tell from her expression: she knows that I know.

I need to call Sam right now. I could excuse myself. Go outside and make the call.

As I think about what I'd say, my gaze drifts toward the doorway between the living room and the kitchen. I can see the side door, the entrance to the house that Ellie led me through that first day when she made me a cup of tea. I see the faded images of rolling pins and sacks of flour on the ancient wallpaper. I see the old wooden key rack on the wall next to the door, two sets of keys hanging from the knobs. I have a sudden thought.

"Mr. Buddy," I say, interrupting whatever he and Daddy are discussing. My voice has a shiver in it. "Where did you keep the keys to your car shop back then?"

"In my pocket," he says.

"Did you ever keep them on that key rack in the kitchen?"

"That ol' rack!" Buddy lets out a laugh that turns into a coughing fit. We wait. Daddy looks at me, eyebrows raised. He's catching on. "I made that ol' thing in a woodworking class when I was . . . I dunno . . . fourteen, maybe?" Buddy says. "Been hangin' there ever since."

"Did you ever keep the car shop keys on it?" Daddy repeats my question.

"Nah, I always kept them in my pock—"

"Yes, you did, Buddy." Ellie leans forward. "Back when I lived here you surely did. All the time."

Buddy wrinkles his brow. Adjusts the oxygen tubing in his nose. "You might be right," he says. "Before I got that fancy lock on the shop door, maybe I did. So long ago."

"Who the hell cares where Buddy kept his keys a hundred years ago?" Miss Pat slaps the newspaper on the end table. "Just listen to yourselves going on and on about the ancient past! I knew as soon as Ellie showed up back here in Round Hill everything would go to hell." She looks at her daughter. "You were a pain in the backside as a girl and you're a pain in the backside now. You're sixty-five years old, for heaven's sake! When are you goin' to grow up? You don't see me moonin' around over your daddy killin' himself, do you?"

"Mama—" Ellie frowns, but her mother plows over her.

"Yes, it hurt, havin' him shoot his damn head off," Miss Pat says. "But I just kept goin', didn't I? Put one foot in front of the other." She shakes her head at Ellie. "Why do you always think the world revolves around you? What the hell's wrong with you that you're so stuck in the past?" She points a trembling finger toward her daughter. "If you *must* know, Eleanor," she says, "*everybody* was there that night. Back in the woods. Every goddamn body! Everybody was disgusted by you and that boy." She shudders, as if sickened by the thought of her daughter and Win together. Then she turns to Brenda, who looks like a deer caught in headlights. "Even Brenda was there that night," she says, "though she stayed in the truck, her bein' expecting and all. Didn't you, honey?"

"Mama . . ." Brenda's voice is small, but the word sounds like a warning.

"Mama *what?*" Miss Pat asks, but it's not really a question. She frowns at Brenda, who seems frozen in her chair. We're *all* frozen. But then Brenda suddenly finds her voice. She looks directly at my father.

"Just admit you were driving your damn truck and get it over with, Reed," she says. "Everybody knows it. They've known it for forty-five years."

Next to me, my father stiffens. "That's not true," he says.

"Oh, bullshit." Miss Pat wears a mocking smile, and for the first time, I have the tiniest sliver of doubt about my father's innocence.

"I was *not* driving that truck," Daddy says. "I had nothing to do with whatever went on in the woods."

Ellie doesn't seem to hear him. Her face has gone white. She's looking across the room at Brenda. "You were my best friend," she says. "How could you have been part of it all?"

"Mama's not well, Ellie," Brenda says. "She doesn't know what she's saying." She rests her hand on Miss Pat's arm, but Miss Pat snatches her arm away from her.

"I'm perfectly fine," she says. "Sane and sober."

"Her memory is off," Brenda continues. She looks at Miss Pat. "You know how you are, Mama. You can't remember where you put your glasses two seconds after you take them off."

"*You're* the one with the memory problems," Miss Pat argues.

My father leans toward me, hand on my shoulder. "Are you all right, Kayla?" he asks softly.

I don't answer him. I glare at Brenda. "You're the woman who took my daughter," I say. "You were the woman in my office who tried to scare me away from Shadow Ridge."

"What the *hell* are you talking about?" Brenda snarls, and I hear a bit of the gravelly voice she used in my office. "What is *wrong* with everybody today?"

"Seriously, Kayla." All of Ellie's attention is on me. "What do you mean?"

"You shot a bunch of squirrels with a pellet gun and threw them on my redbud tree." I'm guessing now.

"That was *Brenda?*" My father sounds astonished. I don't answer him. I'm too busy staring her down.

"You're insane," she says.

"Leave Brenda alone," Miss Pat says. "I thought you were a nice girl, but you—"

"You went to tremendous lengths to try to prevent anyone from finding that grave," I say to Brenda. "Why? What's your connection to it?"

Brenda laughs. "You're completely out of your mind," she says. "You're so obsessed with your 'Shadow Ridge Estate' that you can't think straight."

"You tried to scare me away," I say. "It had to be because of Win."

"Don't say that name!" Miss Pat nearly shouts, and I ignore her.

"You didn't want anyone to find him," I say to Brenda. I'm trembling, afraid of her. She took my daughter. She told me she wanted to kill someone. What is she capable of? Yet, I can't stop talking. "You probably *were* there the night everything happened, like Miss Pat said. You knew Win was buried in my yard, didn't you?"

She glares at me, opening her mouth as though she's about to say something, but she can't seem to find the words, and I keep talking. I look at Ellie.

"Your uncle Byron," I say. "Remember how he wanted to buy my lot?"

I can practically see the light bulb going off in Ellie's brain. Her eyes fill with horror.

"Uncle Byron?" Buddy asks. "Why the hell would he want land in Shadow Ridge? He was knockin' at death's door for two years before he passed."

"Byron knew the grave was there," Daddy says quietly.

"Well, you figured it out. Congratulations." Miss Pat slaps her hands on her thighs. "Of course Byron knew the grave was there. He should have. He's the one who dug it."

"Hush, Mama. You don't know what you're talking about." Brenda tries once more to put a hand on Miss Pat's arm, but the old woman slaps it away.

"But Uncle Byron was at a poker game with Daddy that night." Buddy looks perplexed. "He and Daddy took Garner to the hospital."

At the mention of her husband, Brenda leans forward, her cheeks suddenly bright red. "They *did* take Garner to the hospital," she says, "but not from our *house*." She turns to look at Ellie. "Garner didn't fall off the ladder at our house! That was a made-up story we told the hospital. He was with everybody else at the circle in the woods, ready to put an end to you and your so-called boyfriend, and *you* killed him!" She picks up her bottle of iced tea and throws it at Ellie. Daddy is quick to get to his feet as though he can somehow reach Ellie in time to protect her, and I suddenly realize that after all these years, all these decades and all her distrust of him, my father still cares about her.

The bottle strikes her on the shoulder. She's stunned but not hurt, but I feel the shock wave in the room. Dead silence follows Brenda's words as we all try to make sense of them. I reach for my father's hand. Tug him back to the sofa again.

"What is *wrong* with you?" Ellie leans toward Brenda. "How could I have killed Garner? I would never—"

"Listen to what she's saying, Ellie," Buddy interrupts her. "She's sayin' there *was* no poker game. It was made up to . . ."

"As a cover-up," Daddy says. "Because Byron and your father . . . they were there in the clearing. So was Garner. It sounds like the whole damn town was in the clearing, like your mother said."

"Except you!" I add, because I'm completely certain now that whoever drove my father's truck, it wasn't him.

"But why would you say I killed Garner?" Ellie turns to Brenda, who's gripping the arms of her chair now, her knuckles white.

"*You* killed him, Ellie. *You* killed Garner and made me lose my baby— the only child I'd ever have! Garner was climbing the steps of the tree house and you kicked him off and destroyed my whole world, all for that stupid boy you'd only known for a month."

Ellie gasps. "That was Garner?" she asks. She sounds like a wounded child.

"Oh, don't give me that innocent crap!" Brenda stands up. "And then you have the nerve to show up here, all these years later, saying 'Can we be friends again? Can we start over?' Like hell! I would just as soon *kill* you as be your friend! God, I loathe you!"

"That's enough, Brenda," Daddy says. He's on the edge of the sofa as though ready to jump up again. His voice is firm, but not angry. I hear pity in it.

"Don't you get it, Ellie?" Brenda asks. I feel her shaky rage, though her voice isn't loud now. It's worse than that. The rage is coiled inside her, ready to spring. "Your father couldn't wait to put an end to the boy who was dragging his family through the mud, and he had a whole lot of help from the rest of Round Hill."

Buddy makes a gasping sound as he tries to sit up straight in the recliner.

"Daddy could've gotten the key to my shop off the rack in the kitchen, like Kayla said." He looks at Brenda, a wounded expression on his doughy face.

Ellie's cheeks are shiny with tears. "I can't believe Daddy would do that."

"You're right about that." Miss Pat nods. "He was a weak man. He went along with it, but he didn't know the whole plan. We kept it from him. He didn't know that boy would end up killed. He couldn't take it, either. He wasn't the same afterward."

My father frowns. "But if he drove my truck, he had to know—"

"I just said he was a coward, didn't I?" Miss Pat sounds impatient. "*I'm* the one who drove your damn truck, Reed! I'm the one who did what everybody else was afraid to do!"

For the first time in fifteen minutes, a hush falls over the room. We stare at Miss Pat, who turns her head away from us, red blotches high on her cheekbones. Still no one speaks. Finally, Brenda reaches over to rest a hand on Miss Pat's.

"Oh, Mama," she says quietly. "Now you've gone and done it."

Chapter 52

ELLIE

I stare out the living room window of my family home. Across the street, where the leafy green dinosaurs and dragons used to roam, sprawling new houses rise from the cold earth. Stone and wood, most of them. When I arrived in Round Hill and saw those houses going up, I thought, *They don't belong here.* Now I can see that my house is the one that doesn't belong. Just like me. In another week, I'll be home in San Francisco. I'll have Christmas with my cherished friends. What I'll tell them about my time here in Round Hill, I don't yet know. All I do know is that I need distance from it. Physical and emotional distance.

I smell the aroma of the leek tart I'm baking and hear Kayla rattling around in my kitchen. She's poking through the drawers and cabinets. I told her to take anything she might need or want and so far she's fallen in love with a big turquoise bowl and a well-worn first edition of *The Joy of Cooking.* Tomorrow, the Round Hill charity shop and Habitat for Humanity are coming to cart off furniture and clothing and kitchen items and who knows what else. It's all going, making way for the bulldozers. Tonight's is the last meal I'll ever cook in this house, and that's fine with me.

With a sigh, I turn around and walk into the kitchen. Kayla looks up from the contents of the drawer she's examining. She holds up an eggbeater with a worn red wooden handle.

"Is this one of those eggbeaters?" she asks.

"Uh-huh," I say.

"Cool." She sets it in the turquoise bowl she's taking. "I've never seen one before. It looks like a great little invention."

I smile. I won't tell her that it was my mother's long before it was mine. She won't want it then, and who can blame her? My mother tainted everything she ever touched. She tainted this entire house. She tainted my memories. She tainted my life.

"This is my favorite thing," she says, showing me an old salt-and-pepper-shaker set I barely remember from my childhood. She laughs as she demonstrates how the magnetized pieces come together to form the shape of a cow. "Rainie's going to love it," she says.

I like the sound of her laughter. She's lighter these days, and I'm only now getting to know the real Kayla. The unhaunted Kayla. She's a lovely young woman and I'm going to miss her. She offered to let me stay in her guest room for the few days between my house being demolished and my flight home, but I turned her down. I'm not the superstitious or squeamish type and I don't like to think I'm still stuck in the past, but beautiful though Kayla's house is, I don't want to stay in those woods. I'd much rather spend these last few days in the second bedroom of Reed's small, new-smelling condominium, with its access to an indoor pool, well-appointed gym, and serene yoga studio.

"Want me to start the salad?" Kayla asks as I lift the foil from the cheese biscuits I baked earlier.

"Sure." I open a cupboard and hand her the salad bowl. "Use up whatever you can find in the fridge."

Kayla talks about a trip to a Christmas shop Rainie's class is taking, but I'm only half in the conversation. I look out the kitchen window into the backyard as I arrange the biscuits in a napkin-covered wicker basket. The day is mild for early December, and Reed and Rainie are out there in sweaters but no jackets. Reed's pushing Rainie across the yard in the wheelbarrow. She's standing, arms out, trying to maintain her balance. I feel the tiniest pang of sadness. Reed's become a good friend. In another lifetime, we might have ended up together. In this lifetime, it's not to be. I know he's quickly grown attached to me and we've enjoyed sharing the bittersweet memories of our years together before SCOPE. Before Win. We even spent a few days in Myrtle Beach, where we danced and ate too much seafood and talked and talked. But Round Hill is his home and San Francisco is mine and nothing is ever going to change that fact.

Reed stops pushing Rainie and she climbs out of the wheelbarrow and runs over to the tree stump that Buddy carved into a chair sometime in the last few decades. She sits in it, kicking her feet against the bark as she chats with her grandfather. The yard is a mess, the grass unkempt and pretty well torn apart from the barbecue we had a couple of weeks ago to celebrate Buddy's life after his heart finally gave out. I opened the house to the whole town. Buddy's friends dug a pit in the backyard and roasted a pig. I tried to put my foot down about that. Even when I was a genuine Carolina kid growing up in Round Hill, I hated those pig pickin's, but Reed settled me down. Buddy would have wanted it, he said, and he was right. He would have loved having everyone packed into our yard, sharing memories. The only person I didn't invite was Brenda. I still remember how she called me a "goddamn stupid bitch" when I went to see her in the hospital after she lost her baby. That is precisely the way I feel about her now. I hope never to lay eyes on her again. She is a sick, sad, and lonely woman, stuck in the past, and I want nothing to do with her.

≈

The salad, biscuits, and leek tart—and Rainie's peanut butter and jelly sandwich—are ready, and Kayla calls Reed and Rainie in from the yard. We sit at the dining room table for the last time.

"Tomorrow this table is going to be gone?" Rainie asks.

"Yup," I say. "Along with everything else."

Rainie pats the tabletop with her small hand. "Goodbye, table," she says. She looks at the wooden light fixture above us. "Goodbye, light bulbs." She's so cute.

"Everything's going to get a second life, though," Kayla says. "Everything will go to a big store and people will buy them and take them home and love them."

Rainie chews her sandwich, considering this. She looks at me with worry in those big brown eyes. "You won't have anything left if you give it all to other people," she says.

"I have a lot of furniture in my home in San Francisco," I say. "I don't need any more."

"Are you keeping anything?" Reed asks. "Memorabilia?"

"Oh, just a few things." My smile is quick and, I suppose, secretive, because no one presses me for more information.

I found, buried in the back of my old closet, the cigar box I'd kept with me during my weeks with SCOPE. It was stuffed with yellowed newspaper articles and photographs that made me weep. Pictures of Win and Jocelyn, Chip and Paul and Curry and Greg Filburn at the school in Flint. Little DeeDee Hunt sitting on my mattress in her bedroom closet. Me, standing in front of the Daweses' house looking serious and so committed. And a picture I'd completely forgotten I'd taken of Win sitting on the porch steps of the Daweses' house, smiling one of his rare smiles at me. It was the night I told him about Mattie Jenkins. My throat tightens as I study that small square photograph of a young man who never had the chance to grow up. To grow old. *I'm so sorry, Win.*

I'll take that box back to San Francisco with me. But first I plan to make copies of all of the photographs and newspaper articles. Reed managed to track down Win's sister, the one who had polio as a child. The one Win cared so much about. I never knew how much Greg Filburn told Win's family about what happened to their son and brother and how much I had to do with it, but I guess it was enough, because when I contacted his sister through email, she wrote back that she didn't want to meet me. I don't blame her. Still, when I found the old cigar box, I knew I wanted her to have a copy of those memories. She has children and grandchildren. They should know what a fine and committed young man their uncle was. They should know what the world lost that long-ago night.

Reed's also helped me figure out how to make my financial plans a reality, now that I have more money than I ever expected from the sale of this property. I want to set up a scholarship in Win's name at Shaw University, the school he attended, and I want to feed money into the community organizations that are my passion back home.

And, of course, I have to pay for the assisted-living place Mama despises. I sent her back there the day after the truth came out, ignoring her protests, her anger, and her panicky crocodile tears of remorse. When the authorities got around to questioning her, she denied everything. Pled ignorance. I shouldn't have been surprised. It doesn't matter. I believe her tiny shared room with its pee-yellow walls and faded blue-striped curtains is better punishment than any prison cell. I'll never see my mother again, and that thought gives me only relief.

≈

Two days after that last meal in my house, Reed, Kayla, Rainie, and I watch from across the street as the bulldozers and cranes pull my childhood home apart, crushing it in mere minutes to a pile of rubble. We're surrounded by a few remaining Shadow Ridge construction workers, who whoop and holler as my red roof crunches like tinfoil and the walls turn to splinters.

"Will they do that to our house, Mama?" Rainie sounds worried. She glances down Shadow Ridge Lane toward her house, all the huge glass windows sparkling in the winter sun.

"No, honey," Kayla says. "We'll never let anybody hurt our home."

I thought I might cry when it happened. In spite of everything, it's a sad thing to see the house you grew up in turn to dust. Yet I feel a weight lift from my heart. I'm finished here. When I look at Reed, I see understanding in his face. His warm blue eyes. His sad smile. He puts an arm around my shoulders. He knows I'm about to leave Round Hill behind me forever.

≈

Three days after my house is gone, Reed drives me to the airport in Raleigh.

"I'll park and come in with you," he offers, but I shake my head. We've already said our goodbyes and I'm ready to be back on my own. Nevertheless, once I'm in my window seat on the plane, waiting for takeoff, I find myself thinking about how nice it would be if Reed visited me in San Francisco. I imagine walking across the Golden Gate Bridge with him. Introducing him to my friends. It will probably never happen, and maybe that's for the best. He deserves someone who can give him all her heart. Although we rekindled a bit of something from when we were young, he will be fine without me. I realized that at the pig pickin'. He knows everyone, and I could tell that there are a few women in Round Hill who have had their eye on him for years. He won't be alone for long.

The flight attendant smiles as she recites her safety instructions. Through the window, I watch the luggage carrier pull away. I smell coffee brewing in the galley and wonder if they have any decent tea. It doesn't matter. I feel very much at peace.

I look down at my wrist. I can barely believe that I found the bangle bracelet Win gave me right where I left it so long ago—between the wall and floorboard of the tree house—on the worst night of my life. I found it the night Kayla sent the police to get me down from the tree house. The silver had blackened with age but I polished it until it shone. Since then, not a day has gone by that I haven't studied it, running my fingers over the engraving. But until today, I hadn't put it on. I needed to get out of Round Hill first. I needed to feel free.

I lean my head against the window now and look at my wrist with a smile.

Ellie—We'll Fly Away—love Win

"Yes, Win," I whisper to myself as the plane shudders, then begins to move. "Here we go."

Chapter 53

———≋———

KAYLA

Rainie runs into the kitchen, where I'm icing Christmas cookies. She grabs my hand.

"Mama!" she says. "They have a little girl!"

"Do they?" I ask. "That's wonderful."

A new family is moving into Shadow Ridge. That will make four houses inhabited and I hope Rainie's right about the little girl. She thought the last family had a girl as well, but it turned out to be an eight-year-old boy with hair down to his shoulders. All of the children who've moved into Shadow Ridge so far have been too old to be her playmates.

I cover the icing with plastic wrap. "Let's go meet them." As the first residents of Shadow Ridge Estates, Rainie and I have appointed ourselves the unofficial welcoming committee.

We bundle up and walk down Shadow Ridge Lane. All of the houses are finished now, and without the constant noise of construction, the neighborhood has become the quietest place I've ever lived. I'd be lying if I said it's the most *peaceful* place I've lived, because there are still nights when the call of an owl or a fox can send chills up my spine, but that's getting better.

The new family is three houses down from ours. Even from a distance, I can see a girl Rainie's age. She looks lost in the midst of the muscular moving men who are lugging furniture between their van and the house. A woman wearing a navy-blue parka and pink scarf is pointing and directing.

"Hi!" Rainie begins to run when we're a house away.

The woman turns at the greeting. "Hi!" she calls back. She looks frazzled—blond hair up in a messy bun, cheeks pink with the cold—but she smiles. She's a bit older than me, but not by much.

"We won't keep you," I say when we reach her. "We just wanted to say hi. I'm Kayla Carter, and this is my daughter Rainie." I look to my side for Rainie, but she's already deep in conversation with the little girl, who appears to be quietly listening to her chatter. "We wanted to welcome you to the neighborhood. Let us know if you need anything."

"Thanks," the woman says. "I'm Paula and my daughter's Tara." She looks at the moving van. Rolls her eyes. "This is overwhelming," she says.

"I know." I glance at our daughters. It looks like Rainie's telling little Tara her life story, expressive arms flying through the air, brown eyes wide with excitement. "There are no other kids my daughter's age in the neighborhood so far," I say. "She's thrilled to meet Tara." I look past Paula toward the house. "Is the rest of your family inside? Do you have other kids?"

"Just Tara," she says. "And newly divorced." She wrinkles her nose at that, as if it's hard to say, but I think, *This is some kind of miracle. Another single woman and little girl.* "I'm widowed," I say. I'm getting more accustomed to the word.

Her face falls. "I'm so sorry."

"Ma'am?" one of the movers asks. He's carrying a small dresser as if it were made of cotton. "Which bedroom you want this in?"

"The front corner." She points.

"You're swamped," I say. This is not the time for deep conversation. "I'm going to let you go."

"Which house did you say is yours?" she asks.

"The one at the end of the street." I point behind me.

"Oh, that's the most beautiful house in the neighborhood," she says. "I love how it's nestled in the trees."

I have to smile. If only she knew how long it's taken me to fall in love with our house. Maybe someday, I'll tell her. As I head toward Rainie, I call to Paula over my shoulder. "Have Tara come over anytime!" I say. "We have a fenced yard!"

I have to practically drag Rainie away from her new friend, who apparently did more talking than I thought, because Rainie tells me they're getting a puppy named Lily.

"Can we get one, too, Mama?" she asks. "Please, please!"

"Maybe," I say. "Let me think about it." Maybe a rescue, hopefully housebroken, would work out. "You'd have to help take care of it."

"Yes!" Rainie says, swinging my arm. She knows I'm already on board. Maybe in the spring.

I imagine two little girls and two dogs playing in our vast forest. They could have all of it except the one spot that will be my private oasis. I hired a landscaper to do something with the empty circle in my woods. He had no idea how much history I was asking him to erase with his horticultural skills. "This is going to be your favorite place on your property," he promised when he handed me his colored-pencil sketch. He's already put the two black cast-iron benches in place at opposite sides of the circle, their curved backs matching the circle's arc. He did some planting in the late summer and fall and will do more this spring. The ground will be covered with moss, and I'll have hostas, colorful astilbe, Lenten roses, ferns, and anything else he can think of that will grow in the shade. A path of decorative stepping-stones will run through the circle. I picture myself sitting on one of the benches with a book. I hope he's right about it becoming my favorite spot. We'll see.

When we get home from meeting our neighbor, Rainie helps me finish icing the cookies. We're running late. I want to make lasagna, my father's favorite dish, for dinner. I think he's going to be a bit down tonight, since Ellie left for San Francisco this morning. He and Ellie rekindled something the past few months, although he balks at the word "rekindle." "Nothing was rekindled," he said with a laugh when I spoke with him on the phone that morning. "This was just two sixty-something-year-old folks enjoying each other's company, knowing it was really never meant to be. I'm a bit too staid for Ellie," he added. "I think I always was."

He may be right, but I love him the way he is. Rainie and I will give him a wonderful evening. We're going to help him start over. We've gotten pretty good at it.

Author's Note

I was fourteen years old during the summer of 1964 when I heard the news about three young civil rights workers who were murdered in Mississippi. Andrew Goodman, James Earl Chaney, and Michael Schwerner were spending the summer in the South to register Black voters. Their disappearance and tragic end may not have been the first time I'd heard about student civil rights workers, but it was the first time their work had an emotional and intellectual impact on me. The junior high school I attended in Plainfield, New Jersey, was well integrated, and I was awakening to the injustices faced by people who looked like my classmates. It was impossible to grow up in Plainfield during that era and be blind to the inequities, even in the North. I was moved by the courage and passion of those young civil rights workers who were willing to face danger to do what they felt was right.

When I reached high school age, I often found myself in the library stacks lost in books and articles about racial injustice. At some point, I stumbled across information on the SCOPE program. The memory of that program stayed with me and inspired Ellie's story in *The Last House on the Street*.

Although much of the story related to the SCOPE program is based on truth, I took liberties with specific facts. For example, while the program was publicly announced by Hosea Williams in late April, Ellie learns of it a few weeks earlier. The orientation dates, however, are accurate, as is the orientation setting of Morris Brown College in Atlanta. Hosea Williams and Andrew Young were at the orientation and Reverend Young's conversation with the young female civil rights workers is based on reality. Martin Luther King Jr. did indeed deliver a speech at the orientation.

The most dangerous work in SCOPE took place in the Deep South, but I wanted to write about my adopted home state of North Carolina, where SCOPE's work was limited to the "Black Belt" counties of Martin and Warren. However, since I was creating my own fictional world, I invented Derby County and its various towns so that I was not constrained by real events. It is true that the KKK had a very strong and growing presence in North Carolina in 1965, inspired in great part by the Civil Rights Act of 1964. It's also true that the registrars' offices in those counties shut their doors prior to the August passage of the Voting Rights Act of 1965, which left the SCOPE students having to focus on community work other than actual registration.

How wonderful it would be to be able to say that the Voting Rights Act signed by President Lyndon Baines Johnson in August 1965 put an end to voting discrimination. As President Johnson signed the bill, he stated that the right to vote was "the basic right without which all others are meaningless." The Voting Rights Act struck down literacy tests and other regulations that blocked the right to vote and also provided federal protection to people as they registered. Most important, it required that states known for impeding voting rights "pre-clear" any changes to their voting laws with the federal government. In 2013, however, a Supreme Court decision did away with that pre-clearance requirement. As a result, as I write these notes in April 2021, Republican legislators in at least forty-three states are considering more than three hundred and fifty bills that will make voting more difficult, particularly for people of color. Several bills have already been signed into law. It's distressing that politics continues to play such a pivotal role in what should be a basic American right.

For those of you interested in learning more about SCOPE and the era surrounding it, here are some suggestions. A great introduction to the tenor of the times is the 2014 movie *Selma* about the 1965 Selma to Montgomery voting rights marches led by Martin Luther King Jr., Hosea Williams, and John Lewis. The first march was halted by a violent attack on the marchers. The second was aborted out of fear of more violence. The third was successful, thanks to federal protection ordered by President Johnson. The marches took place only a few months before the beginning of the SCOPE program.

For an honest and informative accounting of one young college student's experience with SCOPE during the summer of 1965, I suggest reading Maria Gitin's *This Bright Light of Ours*. I devoured this book and corresponded with Maria, who was generous with her time and the sharing of her experiences. One of the many things I most admire about *This Bright Light of Ours* is Maria's honesty. Nineteen-year-olds don't always make the best decisions and often operate out of idealism rather than realism. Maria doesn't sugarcoat her experience of that summer, yet what comes across most strongly is her passion. That passion combined with youthful naïveté is what I hoped to capture in the character of Ellie.

The late Willy Siegel Leventhal was a SCOPE worker that summer as well and he assembled hundreds of SCOPE-related documents into a massive tome I was able to find on eBay. It was fascinating to read through the contemporaneous letters, messages, and notes related to the program as well as the students' own assessments of what worked and what didn't.

A book that describes the heart of the voting rights movement in North Carolina is *The Williamston Freedom Movement: A North Carolina Town's Struggle for Civil Rights, 1957–1970* by Amanda Hilliard Smith.

One final resource played a part in my research and that is the 1965 book *The Free Men* by the late John Ehle, which covers the 1963–1964 civil rights protests by students at the University of Carolina at Chapel Hill, including the "kneeling in the street" protest Ellie takes part in.

Acknowledgments

In addition to Maria Gitin, whose firsthand experience of SCOPE was invaluable to me, I'd like to thank Cynthia Lewis at the King Center in Atlanta; my research assistant, Kathy Williamson; my ever-supportive significant other, John Pagliuca; and my phenomenal agent and friend, Susan Ginsburg from Writers House. I'm also grateful for everyone else at Writers House for their hard work and enthusiasm, especially Catherine Bradshaw and Peggy Boulos Smith.

I'm delighted to now be working with my enthusiastic United Kingdom editor at Headline Books, Sherise Hobbs, as well as with Headline's marketing director, Jo Liddiard, and all the behind-the-scenes Headline people who have embraced *The Last House on the Street* with such dedication.

As usual, my U.S. editor Jen Enderlin zeroed in on the heart of my story and helped me bring it to life. Jen both challenges and inspires me. She is now the president of St. Martin's Press and it's a huge honor to be able to continue working with such an amazing editor.

Thank you to my publicist, Katie Bassel, who would never let a little thing like a pandemic get in the way of her already challenging job. I'm grateful to all the other supportive folks at St. Martin's—Sally Richardson, Erica Martirano, Brant Janeway, Sallie Lotz, Jeffery Dodes, Lisa Senz, Erik Platt, Tom Thompson, and everyone in the sales department who does so much to get my books into the hands of my readers.

Special thanks go to sensitivity reader Grace Wynter, for her insight and encouragement. As a white author writing about racial issues in the South, I was very grateful to have Grace's input.

Finally, I'm grateful to the civil rights workers of the past and the present who continue the fight for voting equality in America.